GRAVES' END

GRAVES' END

-A NOVEL-

SEAN PATRICK TRAVER

R|S|B
LOS ANGELES

Magic (maj'ik), *n*. **1.** The art and science of causing change to occur in conformity with will (Aleister Crowley). **2.** The manipulation of symbols, words or images to achieve changes in consciousness (Alan Moore). **3.** A basic imagination technology (Grant Morrison). See **WITCHCRAFT**.

Prologue

The only cat Tomas Delgado could find, before his old ride died out from under him, was a young tom. A black one this time, barely weaned. Weak. Not long for this world, most likely.

Still, it was all that was available on this rainswept night in Valley Village, early in the Year 2000.

'*The Year 2000*,' Tom mused. It was hard not to think of it in capitals and quotes. He'd never imagined that he might see the calendar roll over to that science fiction date for himself, not in all the decades of his unnaturally-prolonged existence. It was the symbolic start of The Future, and had been the focus of anticipation and dread across all the worlds in almost equal measure.

The former necromancer could likewise never have guessed that this zero-year sandwiched between two colliding centuries was also apt to be his last.

Some nights he might've found a dozen cats or more congregated behind the Ralphs supermarket at the intersection of Magnolia and Coldwater Canyon, but this evening the inclement weather had driven them all away. The housecats had retreated to their homes and the ferals to whatever dry hideaways they were able to find.

Tom stood up in his scrawny new body and stretched hugely, testing it out. The kitten had sheltered under a lean-to accidentally erected when a stockboy propped a number of wooden shipping pallets outside the market's rear delivery entrance, so its fur was relatively dry.

The stomach was empty and knotted with cramps, though, and the joints ached in the cold. The musculature had had neither the time nor the nutrition required to develop well.

This kitten might do for a few hours, old Tom thought, but if he couldn't find something with better prospects for survival soon, he was finished.

He couldn't believe there wasn't another, stronger cat somewhere within the range of his perceptions. It was his own fault, really. He'd stayed with his last form too long, past the point of its realistic hope for recovery. But dammit, he'd *enjoyed* his fourteen years spent playing the ragged neighborhood scrapper called One-Eyed Jack by the locals who left food out for him on their back stoops. For him, or for pets of their own, all of whom had learned to leave such offerings alone until Tom/Jack had eaten his fill.

It had been a simple life, rough and close to the bone, but a good and free one for all that, and Tom had hoped to prolong it for one more summer, if he could. He'd hoped for so long that he let himself get caught out unawares, like a movie vampire too stupid to buy a watch or an almanac, one who finally gets crisped by an unanticipated sunrise as the contrived culmination of a film's last act.

Tom had loved films since their invention, and he'd continued to watch them over the decades. Even in catform he'd always had access to television in living rooms or store windows and movies at the drive-in theater that used to be up on Roscoe Boulevard, so he really should've known better than to make such a classic blunder by now. But hope had made him stupid, and he'd stayed with old Jack until the frail feline body lacked the strength for him to send his mind out very far.

This sickly black kitten, this unfortunate runt that was all he could reach, wasn't doing a hell of a lot to boost his signal, either.

Tom was tired, but he figured that if he went to sleep now his odds of waking up dead in the second chamber of the Temple of Mictlantecuhtli were pretty damn high. And, even though he was ninety years late, he knew that *el Rey de Los Muertos* would still be waiting at the door to greet him.

And yet... he was so weary that he didn't know if he cared anymore. He couldn't really keep this cathopping business up forever, could he? At some point he'd have to face the King.

The Great and Powerful Mictlantecuhtli's wishes might be deferred, but never denied. The strange new form his temple had assumed in the modern-day world was proof enough of that.

Old Tom had spent too many decades avoiding that odd building in Hollywood to want to curl up and die *quite* yet, however. The Silent Tower, people had called it for a while, though Tom had never known the reason why. He'd heard the place was truly quiet these days, perhaps dormant, and had been that way since at least the early 1950s. The apparent stillness could well have been an illusion, however, if not a trap, and Tom had little desire to challenge it. He'd cheated King Death at his own game long ago, and Mictlantecuhtli's ire over that insult was not apt to have lessened with the passing of the years. Time meant very little to him.

Maybe if he could get some food into this new catbody, Tom thought, that might be enough to keep it going till he could find himself a sturdier replacement.

There was also a dumpster behind the supermarket, one piled so high with soggy boxes and bags of crap that its lid sat ajar by a good four inches.

It was a pretty slight gap; but then, he was a pretty slight cat.

Tom laddered up the outside of his shipping pallet lean-to and leapt onto the closed half of the dumpster's plastic lid. It was slippery and his legs were shaky—he almost slid right off the side. But his paws found purchase just in time and then he'd made it; he was up there. Soaked to the skin already, with his small heart rabbitting along... but one step closer to nourishment, of some sort.

The market boasted a new service deli, serving soups and sandwiches and chicken and coldcuts, and Tom could smell the lukewarm remainders of several people's comingled dinners down there in the trashbin's shadows.

He shoved his small head under the lid at the gap's widest point, then weaseled the rest of his body through.

It was actually not so bad in here, Tom thought as he picked his way down into the tight crevasses between the dumpster's contents. The bin was full of smells that would appall a human being, but didn't draw the same negative value judgments from a feline palate. Besides, it was relatively dry, and dark, and private. The drumming of the rain on the plastic lid was a cozy, comforting sound.

Tom felt like just another shadow, in here.

He found a three-quarters-eaten breast of fried chicken at the bottom of a trashbag and clawed open the thin plastic to get at it. Some satiated human had left good white meat on the bones. Only a bite or two, but it might be enough to keep a small cat alive, for a little while, if he could manage to digest it.

Tom was making the experiment in small bites when the plastic lid overhead swung up and away, gonging a second later against the back of the metal bin.

He jumped and fled, bounding out of the dumpster on some last reserve of strength and eliciting a brief, cutoff shriek from the young woman who'd torn the roof off his sanctuary when he darted past her and raced away, across the wet blacktop.

Tom scrabbled up into the ivy that topped the painted concrete retaining wall separating the market's parking lot from the houses and apartment buildings that filled out the rest of the city block.

Figuring he'd reached a minimum safe distance, Tom turned back to see what sort of intruder had just deprived him of a last meal.

It wasn't really a woman at all, he saw, but more of a girl. Maybe fourteen or fifteen years old. On the cusp. She was looking right up at him, having tracked his brief flight across the lot. Tom glared back at her with his new kitten's baleful green eyes.

"I'm sorry, little cat," she said, standing in the rain like it wasn't even there. "I didn't mean to scare you. Come back down, if you want to. We can share."

Tom knew she had no way of knowing that he understood, but he saw that she was a tenderhearted little thing, alone and afraid and out of her element, and he was moved by her offer of generosity. He didn't take her up on it (his legs felt too much like old, loose rubber bands to try climbing down again), but he lingered in the plant cover at the top of the wall, waiting to see what she'd do next.

For the moment, he was more interested in her than he was in his own imminent demise.

The girl waited for more than a minute, cooing to Tom and trying to coax him back down. She was cute, with long black hair and large dark eyes. Too young and too pretty to be safe alone out here on a night like this.

When it was clear he wasn't coming down, she turned back to the dumpster and hauled herself up onto the thing's slick blue side so she could bend in at the waist to scrounge.

She came back up with the chicken breast Tom had been nibbling, as well as part of a ham sandwich. She used the bread to swipe yellowing mayonnaise off the scrap of gray meat she seemed to have deemed edible, then flapped it in the rain to wash it off a little more.

She crouched down in the lee of the supermarket building, trying to take advantage of the minimal shelter it provided, and tore a small strip of meat from her piece of reclaimed ham. She raised it to her mouth with a shaking hand and forced herself to chew it. Swallowing took an obvious effort.

Eating from the trash was a new experience for this girl. Tom had to wonder what had happened in her world that she was out here like this, suffering like a miserable stray. She had her eyes squeezed shut tight and her breathing turned shallow as she fought to keep down the morsel she'd managed to eat.

After a minute or so her shoulders began to shake, right before she lost her struggle with nausea and gagged up her one bite of dumpster ham.

She started to cry, hugging her knees to her chest.

This was nothing old Tom wanted to see. His heart went out to the little one, and for a second his slow blood boiled with rage against the ugly, poisoned realworld that would throw this child away, leaving her to eat other people's garbage and sleep out in the rain.

You know what? Tom thought then: *fuck it.* He was done for anyway. He might as well make his last act in this world one of kindness.

Why not?

He drew back deeper under the ivy, and sent his mind out. His kitten wouldn't survive this effort (meaning his mobile old soul would die with it, once and for all), but right now, he didn't care.

He found the market warm and bright inside, the aisles mostly empty of shoppers as the rainy evening gave way to an inhospitable night.

Tom condensed his awareness down near the express checkout lane, the one closest to the store's front entrance.

He didn't like to steal, but when the checker got distracted by some old bat's raft of questions regarding a fifty-cent detergent coupon, he delved into the cashdrawer and popped the mechanism that held it closed. Tom had always had a knack for getting into things. He'd studied the locksmithing trade for a time, in his youth.

He raised the springclip that held the ones down in their slot at the same moment he sent out into the electric eye that controlled the market's automatic door, triggering it and letting in a well-timed gust of cold, wet wind.

A single crisp dollar bill fluttered out and landed in the next lane, unseen, before the checker nudged the errant drawer shut with her hip and made some comment about the weather to the crusty old coupon-hound who had begun to laboriously count out her purse full of dimes.

Tom's formless point of awareness tugged the dollar under a nearby rack of chewing gum and trashy magazines, and then he marshaled his strength.

When the aged cheapskate left, lugging her discounted soap out toward her Mercedes, Tom floated the pilfered bill out after her, like a tiny magic carpet.

The wind outside blew it to the ground, where it stuck to the wet sidewalk.

Someone other than the intended beneficiary might find it at any minute, and he wouldn't get a second chance at this.

Behind the market, Tom's cat took a deep breath and let it out, very slowly.

He sent his mind out as wide as he could and then pulled it back in tightly, drawing fine particulate matter off the ground and out of the air, coalescing the dust down into a form that reflected light and possessed at least a little bit of mass.

Tomas Delgado (or at least a pretty good approximation thereof) reached down and peeled the damp dollar bill up from the sidewalk. He felt his blood pounding through his distant kitten's ears as his projection of a human form strolled nonchalantly around the side of the market, leaning on a cane.

Just the way he remembered himself.

The crying girl looked up to see a hunched old man with kindly eyes and a wry grin standing over her. He could tell she hadn't even heard him walk up. Her emotions were very palpable, to him.

He held out a dollar bill.

Tentatively, the lost girl took it. "Th- thank you," she stammered, her sinuses well clogged from weeping. She wiped her eyes. "Thank you."

The old man nodded and tipped his hat, then turned and walked away from her, without ever having said a word. The girl watched him go. He seemed somehow to vanish into the rain and mist before he'd made it all the way down the alley that exited onto Coldwater.

Tom managed to open his cat's eyes again, with an effort. He was lying on his side in the mud, panting shallowly. The effort of appearing as a man for a minute or two had depleted the kitten, used it up, and Tom knew he wouldn't be able to send himself out again.

So this was it. His long, strange sojourn on the earth plane would finally draw to an end, before this night was through.

Still, as Tom watched the young runaway or whatever she was hurry around to the front of the store with her newfound money, he was comforted to know that his last act of will in this world had been a good one.

He'd always been a sucker for a pretty face. He didn't regret the action sentiment had prompted him to this time, though. Not one little bit.

The girl came back in less than two minutes, clutching a small paper bag.

She approached his hiding place in the wall-topping ivy carefully, and Tom managed to sit up, wondering what it was she thought she was playing at.

When she took a can of cat food out of her shopping bag, Tom felt the weary old heart he'd been carrying around for better than a hundred years shatter within his fragile cage of tiny kitten ribs.

This starving girl had gone and spent her single dollar on *him*.

"Hey there, little cat," she said, peeling the pulltab-equipped lid off the top of the can and setting it down in the relative shelter of an overhanging tree branch. "Come on out. I thought this might do you some good."

And then, at that point, although he wouldn't have thought it possible thirty seconds before, Tom found he had the strength to run to her.

He clawed his way right up the front of her jacket to nuzzle in against her neck. Her skin was warm despite the chilling rain, her cheeks aglow with mild fever. Still, she laughed delightedly and put her hands around his tiny body. He thrilled to feel her gently stroke his fur.

Shelter, then, was the first order of business regarding this one. Warmth, then food, and not garbage from a can, either. No more of that for her, not ever again. If Tom had to hunt down a live chicken to provide a decent goddamn meal, then he fully meant to do it.

When the girl set him down, he ate the food she'd purchased for him. He *would* be surviving this night, he'd decided after all, and he was going to need his strength for the days ahead.

Old Tom had remembered that he used to be a lion, in his dreams.

Then he became a cat that only dreamed he was a man. And he'd stayed that way for so many years, hiding from the King through four decades of bobcats and panthers before the encroaching city drove those so deep into the hills that common housepets became his most reliable vehicles into the modern era.

But now he'd be that lion again, on behalf of this generous girl who needed an ally in this world as much as anyone Tom had ever seen. She would never walk alone again, he vowed, or be without defense. He'd teach her every secret he had ever learned. He'd arm her up with magicks so old and deep and true that she'd be the match of any operator, imaginal, or ordinary jerk that fate could ever throw her way.

Tom was prepared to trust her with everything he knew, worlds be damned, after fifteen minutes of acquaintance.

The child may not have known it yet, but her initiation as a witch had already begun. Her teacher had selected her as his pupil, and an ancient pattern might now play out anew.

Assuming the girl wanted to learn, that was. She had to be willing, as the sorts of truths Tom meant to share couldn't really be transmitted, but only received. The skills he had to pass on would change her, divert the course of her destiny off from where it might otherwise have led, but then again, she'd never have her native kindness shamed out of her by a wicked world this way, either. The power that comes with knowledge would make her strong enough to keep it, and that seemed to Tom like an excellent thing.

For the first time in the gods only knew how long, the old ghost in a cat actually felt *excited* about something.

He refused to let himself be troubled by the thought that one day, for her own safety, his girl might need to know the secret of the King's Chambers and the building—the Silent Tower—that now concealed them. Tom knew the consequences of that revelation could be as dire for this new child as they'd once been for his lost love Dulcé… if he wasn't just as careful about it as he could possibly be.

But that theoretical occasion was many, many years off; a decade or more before she'd be ready, and for now there were far more immediate plans to be made.

Tom knew the Valley incredibly well after a fifty-year career as a backyard mouser. He knew the secrets cats knew, the hidden paths and the rarely-traveled roads, the forgotten tunnels and the rooftop hideaways.

There was a certain place he knew of, not too many miles distant. A place many cats knew, that literally thousands of them had visited or lived at over the past forty years or so. It used to be a farm-supply depot, a rather remote one, in the dimmest days of Tom's human memory. During his bobcat years it'd been a small farm itself, or maybe a large garden would've been a better description, growing corn and strawberries and selling them all summer long from the property's original wooden shack. It saw a couple of seasons as a Halloween pumpkin patch in the late 1950s. Then, in the years after that Cuban Missile thing Tom absorbed some news about in passing, the patriarch of the family that owned the place had sunk a bunch of money, literally, into an underground nukeproof bunker in which to wait out an anticipated Apocalypse that never quite came.

The bills for the project kept coming, though, and apparently they'd never gotten paid.

The acreage was abandoned to this day, its future tied up in legal limbo while the original paranoiac's distant heirs squabbled over their inheritance, none of them even aware, at this point, of the big bomb shelter that had bankrupted the family business so many years ago.

Forty years worth of Valley cats would've brought their every half-eaten trophy to these people's doors in gratitude, if any but Tom had been able to find them by reading a street address. Rumors that the property was soon to be sold off and either developed or reopened as a nursery continued to circulate, but so far they'd come to nothing.

Tom felt certain he could find a way to lead his new protégé out there, even without a voice to guide her. He'd been robbed of his capacity for words along with his living body almost a century ago... although that, too, was another story. One he supposed he'd need to reveal to his new friend, in time, after she'd gotten used to the psychically-projected pictures, sensations, and dreams that were the only vocabulary he had to work with anymore. Their connection would have to be empathic, emotional and visual, as the unfortunate events of Tom's past had eliminated all verbal options.

But that was all right. The bus line that ran past the market would get them close to the place he meant to take her, and he could fox a goddamn mechanical fare counter. That was easy. Once he got his girl out to the hunting-place, he was pretty sure he'd be able to get them into that subterranean sanctuary, too. He was good at getting into things. They might find food down there, cans, military-style rations maybe, or other packages that required opposable digits to open. It seemed likely enough. The place *had* been built with the end of the world in mind, and you'd have to expect that survivors would want to eat.

He was surprised by how much better he felt once his small belly was filled with the preservative-laden bovine mash they sold as 'cat food' these days. The girl seemed pleased and gratified simply to watch him eat it.

When he was finished Tom looked up at her, his ward, his new best friend, and thought that she had no idea what she'd just bought herself, for the price of a can of processed cowlips.

Part One: Halloween Night

Chapter One

A decade later…

Lia Flores made a futile swipe with her coat sleeve against one of the narrow glass panes set into the old building's heavy front door, attempting to clear away what might have been years of accumulated grime. The windows were backed with brittle brown paper, but it had peeled away from their corners, to greater and lesser degrees. Lia couldn't make out anything in the blackness beyond them, however, no matter how hard she squinted. There was nothing to see but her own pale reflection in the smudged window glass—a transparent ghost with black, bobbed hair and large, dark eyes.

She tried the bell, waited for a moment, then tried it again. When nobody answered after a minute or so, she repeated the procedure. There was still no response, but then Lia wasn't really expecting one, either. It was after ten p.m. on Halloween Night, for one thing, and the building itself—a century-old, red-brick office box languishing on an underpopulated Hollywood side street—was the kind that would've looked just as moribund and disused at ten *a*.m. on any given morning.

Assuring herself that no one could possibly be watching, Lia dropped to her knees before the doorknob and withdrew a miniature set of locksmith's tools from an inner pocket of her dark, bulky peacoat. She took a breath and held it as she went to work on the corroded old lock with a slim rake that looked appropriate to the job.

Behind her stood a short, hunched old man. He was propped

up on a walking stick and still wearing sunglasses, despite the lateness of the hour. He wore a white linen guayabera shirt with two rows of extra pockets down the front and a misshapen hat over his gray-streaked hair. Lia knew him as Black Tom, and even though they'd been inseparable companions for better than ten years now, they'd never once had a proper conversation.

Tom raised a hand to bless her lockpicking efforts and the lock gave way. The door before them yawned open onto a shadowy corridor.

Lia looked back over her shoulder at the bright street several blocks behind her. It was packed tight with costumed celebrants, not a one of them aware of her or of what she might be doing back here in the darkness. They could've been in a different world. One they all agreed upon and labeled 'real.'

She was uncomfortable with what she was doing here, to say the least. Breaking and entering was *not* the arena in which she normally applied her skills. This felt more like a job for a detective.

Still, she crept on down the corridor anyway, with exaggerated caution. Skeins of cobweb depended from the ceiling and a total lack of lighting made the obscenities scrawled upon the walls difficult to read. Black Tom trailed after her, a portrait of cool behind his sunglasses. He leaned on his walking stick but didn't bother to creep as he ambled right down the middle of the hall.

Lia knew this place had once had a name, though Tom wasn't able to tell it to her. They were here because she'd been asked to check the location out by a stranger, one whose brother had vanished almost a year ago, after coming here to perform what their so-called client had referred to only as 'some weird ritual.' Lia and her wordless familiar had a bit of experience with missing persons, and a lot more than that when it came to arcane rites. The real reason she'd agreed to this, though, was that Tom had known the place in question immediately. This place, this building, and the story of the missing brother had struck an obvious alarm bell for him.

He'd covered it up with his habitual wry composure right away, but Lia wasn't sure if she'd ever seen him frightened before. Ghosts had little to fear, generally speaking, and yet even now Tom radiated a desire to believe that the story they'd been told was somehow inaccurate, that the location was dormant or otherwise closed down, and the neglected condition in which they'd found the building *would* seem to argue in favor of that possibility.

If something was lingering on here, however, Tom expected it to reach the height of its power during the next two days, a period of time roughly corresponding with the holiday the locals called *el Dia de los Muertos.* That made tonight, Halloween night, the best possible time to observe without putting themselves in unreasonable danger.

It sounded logical enough to Lia, in its way, but she was still unsettled by the fact that her friend had never tried to tell her before about the early twentieth-century skyscraper that now stood on a site once considered sacred to the Aztecs' God of the Dead.

She glanced up, noting a camera mounted in a corner near the hallway's ceiling. Its lens appeared to be occluded by a thick cataract of dust.

She looked over at Black Tom, who shrugged, although he could've sent her reassurance if he'd wanted to. Could've reached out with his mind and touched her nervous system, psychically blunting the sharpest edge of her fear and letting her know without words that everything would be all right. He'd done such things before, when she'd needed them in the past. That he wasn't doing them now told her everything she needed to know about this situation. Tom thought it was more important, at the moment, that she be focused and on her guard than comfortably unafraid.

She did wish he could just *talk* to her about it, though. The wish was a well-worn one, reiterated nearly every day, but she felt her friend's silence especially keenly right now, when even a single word of reassurance would've done something to ease her tension. But Tom was as silent as he'd ever been.

As silent as this empty tower.

Lia decided to push on, assuming the cobwebbed camera overhead had to be a dud. Nothing was working in here, she felt sure of it. Or at least she *wanted* to feel sure of it. All of the evidence before her confirmed the assumption that nobody else had set foot in here for a very long time. Even the graffiti looked pretty old.

Still, she had to force herself deeper into the building, and it did seem like that elderly camera was following her every move. She couldn't tell if she felt watched because she was *being* watched, or merely because she was trespassing in a place she didn't belong. In any case, she was nearly dizzy with it, that feeling was so powerful.

Encountering the otherworld always involved a series of moves and counter-moves, of selective advantages leveraged against specific weaknesses. Head-on confrontations with its denizens were generally ill-advised. But, much as a man in a flame-proof suit might stand beside a conflagration and not get burned, Lia was often able to edge in close to dangerous entities and learn their secrets—so long as she remained aware of their blind spots. This sort of divination was a spy-game akin to chess, and Tom had taught her to play it like a grandmaster (although he'd also trained her to know when it was time to knock over the board and make a run for it, too).

Intuition could be difficult to separate from paranoia, and Lia couldn't tell which one of them was coloring her impressions now.

She clicked on her flashlight as she eased open the solid double doors at the end of the hall, and its beam sliced at the shadows that closed in around her like a silent pack of eager black beasts. The flashlight flickered and wavered as though it were frightened, but Lia shook it and it came back on strong. For the moment. She'd purchased new batteries before driving down here, so maybe it was a loose connection. Maybe. She hated to think the building might be draining her energizers at an accelerated rate.

The wide foyer she and Black Tom found themselves in was dark, abandoned, and liberally vandalized. Lia played her flashlight over the gaping elevator shafts, and then across the door marked 'STAIRS.' Its identifying sign hung askew.

Still, she opted for the stairs. Those elevators hadn't been operated in a very long time.

Her flashlight flickered and stuttered out more warnings of its own imminent demise as she ascended flight after flight of echoing steps, headed up toward the tower's very top floor. Black Tom tagged along after her, ascending easily despite his age. Lia's calves had turned to wood by the time they reached the seventh landing, but she took a deep breath and continued climbing. Her heart thudded against her ribs, and not just from exertion. This place had an aura about it that unnerved her, despite Tom's clear wish to find it empty.

The last stairwell door protested when she pushed it open, its disused hinges groaning over the indignity of being disturbed after so many years of rusty silence. Lia's dimming flashlight beam preceded her as she emerged into a top-floor corridor, followed as always by her Tom.

She skipped her coin of fading, copper-colored light down the corridor's frayed runner of once-red carpet, scanning along the baseboards for anything out of the ordinary. She paused and held the flashlight beam in place when it glinted off some tarnished bit of metal that might've been an old-fashioned cigarette lighter lying on the floor at the far end of the passage.

She and Black Tom went over to crouch down on either side of what did indeed turn out to be a Zippo-style lighter, one that sported a US Navy insignia on its side. An anchor inside a loop of rope. Tom and Lia examined it silently for a moment. Then they looked up at one another, as if on cue, and nodded in agreement. This felt significant to both of them. It was just the sort of sign they'd come looking for, although the lighter itself appeared far older than anything they'd expected to find.

Lia's sepia-toned beam flickered fatally when she bent to pick up the Zippo. She shook the flashlight again, but it was a goner and she knew it. What she didn't know was whether or not Black Tom could lead her out of here in total darkness. She guessed that he could—she was quite sure of it, really—but she still preferred not to put it to the test.

Lia rolled the Zippo's wheel in desperation and, as old as it was, the flint inside of it still sparked. Her electric light would be dead within seconds, so she clicked the Zippo again, several more times, as her depleted batteries failed her once and for all.

In the moment of pure blackness that followed the flashlight's demise, Tom seemed to notice something. Lia felt him frowning in the gloom.

Then the lighter's wick ignited, and she was bathed in its faint, warm fire-glow.

Lia stood up on legs that felt liquid with relief, holding the lighter aloft. Black Tom hopped to his feet and tugged on the back of her coat.

She turned. "What?"

Tom pointed to a closed door at the end of the hall.

Now it was Lia's turn to frown. She hadn't even *seen* a door there, herself, shrouded as it was in cobweb and shadow. She supposed a part of her hadn't wanted to see it.

But she closed the lighter, as Tom indicated she should, and after giving her night-vision a long moment to adjust, she too was able to see the thin seam of light that lined the bottom of the door.

It was only the faintest glow, seeping out from the next room, but it was there, definitely there, beyond any shadow of a doubt. The flashlight and the old Zippo had each provided enough illumination to obscure it.

In the darkness that seemed to iris down around them, Black Tom pointed toward the stairs, punctuating the gesture with a questioning raise of his eyebrows. (He could bypass Lia's retinas when he wanted to, appearing directly on the movie screen of her mind, so her ability to see him wasn't compromised by the dearth of ambient light. It was still disconcerting not to see much of anything *besides* him, however, hovering there in the entoptic murk while he waited for her to make a choice.)

She re-lit the tarnished Zippo and squinted against its bright yellow tongue of flame as she considered her options. There seemed to be a name stenciled on the door in front of her, barely legible beneath what looked like ancient rust stains, even with her nose an inch from it. She held the lighter's flame up before the letters one by one and found they spelled out 'Miguel Caradura,' a name Lia translated as 'Michael Hardface.' It might've struck her as funny at a different point in time, but not so much, right now.

Tom won't fault you if you turn back, she told herself. *He's letting you off the hook. And it's not like he can tell anybody if you chicken out, anyway.*

But Lia shook her head. They'd come up here because Tom needed to know if the rooms at the top of this tower were occupied and open for business once again, yes, but also because they'd been asked. Asked by someone who needed their brand of help and had nowhere else to turn, which was more than Lia could refuse. She knew all too well what it felt like to need an ally.

So they *weren't* leaving, she decided, not quite yet. Not until she'd seen all there was to see, and not before she'd done what needed doing.

She closed the lighter, put it in her pocket, and reached for the doorknob.

Black Tom looked on, radiating his regret as Lia pushed open the door to the rooms he'd once called *las Cameras del Rey*—the King's Chambers—and her startled, wondering face was bathed in dazzling light.

Miguel Caradura's office suite was brightly lit and fully functional, in surreal contrast to the rest of the shabby and apparently abandoned modern-day building.

Lia stepped tentatively into the outer office, shielding her eyes and feeling blown away by the sheer weirdness of it all. Instead of the decrepit, run-down room she'd been expecting, she found herself inside an office decorated to rival any top CEO's establishment. The leather furniture smelled new, and the walls shone with a fresh coat of paint in a designer shade of cool mint green. The waiting room might've been refurbished that very afternoon.

The door to the next chamber stood open, beckoning like an invitation.

The overhead lights in there were switched off, but Lia couldn't miss the huge flatscreen monitor glowing on an executive desktop, so she crept a few steps nearer to that shadowy inner office. The monitor was displaying security-cam angles of locations within the building that were already familiar after her laborious climb up the stairs.

Each window on the display seemed to be showing a short video clip on a loop, in fact, and every clip she saw was of *her*. Lia's stomach tightened at the realization. Black Tom wasn't visible, not anywhere on the screen, but then his presence never had been perceptible by a thing like a camera's lens. Not unless he wanted it to be.

The clips traced Lia's progress upwards through the building. Starting in the upper left corner of the screen, she saw herself down at the front entrance, looking up into a fish-eye lens and seeming to scrutinize it with one huge eye. (There *had* been a stone gargoyle mounted over the door; Lia remembered looking up into its snarling face when trying the bell. The camera must have been hidden inside its mouth.) In the next video window she was pixilated in poor lighting, standing in a downstairs corridor and plainly wondering whether the dusty relic of a camera she was staring up into could possibly still be viable and functioning.

Got my answer on that one now, don't I?

Yet another window showed infrared footage of her brightly-colored silhouette standing outside the office door, minutes ago, flicking the wheel of a cold blue antique lighter and making psychedelic sparks. The tongue of flame they finally kindled made for a dramatic, multi-hued fireball on the feed from the thermal spy cam.

The very last window, in the lower righthand corner of the screen, showed her right here and right now, real time, standing in the well-lit outer office. As her eyes continued to drift south she realized there was a silver tray sitting next to the monitor, one piled high with what looked to be wet, red, and weakly-pulsing human hearts. Her own heart seemed to stop in her chest at the sight of them. A rose in a cut-glass vase stood beside the tray, completing an elegant presentation. Lia hadn't registered the grisly offering immediately because of the bright glow from the computer screen, which made everything else in the dim second chamber difficult to see.

Oh, shitballs, she thought, watching herself assess the situation, live on digital video. *What* is *this?*

Not what she and Tom had been led to believe, that much was certain. This place wasn't dormant at all. It was fully awake. Awake, alive, and *active*. The abandoned-and-vandalized facade it presented to the world was nothing more than stage dressing.

Black Tom faded into a corner of the first room while an appallingly large tarantula descended from the ceiling on a thread of viscous webbing, sinking down to the floor behind Lia. She almost turned, sensing its motion peripherally, but her attention was arrested by the luminous flatscreen on the desk in the darkened second chamber. She paused in the middle of the first room and strained her eyes from where she stood, wanting paradoxically to get a better look at the screen without moving any closer to the next room's doorway.

Tom hung back and watched as bees and beetles and fat red ants poured out from the baseboards and roiled together in silence, as roaches and wasps and tiny white scorpions teemed up into a swaying tower that stood almost six feet high. Right behind his girl. The looming mass of insects and arachnids seemed to be trying as one to copy a human form, clumping together into a vaguely feminine, hourglass configuration, perhaps using Lia herself as a handy example. They organized into a number of long tentacles that the lady-shaped swarm reached out with while her individual bugs began melting together, working furiously to congeal into a single, outsized specimen.

Lia's eyes darted away from the mound of shining hearts beside the bright computer screen when she realized that someone was watching her very closely, even still.

A black-cowled figure seated at the desk—a figure obscured by the high back of his chair—now moved for the first time. She saw the reflection of the creature's robe and his heavy, face-obscuring hood in the dark window beyond the desk when he picked up a half-eaten heart from a linen napkin and tore a squelching bite out of it with his long, gumless teeth. Lia knew immediately that this was not a man, although it still impressed her as being male. The thing's skeletal hand, she noted with hallucinatory clarity, was stippled with clots of blood and fringed with fresh red shreds of flayed tissue. All she could see beneath the shadow of his cowl was a skeletal grin. Dark heartblood dripped down his bony wedge of a chin.

Lia gasped and turned to flee, only to run face-first into the newly-minted bugwoman that was still churning behind her as it struggled to come into focus. She yelped, instinctually throwing up her hands to dampen the collision, and when a stray centipede scurried across the backs of her fingers, she screamed.

The unstable bug-thing lurched after her as she staggered back, grasping with its multiple arms but not yet facile enough on its obscenely long, chitinous legs to catch her.

Lia shouted again when she stumbled, tripping over her own feet and landing hard on her ass. She cringed, expecting the worst, but Black Tom whacked the bugwoman from behind with his walking stick before it could fall on her, and the swaying conglomeration of half-melded carapaces disintegrated into an avalanche of separate insects. Tom must've been biding his time until the demon was solid enough to be attacked. Lia scrambled away from the bugwave that resulted from his efforts, grimacing with revulsion when it washed across the floor and over her shoes.

Tom extended a hand to help her up and together they ran like hell, pursued by the mad, cackling laughter of Miguel Caradura, currently known on the streets as Mickey Hardface, and previously known to the adherents of his ancient cult as Mictlantecuhtli, the Aztec King of the Dead.

Chapter Two

Lia and Black Tom burst out through the old building's front door and back into the unlighted street, pursued by an angry cloud of buzzing, flying, biting creatures. Lia ducked and flailed, trying to keep the insects out of her hair and clothing. They swirled away into three separate funnels that swiftly congealed into lanky, Amazonian female forms. They were a lot faster about it now that they were warming up, she noticed with some concern.

Black Tom turned and stood his ground against them, snarling.

He swung the head of his walking stick up, catching the first of the re-spawned bugwomen under the chin and bursting her into a spectacular shower of insect bodies. He dealt with the other two incipient bug-beings just as deftly, bashing one through the midsection and sweeping the other to the ground, where he stabbed it between its multiple eyes with his cane tip.

Their component colonies began to re-form almost as soon as they came apart.

The bugwomen wouldn't stay down for long.

Lia, having caught her breath while watching the skirmish from what felt like a reasonably safe distance, now sprinted for the better-lighted street a block to the north. She glanced back to see Black Tom grinning and giving the finger to the camera-concealing gargoyle above the building's front door, right before he punctured another nearly-whole buglady and batted her back into a shapeless cloud of gnats with his stick. He *could* reflect enough light to appear on video, briefly, when he made a special effort, so the King was sure to have seen his unambiguous gesture. Lia imagined the robed skeleton at the top of the tower winging his plate of shiny human hearts against his computer monitor in outraged response.

She was almost surprised when she made it to the lighted and pedestrian-packed street up the block without being set upon from behind. This had to be the only Halloween she'd ever been grateful for the Hollywood crowds. The cordoned-off road was awash in masked revelers, mounted police, stiltwalking firebreathers and inebriated hipsters, and the collective mass of them made for at least some cover. The fact that she was still alive suggested the King at the top of the Tower wanted her captured rather than killed, and a crowd panicked by the sudden descent of a biblical plague was something she might well escape into. So the bugs were less apt to attack her directly, now.

Thank the gods for public intoxication, she thought. *Dionysus particularly.* She'd have to make an appropriate offering later, like buying a shot but leaving it on the bar.

Lia glanced back at the bug-beings gathering in the shadows behind her before she darted out into the costumed throng. The tiny insects they were made of seemed to be melting together, like lumps of sugar over heat, and Black Tom couldn't continue fighting them all at the same time.

The old people (she knew, from sources Tom had pointed out), had called them *Tzitzimime.* In the language of the Aztecs it meant 'nightmares of the sky' or 'horrors descended from above.' They were said to be demon courtiers in thrall to the King of Mictlan, the land of the dead, whom Lia still couldn't believe she'd just seen with her own two eyes.

Behind her, instead of a swarm, three fully-formed and solid bugwomen stepped out into the bright lights of Sunset Boulevard. There was an Ant, a Mantis, and a Wasp, each of them at least six feet tall. They looked stately and dangerous—all grasshopper legs, pinched waists, and curvaceous thoraxes. The Wasp's long stinger dripped with viscous venom, and Mantis's snapping mandibles looked as powerful as the jaws on a steel bear trap. Their dramatic appearance drew pleased applause from the crowds.

Shitballs, Lia thought, looking back over her shoulder upon hearing a volley of cheers erupt behind her, rather than a chorus of screams. Those fucking bugs were smarter when they gelled together. At least by a little bit.

They pushed after her, ignoring their admirers. Their fundamental inhumanity was neatly camouflaged by the occasion, and Lia hadn't counted on a factor like that.

She made it to the far side of the street, elbowing through a knot of glitter-covered, gossamer-winged fairies, and up onto the sidewalk. Only then did she pause to look back again.

The bugwomen were coming, all right. They parted the partiers before them, shoving their way through the crowd and recklessly shunting human beings aside. Mantis and Ant were closest to her. The Wasp lagged behind a bit, using the opportunity to look around.

Lia ducked into a dark and narrow alley, as yet unseen by any of the multilimbed predators. Or so she hoped. She immediately spotted a furtive young tagger crouched beside a dumpster down at the far end of the passage, honing his craft on a patch of virgin wall.

"Hey!" Lia called, startling him. "You, there with the paint, let me see that."

The bewildered vandal dropped his spray can and ran away, showing her nothing but the soles of his Nikes.

"That works too," Lia muttered, hurrying over and grabbing up the abandoned can. Glancing back, she spotted Ant and Mantis near the mouth of the alley, scanning and sniffing around for her. There was no sign of Wasp.

Lia turned to the wall and sprayed, in big bold letters:

MADAM, I'M ADAM

—on the theory that palindromes make good imaginal traps.

Semi-intelligent otherworlders, like her current pursuers, were said to get stuck in them, although she'd never had a need to test the idea out before. She didn't know if this was going to work at all.

Ant spotted her as she was finishing off the last letter of her slogan.

Lia dropped the paint and slipped away while Mantis and Ant shattered into a rustling wave of bugs that poured down the alley after her, as fast as a thought. The pair drew themselves back together to concentrate with every modicum of mental acuity they possessed when they paused before Lia's hurriedly-scrawled tag. She knew they had to make themselves as human as possible in order to focus and reason, in even the most perfunctory fashion.

They cocked their sleek heads in eerie synchrony, reading and considering the spray-painted words for longer than they meant to, as Lia'd hoped they would. She paused behind another dumpster to watch them, even though her every nerve was vibrating with a suppressed need to flee. She could see the demons' large, faceted eyes ticking back and forth over the letters that came to the same meaning when read from either the left or the right.

The staring monsters' smooth carapaces soon pebbled and roughened, then separated into tiny bugs that drifted lazily away.

The entities were hypnotized by the words, their simplified minds bouncing back and forth between the strange phrase's beginning and its end, completely foxed by the unexpected experience of finding the same message in either direction. It was like feedback in the symbolism, something entrancing and compelling. At least for them.

Lia knew a child's wordgame wouldn't hold the Tzitzimime forever. It might not even hold them for long. But it was something, anyway.

Within moments all that remained of the statuesque ladydemons were two vague swirls of wan, white light hovering before a nonsensical legend written on a concrete wall.

Lia had to wrench herself away from the fascinating sight of them.

She was shaking by the time she emerged from the alley's far end and onto the next street over, not only from an adrenaline surge that was just now subsiding, but also from the manic, triumphant thrill that always hit her after seeing one of Black Tom's old tricks come off without a hitch.

This block was residential, tree-lined, stacked with apartment buildings and packed with parked cars, but far less crowded with pedestrians than the main drag had been.

So it was no place to linger.

Lia, looking ever over her shoulder, hurried down the sidewalk to her battered gray Mazda. It was identifiable at any distance by its proliferation of stickers proclaiming the names of her favorite bands or displaying slogans that amused her. A vivid purple example on the rear bumper exhorted its readers to 'Visualize Whirled Peas.'

She fumbled out her keys and got in. Tom was already waiting in the passenger seat. He tipped his hat with his customary wry smile before she started up the engine and pulled away from the curb, out onto the dark and traffic-free street, wasting no more time about it. She was opening her mouth to tell him about her success with the palindrome trap when something long and straight and deadly sharp plunged down through the car's roof, barely missing her head. She lost control of the wheel as her eyes tried to focus on the fat black needle that had almost lobotomized her, crushing a trash bin with her front bumper before the car squealed to an involuntary halt against the curb. Its ill-maintained engine burbled, faltered, and stalled.

While Lia twisted the key, fighting to restart the car, the unidentified spike withdrew with a loud metallic screech and slammed down again, punching a second hole in her roof.

This time Black Tom grabbed the thing, whatever it was, and held on. He leaned out the passenger window and looked up.

An enormous wasp/woman hybrid glared back down at him, enraged at having her stinger trapped.

Black Tom pulled his head back into the car when the engine coughed and roared again. Gripping the thrashing stinger for dear life, he frantically indicated that they should go. The faster the better.

Lia floored it and the little car lurched away from the curb, off down the street at full speed, with Wasp pinned to the roof by her considerable, yellow-&-brown-striped ass. Lia could hear her unfurled wings crackling in the wind as she piloted them straight up into the hills, climbing hard, with her Mazda's puny engine howling in protest.

She knew exactly where she was going.

In minutes they were up above the houses, on a rough fire access road that ran all the way through Griffith Park, bisecting the vast swath of undeveloped territory that served as a divider between the city of Hollywood on this side and the San Fernando Valley (where they lived), on the other. Wasp slapped lashing foliage aside as Lia sped them through a tunnel of black nighttime trees.

Stretched across the road ahead was a chain with an ineffectually small 'NO TRESPASSING' sign dangling from it. The chain was set high, for the sake of roving SUVs, and Lia's car was small. Going slow, she might've slid right under it. But she wasn't going slow. Not at all.

The chain starred her windshield and snapped with an audible twang when the Mazda plowed through it at full speed. Lia's hand shot up to shield her eyes.

The broken chain whipped upwards, cutting Wasp in half at the middle while flicking her neatly off the roof. The two pieces of her segmented body fell away to burst against the pavement like a pair of rotten pumpkins, exploding into a dazed-looking swarm that rose and dissipated, reluctantly, after Lia's taillights disappeared over the crest of the hill they'd been climbing.

Black Tom craned around to look back and Lia angled her mirror every which way, but the Wasp seemed to be gone. It was either dead or distracted, at least for the time being. Lia drove on as fast as she dared, down a series of narrow back roads meant only for park service vehicles and the occasional fire truck.

Tom realized he was still holding onto Wasp's severed stinger. He looked down at it, nonplussed, then tossed it out the window. It clattered to the road surface behind them just before an unlighted, off-the-map tunnel swallowed up Lia's car.

Chapter Three

Lia's tires crunched and popped in the gravel when she pulled into the parking lot at the front of Potter's Yard. Her headlights splashed across the Yard's small office shack and penetrated the dense wall of greenery behind it, causing a brief wash of weird, bristling shadows to race away through the orderly ranks of sapling trees.

"Home again, home again," she muttered, then sighed. Peering through the new web of fissures in her windshield during the drive up through the Valley had given her the beginnings of a headache. She gauged how weary she must've looked by the concern she saw reflected in Black Tom's eyes.

She angled into her accustomed spot near the wooden fence and paused to finger the freshly-punched holes in the roof of her car before getting out. "Shitballs," she muttered to herself, feeling fairly certain that demon attacks were not going to be covered by her insurance policy.

Black Tom stepped out on the passenger side and inspected the holes in the roof for himself while Lia pulled the Yard's rattling gate closed along its metal track, then locked it for the night.

All around her, lush and leafy life thrived. There were shrubs, flowers, and mature trees in big wooden bins, as well as a large nursery under green nylon shades, a corrugated-plastic greenhouse, and the tiny cabin that looked to be about a hundred years old, which currently housed the establishment's cash register. Its wood-plank walls were silvery-gray after years of exposure to the weather, and its glassless windows were shuttered closed for the night. Beyond that lay eight full acres of foliage, plants in hundreds of varieties and sizes.

It all felt still, silent and safe—just the way Lia liked it.

She paused to look back toward her car before she'd gotten more than a few feet down a narrow path that ran between two rows of bushy ficus trees.

Black Tom was just then stooping down as if to pet a large black cat that was lying curled up near the gate, as still as a stone. He lifted the feline's pointy chin with one gnarled hand and then dissolved into a substance that might have been either light or mist in order to funnel himself right down into the animal's unblinking eyes, so fast that most people would have been able to tell themselves they hadn't seen it happen.

"C'mon, already," Lia said, then vanished down the darkly verdant corridor. The spirit she called Black Tom trotted after her, re-ensconced within the catbody that kept him anchored to this world. The ink-colored kitten had been so young and so close to death when he claimed it years ago that it had no volition of its own today, and would sit motionless wherever he left it for as long as his conscious mind was absent.

The reanimated animal was leading the way by the time they reached the center of the Yard: a clearing where pots, fountains, and a large collection of garden statuary were displayed. What Lia chose to see was a fairy ring made up of crouching gnomes, spitting mermaids, and concrete bodhisattvas, all of them frozen in their nighttime revels by her approach.

Potter's Yard was a place she dearly loved, especially at night, when it was hushed and lit only by the stars. It felt like a shadowy oasis out here in the middle of the industrial suburbs, one that was always awash in some sort of fecund, flowering life, all year round. She breathed in the familiar olfactory chorus of damp, green, earthy smells, and as always, she felt immediately soothed. She even shivered pleasantly in the chilly air.

Lia knew she couldn't relax yet, however. She might, in fact, never be able to properly relax again, if she wasn't careful. Those insect women were out there somewhere still, regrouping, and they might even know her name. If they did, it meant they'd never quit. She didn't need her Tom to tell her that.

Her eye landed on a number of pale green mantises sitting primly on a palm leaf nearby. They seemed to be watching her.

That in itself wasn't so troubling, but when Lia looked down, she realized that an entire line of tiny red ants trailing across her path had also paused, and every one of them seemed to be staring up at her, too.

Only then did she become aware that the night had gone unnaturally silent around her. There wasn't a single cricket to be heard.

The ants resumed their usual brisk pace as soon as they knew she'd noticed them.

Lia took a deep breath and let it out slowly, forcing down the panic that was rising in her chest. She knew what this was, all right: a witch test. An assessment of her comfort level in the face of wild improbability. Her Tom had warned her about such things, but she'd never been the subject of an otherworldly assessment like this one before. The surreal occurrence had happened so quickly that an ordinary person would've shaken her head, blinked her eyes, and walked away. Someone who knew the Tzitzimime for what they were, however, was apt to react to unusual bug behavior with stark raving terror, thereby marking her sorry self as a holder of occult knowledge.

Black Tom quietly confirmed her suspicions about this, mind-to-mind.

The King's consorts weren't too bright in their insect forms, so Lia figured it was unlikely that this little lapse on her part would catch their attention. Only a big reaction would alert them. Maybe the distinctive stinger-holes in her car's roof had helped them to spot this place from above, but human faces all looked more or less alike to them, and it seemed they didn't know her well enough yet to recognize her by sight alone—which was a good thing. They'd want to be sure to get the right girl, and they wouldn't pounce until they were certain they had her.

If she made a wrong move, though, every bug hidden away within the greenery of Potter's Yard would be on her in the space of a heartbeat.

She forced herself to giggle aloud, as if chiding herself for imagining she'd seen a thing that simply couldn't be, before stepping casually over the ant superhighway and moving on, ignoring the attentive cluster of mantises who rubbed their tiny, greedy hands together. Tom hugged close to her ankles until they reached the very back of the Yard.

Lia knew the only thing she could do now was seal herself in and hang on till daylight. Tzitzimime were insidious things by nature, and they'd get in through vents or under doors—at any place a tiny bug or a point of light could. Hiding out from them was a tall order. Fortunately, she happened to be prepared for just this sort of thing.

The nursery's rear storage corner was packed with pots, planks, bags of soil, and a small forklift. There was also a big, upended concrete cylinder that could've been some sort of a well, all of it situated behind a low chainlink fence with a gate marked 'EMPLOYEES ONLY.'

Lia was relieved to hear the crickets start up again behind her after three points of light that might almost have been mistaken for shooting stars departed from the Yard, rising up into the night sky like meteors in reverse. It meant the Tzitzimime had moved on in confusion, and that she had a moment or two before they'd come around to thinking she might have been their prey after all. But a moment was all she needed in order to drop out of sight.

Lia scooped her tomcat up and tucked him inside her coat. She hurried over to the wide concrete tube that seemed to be planted in the earth, swung her legs over the lip, and climbed down a steel ladder bolted to the inside of it.

Some feet below ground level was a hatch. Lia turned a big spoked wheel to unseal it, then pulled it open and climbed on down, letting the hatch door slam shut after her with an ear-hammering metallic clang. She spun a second wheel, a less-corroded twin to the exterior one, in the opposite direction now that she was inside and underground. There was a bolt that locked the hatch in place and Lia threw it, battening herself in for the remainder of the night.

Lights buzzed and flickered to life when she hit a wall switch before climbing down the ladder's last few rungs and into her home of the last ten years. She thought of it as Bag End, her hobbit hole, buried deep in the sheltering earth. Old signage on the unpainted walls indicated that the big concrete bunker had originally been intended for use as a bomb shelter.

Lia opened her peacoat, letting her tomcat out. She dumped the coat over the back of a chair and kicked off her Chuck Taylors as she picked her way over to the dark corner of the room that housed her bed.

The furnishings she twisted past were all cleverly repurposed objects. There was a dented surgical crash cart for a dresser, while a pharmacist's cabinet with cracked, chickenwire-embedded glass doors served as an overcrowded bookcase. Her table was a carved mahogany door she'd topped with a salvaged slab of green-edged glass. There were pictures, toys, and bits of statuary all over the place. Many things that looked alive, as Lia was an animist by inclination and therefore always felt a need to make objects with personality feel welcome when they showed up, wanting to spend a part of their long, strange lives with her. As a result her place felt funky, weird and witchy, although it was undeniably cozy, too.

Lia stopped by her bed and took the tarnished, Navy-crested Zippo from her pocket. She considered it for a long moment before setting it on a wooden shelf stuffed with secondhand books, wondering who might've owned it before her and how they'd come to leave it outside an office belonging to the Aztec God of the Dead.

She didn't imagine the antique's previous steward was apt to come looking for it, in any case.

Lia flopped down onto her futon, fully clothed, on top of the covers. Tom curled up next to her and purred loudly. Within minutes they were both asleep.

Ignored and unnoticed, the dead man's lighter warmed up by gradual degrees, until its case smoldered in an ominous shade of orange. Slight curls of smoke rose from the shelf it sat on.

Now that its dormant magic had been kindled by a witch's touch, the heated anchor on its side pulsed like the slow and steady beat of a living heart—*bumpbump, bumpbump*—as it silently called out to its former owner.

Retrospective No.1 ~ 1950

Six decades ago…

Dexter Graves lit a cigarette, snapped his lighter shut, then tipped the brim of his fedora back so he could look all the way up the tall front of an old, brick office building located on the southern edge of Hollywood. A few of the local oldtimers still called it the Silent Tower, though Graves had never learned why. The sky was clear and blue above it, and the structure itself was as silent as a tomb, lacking identifying signage of any kind. It was in obvious use and good repair, however, despite its half-century of wear and weathering. Most of its neighbors were newer by decades, and in truth next to nobody remembered its name anymore. Graves had done a fair bit of digging before turning it up himself. At thirteen stories high, the Tower must've been one of the first tall buildings erected in this area, back in its day, but the public records regarding it were as sketchy on that score as they were on any number of others.

As soon as the little-used street in front of it was entirely clear of both pedestrian and motor traffic, Graves ambled across with perfect nonchalance, making a low-key beeline for the building's front door. He drew a leather wallet that bristled with lockpicking rakes from his trenchcoat's inside pocket, meaning to admit himself to the so-called Silent Tower on his own recognizance. He was aces at getting in where he hadn't been invited. But then the only tension bar in his entire goddamn pick set broke off as soon as he leveraged it against the lock's sturdy tumblers, and that was it for the subtle approach. Graves snarled a curse, glanced around, then just kicked the door right the hell in.

He dove for the deck when a startled thug stationed in the front hall reflexively unloaded a shotgun in his direction, and a burst of jamb shrapnel filled the air.

The wild blast tore the fedora from Graves' head, but he managed to tackle the gunman around the knees (aided greatly by gravity and luck), and took him down to the polished parquet floor. The scattergun discharged a second time, causing jagged chunks of ceiling plaster to rain down on the guard's undefended head. He was knocked senseless.

Graves stood up and dusted off his coat, taking his good luck in stride. He claimed his adversary's plaster-dusty hat to replace his own, shook it off, and put it on his head. Then he picked up the man's shotgun, cocked it, and pushed forward before nerves could get the better of him. He knew full well that he wouldn't get another chance at this. Not now. But he had reason to believe that a lady of his acquaintance was being held here against her will, and that was the sort of thing Dex Graves wouldn't let slide.

He heard footfalls and ducked behind a potted palm situated outside a fancy set of double-doors at the end of the hall. A bare instant later three new thugs in big-shouldered suits burst through them at a full run, but failed to see him.

Graves was grinning when he darted through the swinging doors, wholly unnoticed by the trio of Johnny-come-latelys—only to run smack into a man he recognized as Juan San Martín, Miguel 'Mickey Hardface' Caradura's chief enforcer. Big Juan, as they called him, was an ugly mountain of muscle overlaid with flab and wrapped in dark blue pinstripes. They'd never met before, but Graves knew better than to mount an assault on somebody else's turf without doing his homework.

Big Juan grabbed hold of Graves' shotgun before he could bring it into play. With his other hand he hoisted Graves up by his shirtfront and hurled him back through the double doors, separating him from the weapon. Big Juan raised the gun as Graves tumbled ass over tits back down the hallway he'd just escaped. The doors banged off the walls and bounced shut again, catching Big Juan's shotgun barrel between them. The noise made the troop of lackeys who were almost out the front entrance realize they'd missed their quarry, and they came running back in Graves' direction at full tilt.

Graves hurled himself against the double-doors, down near floor level, pinning Big Juan's gunbarrel between them. He clamped his hands over his ears (as well as over the brim of his fedora) a split-second before Juan let off a deafening, double-barreled blast, scant inches above his head.

Big Juan's blind shotgun barrage splattered the fastest of the three returning goons right out of commission. Graves winced and the other two men dove aside, out of the line of fire.

He reached up, grabbed hold of the trapped gunbarrel with both hands, and yanked on it viciously, with all the force he could apply. He felt an unbalanced Big Juan topple face-first into the closed doors, and heard him bellow when his nose made solid, crunching contact with the heavy planes of polished wood.

In the instant after he felt the impact and heard Juan's resultant shout, Graves was able to rip the shotgun right out of the big man's hands with a second, well-timed pull. San Martín grunted, stumbling to his knees as the doors swung open before him.

Graves kicked one of them hard, whacking Big Juan square in the face with it for a second time. The human mound fell backwards into the foyer as Graves whirled, cocking the shotgun he'd recaptured from his oversized adversary, and fired twice after the two henchmen who were caught in the front hallway.

The swinging doors fell shut.

An instant later they banged open again and Graves strode into the foyer. Big Juan looked up as Graves loomed over him and trained the shotgun's long barrel right down between his eyes.

"Where's Caradura?" the detective asked, getting to it without preamble.

Juan, dazed, his nose bleeding freely from its two collisions with the door, reluctantly pointed upwards. Graves looked across the foyer. There were three elevators and a door marked 'STAIRS.' He nodded, and then looked back down at Big Juan. "Good talk, amigo," he said.

Graves flipped the shotgun upside down and whacked Juan San Martín decisively in the face with the stock. The fat henchman's eyes rolled back to the whites, and then he lay still. Graves didn't like to kill people if he didn't have to (although if he *did* have to, he could make his peace with it). He'd figured gunplay might be a part of this deal—he just hadn't expected so much of it so soon.

Graves lit another cigarette while his elevator car noiselessly ascended, using his silver Zippo with the gold US Navy insignia on its side.

Now this, to say the least, was not how he would've chosen to spend his day. His PI work tended to be staid and predictable. Embezzlement, infidelity—those were his normal bread and butter. Cheating husbands and crooked beancounters. Stakeouts and papertrails. A snore sometimes, sure, but frankly, Dex Graves had worked the need for thrilling heroics out of his system back in the war.

The only thing was, he'd recently shared a cup of joe at an all-nite diner with a woman he knew, an occasional singer at his local watering hole, and she'd chosen that moment to confide in him. At least in part. It seemed she'd had an affair with a shadowy underworld character named Mickey Caradura, given birth to his baby in secret, and then put the kid up for adoption to keep it safe from its psychopath father. After all the regrets and second thoughts settled in, however, she'd gone and tracked her baby down again, through whatever orphanage had taken it in, and Hardface had somehow gotten wise. Now that he knew the kid existed, Caradura meant to claim and raise it as his heir. Ingrid (that was the mother's name) told Graves she was planning to go and talk with her former fiancé, to try and convince him to leave the child alone. Then last night she hadn't shown up for her set at the joint where Graves liked to listen to her sing, and it didn't take a mathematician to put two and two together. He didn't even know this Ingrid person all that well, but he'd grown up an orphan himself, and he'd be damned if he was going to let any kid get snatched away from a mom who cared about it.

So here he fucking was, despite all his better judgment.

Still, he was in it to win it now, as somebody once said. Not in the name of action or glory or any other idiot ideal, but because he was the only person in any position to clean up this shit. The proper authorities wouldn't even try to touch the mysterious man called Hardface, and that was a fact.

In it to win it, then, Graves reminded himself, *and to hell with the goddamn odds.* That philosophy might not've been designed to maximize longevity, but it had somehow carried him through the Pacific Theater just the same. The guys he'd served with had even come to call him 'Death-Proof Dexter,' in honor of his uncanny ability to dodge the Reaper time and time again. It was as though he were drawing from a Tarot deck with no Death card, only Jokers. And now he was gambling on that odd imperviousness once again. He could only hope he hadn't played his lucky streak out yet.

So musing, he cast a glance up at the trapdoor in the car's roof.

A moment later, the bell over the middle of the three elevators dinged. The doors slid open onto a top-floor hallway, and another waiting pair of Mickey Hardface's enforcers unloaded their sawed-off shotguns into the car. They each got off three or four noisy rounds before realizing there was nobody in there.

The pudgy palooka in charge (the man was nowhere near as hefty as Juan San Martín, but *still*) raised a hand to signal a cease-fire, and then he crept up to the car while the second clown covered him. It looked as though they expected Graves to be hiding inside the door. The fat guy darted in with his gun at the ready, but there was nothing to see. No Graves.

"Look out! Above you!" the taller, skinnier mug shouted. So *he* was the functioning half of this dyad's brain. As a pair they reminded Graves of an unwholesome Laurel and Hardy.

'Ollie' complied with his partner's directive just in time to see Graves' face and hat dart back from the edge of the open trapdoor in the elevator car's paneled ceiling.

Ollie jumped, grabbed the portal's lip, and started to pull himself up. 'Stan' scrambled to boost him. "Get *up* there, already," Stan squealed, sounding keyed up with murderous excitement. "Get him, he's trapped up there!"

Up in the dark and narrow elevator shaft, Graves jumped across to the top of the next car, catching hold of the taut, greasy cables it dangled from for balance. There was no way he could see of escaping this vertical tunnel, not with another armed man waiting out in the hall. As Ollie began cramming his well-fed bulk up through the middle car's trap, he craned his sweaty, porcine face up towards Graves and grinned.

"Give it up now, why dontcha?" Ollie said. "Ain't no place left to go—"

"But down," Graves supplied, as inspiration struck him and he blasted the elevator cables above the fat man's head with the one shell he had remaining in his shotgun.

They twanged and frayed dramatically, down to a thread.

The elevator car lurched and skinny Stan had sense enough to dive back out of it, into the hallway. Graves heard him shouting. Ollie had one single instant in which to favor him with a look of horrified dismay before the last steel strand holding his perch aloft snapped and the car fell away, noiselessly, down into the engulfing darkness below it.

Some seconds later Graves heard a decisive *crunch*. He nodded in satisfaction, pried open the new trapdoor at his feet, and dropped down into the next wood-paneled carriage over from the one in which he'd ascended, absorbing the impact with a bend of his knees.

The elevator to the left of center dinged and its doors slid apart. Graves stepped out into the hall, leaving the trapdoor hanging open from the carriage's ceiling behind him.

The middle elevator's big doors were still gaping wide, although there was nothing to see through them now but an empty shaft and a snarl of shredded cable. The guy Graves had nicknamed Stan was staring right down into the chasm, looking about as aghast as a man can be. He whipped his head up when Graves strode toward him.

Before he could get his gun into play, however, Graves flicked a smoldering cigarette butt into his face. The skinny henchman staggered backwards, flailing, and fell right into the open, empty elevator shaft.

His scream echoed all the way down, until a muffled thud abruptly cut it off.

Graves didn't look back, but he grinned an ugly grin as he walked on down the hall. He paused to pick up a still-loaded shotgun one of the now-dead guards had dropped, as a replacement for the one he'd emptied.

He was about to throw open Miguel Caradura's office door, the only one down at the far end of the hallway, but he stopped in his tracks at the sound of a woman's dulcet voice behind him.

"Dexter."

He spun around and Ingrid Redstone stepped out from a recessed doorway, as if into a silver spotlight. She was a vision: in her late twenties, with ivory skin, fox-red hair, and a body to make any man want to run screaming through the streets with his balls in a bucket of ice. Graves found it incredible to think that she'd given birth not too many months ago, as she in no way resembled any matron he'd ever met. Her missing kid was bound to be a looker too, if precedent meant anything. The tall redhead (who was packed into a black satin evening gown even though it wasn't much past eight in the morning) regarded Graves with troubled blue eyes.

"You really came," she said.

Graves' face tried to light up with relief and pleasure as he started toward her, but Ingrid's look of brokenhearted sorrow kept it from doing so. "Ingrid, holy shit, are you okay?" he blurted. "Did they hurt you? How'd you get away?"

Ingrid shrugged him off when Graves tried to embrace her. "It doesn't matter, Dexter, there isn't time," she said. "You have to get out of here."

"*We* have to get out of here," he corrected. "Soon as I've seen to Caradura."

"Dex, no," Ingrid said, her eyes widening in shock at the very idea. "He'll kill you. Or something worse. Let's just go, please, while we still can..."

She pulled him back toward the elevators by the sleeve of his coat, but Graves stopped and held his ground.

"Ingrid, listen to me," he said. "He's not gonna hurt you, not ever again. You or anybody else. You wanna know how I know?"

Graves drew a loaded .45 from a shoulder-holster he wore inside his jacket, racked it, and handed it to Ingrid, who took it in spite of herself. She looked down at it, seeming to marvel at its weight and the coldblooded elegance of its engineering.

"Cause we're gonna go make sure of it together," Graves told her. "You'n me, sister. Let's finish this thing."

He turned and marched back toward Caradura's door, holding Stan's dropped shotgun at the ready. Ingrid was still looking at the pistol in her hand.

"I can't do that, Dex," she said, and her tone stopped Graves cold. He whirled around to see her pointing his very own gun at him. She looked distressed by what she was doing, but her aim was all too steady. "And I can't let you."

"If this is a comedy act, it needs a lotta work," he said.

"Let's just go, Dexter. Right now. I'll go with you. But you can't... You just *can't*..."

"Why are you protecting him?" Graves asked, in a low and ominous growl.

"I'm not," Ingrid said. "I'm protecting *you*."

Graves glanced pointedly at his pistol, clutched there in her unwavering hand. "Yeah, how could I have missed that?" he said. "Haven't felt quite *this* safe since my time on Okinawa."

"Don't joke."

"Is it Martin or fuckin' Lewis that I look like to you?" he snapped. Before Ingrid could respond, he continued: "No, now you *listen*, sister, I came to get you outta here—"

"Then let's *go*," Ingrid said, sounding exasperated.

"But I'm not leaving this place till I know this thing is done. You get me? I am not walking outta this building while Mickey Fuckin' Hardface is still around to walk this *earth!*"

Ingrid cringed at his vehemence, and he relented.

"You don't wanna watch it, then wait here," he told her, softly. "But don't stand in my way."

With that he turned and started for the door at the end of the hall.

"Dexter, don't you go in there," Ingrid half-warned and half-pleaded, her voice quavering as it rose by an octave or two. "I'm telling you, don't do it!"

Graves stopped before Caradura's door, but he didn't turn back. He shook his last cigarette out of the pack and lit it with his Zippo, crumpling the empty cellophane in his other hand before tossing it aside. "I gotta do what's gotta get done, Ing," he told her. "You go ahead and do the same."

He put his hand on the doorknob and the gun went off behind him, explosively loud in the narrow hallway. Graves' brains blew out his forehead and spattered against the door, obscuring Miguel Caradura's painted name.

His last coherent thought was that he really hadn't seen that coming.

He stared for a disbelieving moment at the bloody gray matter that now decorated the door's varnished surface, before his knees buckled and he slumped forward, shot dead. The boneless weight of his collapsing corpse pushed the door open even as it twisted his neck back at an angle that should've been painful, so that the last thing his dying eyes registered was Ingrid, still holding the smoking gun she'd used to murder him. Her eyes ticked to the floor when his lighter tumbled from his slackening hand. Graves was barely aware of it, himself. He couldn't feel his hands anymore, or any other part of his body, either.

The final image that dissolved from his mind—as his scrambled brain sputtered out its last erratic signals and his vision faded away to black—was one of Ingrid, lovely Ingrid, anguished and sinking down to her knees.

Some unacknowledged span of time later the bell above the elevator bank dinged and its last undamaged door slid open, disgorging Juan San Martín. There was clotted noseblood all down the front of his expensive, custom-made suit. He looked to Ingrid like a man who'd recently been cracked in the face with a gunbutt.

He stopped dead as soon as he stepped out of the elevator, taking in the gory scene.

Ingrid turned away from him. She'd been sitting on the floor and silently weeping, some feet away from Dexter Graves' cooling corpse. His .45 lay forgotten on the carpet beside her.

Beyond her, however, and just beyond the detective's occasionally-twitching body, the door to Miguel Caradura's office was still standing open, and there didn't seem to be anything remotely resembling a conventional workspace in there, at the moment.

Big Juan gulped hard as he confronted the truth that lay behind the visual illusions his boss habitually kept up. Behind Caradura's door was what appeared to be the inner sanctum of a pre-Columbian Aztec temple: two small, firelit rooms fashioned from stone and brown mud bricks. Torches soaked in pitch flickered on the walls and a round, blood-blackened altar stone dominated the second chamber, hulking in the spot where an executive's desk might otherwise have stood.

Ingrid couldn't be bothered to look, herself. She'd seen it all before.

Besides which, the cloaked figure of Mictlantecuhtli himself was currently standing in the rough doorway on the furthest side of his altar room, looking out over the miles upon miles of chaparral hills that rolled away under a leaden sky, in sharp contrast to the bright LA morning in 1950 that Ingrid knew was going on outside the Tower even now. She could sense Mickey's quiet fury, and she didn't want to risk making eye contact with him, should he happen to turn around. It was as much as she could do to remain composed already.

She therefore chose to concentrate on Dexter's silver cigarette lighter, the last thing he'd held in life, lying where it had landed on the carpet, because looking at his inert body was also more than she could bear.

She'd never intended for him to follow her. She couldn't even imagine how he'd ever *found* this place. But then, Dexter was different. Special. She was appalled by what she'd done to him, but when he turned up the way he had, unannounced and out for blood, she hadn't known how else to stop him from going through that door.

Big Juan stepped around Ingrid, grasped Dexter by the ankles, and dragged him back the few inches he needed in order to close the office door again. Ingrid felt him pause for a moment before he did so, presumably taking one last look at Mictlantecuhtli's shrouded, broad-shouldered back.

Then he eased the door shut and turned to face Ingrid, clearly at a loss in regards to her. "I- I'll go get some stuff to clean up the, ah… the mess," he said lamely.

Ingrid nodded, avoiding eye contact with the henchman the same way she had with his boss, and Big Juan took this as permission to flee the scene. He managed not to run, but he couldn't keep the evidence of rubbery relief out of his posture entirely, as Ingrid observed once his back was turned.

She didn't know for sure what happened next, but she found she could make some educated guesses. Her dreams that night were filled with her imaginings. The pictures waited in the wings of her mind until she was helplessly asleep in a lonely corner of the Silent

Tower and unable to push them aside through conscious effort anymore.

In them, she watched Big Juan San Martín dump Dexter's body into the middle of an old, paint-stained dropcloth and bundle him up like so much meat in a burrito. Blood from the bullethole in Dex's head soaked through the canvas, but it was just one more stain on the Jackson Pollock cloth.

Even in her sleep Ingrid tried to banish such images, but she couldn't help seeing Juan turn on his headlights as he rolled down out of a tunnel high up in the hills of Griffith Park. He was driving a bulky black Packard and taking an obscure route out of Hollywood in order to minimize his chances of encountering the police. She pictured him cruising through acres of San Fernando Valley orange groves, with the ripe fruits on the trees glowing like warm coals in the last of the day's dying light.

He wended his way through oak-dotted hills on a dirt road as the sky darkened and the first stars began to appear.

Finally he was out in the roadless desert, miles away from civilization, alone in the flat and ugly scrublands where no sane person would ever want to live, not in a hundred years. His tires kicked up moonlit plumes of pale, dry dust while he looked around for a suitable spot to dig.

Part Two: All Saints' Day

Chapter Four

Six decades later...

The Bindercotts' aged Latina housekeeper was vacuuming, alone, mid-morning, in bitchy Bethany Bindercott's outgrown frillygirl bedroom. She bumped the noisy vacuum against the leg of Bethie's canary-yellow dresser, dislodging a baggie of *mota* that had until now been taped up underneath it.

Pilar, the housekeeper, shut off her roaring machine and picked up the baggie, considering it in the bright, suddenly silent bedroom.

Ten minutes later Pilar was parked out on the Bindercotts' back deck, toking up in the clear autumn sunshine.

The hills just outside the irrigated housing development in Santa Clarita that her employers called home looked dusty brown and about as dry as kindling. As little as ten years ago, she remembered, this whole area had been a waterless wasteland, fit for little more than the surreptitious disposal of inconvenient corpses.

On the big green lawn in front of Pilar—right out in the center of Big Bill Bindercott's personal practice putting green, in fact—something broke through the sod.

A gopher, maybe? If so, it was a damn big one. Whatever the thing was, it seemed to be forcing its way up from underneath the lush, professionally-tended lawn. Pilar squinted to see better, shading her eyes against the sun's glare.

Out on the putting green, skeletal hands and arms emerged from what looked increasingly like a small sinkhole, clawing and scrabbling at the grass around it. A grimy skull popped up, one with a distinctive exit wound above the right eye socket.

Pilar's own eyes widened. She looked down at the ineptly-rolled joint in her hand.

Dexter Graves (or what little remained of him after sixty years in the earth) hauled himself out of his grave and came staggering across the broad back lawn he found himself on, holding his cracked braincase like a drunk wallowing in the throes of crapulence. Up the steps and onto a redwood deck he went, where he stopped, looking down at an older woman in a light-blue uniform with bulky white sneakers on her feet who was parked in an Adirondack chair. A maid, Graves surmised, judging by her attire. The housekeeper was frozen, looking back up at him with a forgotten smoke dangling from her fingertips.

Must've scared the living shit out of her, Graves thought, *wandering in from the backyard like this.* Hell, he could've been anybody! A certain comfort level in the face of wild absurdity had often helped him keep hold of his wits, both during the war and several times thereafter in his current line as a PI, but he knew not everybody could roll with the punches in a similar fashion. He was still a little confused himself after waking up underground, not quite sure of where he was or exactly how he'd gotten here.

"Estoy muerta?" the maid whispered, looking up at the dirt-encrusted skeleton who wasn't yet up to speed regarding his own situation. "Usted es la Santa Muerte? Esta esto la Apocalipsis?"

"Sorry, sister," Graves' reanimated bones replied, in a predictably gravelly voice. "Never did learn to habla the old es-pan-yol. Wouldn't mind a puff on that smokestick, though. I have *never* had a hangover like this before."

Graves plucked the hand-rolled cigarette in question from the lady's fingers and put it between his teeth. He expanded his ribs as if to inhale, but with no lungs to pull air, nothing happened. Graves examined the joint critically while patting around the region where his pockets should've been. "Guess it went out," he said absently. "Don't know where my lighter got to, either. Hell, I'd hate to lose that thing *now*..."

Graves offered the joint back to its original roller. She stared at his skeletal hand. "De nada," she managed to croak.

Graves thought she looked sort of shellshocked, for some reason. She had that sort of half-comprehending stare. He shrugged and went to stick the reefer behind an ear that'd turned to dust years ago. It bounced off his collarbone and tumbled to the deck.

"What the…?" he muttered, turning to look at his reflection in the house's glass back door. His appearance came as a bit of a shock, to say the least.

"*Holy* hell, wouldja look at that?" he shouted, reeling back in bewilderment. He was nothing but a string of bones, literal bones, and the smooth, soil-blackened plate of his forehead was marred by what looked suspiciously like an exit crater. "Geez, no wonder my head feels like it's got a goddamn hole in it. Now how in the—?"

He remembered.

"Oh, yeah. Ingrid."

Leaning back in to examine the reflected bullethole in his fleshless brow, he murmured to himself: "How could you, Ing?" He hadn't known the woman excessively well (certainly not in the biblical sense), but he'd imagined she thought more of him than *that.*

Behind him, that hapless housekeeper dumped what she must've assessed as a sack of psychotic locoweed out into the bushes. She skirted as wide a berth around Graves as she possibly could and slid a big glass panel in the house's back wall aside so that she could scurry indoors, leaving the modernistic entryway open in her haste.

Graves followed after her.

Crossing a vast family room that had what looked like a mid-sized movie screen mounted up on its most prominent wall, he said: "Listen, lady, I gotta go find my lighter. It's important to me. You think maybe I could—"

But the cleaning woman waved him off without so much as a look back. She was done. Just done. He knew *that* look, too. She gathered her purse and her jacket from the kitchen and exited right out the front door, closing it quietly behind herself this time around.

"Oh. Okay. All right," Graves said after her, feeling affronted.

He went to the window and watched the house's custodian

drive away in a weird, rusty little car of some sort, one that seemed to have a great big hatch on its back end.

"Then I guess I can," he opined, standing alone at the kitchen window.

Graves ransacked an upstairs closet, tossing clothing aside. Old stuff, winter coats and ugly sweaters, mostly. He came up with two reasonably familiar items: a ragged raincoat and a battered fedora. The hat said 'Indiana Jones' around the inside of the band. Graves didn't know what sort of a name that was supposed to be, but Mr. Jones' garage-sale candidates were close enough to the clothes he remembered wearing, and he nodded over them in satisfaction.

Standing in front of the master bedroom's full-length mirror a little while later (after having hosed the worst of the yard dirt off his bones in the attached bathroom's shower), Graves stepped into a pair of sweat pants and cinched them all the way down to the fattest part of his spine. He shrugged into his borrowed raincoat, donned his found fedora, and spent some time tilting the brim to his liking.

With big sunglasses taped to the sides of his skull and his coat collar flipped up, he was almost able to believe he wouldn't draw much notice.

Next, he raided the kitchen drawers. He was flying more or less on autopilot now, distracting himself while he figured out how to proceed. He didn't know why he was up, out of the dirt; he'd just felt a sudden need to be, and acted upon it. There'd been no real *thinking* involved. He didn't care to lament his death or mourn his appearance—he just wanted to know why he was back, and how in hell it was possible. He felt almost more upset over the loss of his old Zippo than he did over the loss of his life, as strange as that sounded, even to him. This was nothing if not a weird situation, though. His first responses to it were bound to be a little wonky.

The drawer he was dredging yielded up an ancient pack of cigarettes wrapped in a clear, rubbery-feeling bag, on which some suburban wit had jotted 'IN CASE OF APOCALYPSE,' in bold black ink. Graves figured today came close enough. There was also a cheap-looking plastic lighter in the bag. He felt heartened at first and clicked the 'bic' to life, but then he sighed in disappointment at the device's meager flash of blue-tinged flame.

"Just ain't the same, somehow," he muttered.

Graves kept the cigarettes but chucked the worthless lighter back into the drawer. It landed on what was obviously a spare set of keys to something, jingling them brightly.

They were unlike any other keys Graves knew, with chunky plastic bases and strange grooves down their shafts rather than the little cutout mountain ranges he remembered. Graves picked them up, curious about what sort of vehicle they started, or which door around here they might unlock.

He glanced back out the front window.

A fancy-looking, carlike thing sat parked out there in the driveway. A tiny, rounded, streamlined capsule that would've made a lot more sense with wings than it did on wheels.

Graves looked again at the keys.

A minute later the fedora-wearing skeleton closed the fancyass car's door behind himself, muffling the neighborhood's sonic backdrop of distant leafblowers and bright birdsong.

He took in the dashboard, with some trepidation. There were more dials, gauges, and knobs in here than you'd find in a goddamn experimental aircraft. And he'd been in Naval intelligence even before the war, so he knew from whence he spoke (*or thought, or recalled, or whatever*). In any case, he'd been around a lot of complicated control panels in his day. He thought he'd be able to manage.

"Still feel like I oughta have a pilot's license here, though," Graves said, talking aloud just to hear a human voice—even his own raspy approximation of one—within the unnatural silence of the cushioned cockpit.

The goddamn grave hadn't been this quiet.

"But it's just a car, right?" he said, reassuring himself. "May look like something outta Jules Verne's hangover, but it's still just a car..."

He put a key in the ignition and started her up. That much, at least, went according to plan. Graves felt heartened. "Okay, then," he murmured. "Here goes nothin.'"

He backed successfully out into the road. A dashboard

compass swung round to south, and that pleased him, for some reason.

Pleased him deeply.

"Yeah, southbound..." he breathed, enraptured by the bobbing of the compass ball within its shiny, fluid-filled globe. It seemed to ease some of the knotted tension in his nonexistent gut, the tension that was nagging at him to go and find his goddamn lighter, wherever the hell it may happen to be. This new sense of direction so thoroughly eclipsed all the rest of the anxiety and astonishment he was feeling in regard to his situation that it was almost like... well, magic.

Graves would've been more impressed, but in truth he barely noticed. He only had eyes for that compass.

"Okay, that feels right," he muttered to himself. "Due south. Retrace my steps, find my lighter. Figure the rest out later. I can do that. Yeah. But for now, due south. And awaaay we go..."

Graves tipped his hat to a stupefied gardener at the corner as he lurched down the street in his commandeered vehicle, following the compass south toward what he remembered to be the farmlands and citrus groves of the northern San Fernando Valley.

Chapter Five

Lia emerged from Bag End's doortube, followed a moment later by her Tom. She was freshly dressed in a knee-length skirt and a light sweater, in deference to the cool November weather. Tom wandered off, still in his cat-form, while Lia wheeled the hatch shut, stretched, and looked around.

Potter's Yard was bright green and peaceful in the pure morning light. All clear of ladydemons, as she'd expected it would be. Tzitzimime were nighttime things, drowned out by the sun. They'd be back tonight, she had no doubt, but that was then. There was time. Right now Lia had an appointment to keep, and at it she firmly intended to extricate herself from the situation that had brought those things down on her in the first place.

The memory of insectile legs tickling her skin made it crawl all over again. She couldn't help but think back on the narrow escape she almost hadn't made the night before. Tom, who never let her go anywhere ignorant or unprepared, had informed her as best he could about the secret history of that shabby brick building, but now, because of the creatures they'd encountered up there, she might never be able to go out after dark again. That seemed to her like a harsh restriction to live under. No more dinners or drinks or decent music, all of which occurred under the cover of night. If Lia couldn't do something about this, she feared that her already truncated social life would soon be limited strictly to brunch.

She sighed. What she'd wanted out of last night's adventure was not only to learn something new (which she'd accomplished, all right), but also to help someone out, if she could, and she didn't feel she'd managed that. She hated to admit defeat, but now, in the light of a brand new day, all she really wanted was to put the experience behind her. Jeopardy so physical and consequences so real were not what she was used to dealing with. Black Tom's tutelage may have led her into some unusual experiences over the last few years (including arming law enforcement officers with information about closed-off places they needed to enter, on an occasion or two), but reviving people's flagging houseplants was still far more familiar and comfortable territory.

Lia never advertised her services, exactly, but word still got around. People knew there was a girl in a garden who could do the things that witches did, and would... provided you asked her nicely and really needed the help.

There were definite limits to her beneficence, however. Lia was neither a saint nor a martyr. She was only herself, and while she might've wished there was more she could do in this circumstance, she also knew when to cut her losses. If she and Tom kept poking around, someone was apt to get hurt. Or worse.

As afraid as she was for herself, though, Lia couldn't up and quit without doing *something* to ensure that the person who'd requested her help didn't fall prey to the mortal threats involved. That wouldn't have been right, in her book.

She brushed her fingers through glowing, sunlit foliage as she made her unhurried way across the Yard. The morning's handful of wholesale buyers were still loading up their small trucks with flats of seedling plants and other landscaping necessities. The last of them would be gone in an hour or so and then the rest of the day would be quiet, with perhaps a little bit of retail business trickling in later on. They'd be closed tomorrow and Wednesday as well, as there wasn't enough trade in the fall to bother staying open to the general public in the middle of the week.

Lia liked this time of year, when the weather was crisp and on a normal afternoon there would be little to do beyond the comforting ritual rounds she habitually made in the course of tending to the Yard's myriad of plants.

Hannah Potter was busy ringing up a purchase in the office shack. She'd been the sole proprietor of Potter's Yard since purchasing the abandoned property it now occupied about seven years back. These days she was Lia's boss and nominal landlord as well as her dearest friend, despite a near thirty year difference in their ages.

Lia waved to her through the shack's un-shuttered window and pointed toward her car, implicitly asking if any help was needed before she took off, even though she'd told Hannah yesterday that she had an appointment to keep this morning. They had a part-time crew that came in during their busier seasons and on weekends, but right now, mid-autumn and on a Monday, it was just the two of them.

Hannah waved back, nodding to indicate that all was under control, and gave her a thumbs up to punctuate it. The canvas gardening glove she had on looked like a big cartoon hand.

Lia's black tomcat crouched down beneath a distant rhododendron bush and went as still as death (although its eyes remained open), even as Lia slipped in behind the wheel of her Mazda.

Black Tom appeared in her passenger seat, nodded to his girl, and they drove off together.

Twenty minutes later they walked into Paty's, a little coffee shop Lia favored, down near the film studios in Burbank. The restaurant was quiet now between the major mealtime rushes, an hour at which she might normally have come in to sit for a while and snack and read a book, especially on a rainy day. There was little she found cozier than lingering over a warm cup of tea on a gray morning. She wished she was here on that sort of pleasant errand right now.

But no. Business first.

Lia spotted her contact waiting in the furthest booth. Alone. Back-to. With a shawl over her blazing red hair. She went over and sat down across from the unmistakable woman, regretting for the first time that she'd chosen to meet at a place she wanted to come back to.

"Ms. Redstone," she said, by way of greeting.

Ingrid looked up.

She was shockingly gorgeous, in Lia's opinion, with gleaming copper hair, a porcelain complexion, and curves everywhere you looked. Although she appeared to be just a few years older than Lia herself, she affected a sort of old-Hollywood glamour in her stylistic choices. Retro all the way. It really did work for her, though. Ingrid Redstone was a hard one not to look at. She should've been a movie star.

Black Tom sat down right next to the radiant lady, who failed to acknowledge him. Making himself solid enough to be seen by ordinary folks depleted Tom's energies fast, so he usually appeared only within the confines of Lia's trained and receptive mind. She'd long ago taught herself not to focus on him when she was out in public.

Ingrid smiled through her aura of elegant sadness. She was actually wearing white satin gloves that went all the way up to her elbows. Lia had to imagine she'd also have an ivory cigarette holder secreted away inside her tiny purse.

"Lia," Ingrid said. "It's good to see you again. Please, don't make me wait. Were you able to find anything?"

"I- I'm afraid not," Lia said.

Ingrid stared at her. It was clearly not the answer she'd expected.

"*Nothing?*" she said at last, her tone filled with disbelief. "Nothing at *all?*"

Lia looked down at her hands, which were folded on the tabletop. "I'm sorry, no," she said. "The building was abandoned. Completely empty."

"Yes, but—"

"Listen, Ms. Redstone," Lia interrupted, before Ingrid could protest further. "I don't think your brother was ever up there. I don't think *anybody's* been there, not for years and years."

"But... no," Ingrid insisted. "I'm *sure*—I mean, there wasn't *any* sign of him? Any little thing? He's a smoker, he's always leaving nasty cigarette butts behind, and he, he was in the Navy... Oh, I don't know *what*, but didn't you see *any*thing?"

Black Tom raised an eyebrow, but Lia shook her head. "I'm sorry," she lied.

Ingrid hung her head, struggling not to cry. Black Tom mimed a clicky-clicky motion, in reference to the cigarette lighter they had indeed found the night before. Lia glared at him for a split second, though she was certain Ingrid couldn't have seen it.

"But…" Ingrid's voice quavered, on the verge of breaking. She took a deep breath, keeping her eyes downcast. "But I *know* that's where he was going. He gave me that exact address the last time I saw him."

"The lock I jimmied hadn't been touched in twenty years, probably more," Lia said, and Black Tom nodded his expert concurrence with that opinion. "And besides, I didn't see any evidence of the sort of thing you thought your brother was involved in. Believe me, it leaves evidence. If what you're worried about *had* happened up there, I would've been able to tell."

Ingrid nodded, trying to pull herself together. "That's about what the private investigator said, too. The regular one. I just thought maybe you… someone like you…"

"I thought so, too," Lia said. "But there wasn't anything to see."

The disappointment visibly crushed Ingrid's frail hopes. She choked on a sob before she buried her face in her gloved hands and moaned: "Then he's just *gone*, isn't he?"

The woman was desolated, her shoulders quaking as she hid her face and fought not to make a public scene. The manager and a busboy were both looking in their direction, aware of Ingrid's distress though not yet concerned enough to intervene.

Lia felt sick, but she still had an uncomfortable agenda here. "It—it's important…" she began carefully, looking at a large, wine-colored garnet that Ingrid wore on a silver chain around her neck, instead of up into her eyes. "I mean, it's probably best that you don't, you know… go back there. Or send anyone else."

"Oh?" Ingrid said, a touch of suspicion drawing her sable brows together into the slightest hint of a frown.

"Yeah," Lia said. Rather lamely, she thought. "It's just… well, I know it's hard, but sometimes, if people who get involved in these sorts of things need to disappear… it's really better to let them."

"I see," Ingrid said, sitting back and dabbing at her eyes with a paper napkin. "Well. We never did properly discuss your, ah… compensation. For your efforts. Did we?"

Lia uncomfortably waved off the suggestion of money. "Just move on," she said. "For your own sake. That's all I ask."

Ingrid seemed about to protest, but then she crumbled and nodded in miserable resignation.

Lia got up. "I wish there was more I could do," she said.

"Thank you," Ingrid replied. "Anyway."

Lia nodded and hurried out of the restaurant.

Black Tom lingered on in the booth next to Ingrid, watching Lia go.

Ingrid sat there, quietly weeping, until Tom eventually got up and left her, too. If her tears were insincere, he thought, then she was one hell of an actress.

Around the next block, he walked up to Lia's vehicle as she was unlocking it. She looked at him across the roof. He looked back benignly.

"Shut up," she told him. Then she got into the car. Impassive, Black Tom did likewise (without going to the bother of opening a door).

Inside the Mazda, where people were less likely to notice her talking to herself (not that it made much of an impression anymore, since the advent of cellphones and Bluetooth earpieces), she turned to Black Tom and said: "What do you want me to do? Really?"

Black Tom, predictably, said nothing.

"The important thing is that nobody else goes up there, isn't it?"

Black Tom shrugged and Lia grew quiet, thinking about it. "What's up in that office is beyond us," she murmured. "You know that better than anyone."

Black Tom conceded the point with the barest of nods.

"And we need to look out for *us*, too, don't we?"

Black Tom nodded again.

"Well, then? That's what I'm doing."

Tom nodded a third time, but with much less certainty. It was still affirmation enough for Lia. She started up the car.

When they drove past the restaurant, headed westbound down Riverside, Tom glimpsed Ingrid through the establishment's big front windows. Just a flash of her, like a snapshot. The astonishing redhead was still sitting in their booth, dialing a cellphone and raising it to her ear.

Then she was behind them, and gone from sight.

Chapter Six

Dexter Graves blew past a cop in his stolen car, doing ninety down the 170, racing in the direction indicated by the dashboard compass like his life—ironically—depended on it.

The instrument was on the fritz, Graves had already realized, spinning around with no regard for true north, and yet it somehow seemed to be leading him on. He couldn't question it; he didn't have the time. Interpreting the compass's directives required all his concentration. When he saw police lights flashing in his rearview mirror he dutifully pulled over, more irritated by the interruption than anything else.

An imposing CHP officer got out of the cruiser behind him and sauntered up to Graves' open window. "Please remove your hat and eyewear, sir," the officer said in a bored, no-nonsense tone, as he flipped open his ticket pad and portentously clicked a ballpoint pen.

Graves' distracted, six-decade-dead skeleton complied with the order.

The cop had no immediate response to the sight that confronted him when he looked up from his pad. He seemed about to say something, then thought better of it. Graves waited, cocking his skull at a quizzical angle. In his weirdly-consuming frenzy to find his lighter he'd almost forgotten what state he was in, physically speaking, and he couldn't even imagine what this must look like to an officer of the law.

"You know what?" the cop said, after a long, long pause. "No. Nuh-uh, no way, just no. Not today. Fuck *this*."

He walked stiffly back to his car, got in, and drove away. Graves shrugged, put his hat back on, and zoomed back onto the highway himself.

He exited at Roscoe Boulevard and headed east into an area he remembered as North Hollywood, a small incorporated city within the Valley's patchwork of communities that bore no legal or geographical affiliation whatsoever with its better-known namesake on the far side of the Hills. In Graves' day the area had been a thriving business center and transportation hub, serviced by a Red Car line that ran down to that other Hollywood, as well as by regular rail to Union Station, downtown. The old groves to its north had even then been giving way to housing or industry, and now, today, they were pretty much gone. So was most of the area's vivacity and that early sense of promise.

The dashboard compass guided him through run-down residential neighborhoods and stripmall-strewn commercial stretches that he barely glanced at, and before he knew it he was pulling his stolen car into the parking lot at a place that looked a little more like the Valley he remembered. It was called 'POTTER'S YARD,' according to its hand-painted sign.

Graves got out and sniffed at the chlorophyll-scented air, feeling dimly amazed for the first time since digging himself up that he *could* still smell things. Or speak, or think at all, for that matter. This was the spot all right, though. He'd never been here before in his life, as far as he recalled, but somehow he knew that this was it. He supposed he felt it in his bones.

It was a nursery, obviously, and a damn big one. Like some kind of a woodland glade right smack in the middle of a dusty beige industrial zone. It seemed very quiet for such a large place. Because of its size Graves figured it might be a wholesale operation, and maybe the buyers came earlier in the day. The stillness didn't feel suspicious to him.

A woman came out of the small office on the far edge of the parking lot and Graves sized her up at once with his investigator's eye. She looked to be in her late forties or early fifties, with long streaks of gray snaking through honey-blonde curls and pretty crinkles around perceptive blue eyes. They made her look like she'd be quick-witted, kind, and prone to laughter. She wore faded dungarees with a flannel shirt and a necklace of tiny alphabet beads that spelled out the name 'HANNAH.' The necklace looked like something a girl might make to give as a gift. Maybe a niece or some other relation had strung it together, Graves guessed, because if Hannah's own kid had done it, the thing would've read 'MOM.'

"Hi there," the lady said, crunching across the gravel lot to greet what she clearly believed was just another customer, out shopping for dirt or flowers or whatever the hell it was that people bought at a place like this. "Can I help you find any... oh."

She stopped and trailed off when she got her first good look at the skeletal remains of Dexter Graves.

"I'm guessing you came to see Lia," she said.

If he'd had any, Graves would've raised his eyebrows. This woman seemed like she practically expected him, even as shocked as she was by his appearance. "I lost something," he explained, and cocked a bony thumb back at his stolen car. "Compass in the rocketpod led me here."

"Definitely, you want Lia," the woman called Hannah told him. "She left, a little while ago, but if you'd like to wait—"

"I'll wait."

"Thought you might," Hannah said, nodding. "You've got a patient look." She examined him critically, doing her best to take him in stride. "Well, I guess you might as well come inside, then," she decided aloud, perhaps assuming it was best to be polite when confronted with something you couldn't understand. "I'd offer you a cup of tea, but it looks like it'd go right through you."

Graves followed Hannah back into the weathered little office shack. "Yeah, well," he said, "I'd ask ya for a belt of scotch, except you're right—I don't have the stomach for it anymore!"

Hannah laughed, brightly if a little nervously, before the old screen door slapped shut behind them.

Chapter Seven

Lia mentally ran through her checklist for 'going dark,' as she conceived it, during the short and familiar drive home. She barely noticed the light traffic on the move all around her.

First and most vital to the things she meant to do was to understand exactly what they were up against. According to Black Tom and the notions he sent into her head, Tzitzimime and all things like them had once been summed up by the old people as 'Those Who Are Not Our Brothers,' because their experience of the worlds is that much different from our own. Symbols were their points of reference, rather than places or things. Meaning, to Lia, that the insectile entities might find her on a symbolic model like a map more easily than they could find her on the street. Their minds were simplified mechanisms, and she figured it shouldn't be too hard to hide from things that couldn't hope to find the same 7-11 twice without being given new directions.

Deflecting them was sure to be safer and more effective than making some sort of desperate stand. If she confused them badly enough, they might forget what they already knew about her. That was possible. If not, she knew of a trap more elaborate than a three-word palindrome that had the potential to pick off the bugs one by one. Such work left no margin for error, but precedent led her to believe that the Aztec entities should be vulnerable to it... assuming she got every detail of the experimental spell's construction right.

The term 'Tzitzimime' itself was one Tom had guided her to on the internet several nights before, filling her mind with the knowledge that the beings so-named were something they might expect to see when they ventured up to the top of the Tower, in a worst-case scenario. Lia kept a whole raft of mythology websites bookmarked on her browser, and today she was glad she'd studied them, as every scrap of knowledge about the history or behavior of Mictlantecuhtli's demon slaves improved her sense of how to deal with them. Tom assured her that all of this was so, and that her understanding was well in place.

Secondly, then, she needed a way to lose focus. Not a distraction or a diversion, but a systematic approach to fuzzing the mantle of symbols that make up an identity, such as our names. The ones we choose, the ones we're given, and the ones that just evolve. Blurring such signifiers would make it hard for otherworlders to perceive the actuality behind them, the things most people would've said were 'really' there. (Although the 'real,' as Lia knew, was often less defined and more slippery than those same people would ever care to imagine.)

At any rate, collecting extra names was a good place to start.

Lia checked the list of voicemail messages waiting on her phone as she drove. There were quite a number of missed calls, as she tended to leave the ringer off. Many of them were from a number identified as belonging to ATLAS RECOVERY ASSOCIATES.

Lia hit the reply button. Moments later a voice chirped in her ear: "Atlas Debt Recovery, is this Ms. Camellia Flores speaking?"

"Yeah, you guys called me, I think?"

"Yes, Ms. Flores, we've left a number of messages," the bill collector said, managing to sound both solicitous and judgmental at the very same time. "I'm Marco, by the way. Is it all right if I call you Cammie?"

"It sure is, Marco," Lia said.

"Good, Cammie. Thank you. Well, then, were you aware that you still owe—"

"Y'know," Lia said, losing interest in his spiel now that her goal in calling back had been achieved. "This isn't really the best time after all. Call ya back."

"Cammie, wait!" Marco cried, with real desperation straining his voice. "Camellia, Ms. Flores, please, it's *extremely* important that we—"

Lia folded up her phone as she came to a red light at Magnolia. *More of that later*, she promised herself. She had a long list of people she could count on to call her by something other than her personal name, and every time one of them did so it made her a tiny bit harder for imaginal eyes to see.

Glancing in her rearview mirror, she noticed two plain, almost identical black cars idling amidst the ranks of traffic that had lined up behind her at the light. They looked like a pair of unmarked police cars, although she somehow didn't think that was what they were.

"Have they been following us?" she asked of Black Tom. He looked in their Mazda's side mirror and raised an eyebrow.

Something about those cars made her nervous. Just in case, just to see, she turned right without signaling and headed east on Chandler, where a two-lane bike path had replaced the train tracks that once ran down the middle of the extra-broad street. She was going out of her way to see if they'd follow.

They followed, all right. Both cars.

"*Shit*balls," Lia said, her brow tightening with worry as she looked over to Black Tom, only to find that he'd already vanished.

T om faded into a state of semi-solidity in the back seat of the closest of those two black cars when it rolled to a stop behind Lia at the next red light. There were two shaved-headed men sitting up front, and neither of the stalkers noticed his silent appearance. He reached out and put a hand over each of their faces.

They dropped into sleep so swiftly that it looked as though Tom had pulled their power cords. He dipped into their undefended minds, ascertaining that they and others like them were, as far as they knew, on the payroll of a powerful 'businessman' they never expected to meet. Even their dealings with his lieutenants were transacted mostly by phone. When they dared to whisper about their boss, the name they used was 'Mickey Hardface.'

Or, in Spanish, 'Miguel Caradura.' The very name Tom and Lia had seen stenciled on the door to what he'd called *las Cameras del Rey*, the King's Chambers, back when he'd been alive.

This was getting serious, then. The nocturnal Tzitzimime, worse than useless when it came to numbers and addresses, must at least have furnished el Rey with a description of Lia's car and the general area they'd chased her to last night. He couldn't tell when or where they'd picked up their current tails, only that it must have been within the last few minutes, since departing from the coffee shop. His sentiments fell somewhere between a hope and an assumption that their pursuers hadn't seen Lia meeting with Ingrid Redstone, the woman who'd asked her to help find a missing member of her family. A relation claimed by Mictlantecuhtli wasn't one the lady would enjoy seeing again, although even if Tom could have told her so he doubted it would've brought much comfort. He had to admit that Lia might be right, that the lovely Miss Redstone was better off being encouraged to walk away. He presumed she'd be all right as long as she did so.

A left-turn arrow flashed green in front of them and Lia drove on. The second black car followed after her, although the one Tom was in did not. Traffic piled up behind it, and it wasn't half a minute before an angry horn sounded, waking the pair of napping henchmen in the front seats with a violent start. The driver stomped on the gas, taking the turn onto Vineland a hair's breadth ahead of oncoming traffic while he scanned for Lia, and promptly plowed them right into the tailgate of a pickup truck that was making a slow turn at the end of the next block.

Lia's little car was long gone, the goons noted in dismay. They exchanged an uneasy look as two big, angry rednecks stepped out of the truck they'd collided with and started toward them, displaying prison tattoos along with an unfriendly attitude.

Feeling satisfied with his work on a deeply personal level, Black Tom moved on.

Lia's car picked up speed as she headed up Vineland. The remaining pursuer followed, tailing her much more aggressively now and cutting people off to do it.

Black Tom poked his head out from under the front end of this second black sedan, as though he were somehow clinging to its undercarriage. Neither his clothes nor his gray-streaked hair moved in the breeze generated by the car's momentum. Even his hat stayed firmly planted atop his head, as if wind resistance meant nothing to him at all. Which, in fact, it didn't.

Tom reached up the black car's grille, found the hood release, and popped it. The hood flew up, blocking the entire windshield and obscuring the occupants' view of the road. Tom heard two grown men yelp in surprise from inside the car.

The unseen driver slammed on the brakes. Tom became diffuse, letting his awareness rise up above the scene while the vehicle he'd been hovering under fishtailed to a stop in the middle of the road, snarling traffic in both directions. Horns blared. Curses were shouted. Both lanes clogged up, making the street impassable. The man in the dark sedan's passenger seat jumped out to slam the hood closed, but Lia had already zipped through the next light up the street as it changed from yellow to red, and was gone.

She bumped fists with Black Tom as soon as he re-appeared in the seat beside her and they made their getaway, leaving busy Vineland just above Burbank before heading further north on Lankershim.

Some little bit of time later they pulled into the lot at Potter's Yard. Lia parked next to a gleaming new BMW, a sporty little thing, and eyed it as she got out. It probably belonged to some production manager looking to rent plants at a later date, she guessed. She couldn't imagine anyone stuffing sacks of fertilizer into that trunk, or cramming potted seedlings into that luxurious back seat.

Lia's black cat blinked at the sound of her car door closing—a sound its sensitive ears registered and recognized even from the distant, shady pocket of the property where Tom had left it earlier. The cat shook its head and stretched as the ex-necromancer's wandering mind reassumed control of its nervous system, his ghost relaxing into its skin after the strange, yoga-like exertion involved in sending himself out.

Comfortably planted back in the only body he had left to call his own, Tom trotted off to greet his girl.

He ran up as Lia was crossing the parking lot. Her mental image of 'Black Tom' had vanished from the passenger seat at the instant the cat awoke, which Lia accepted as a matter of course. She didn't even think about such things anymore. She crouched down to pet the cat, her Tom in any form, while he purred and nuzzled at her ankles, making her feel at home.

This, she thought, returning to the checklist in her mind, was the third and final thing she required for her planned operation: a place to go to ground. A base of operations, a place to protect and be protected by.

This, right here, Potter's Yard, was hers. Her roots were here (at least those she'd set down for herself, with Tom's assistance), and by nightfall she intended to have the place hexed up so tight Saint Anthony himself would never be able to find her. Nothing was going to track her back here, not ever again. Not if she had anything to say about it.

She looked up at the sky before she started across to the office shack. There were still a few hours left before dark. *Should be time enough*, she thought. If she hurried.

Hannah was nowhere to be seen when she entered the office, and Lia frowned. Absence wasn't Han's style. She was the lynchpin of the operation here (although Lia knew Hannah would've modestly claimed that it was *her*, Lia's, green thumb that kept the place afloat).

"Hannah?" she said, uncertainly.

Then, from the back room, she heard the low rumble of a male voice, and it was followed by a pretty peal of Hannah's irrepressible laughter.

Lia smiled, feeling impressed, surprised, and pleased to think that Hannah should have a gentleman caller back there. A gentleman of means, too, judging by the deluxe piece of German engineering he'd left on display out in the parking lot. She headed in the direction of the voices, parting Hannah's Japanese, *noren*-style half-curtain with Hokusai's famous wave printed on it before stepping into the shack's back room.

She was halted in her tracks by the remarkable sight of a well-rotted cadaver in a toy hat and a torn raincoat lounging at the table with her boss, who had a very full glass of red wine in her hand.

"Oh, Lia!" Hannah said cheerfully. "Good, you're back. This is—or, this *was*—Dexter Graves."

"Miss." The thing called 'Graves' stood up and took off his

fake fedora. He offered a skeletal hand to Lia, who dumbly took it, despite herself.

Hannah grinned. "He's come a hell of a long way to find you," she said.

Chapter Eight

Ingrid stood on the trash-strewn sidewalk and looked up as the limousine that had just dropped her off pulled away from the curb, leaving her alone on the deserted street. The century-old office building before her still seemed to stretch into the sky, even though most of its neighbors rivaled it in height, these days.

Silly girl, she thought, smiling gently as she recalled Lia's well-intentioned warnings about returning here. As if such efforts at deflection would keep her away from this place. As if anything ever *could*. The building was even named for her, in a manner of speaking.

The Silent Tower.

Trying the knob on the front door, she found it unlocked. Entering, she found the interior looking... new. Clean and pristine. Not at all the way she'd left it earlier that morning, when she went out to meet with Lia. The potted palms on either side of the double-doors down at the end of the entryway were green and thriving. She fancied she could even smell a ghost of fresh paint.

You're too good to me, Mickey, she thought.

She knew she was expected, but a welcome mat this impressive still came as quite a surprise. The place hadn't looked this slick since 1950, when Mickey locked the doors rather than risk having the last object Dexter Graves ever touched—a cigarette lighter he'd dropped while dying—disturbed by the wrong sort of hands. Mictlantecuhtli's reach had always been at its longest this time of year, close to what the locals liked to call *el Dia de los Muertos* (and her own, more northerly ancestors had once celebrated as Samhain, or All Hallow's Eve), but this was getting out of hand. The King's power in this world remained limited, for the time being, but Ingrid had to wonder what would happen when his influence was strong enough to spill out into the street.

She felt unsettled, but she had a purpose here. There was no sense in putting it off.

When she clicked down the hall on her dramatic, blood-red heels, the front door closed on its own and the lights behind her went out, one by one.

She made it a point of pride not to look back.

The foyer's double-doors opened before her and she saw that the downstairs lobby was also in perfect repair. The floorlamps glowed a mellow yellow, and the floor tiles were polished to a mirror sheen.

Ingrid crossed to the bank of three elevators waiting on the far side of the room and stepped into the center car. The doors closed behind her, and as soon as they did so, the vitality drained out of the foyer. It decayed back into the dusty, ravaged ruin that lay underneath the King's illusions, now that she wasn't there to see them anymore.

Starting off as a similar sort of moldy wreck, the upstairs corridor brightened and restored itself in perfect anticipation of the elevator's bell.

Ingrid stepped out of the car and into the hall, onto carpeting that matched her shoes. She hadn't seen the transformation occur, but she sensed that it had. The magic left a charged, electric feeling hanging in the air. She went straight to Miguel Caradura's office door.

The name painted there at eye level was still marred by Graves' bloodstain, even after the passage of more than sixty years. That much had *not* been cleaned up in honor of her visit. Ingrid contemplated the rusty smear for a moment before opening the door. She knew better than to think that leaving it there had been an oversight.

The outer office she walked into looked mostly appropriate to the modern world, although its far wall was constructed of rough mud bricks that didn't match the rest of the décor one bit. Ingrid could see Mictlantecuhtli's bloodcaked altar through the doorway in the adobe wall: a round slab of limestone carved with hearts, skulls, and others of the King's symbols. Beyond that was yet *another* doorway—a doorless portal to the outside world, ancient and simple in its style—one that admitted a sort of weak, gray daylight into the sacrificial room.

"Hello?" Ingrid said.

There was no answer. The place was empty.

Ingrid frowned as she stepped through the doorway between the Chambers and into the inner sanctum. She gave the altar a wide berth on her way to the far door.

Then she stepped outside and found herself on the top level of a monumental Aztec pyramid. It was the only structure of any kind anywhere in sight.

Silver stars and a line of moons in progressing phases hung motionless across a matte gray sky, above her. Pale, fog-shrouded suns hovered at either horizon, and the untrammeled landscape looked like the Los Angeles area would have back in the days when the world was still flat.

This was Mictlan, the Realm of the Shades, where Time did not apply. Which meant that events here felt like they were either taking forever or happening instantaneously, and sometimes both at once.

Ingrid sighed, looking down the excessively long and steep set of rough stone steps that lay at her feet. There was no other way down the side of the pyramid.

"Dammit, Mickey…" she muttered, taking off her impractical heels. She carried them by their thin straps as she began picking her way down the precarious stairs in nothing but her stocking feet.

Some indeterminate and utterly meaningless span of the pseudotime Mickey insisted on playing around with later, Ingrid reached ground level.

Her hair was mussed, she was out of breath, and her feet were screaming. Her silk stockings were a total write-off. She sat down on the last step and considered putting her pumps back on, then just threw them aside instead.

"Lady Redstone."

Ingrid looked up. Standing a few yards away from her was a tall and dignified-looking skeleton in dapper black tie and tails. This was Winston, Mickey's majordomo and the overseer of his affairs out in the realworld. Ingrid knew him all too well.

"Winston," she said.

"Mictlantecuhtli would see you," the dead manservant told her.

"Good for him," was her terse reply. She was still irritated over having been made to climb down the pyramid's side when Mickey normally met her at the door between life and death, the one between his Chambers. These games of his were *so* uncalled for. Being pawned off on a servant was nothing she appreciated, either.

Winston made a casual gesture and a palanquin composed of smoke swirled into view behind her, along with a team of eight skeletal porters. One of the porters slid open a diaphanous door in the box's misty side, revealing a solid and comfortable-looking interior. A space upholstered in silk and red velvet. A magnum of wine, an elegant hookah, and lush cushions all awaited her within.

It looked like heaven after her long hike down the side of the pyramid.

Winston offered a hand to help her up, and Ingrid took it. With a smile. "Thank you, Winston," she said.

The well-dressed skeleton followed her to the insubstantial conveyance and helped her in. He slid the smokedoor shut behind her. "The pleasure is most assuredly mine, Miss Redstone," he said.

Winston clicked his bony fingers and the porters bore Ingrid away. The ghostly palanquin faded rapidly into the thin but omnipresent fog. Winston turned into a wisp of smoke himself in order to follow on the breeze.

Ingrid had no trouble making herself comfortable inside the palanquin. She blew languid smoke rings while it rocked and bobbed with the rhythm of her porters' gait. Time that wasn't really time seemed to slowly pass.

Growing bored, Ingrid slid a window panel open for a peek outside.

Superimposed over the vast chaparral plain was a faint, barely-there street made of thin smoke and populated by clothed skeletons, all of them going about their everyday business— whatever they remembered that to be. Ingrid perceived gossamer suggestions of buildings and cars from different eras, from horses and carts to vehicles far ahead of any age she knew. An instant after they congealed they were gone again, absorbed back into the mists. The geography over here could be uncertain and unstable, changeable like the weather. Landmarks didn't like to stay where they belonged, and the fashions she saw cut across the centuries.

She'd often wondered how that sort of thing worked, exactly. If the future dead were here in this timeless realm (as they plainly were, at least from her perspective), then might it not be possible to meet her future dead self?

Questions like that only irritated Mickey. His answers to them were vague, full of paradox and what he imagined to be poetry, leading Ingrid to suspect that even a god might not always understand as much as he pretended. The King of the Dead's best explanation was that the phenomenal world, as he called it (which was not some fabulous location, as Ingrid first thought, but simply the regular human world where phenomena occur, otherwise known as the *real* world), is something that exists only as a single anomalous bubble of change and alteration amidst the vast timelessness of Mictlantecuhtli's territory, where all possibilities exist at once. Chronology itself was the illusion.

As with most things Mickey told her, she wasn't sure where the truth ended and the self-aggrandizement began. She knew he'd long since cornered the afterlife market, subsuming competing death-deities into himself, and that he'd also conquered any number of mythological territories beyond his native one, through sheer ambition. And yet he was hardly the almighty ruler of everything that he aspired to be. The realworld, for example, remained out of his reach, as did the more distant shores of the vast imaginal sea in which the realm of the dead was still just one of the islands (all right—one of the *continents*, Ingrid conceded), no matter what el Rey de Los Muertos had to say about it.

She only stared out the window for a minute or two (or so it seemed—the action may have taken a century or a second in relative time, and there was no meaningful way to gauge it), but skeletons on the sidewalk started to notice their world's living visitor just that quick.

They pointed bony fingers and followed along with the palanquin, in rapidly increasing numbers.

The skeletal citizens and their surroundings became more solid as the crowd grew, as though they were remembering form and vitality through Ingrid's example. Even glimpsed through the slit of a window, her dark red hair and jewel-like eyes were the most vivid sights available. Arresting enough in the realworld, Ingrid's beauty was almost shocking in this gray and faded place.

The locals were more than seduced.

Ingrid, feeling uncomfortable, slid the window shut. Alone again, she sucked on her hookah for reassurance.

As the tireless porters carried her down the chronologically-promiscuous, half-substantial street, it swirled away to nothingness behind them.

Finally—although any appearance of time here was really just for show—Ingrid's porters set her palanquin down in front of a smokesketch of a cozy restaurant. Ingrid recognized it as a flawless simulacrum of Tom Bergin's House of Irish Coffee, down below Wilshire on Fairfax, right here in Los Angeles. It was a favorite realworld pub of hers, a place she'd visited in seven different twentieth-century decades. Only the faces of the bartenders had ever seemed to change, and even those were apt to take their time about it.

In a world where so much was in flux, Ingrid took comfort in that type of continuity.

Winston reappeared to slide open the palanquin's door and help her out, onto a misty sidewalk that felt more like cold, bare earth than concrete against her soles.

A ring of skeletons watched in awed silence, from a respectful distance. A number of ossified paparazzi snapped pictures, one with an old wooden box camera balanced on a tripod. His hand-held flash apparatus went up with a soft *flump*, in a puff of desultory smoke.

Ingrid spared them one glance, then turned and walked into the restaurant.

Winston held the heavy front door open, and then closed it again behind her.

Like the palanquin, the inside of the public house appeared perfectly solid and real. Winston led Ingrid past the central bar and across a front room crowded with gregarious skeletons in vividly realized Prohibition-era attire.

By the time they reached the back of the bar, the skeletons had all become real-looking, fully-fleshed people from the Jazz Age.

Winston admitted Ingrid to a boisterous private party going on in the back room, ushering her past a pair of stone-faced bouncers.

Wild flappers in slinky dresses and bootleggers in suspenders, flatcaps, and rolled-up sleeves all laughed, danced or drank to the hot jazz provided by a combo in the corner. Several brands of fragrant smoke hung in layers in the air.

The crowd parted readily for Winston, revealing Mictlantecuhtli, in full cowl, sitting at a big table against the back wall.

Two sloe-eyed lovelies she'd heard him call Nyx and Lyssa on previous occasions sipped at opium pipes as they lounged on either side of him. He ran a flayed finger down Nyx's throat and breastbone, playfully. She smiled.

Ingrid, who wasn't into this at all, rolled her eyes, stepped past Winston before he could announce her, and walked right up to the King's table.

"Mickey," she said.

Mictlantecuhtli turned his head to look at her. All she could see beneath his heavy cowl was his jawbone and his bloody lower teeth. "My love," he greeted her, in a voice that echoed like eternity.

"I did it," Ingrid said. "I've done it. It's done."

Mictlantecuhtli tipped his head in the barest nod of acknowledgement.

"So. Are we square?"

Mictlantecuhtli didn't answer. Instead he tipped his head forward and put his hands under his cowl to push it back. In doing so he revealed his 'Miguel Caradura' aspect: that of a powerful, dark-skinned man with small, intense eyes and a prominent nose, wearing a broad-shouldered Italian suit and a necklace of human eyes. If Rudolph Valentino had been an Aztec king...

"I can't help but think you don't care for my party," he chided Ingrid, in a low whisky growl of a voice. "And I thought this was your favorite era?"

"It's great, Mickey," she said, not taking any special pains to conceal her impatience with his theatrics. "It's fine." If he'd bothered to look a little more deeply into anyone's mind, he would've known this bar had never been a speakeasy. It hadn't even opened till the 1930s. She cast a glance at Lyssa, who looked back with heavy-lidded, contemptuous eyes. "Really nice."

Mickey snarled. He didn't like being patronized. He never had. "I think perhaps you would prefer something different," he murmured acidly.

'Miguel Caradura' stood, and his coat and shirt rotted away to reveal a muscular torso. He donned a ludicrous, floppy top hat and pumped his fist to a house beat that seamlessly supplanted the 20s-era jazz. Even the crowd changed around them, into rave kids with light sticks and water bottles clutched in their hands. Blacklight-reactive bodypaint designs appeared all over Nyx and Lyssa's glistening flesh, like luminescent tattoos.

Mickey grinned. "Yes?" he asked. "No. A bit past your time, isn't this, my love? How about this, then? Any better?"

Even as he spoke the music changed to disco and Mickey's clothes grew back into an outfit Tony Montana might've worn to a cockfight: an awful leisure suit in a shiny white synthetic fabric. Only his garland of eyeballs remained unchanged, while styles all around them morphed over into Afros, miniskirts, and paisley polyester.

"Mickey, stop," Ingrid said. "It doesn't matter."

"But I will have failed as a host if I cannot please you."

Ingrid sighed. There was no talking to him about things like this. "Ago, then," she suggested. "Can we try that?"

Mickey looked displeased, but he waved a hand and the restaurant, the crowd, and the band all vanished around them on the wind. Everything and everyone except for Lyssa and Nyx, who retained their stupid 70s outfits even out here on the chaparral plain, under the flat gray sky.

Mickey himself was now the Aztec king in every detail, down to an owl-feather headdress, golden ornaments on his arms, and an abbreviated loincloth that tied in the front, one woven from coarse but colorful threads.

"Happy now?" he asked.

"You know I didn't come to play," Ingrid said.

"Time was you wouldn't come for any other reason."

"Times change, Mickey."

"So I hear," the King said wistfully, looking off toward the horizon. "So I hear..."

Lyssa twirled away from them, dancing to a tune only she could hear. Nyx lay on the ground, rolling around and stretching her limbs out sensually.

Ingrid eyed them, nonplussed. Turning to Mickey, she said: "Your new witch took the bait. I'm certain she did. So can you please just tell me now, are we square?"

Mickey shrugged. "When *they* come back, *we* will be."

"But that isn't fair," Ingrid protested. "I've done my part."

The King, however, could not have cared less. He smiled, watching his concubines cavort in the near distance. Ingrid had to struggle not to get shrill. He was trying to goad her into losing her composure, and she knew it. These were the games he played.

"He'll go to the girl first," she said. "You know that's how this has to work. She could be anywhere in the city, and it's not my fault if your... your *bugbitches* can't track her, Mickey."

"Not your fault, no," Mickey said calmly. "But still your problem."

Ingrid was angry enough to cry, as he knew she would be. She clenched her jaw and stayed silent.

Mickey, pleased with her show of resolve, turned and put his hands on her shoulders. "Be soothed, my love," he said. "My living soldiers search for them even now, and my Tzitzimime will soon rejoin the hunt."

Ingrid looked away. "Wonderful. The ignorant backed by the incompetent. My fate's never felt more secure."

The King let her go and stepped back, looking irritated. "You make a point," he said. He considered for another moment, then turned and clapped his hands for his concubines. "Lyssa!" he called. "Nyx!"

They vanished from where they were and reappeared right before him, submissive and attentive, with their 1970s attire now abandoned in favor of simple linen shifts and pulled-back hair.

"You are to go and lead my Tzitzimime in their task," he told them. "Yes?"

They answered in unison: "As you would have it, Mictlantecuhtli."

They vanished again, and this time they didn't reappear.

"Is that supposed to make me feel better?" Ingrid asked, folding her arms once they were gone.

"It should, I think, yes," Mickey said. He grinned in a way that chilled Ingrid's blood. "Madness and Darkness, Lyssa and Nyx," he continued, looking off to the horizon again, as he was wont to do. "If he's above ground, those two will have him."

Chapter Nine

L ia picked up the lighter she'd found the night before from its new resting place on her bookshelf. She noted the burnt spot beneath it with a frown. But no matter. She turned, holding up the Zippo as a skeleton who dressed like a detective from a black-&-white movie came climbing down the tube ladder and into her underground home. Graves' bony, segmented fingers clicked and rang against the ladder's metal rungs. Hannah descended after him. Black Tom was down here already, projected from his catbody and appearing human again to Lia (although he remained invisible to everybody else). He kept one censorious eyebrow arched in the undead thing's direction, but Mr. Graves' courteous attitude was so different from that of the Tzitzimime that it was hard for Lia to believe he might be in league with them, despite the probable origin that his raw-boned appearance hinted at.

Whatever he was and wherever he'd come from, all he really seemed interested in was finding his cigarette lighter.

"Is this it?" Lia asked.

The skeleton raced over and snatched the Zippo from her hand, Sméagol-like, as soon as his shoeless, skinless feet hit the concrete floor. "*Yes!*" he shouted. "Oh, man, it is *good* to have this back." Graves flipped the lid a couple of times, clicked the wheel to light the device and snuffed it out again, nodding happily. "Ohhhh yeah, that's the stuff," he crooned. "That's just, I dunno... *satisfying*, somehow."

He became aware of the strange looks the women were giving him and straightened up to recover his dignity. "Uh... yeah," he said. "Sorry. I'm not, y'know, section eight or nothin.'"

"I'd never think it," Lia said.

"It's just got personal meaning for me, this thing," Graves explained, contemplating the tarnished old lighter.

"Then I'm glad I can give it back to you."

She meant it, too. The raggedly dressed skeleton looked up at her and seemed in a way to see her for the very first time. It was hard to tell without facial expressions, but she thought he looked surprised, and maybe even humbled.

Then his swagger reasserted itself. Grinning (again, insofar as that could be done without facial muscles or lips—it was mostly a matter of skull positioning), he sauntered over to take Lia's hand, clearly and perversely attempting to charm her pants off. That he now conspicuously lacked the endowments needed to follow through on his compulsion didn't seem to faze him at all.

"Well, listen, dollface," he drawled. "I am in your debt here, so if there's anything, and I do mean *any*thing that I can do—"

Lia recoiled when Graves took her hand and attempted to kiss it, jerking it away and shying back with a startled hiss.

It made for an awkward moment between them, to say the least.

Lia regretted her reaction as soon as she sensed Hannah's mounting alarm over it. If Lia turned frightened of this thing that called itself Dexter Graves, then Mrs. Potter might well freak out. And who'd be able to blame her?

Graves looked down at his own fleshless phalanges. "I keep forgettin' I'm not as pretty as I used to be," he said quietly, by way of apology.

Lia felt guilty enough about her discourtesy to a guest that she began to protest automatically, in spite of her genuine consternation. "No, no, it isn't that," she said, groping for words even though she wasn't sure what she meant to say. The man *was* a walking cadaver, after all, and Miss Manners was sure to be silent on subjects like these. No index entry for 'undeadiquette,' Lia would've wagered. She didn't like to hurt feelings, though, if she could help it, no matter who or what those feelings might belong to. "It's just—"

"Guess I could be crawling with disease, too, couldn't I?" Graves mused, talking over her and rubbing it in a bit, she thought, now that he could see she felt bad. "After being planted for… well, hell, how long *has* it been, anyway?"

Lia didn't know. How on earth could she? She shrugged and shook her head, still feeling quite bewildered by him. By the incredible fact of his existence, as well as the sheer undeniability of his presence. Desiccated Dexter Graves represented a new phase in her experience, all right. A mindblowing one, even for a woman with interests and predilections like hers. He looked like a Day of the Dead decoration come to life. "When did you, umm…?"

"Buy the farm?" Graves teased, trying and failing to cajole her out of her obvious discomfort. "Cash my check? Shuffle off my—"

"Yeah. That."

"1950 or so, I s'pose," Graves said, thinking about it. He scratched at his fractured skull, tipping back his hat and revealing a ragged crater in his forehead, like an off-center third-eye socket. "Memory's a little cracked, y'know. So, when is it now?"

Lia hesitated. She didn't want to deliver this sort of news.

Hannah stepped in, seeking to take the pressure off her rattled friend, and Lia was more than willing to let her. Han took Graves' reclaimed lighter from his hand and set it aside, then urged Graves to sit.

He did so compliantly, settling his assbones onto one of Lia's scavenged chairs with a trenchcoat-muffled thump. Hannah crouched down in front of him, took both of his hands, and looked him square in the eyeholes.

"Dexter…" Han said. "Brace yourself, okay?"

"I'm braced," he said, and Hannah told him what she knew.

Graves looked overcome.

"No fooling?" he said wonderingly, after a moment or two. "Sixty *years?*" He thought about it for another beat, and some of the straightness went out of his spine. "Everyone I ever knew is dead," he murmured.

"Probably," Lia agreed, perhaps tactlessly, but it was out there before she could think better of it.

Graves shook his skull as the full weight of his existential conundrum crashed over him. It was as though a spell that'd been keeping him from thinking too deeply about his circumstances had evaporated, probably at the instant she gave him back that lighter.

His cervical vertebrae crackled.

"Holy hell," he said. "I never thought... I mean, how could I have, it's not, it, it—oh God what's *happening*? *What the hell is going on?*"

He jumped up, beseeching, and this time both women recoiled in fear. Lia pushed Hannah aside to grab up Graves' Zippo from the pile of books Han had absently set it on top of. Graves lurched away after Hannah, who shrieked at full volume, her voice echoing painfully off the close concrete walls.

"Lady, come on, you gotta tell me, how is this happening?" the skeleton pleaded, backing Hannah into a corner. "Why did I *come* here? Who the hell *are* you people? *Come on, I need to know!*"

All right now, Lia thought. *Enough's enough.*

She deftly wrapped Graves' lighter in twine that she snatched up from a handy box of craft supplies, then nipped it off with her teeth and knotted it. She dumped the stagnant remainder of a beverage from a nearby drinking glass and clapped it down over the lighter. She put her hands over the glass, closed her eyes and concentrated hard to charge her intention. She gasped sharply and straightened up like she'd been jabbed in some invisible way when she felt the psychic circuit close. It would've been difficult for an observer to guess whether this was painful or pleasurable for her. She wasn't always so sure herself.

At the instant her eyes flew open, Dexter Graves tumbled into a heap of bones and clothes on the floor behind her. His ongoing rant was silenced mid-shout. Lia heard the bones clatter, and the coat whispered as it deflated.

Hannah, cowering against the wall, likewise sagged with relief. "Is he gone?" she asked in a shaky voice.

Lia turned around, feeling woozy, and smoke rose up from Graves' disarticulated bones. It coalesced into a vivid ghost right in front of her, one that looked the way Graves must have before he died: smug and cool in his coat and hat. "Not gone by a long shot, sister," he said to Hannah, who yelped and clutched at her breastbone when he spoke to her. "Not forgotten either."

"Oh, my God, it's a ghost," Han said.

"It was a talking skeleton when you were having a drink with it," Lia observed.

"Yeah, but... I've never seen a ghost," Hannah said,

prompting Lia to roll her eyes and abandon the conversation.

"Listen," Graves said. "I don't know what you dolls are tryin' to pull here, but—"

He took a step toward Lia and bumped against an invisible barrier, like a mime in a box. Or under a big drinking glass.

"Heyyy," he said, scowling and testing the unexpectedly resistant air before him. "What gives?"

Lia pointed to her arrangement of glass and lighter and string, nestled up on her overstuffed bookshelf. "I've bound you, Mr. Graves," she explained. "I'm sorry, you seem like a very nice man, but… you're scary."

Graves shrugged. He couldn't argue that one.

"What I mean is, we don't know what you are or why you're here, any more than you seem to. And until we figure that out, I think it's best you stay right where you are."

"You've gotta be kidding me," Graves said. "What, you're just gonna *leave* me here? For how long?"

"I don't think time is exactly of the essence with you, Mr. Graves," Lia said.

The ghost put his hands on his hips and looked for a retort, but he couldn't seem to find one. "Yeah, well, maybe not," he said, and sighed, looking defeated. "Will you at least call me Dexter, then? I like to be on a first-name basis with all my captors."

"I will do that," Lia agreed with a nod. "And… you *are* right about one thing, Dexter."

She looked Graves'—*Dexter's*—ghost up and down, with an approving lift of her eyebrows (a mannerism she'd half-consciously adopted from Tom). In life Dex had been tall and solid, with dark hair, nice eyes, and an affably bemused expression. He looked damn good in the suit he'd manifested, too.

"You *were* prettier before you rotted," she told him.

Then she sashayed over to the tube and climbed up without another look back. Hannah waved an awkward goodbye before she followed.

Graves heard the hatch clank shut and the wheel squeal, above. He reflected that this, then, was the *second* time he'd ever been dumped in a hole for safekeeping. At least he had dim electric light and a little bit of elbow room this time around. His invisible cell allowed him almost five whole feet of leeway. Enough space to dance a goddamn jig, should the spirit move him.

He wanted to be angrier about all of this than he was really able to manage. That Lia was smart to be cautious, as well as far too cute for him to stay mad at. Her oversized eyes glittered like balls of dark glass, and her pert little figure looked generous in all the right places.

While *he'd* looked like something a dog might dig up and barf onto a kitchen floor, when making his first impression.

Frustrated, Graves sat down crosslegged amidst his own dusty bones, with his ghostcoat pooling out around his insubstantial shoes. This whole deal felt backwards to him. Clients were supposed to walk into *his* office, looking for help from a man who knew the score. Not the other way around. Miss Lia seemed at least to know the name of the game they were playing, which was far more than Graves could currently say for himself. She'd also dealt with his little outburst pretty efficiently, as soon as she felt the need. He couldn't help but be impressed with that, despite the resulting inconvenience. She was like nothing he'd ever seen before.

Letting his thoughts drift back toward the girl wasn't as distracting as the weird compulsion that had left him like a dream as soon as he touched his lighter, but it was a perfectly kosher way of occupying his mind while he waited for a plan to occur to him. Habit made him pat his breast pocket and he was pleasantly surprised to find a pack of ectoplasmic cigarettes in there.

Talk about coffin nails, he thought dryly.

He patted again, his hopes rising, but he no longer seemed to have his lighter. He remembered why and looked over at it, tied shut and imprisoned under glass up on Lia's crowded bookshelf. He sneered bitterly.

"Story of my goddamn life," he muttered.

Chapter Ten

Potter's Yard was fast becoming a seductive oasis of deepening shadow and saturated color by the time the women emerged from the doortube, swinging first one leg and then the other out over its concrete lip, but Lia could only look pensively up at the still-bright sky. Her tom twined about her ankles, anxiously.

Hannah, as shaken as a martini by the experience of meeting Dexter Graves, didn't quite know what to say.

"We don't have much time," Lia murmured, talking mostly to herself. There were only a few hours left before dark. It wasn't yet two in the afternoon, but night fell early at this time of year.

Hannah looked back at Bag End's doortube: that innocuous concrete cylinder poking up out of the earth. "Are you really gonna leave him down there?" she asked, in reference to the magically-incarcerated Mr. Graves.

"I guess," Lia said absently. "It'll keep him out of the way. Right now I've got other things to worry about."

Hannah followed when Lia strode off through the plants, headed toward the parking lot and the distant office shack.

"Lia?" she said tentatively, brushing aside the foliage that swatted at her as she hurried to keep up. "How'd you know you could, you know, do what you did? To him, back there? Trapping him like that, I mean. Dexter."

"I could do as much to you if I wanted."

Hannah stopped in the middle of the path.

Lia realized what she'd said and stopped, too. She turned and saw that her friend was genuinely frightened—this time of her. It was not a nice feeling. "I don't, though," she said quickly. "Want to. I won't. I mean, I *wouldn't*. You know that, right?"

"I don't know what I know right now," Hannah said.

Lia winced. She wondered, not for the first time, if telling Hannah the truth about what she was had ever been a good idea. They'd discussed it before, a time or two, but the poor thing had never fully accepted that being a 'witch' entailed more than wearing too much black and enjoying books about mythology.

"Hannah, look, I'm sorry," she said, striving for patience despite her own growing anxiety. "But there're more things like your pal Dexter on the way and I have to be ready for them. Before dark."

Hannah looked unwell. "More?" she gulped.

"Yes, and we can talk about it all later, but right now I have a lot to do and it might be safer if you're not here."

"But... I can help," Hannah said. "I can stay. I *should* stay."

"You don't have to."

"I want to, though. I do." She added: "I can't just *leave* you."

Lia had to smile. Hannah was more fascinated than afraid. Lia was both touched by her concern and proud of her excitement in the face of events that went far beyond the scope of her previous experience. "Okay. Good," she said. "I don't really think I have time to finish everything by myself anyway. I can use a hand."

Hannah nodded, looking both pleased and apprehensive, like a soldier hand-picked for dangerous duty.

"You go home, though, if you get scared, okay? I won't hold it against you."

Hannah nodded again. "Just tell me what we need to do," she said.

Lia tied a hasty dreamcatcher from red thread and gave it to Hannah, who hung it, alongside many others, high up in the trees. They looked like scarlet webs spun by nightmare spiders.

It was arts and crafts time for Lia, with an emphasis on the Craft.

Tom hung about, watching the women work as the day's late light grew warmer and the shadows grew longer, pointing like heavy, black fingers toward the east. There wasn't a lot he could do to assist; it was now up to Lia to apply the knowledge he'd given her over all the years of their acquaintance.

The first task she assigned herself was to spraypaint creepy, staring blue eyes, dozens of them in many sizes, all down the outside of the nursery's wooden fence. Hannah consented to the vandalism without so much as a word about property values.

Tom's (and now Lia's) theory was that to 'Those Who Are Not Our Brothers,' even rudimentary symbols are alive and imbued with power. It meant that the unblinking stares of her warding eyes would be agony for Mictlantecuhtli's demon women to endure, and best of all, with a little deflective hex added in they wouldn't even understand why.

Lia next decided a little math magic might be in order. The number Pi, she'd been told, represents a crack in reality's mathematical rationality, one that unwary otherworlders might easily stumble into. She therefore instructed Hannah to paint a string of red numbers all around the eyeball-bedecked fence. 3.1415etcetera, etcetera, etcetera, and so on. Han checked the digits against a computer printout as she went, starting at the top of the front gate and spiraling them around the Yard's perimeter in descending rings, all the way down to the ground.

Encountering such a sequence, the cut-down consciousness of a typical imaginal feels compelled to follow it all the way out to its logical end. Pi, as far as Lia knew, had been calculated well past its billionth decimal, although the actual end was nowhere in sight.

Have a nice trip, was her thought on *that* matter.

Next, she stuck a USB drive into the aging computer attached to the office cash register. A Solitaire window popped up on the screen and laid out a game, seven cards, face up. Lia saw a story in the sequence. A beginning, a middle, and an end. Then the program glitched, blanked, and restarted in a new window, laying out a new game. Another window popped up, and then another, each dealing out a hand of cards and disappearing, but not before two new games opened in its place. They rapidly filled up the screen.

The program on the portable drive was something she'd gotten from her old friend Riley, who was, by his own description, an accomplished mathmagician. (Or technomancer—he'd vacillated between the terms for years, like he meant to put the to-be-determined favorite on a business card someday.) It was essentially a magic trick, an illusion, one designed to make the area around its point of deployment look like Union Station at rush hour, to a certain sort of eyes. It made the cash register's old computer system into a large-bore conduit for a constant stream of fresh identities—symbolized lives dealt out by the score and swept away again just that quick. Playing cards were originally derived from the symbols of the Tarot deck, and so otherworlders feel inclined to link them with personality traits and potential destinies. The point of the buggy software was to weave an opaque curtain from false threads of fate.

Lia watched hand after hand, life after life, cluttering up the computer screen. She nodded in satisfaction and quit the office, leaving the program to run unsupervised. Finding her through such an elaborate screen of semiotic disinformation should've been impossible, now.

But then, these Tzitzimime were surprising things. Witless and not that hard to manipulate, but surprising, too. It was hard to know if what she knew was going to be enough to deal with them.

She sat down in a little clearing she'd arranged at the quiet center of the Yard, on the bare ground and amidst a profusion of foliage that blazed in tones of green, gold and delicate orange as the smoldering, late-day light poured through it. She closed her eyes to compose herself. Her tom sat down beside her and dropped into a similar state of psychic quiescence (which comes naturally enough to a cat), and together they activated Lia's symbolized intentions.

It was a sacred, silent moment for the both of them. Lia fancied she could feel the pull of the imminent moon in her blood, as well as the terrifying velocity of her vast world as it ground its relentless way around the tiny spark of light and warmth that kept it alive in the never-ending blackness of space. Her mind kept on expanding, out beyond the galaxies and down through the microcosm, too.

Faint but luminous perspective lines bled out from Lia's imagination and into the real world, stretching away toward all horizons. Their bright point of convergence was her third eye, her Ajna chakra, right in the center of her forehead. The lightlines undulated all around her, as if stirred by deep currents in the imaginal sea. Faint auras also faded in, one around Lia's body, and another, brighter circle around her head.

Hannah wouldn't have been able to see these effects if she'd been looking on (although she would've readily sensed and respected Lia's deep state of meditative focus). Still, seeing more than consensus reality allowed for was mostly a matter of experience, in Lia's opinion. A skill, not a power. After Black Tom, it was the ritualistic nature of her work with the plant life at the Yard that had taught her the fundamental trick of looking at the world around her, moment by moment, and knowing it for the work of art that it was.

She was never less than grateful for her unique perspective, even if it did set her apart from other people.

Out beyond her and Tom, unseen by anyone else, an imposing ring of silent, jointly-imagined flames licked up toward the sky, from all around the Yard's furthest boundaries.

Lia wondered if her collection of improvised wards would do the job. She truly wasn't sure. But she swore that if this all went wrong tonight, it wasn't going to be because she hadn't done every single thing she could think of to do in the name of defending her home.

She let her thoughts uncouple from her brain and rise up, into the indigo twilight. She knew the sun was on the verge of setting, and that lights were starting to come on across the Valley floor. She could envision it easily, as though she were physically flying.

Potter's Yard blazed bright down below, with her imaginal effects visible across the worlds for one brief flash—right before it all went completely dark.

Chapter Eleven

Three identical points of light that might have been cold, distant stars appeared in the eternally gray sky that hung over the land of the dead and dropped down from it, like phosphorescent spiders descending on unseen webs. Smoky, wispy skeletons on the ground scattered like herds of cattle spooked by aircraft as the falling stars converged upon the mountainous step pyramid that was always visible on Mictlan's horizon. The Temple of Mictlantecuhtli. The trio of swift sparks funneled themselves into the squat, square structure that topped the pyramid, shooting in under its doorway's carved limestone lintel.

Lyssa and Nyx were waiting inside. They were amongst the King's elite creatures, conscripted from one of the all-but-forgotten pantheons he'd conquered in his campaigns. Each of them was intimidating to look upon, with curling tresses, full red lips, and a haughty expression on her exquisite, angular face. They were each clad in sleek, dark, twenty-first century business attire, and Nyx wore an enormous pair of black butterfly sunglasses over her eyes. Lyssa was sprawled across what now appeared to be a mahogany desk, even though it normally looked like a large stone altar.

As soon as the three formless Tzitzimime arrived via the doorway from Mictlan it disappeared behind them, becoming a plate glass window-wall that offered up a kingly view of the Angels' City. LA's clumped-together business towers draped elongated shadows over traffic arteries that glinted and sparkled in a wash of warm, westering light. The panorama and the executive office were both illusions arranged for the group by their King: images he'd laid over the inner sanctum's flickering torchlight and bloodsoaked stone as an example of the era he wished them to go out into and hunt. The door between his Chambers had been left aligned with the very moment in time they saw mirrored in the office's big glass wall.

Insects began to crawl from the illusory woodwork as soon as the realworld's sun began to set. Then they boiled out, pouring from the walls and dropping from unseen cracks in the ceiling. The bugs lumped up around the floating points of light into three semi-feminine clouds that writhed and churned as they worked to solidify (although they wouldn't be able to manage it until after the realworld's night had fallen).

Nyx took off her eyewear as soon as the sun's upper arc dipped below the horizon, revealing eyes as black as the night she embodied. They were all pupil, devoid of either whites or irises. She looked over at the others. "It's time," she said.

Lyssa sat up from the desk and nodded her assent; then she, Nyx, and the incomplete Bugwomen headed for the exit door, *en masse.*

As they crossed into the outer office, passing through the barrier between the worlds of life and death, they changed. Everything that passed through there did, in one way or another. The two chambers were something like an air-lock between realities, one room in either realm.

Nyx became a flattened, two-dimensional outline of herself that filled up with stars and swirling galaxies when she stepped through the portal, while Lyssa changed into a similar silhouette containing only mad static and twitchy silver flickerings. The unfinished bugwomen finally came together into their distinct, hard-shelled, long-limbed avatars: a Wasp, a Mantis, and an Ant.

Nyx threw open the door to the wider world—the door that read 'Miguel Caradura' on the outside—and the surreal quintet strode down the hall, toward the elevators, looking like danger and glamour personified.

Chapter Twelve

Lia, done meditating upon the now-active and empowered symbols she'd set up to defend her home, opened her eyes. It was just after sunset at Potter's Yard. The sky was a pool of blue ink above, flecked with a first dusting of tiny silver stars. The trees were black silhouettes set against a backdrop of luminous twilight. Lia's expression remained blissfully serene and untroubled for one instant, until she remembered something, and frowned.

"Hannah," she said to herself, then leapt to her feet and hurried off toward the front of the Yard.

Tom followed, after resuming control and stretching the muscles of his waiting catbody.

Hannah picked up a paper plate with a piece of withered fruit on it that was lying on the ground inside the Yard's front gate. She dumped the old fruit into a green plastic trash bin, then set the plate back down and fanned a newly-sliced apple out onto it. Lia had left her in charge of this one final task.

Within seconds, the apple wedges withered, browned, and visibly began to mold. Hannah watched the accelerated process of decay in total mystification.

"What makes that happen?" she asked, looking up when she realized Lia had emerged from the foliage behind her, with her tomcat close at her heels.

"Crouchers," Lia told her. "Doorway demons. You buy their loyalty with snacks. That's why I had you do this."

"So there's something there... eating it?" Hannah said, eyeing the sliced fruit uneasily.

Lia shrugged. "The part that counts, yeah." Then, before

Hannah could pose a follow-up question, she said: "Listen, Han, you've gotta get out of here, okay?"

"What, now?" Hannah asked, looking bewildered. "But I thought—"

"We've done everything I know how to do," Lia told her. "But I've got no way of knowing if it's gonna be enough."

She knew it scared Hannah to see the worry in her eyes, but she also knew Han really believed what she said when she spoke so nakedly.

"I couldn't live if something happened to you," she said, her voice tightening up as she forced one of her worst fears into words. "And I might not be able to keep my guard up properly if I've got too much on my mind."

Hannah stared at her for a long moment, unsure of what to do. Unsure of everything, it looked like. "Okay. I understand," she said at last, although she clearly didn't.

Lia wanted to hug her, but she could be awkward in her expression of feeling (having been socialized under some fairly unusual circumstances), and the appropriate moment for it passed her by.

It was plain enough that Hannah's experience of meeting Dexter Graves had called her basic picture of reality into question, sparking an agonizing reappraisal of her entire belief system. Lia felt her searching for words to express herself. She *did* understand what Hannah was going through, from personal experience, and so she chose to let her friend talk through it, for a minute, despite the approaching darkness.

"Lia?" Hannah ventured in a troubled tone. "This's all been, I don't know... so *different* from the things I've seen you do before."

Lia smiled. "Like getting plants to grow and reading people's tea leaves?"

"Yeah. I guess," Hannah said. "And those sorts of things are impressive enough, believe me, but *this*, this has been... I don't even know. On another level."

"C'mon," Lia said. She helped Hannah up and guided her toward her car, which was parked on the far side of the gravel lot.

"Where'd you even learn these things?" Hannah asked.

Lia shrugged, glancing down at her black cat. She'd never figured out how to explain her teacher, or the relationship they had. It was something else she'd never found the right moment or the right words for.

"The earth," she said, in partial answer to Hannah's question. "Books, certain plants…" She hesitated, then told her friend the simple truth: "Black Tom's taught me more than anyone."

Hannah's eyes widened, as eyes do when the people behind them are told something crazy. "You mean your *cat?*" she said, making no attempt to disguise her knee-jerk incredulity… until she saw how it abraded Lia's feelings. Then she paused, as they reached her Volvo, and looked down at the animal in question. He blinked back up at her with his bright green eyes.

"He's not really a cat, you know," Lia said, trying not to sound defensive. "I mean, yeah, of course that's a cat, but a cat's not all that's in there. If you know what I mean."

"I… I did not know that, no," Hannah said. After a beat she admitted, very softly: "Nothing looks like it did to me this morning."

Lia did hug her then, feeling for her but also feeling the pinch. "Hannah, honey, I know," she said, into the older woman's ear. "But we'll have to talk about it tomorrow."

Hannah pulled back and offered an awkward smile. "I kind of want to stay and see how some of these things work," she said, sweeping a hand around in general reference to the nonsensical projects they'd labored over all afternoon.

"But you won't want to be here if they don't," was Lia's terse reply.

Hannah understood that this was probably so, and nodded reluctantly. Lia herded her into the old Volvo and closed the door behind her. Hannah's driver's side window was already down.

"Go home," Lia told her through it. "And call me when you get there, but don't call me by my name when you do. Okay? That's important."

"Okay."

"Go on, then," Lia said. "Get out of here." She slapped the top of the car like a cowpoke motivating a sluggish steer and then hurried off, back into the darkening Yard and onto other last-minute errands.

Chapter Thirteen

Lia sat down again, crosslegged, cat in her lap, back in the cozy bower where she liked to do her psychic exercises. It was fully dark by now, just after nightfall. She set a notebook computer she'd retrieved from the trunk of her car next to herself on the bare earth. It was on, but closed and quiet, waiting for her in standby mode. She closed her eyes, controlled her breath, and within moments she was able to send herself out, leaving her own body in a sort of standby mode, as Black Tom had long ago taught her to do.

'Sending out' was Tom's term (or at least one he'd surrounded with an aura of approval back when she first thought of it, the same way he once had with his own name). The ever-informative internet had the technique labeled in various places as scrying, astral projection, remote viewing or skywalking, but they were all names for a more or less identical concept. Lia wasn't as skilled a sender as her Tom, who'd been practicing the art for well more than a century, long outlasting his original body in the process, but Lia didn't need to be a master in order to help him watch over the Yard's new fortifications.

She rose up—at least the invisible, non-physical part of her did—nearly to the tops of the Yard's tallest trees. Tom left his catbody and rose up with her. There was nothing of him to see, nothing of either of them, and yet they each felt the other hovering close by as they chanced a look around.

Potter's Yard was situated in a semi-industrialized area in the northernmost part of North Hollywood, right before it became Sun Valley on the maps, so there were few homes nearby and little traffic to be seen on a weeknight. Not too many people around.

The area managed to feel surprisingly isolated and almost rural, despite being set right in the heart of one of LA's largest suburbs.

Both Lia and Tom were careful not to rise too high or to extend their awareness beyond the psychic barriers they'd erected earlier in the day—barriers that rippled when the evening's first otherworlders arrived in the neighborhood like day-late trick-or-treaters, causing Lia's distant body to break out in gooseflesh and dashing her last faint hopes that the Tzitzimime wouldn't manage to find their way back here at all.

A striking set of Mictlan's minions stepped into the nearest lighted intersection, a few dozen feet from the Yard's front gate. They seemed almost to coalesce out of the shadows themselves. There were two new creatures in the lead, Lia noted. Not Tzitzimime, although, like the bugwomen, these were also doing their best to appear human. With a heavy emphasis on 'their best.' In practice, the only disguises the new additions to the crew seemed able to manage were woman-shaped outlines: one of them ink-black and flecked with stars, like the night sky, while the other crackled with a sort of mad static that jumped and flickered in an unhealthy-looking way.

These two were more than demons. They were Archons, Lia guessed—ancient embodiments of fundamental concepts, and who knew how old or how powerful they might be?

She dropped back into herself and flipped open her computer.

Tom gave her a sense that entities such as these Archons were free to pretend to be anything they liked (such as human women) on the other side of the door between worlds, but over here they were compelled to appear more or less as they actually *were*. They could never completely conceal their fundamental natures out here in the realworld. Lia scanned a webpage or three with that in mind, until she felt reasonably sure she'd pinned down the one who looked like she'd been airbrushed with stars as the goddess of darkness and night. Nyx, the Greeks had called her. The staticy one she was less sure of, although she felt no less threatened by her. The pair might've been able to project those womanly forms, but it seemed they couldn't finish them off with crucial details like hair, clothing, or facial features. Or maybe they were simply too far removed from humanity and its concerns to know how to draw up more than simple representational sketches.

Lia sent herself out again. Carefully, not wanting to be picked out by otherworldly eyes, which could be exceptionally keen under certain circumstances. She rejoined her disembodied Tom, who'd never stopped monitoring the situation from above, and he let her feel that nothing much had changed, as of yet.

She watched as Ant, Mantis and Wasp, the original Tzitzimime, hardened into their three distinct avatars out of an amorphous swarm of gnats.

Lia felt ill with anticipation as the five otherworlders paused to look around. From her projected perspective, she saw her own defenses more clearly than they did. The ring of ghostly flames around the property shimmered, although it would be opaque like a one-way mirror from the other side, and a challenge even to perceive. The eyes she'd painted all down the fence appeared to be blazing like halogen lights. The two flat, feminoid shapes—the Archons—exchanged a look, and Lia felt her earthbound body's heart speed up in terror when they chose to head in the Yard's direction, despite the wards intended to shunt their attention aside. The three Tzitzimime trailed after their new leaders, and Lia readied herself to drop back into her head and make a dash for her bomb-shelter home (skeletal prisoner notwithstanding), should such a drastic retreat prove necessary.

The team of otherworlders spread out as they approached the simple spraypainted eyes that they experienced as blinding floodlamps. The Tzitzimime spread out literally, separating into many thousands of tiny flying and crawling creatures, in order to cover the widest area possible.

It was then that Lia realized her barrier was working after all.

The otherworlders looked confused, and were clearly not able to penetrate her concentric rings of influence well enough to find the gate. For them, the painted eyes and the glitchy Solitaire game running on the office computer conspired to create the impression of a raging party going on inside the fence. The soft music pouring from Lia's cheap boombox sounded like a live and amplified band. The demons had come here expecting to find a lone girl in a deserted grove, so this trick alone might convince them to retreat, shaking their misshapen heads in frustration.

The bugs couldn't even feel the subtle deflective hexwork that rendered the Yard's green canopy of treetops totally opaque to them when they flew over. They couldn't sense Lia or Tom at all.

Everything was working *beautifully*.

Lia's body grinned, even though it was down on the ground and mostly detached from her spirit.

Around the back of the property, Nyx (the black outline comprising the goddess of night), tried to peer into the lights along the fence. She shied away, however, shielding her featureless face with a hand made out of stars and nothingness, which pleased both Lia and Black Tom to see. Bright light was obviously not Miss Nyx's thing.

The Archon looked away, down darker streets, bewildered.

Around the front, near the northeastern corner of the Yard, some of the insects swarming in the street pulled together and solidified into the same giant, bipedal, red Ant-woman that had chased Lia the night before, which she took as a probable sign that the creature was trying to think. The bug-based entities couldn't concentrate without assuming a humanoid form. Intellect just wasn't an insectile trait.

Ant tried harder than the Archon of Night had against the lights, edging into the hot glare around the fence that the painted eyes provided. She cringed, but forced herself closer, and stopped when her thorax brushed up against solid wood.

Uh-oh, Lia thought. She realized she was biting her lip only when the pain surprised her and she had to force her remote body to quit it.

Ant stepped away from the fence and immediately began blinking her stalky, wavering eyes—clearly feeling the imaginal incandescence once again. Lia and Tom had a moment to hope before the Ant cautiously pressed herself back against the boards, in defiance of all their wishes.

The demon had figured out that the warding eyes' deflective power was cancelled when she touched the fenceboards and felt what was *really* in front of her: nothing but cleverly-painted wood. The first of the otherworlders had breached the outer defenses and it was creeping down the fence already, feeling for an opening.

The Ant, at least, knew Lia was here.

Shitballs, she thought, preparing to fire her awareness back down into her motionless body.

Then she froze in mid-air, arrested by the sight of movement *inside* the gate.

Oh, Hannah, no, she wailed without using her voice, upon realizing who it was she saw walking from the office shack and out toward her parked car. Han must've left her keys behind in the office. Again. It happened so often that it was a joke between them, and Lia castigated herself now for not remembering Hannah's absentminded habit.

She could still be all right, though, if she'd just get into her car and drive away. The barriers would still be in effect against all the other entities, since Ant hadn't yet shared her strategic intelligence with them. The Tzitzimitl (singular for Tzitzimime, according to sources) might try to follow her, but since Hannah didn't fit Lia's description it would forget why it was doing so within seconds.

She therefore willed Hannah to go on, to get out of here without delay, before the big Ant could find its way in through the gate to attack her.

Han had her fingers wrapped around her Volvo's door handle before she looked back longingly, first toward the corner of the Yard that Lia called home, and then over toward the still-open gate. Lia's diaphanous firewall was the only ward covering the gap, and it alone wouldn't stop something that really meant to step through. It was little more than a scrim of imaginal camouflage.

Hannah trotted back past the gate and picked up the paper offering plate she'd left beside it earlier, meaning, Lia assumed, to provide the fascinating Crouchers with one last snack before calling it a day.

She certainly could've picked a better moment to indulge her sense of wonder.

Lia gritted her distant body's teeth while she simultaneously tracked both her friend and the menacing Tzitzimitl outside the fence with her mind's eye, uncertain of what to do. She might *invite* an attack if she intervened now, and if Hannah would hurry the hell up and drive out through the wards without doing anything else, there might not be a need for it.

Hannah bisected an orange with her pocketknife and set the two halves down atop the paper plate, leaving them like a tip for the unseen guardians of the Yard's front entrance, hoping they'd work extra hard at their jobs tonight because of it.

She thought she saw something move when she stood up, in the deep shadows outside the Yard's well-lit parking lot.

"Tom?" she said uncertainly, stepping outside the gate. She peered down the street, looking for Lia's cat, although a cat was not even close to the sight that confronted her when she turned around and looked up.

Lia slammed back into her body as hard as she could, feeling hot blood surge up into her ears with an oceanic *whoosh* a second after jumping to her feet from a full lotus position. "*Fuck!*" she shouted. "Why didn't she just *leave?*"

Tom, back in catform, flattened his ears and offered no answers.

"*Han, get back inside,*" Lia shrieked, sprinting for the front of the Yard. She couldn't see Hannah anymore, not now that she was back in her head and down on the ground, so she ran at full speed, unmindful of the many obstacles that might trip her up in the deepening darkness.

She heard a scream before she was halfway there.

"*No!*" she shouted again, feeling frantic with terror, her lungs burning as she and Tom raced toward Hannah's last known position at the front gate. Lia muttered "Oh, Hannah, no, oh gods no..." under her breath as they went, without even being aware of it.

She grabbed hold of a fat cherry branch and ripped it loose when she passed by, trusting that the assaulted plant would be willing to forgive her under the circumstances. She and Tom emerged into the parking lot and she swung the wrist-thick branch around, wielding it in a way that suggested she meant to do something pretty impressive with it.

But she pulled up short instead, before the intention she meant to symbolize with the weapon could click in.

Hannah stood framed in the open gate on the far side of the parking lot, frozen in terror in front of the Ant.

"Liiaaaaaaahh," the six-foot-tall upright female insect hissed, waving her razor-edged mandibles in Hannah's face. "*Where?*"

Hannah held her hands up, backing away from the first embodied demon she'd ever had the misfortune to see and triggering its aggressive inclinations. The thing looked strong enough to pull a human being apart without making any particular effort. Lia was about to shout a warning, to try and distract the creature, when the Ant paused of her own volition, staring down at Hannah's chest and cocking her head in a quizzical manner. It was an expression that might've looked cute on a puppy, but not on a murderous, monstrous insect.

Tom touched Lia's mind and urged her to stay perfectly still. The thing hadn't seen her yet.

"Han...nah?" the ant demon said. She tried out the name again, saying it backwards this time: "Han-nah."

Lia sucked in a quick breath. She understood what was happening when she saw the Ant's eyes tick back and forth across the alphabet beads that made up Hannah's necklace. Little square plastic ones that spelled out her name. Hannah wore the old thing almost every day.

Ant's exoskeleton pebbled and turned to individual bugs while she stood there ogling the beads, forgetting to concentrate on holding her body together. Hannah shuddered over this new development, gasped, and turned to flee.

The demon's forelimb re-solidified in the flash it took to shoot out and snag Hannah's wrist. The disproportionately-strong insect jerked her around like she was nothing but a ragdoll. Ant caught sight of the alphabet beads again and lapsed back into her trance before she could bite, although she didn't let go of Hannah's arm. Lia could tell the tall Tzitzimitl was fighting hard to shrug off the palindrome-induced cognitive dissonance the necklace beads caused her and retain her physical form.

Lia also understood that Hannah was stuck. Hopelessly stuck, because Ant would snap back to herself at the instant those beads were out of her sight. Hannah seemed to understand at least some of this when she looked over toward Lia with wide and horrified eyes. "Little help? Please?" she said in a tiny voice, as if afraid to disturb the distorted, shimmering Ant in even the slightest of ways.

Lia set her broken-off branch aside and approached her friend with a bomb-squad degree of caution, sizing up the situation. "It's gonna be okay, Han," she reassured, and thought she sounded at least mostly convincing. "It's all right. Just don't move until I say. But then be ready to do it *fast*."

She edged in carefully, meaning to untie Hannah's necklace at the nape of her neck and remove it without taking it out of the Ant's eye-line.

"I'm sorry, L—"

"Stop, right there, just shut up," Lia said harshly. Then she whispered, "The instant you say my name we both die, so be very, *very* careful when you speak. Okay?"

"O- okay."

Lia undid the necklace and lifted it off Hannah's chest, leading Ant away with it as though the string of beads were a carrot on a stick. She hung the necklace on a nail just outside the gate. It was still holding Ant's attention, but only barely. The creature almost seemed to understand that its quarry was within reach, and yet it couldn't quite force itself to ignore the series of lettered beads that spelled out the same word in either direction.

"Get inside," Lia said.

Hannah complied, springing over the property line like a schoolgirl skipping rope. Lia jumped back alongside her and threw the gate shut, shoving the wheeled length of fencing down its uneven track with all her might.

Ant shook off her paralysis and lunged, but she was a moment too late. The corrugated sheetmetal gate rattled shut, nearly cutting off two of her six limbs. She yanked them back with an ugly, high-pitched shriek.

A sequence of red spraypainted numbers rolled in front of her eyes along with the closing gate:

3.14159265358979323846264338327950288419716939937...

...and Ant jerked like she was having a seizure.

Her bugbody burst apart and the white light at her core rocketed down the line of numbers (which started at Hannah's eye-level and went around and around and around the fence, all the way down to the sidewalks), scorching the digits onto the wood planks as it went. Ant's inner light whizzed around the Yard's perimeter multiple times in less than a second, chasing the Pi line like a firework flower, and then it winked out in a flash.

She was gone, just like that. Pursuing Pi into eternity.

Inside the fence, night's stillness resumed. Crickets picked up their interrupted songs. Woodsmoke rose lazily from the outer side of the fenceboards, and Lia thought it smelled bizarrely nice.

She turned to Hannah. "You okay?" she asked. She figured her face was waxy pale, bloodless, and her wide, frightened eyes felt like they took up half of it.

Hannah nodded vigorously, assuring her that she was indeed unharmed, to the best of her knowledge.

"Okay, good," Lia said. "That's good. Yeah."

Now that the crisis had passed and they were both provisionally safe, she turned away from Hannah and went over to the cherry branch she'd dropped in the parking lot gravel, where she sat down beside it and burst into a wrenching squall of post-traumatic sobs.

Being in danger herself was one thing, in Lia's mind, and bad enough, but seeing that danger threaten someone she loved was *entirely* another.

Hannah all but slid into home in her rush to throw her arms around her friend. Tom ran up too, offering his feline brand of comfort. Lia let Hannah squeeze her fiercely for a moment, soaking in the concern and affection, then pulled herself together and drew away, feeling self-conscious.

She swiped at her nose and looked up at Hannah from beneath the fringe of her thick, black bangs. "I really hope you and Skeletor didn't finish off that bottle of wine," she said.

Chapter Fourteen

Graves' ghost tapped its way around the circumference of his invisible prison with vaporous knuckles that felt solid enough against the symbolized glass, looking for a weak spot in the force-field and growing increasingly frustrated with each rotation. He didn't know how long he'd been down here, interred within Lia's underground bunker. It seemed like hours had passed already. He could've used a cigarette or a drink, and he would've settled for something to read. No dice, though. He began to curse as he tapped, under his breath at first, but then with more volume.

Tap tap tap. "Dammit." *Tap tap tap.* "Dammit." *Tap tap tap.* "Dammit." *Tap tap tap.* "*Dammit!*"

As Graves grew angry, the bound-up lighter Lia'd stowed away on her bookshelf grew hot. The twine began to smoke, and the smoke swirled inside the inverted water glass.

Graves noticed this. He paused, getting an idea, and then strategically went nuts, bellowing at the top of his lungs and hammering on the psychic boundary Lia'd trapped him under, getting just as mad about his confinement as he possibly goddamn could.

The twine flamed and went up in a flash. Smoke filled the interior of the glass. The red-hot lighter pulsed deep within the gray miasma, glowing like a ruby beacon in a fog. Graves' bones stood back up inside his stolen coat as his ghost evaporated. The transition from spirit to solid happened instantaneously, requiring no further effort on his part.

"Now that's more like it," his restored-to-animation skeleton said aloud.

Graves peeled off his tangled raincoat and tossed it aside. He stretched, groaning, and his spine crackled all the way up. The lighter's glow faded away in the dense cloud of smog still lingering under the glass.

"All righty, then," Graves said. "If nobody minds, I think I'll just be on my—"

Clink. His fractured forehead tapped against Lia's barrier when he tried to walk away.

"Oh," he finished. "Ow."

He rubbed the exit crater above his eye as he looked over at the smoke-filled glass up on the shelf. The twine was long gone, burnt away, but the intention symbolized by the glass itself apparently remained in effect.

"Dammit," Graves said, like he was picking up a refrain.

He sat his bones down on the floor in the same posture his ghost had assumed while ruminating and drummed his fingers on his kneecap. An air exchanger of some kind went on with a soft *whoosh.*

A lone dust mote drifted down from an air vent, floating right past Graves' nosehole. He followed its drift with his finger until the bone clicked against Lia's magic field... even as the mote sailed lazily on toward whatever corner it would finally fetch up in.

"Hmmm."

It was only then that he noticed the coat he'd tossed aside was lying on the floor, well outside his established circle.

Graves thought about this. Thought hard. He looked up at the glass on the shelf, wondering if he might be able to knock it off.

It would take a little experimentation to find out.

He took off his hat and moved it toward the barrier. The felt brim crumpled against empty air at exactly the point he expected, the crown bunching up into his bony hand.

He pulled it back, then tossed it gently, like a kid flying an overturned pie tin. It sailed easily outside the barrier this time around, now that he wasn't in contact with it.

"Well all right," Graves said. If he threw hard enough, he might have a chance at hitting Lia's voodoo waterglass. He bent to retrieve the hat, but his forehead and hands clinked against the magic boundary once again.

The hat, he understood in dismay, was out of reach, and he had nothing else to throw.

He sagged against the unseen barrier in defeat. "Coulda planned that out better, couldn't I?" he muttered.

Chapter Fifteen

An hour after dark, Lia and Hannah sat sipping pinot noir under the stars, surrounded by the Yard's dense, potted wilderness while they lounged around on last season's unsold garden chairs. They had citronella candles burning for light (and irony, considering the bugwomen they were trying to repel). The music was turned down to a whisper, though prowling imaginals would, thanks to Lia's efforts, still perceive a full-volume blare. Tom was curled up nearby, catnapping.

Lia had her laptop open with a number of IM windows displayed on the screen. A collection of internet pervs addressed her variously as Cammie, Chloe, Zoe, Lisa, and Mia. She paid them little mind, typing just enough to keep them going. Which wasn't much, as the men on the other sides of the message windows needed just a touch of believably female participation to fill in the gaps in their fantasies.

All Lia needed out of them was to be called by the wrong name.

She had the branch she'd torn down earlier propped up next to her chair. She was still prepared for the worst, but she felt far more relaxed now that she knew Hannah, at least, would be safe here until morning.

The rest of the otherworlders must have known the Ant was gone, but they couldn't know if she'd been destroyed, captured, or if she'd run off of her own accord. The deflective eyes and other wards had neatly concealed the Tzitzimitl's demise, and they were still preventing the rest of the entities from seeing anything that happened within the fence's perimeter. The party the otherworlders thought was going on inside the compound still seemed loud and lively.

Lia could imagine the remaining Tzitzimime stalking the streets and scratching their freakish heads, although she didn't send herself back out to observe them. Better to lay low, at this point. And besides, she knew Black Tom was out there keeping watch around the edges of things, even if his catbody seemed to be asleep beside her.

Hannah leaned back in her chair and looked up at the bright splash of stars overhead. "So, where are we supposed to sleep tonight?" she asked. And then, after a pause, "*Are* we supposed to sleep tonight?"

Lia looked over. She was feeling better by now, over the shock of Hannah's close call, soothed by the wine and the quiet. She decided she liked having Han out here for company. Lia tended to protect the Yard like a secret, and therefore rarely entertained. Hannah may have owned the place on paper, but after dark, the territory still belonged to Lia and her Tom. This change of pace was nice, though. Cozy and convivial, in an eye-of-the-hurricane sort of way.

"I was thinking right here, campout-style, if you want," she said in belated response to Hannah's query about the sleeping arrangements. "I've got sleeping bags, I've just gotta go down below to get them."

"Is it... you know, safe? To go to sleep?"

"Sure," Lia said. "Everything's holding. And I can keep an eye on things from my dreams."

"Can you really?" Hannah seemed charmed by the idea.

Lia nodded, sipping her wine and smiling. She liked the odd combination of candle-and-computerlight. It seemed both warm and ice-cold at the same time.

"That's amazing," Hannah said.

"Just something I learned. You could learn too, if you wanted."

Hannah snorted at the idea. "Yeah, I can see the marquee now: '*Hannah Potter and the Angry Ant*...'" She shook her head and smiled wistfully. "How weird that that's really my name, though, huh? Like Harry's long-lost aunt or something."

Lia grinned back. "That's a synchronicity," she told her. "You should take it as a sign."

Hannah laughed again, but shook her head. "I could never be like you," she said quietly, seeming to consider her young friend in a brand new light. "You saved my life tonight, I think."

Lia blushed. "That necklace did," she said. "Your name did. The palindrome. Just lucky, is all."

"But *you* gave me that necklace!" Hannah said. "You made it for me, years ago."

"Yeah, that's right, I did, didn't I?" Lia teased, waggling her fingers in a mesmeric manner. "All part of my master plan."

"See, now, I can't even tell if you're kidding or not."

"I am," Lia said. "But that's still sort of the way these things work, sometimes."

"Oh." Hannah seemed unsure of how she wanted to feel about that piece of information. "Well… what about whatsisname, then, down in your place? Dexter?"

Lia waved off the question and refilled her wineglass. "Let's not worry about that right now," she said. "He's not going anywhere."

Graves' first throw bounced off the waterglass on the shelf with a musical *clink*, down in the old bomb shelter. The glass resounded with a deeper note in response to his second bullseye, something more like a *clank*, but the force of the hit only tipped the inverted tumbler back on the shelf for an instant, failing to overturn it.

His third throw went ludicrously wide, knocking some other, untargeted knickknack right off Lia's crowded shelf. He didn't know what it'd been, hadn't been looking at it, and couldn't even hope to guess at the object's original form after it crashed to the concrete floor and exploded into a thousand ceramic shards. Graves cringed, but he worked yet another small bone loose from his left hand and threw again, harder still. So hard that momentum unbalanced him and his full-body, forward-hopping follow-through left him staring down at the floor between his feet by the time he caught himself against the transparent magical barrier. He heard rather than saw his knucklebone hit the symbolic dome that kept the barrier in place (it made a dull *clunk* against the glass), and the force field scraped a few encouraging inches across the floor under his weight.

He looked up, his hopes on the rise, but they crested and

plummeted when he saw that the impact had merely driven the overturned waterglass further in amongst the books behind it. It was socked in there but good, now, nestled into a pocket of cushioning paper on three sides.

"*Oh*, for cryin' out loud!" Graves yelled in frustration. His tiny handbones weren't cutting it, weight-wise, and he was almost down to throwing toes. "All right, nuts to this."

He reached down and detached a kneecap. His lower leg promptly fell off, but he ignored it. One problem at a time. Balancing like a flamingo, he hefted the weighty patella in the still-assembled palm of his bony right hand, wound up, and fired off his most forceful fastball.

This time he nailed it. The glass broke and crumpled inward with a satisfying crunch. Graves threw his arms (minus most of his left hand) into the air in triumph. "Steeeeeerike one!" he cried, feeling entirely too pleased with himself. Then, with only one leg left to balance on, he toppled right over and sprawled to the floor with a hollow xylophone clatter.

He was outside that magic circle, though, he noted with satisfaction upon looking up from the smooth concrete. *Well* outside that circle.

He scrambled over to the shelf and began sweeping up his bones, fitting them together like puzzle pieces as he came across them. "Now I just gotta pull myself together, here," he muttered to himself.

In one of several open message windows on Lia's laptop screen, someone using the imaginative nickname of 'ASSLVR69' asked 'Mia' what sort of panties she was wearing, and Lia responded by pecking out '*blk lace frm vic scrt,*' although white cotton from Target was, at present, closer to the truth. Not that it was really any of his business.

As if, she thought with a frown, before hitting enter.

She didn't like doing this at all, using people (even these people), as it felt sordid and made her sad, but she couldn't argue with the results, either. The Yard hadn't had another demon problem since they'd exterminated the Ant, and the false names her correspondents addressed her by helped to keep her real one safely obscured from the quartet of creatures that still remained in play.

Hannah stood some way off, leaning against a redwood arbor and gazing up at the stars. There was no moon in the sky this early in the evening. It wasn't quite eight o'clock.

Hannah shivered. Only slightly, but Lia noticed. "I can go get those sleeping bags now, if you're cold," she offered.

Hannah looked over. "I can wait, if you don't want to, you know, go back down there yet."

Lia set aside her depleted wineglass, then stood and stretched. "I don't mind," she said. "I'm getting hungry anyway. Here, watch my names for me."

Neither of them mentioned Dexter Graves, but Lia assumed they were both thinking about him. His imprisonment within her hobbit hole was the only conceivable reason why she might not feel comfortable going underground. Hannah came over to the tiny bistro table Lia'd been sitting at to monitor the laptop as Lia headed off, feeling the black, nighttime foliage engulf her when she waded into it. She found the sensation more comforting than intimidating. This was *her* darkness, and she felt perfectly at home within it.

The first joint of Graves' left pinkie fell off as he was reaching up for the hatch's wheel. He caught it, nearly falling off the exit tube's ladder for the effort, and stuck it back into place. It stayed, like his bones were magnetized or something. He was already back in his coat and hat, with his left shinbone and the corresponding foot similarly reattached.

He was making his break.

The hatch wheel turned on its own before Graves could take hold of it. He almost fell again, cringing back as the hatch cover groaned open on its heavy-duty hinges.

Lia, above, turned away before she could see him dangling there from the tube ladder, framed in the hatch's mouth like a goddamn portrait.

"Hannah?" she called back into the darkness. "Would you rather have banana chips or cereal? I don't have much." She paused, then called again. "Han?"

There was no response from Miss Hannah. The older lady must not've heard. The nursery *was* large, and this Lia didn't seem like she'd be given to shouting. Graves' assessment of her modest nature was confirmed when she headed back the way she came, out of his view, rather than standing there and bellowing her question until she got an answer.

He hurried up, scrambling out of the tube she'd left open, then scurried around behind it and watched Lia disappear back into the bush.

Hannah was still stargazing, leaning back in her chair when Lia walked up.

"Hannah? You want something to eat?"

"Weird moon tonight," Hannah said idly, shaking her head in distracted answer to the question. "Came up fast. In just the last few minutes, it seems like."

"Shouldn't be much of a moon tonight," Lia said. "Just a tiny sliver."

Hannah looked over at her, letting the front legs of her rocked-back chair touch the earth before she sat up straight. She pointed just above the horizon, through a loose screen of leaves and branches. "Then what's that?" she asked.

Lia squinted to see. There *was* something out there, hovering beyond the canopy. The small, bright, full 'moon' behind the trees seemed almost to flicker with gray static. Lia frowned, suddenly on her guard. "I don't know what that is," she said in a low voice. "But it's not the moon."

Hannah stood and looked up with Lia.

As they watched, the staticmoon shuddered drunkenly to one side, leaving a still, black shadow of itself behind, superimposed on the sky.

Lia and Hannah exchanged a nervous look. They both saw it. It was happening. Tom's catbody woke with a start, and his tail puffed up with panic as he leapt to his paws. Lia knew her defenses had been breached again even before the two basketball-sized orbs (one ultrablack and the other staticy silver) descended into the foliage. The black one came down quite close by.

"Oh, shit," Hannah said, and seized Lia's hand. She was galvanized with fresh terror.

Lia put a finger to her lips as the black orb unfolded into the outline of a woman, one who seemed to have been hollowed out and filled with the night sky. The sky-woman paused and seemed to look around. It was difficult to tell, as she didn't have any eyes.

A second form, this one flickering with static, appeared some distance away, amidst the rosebushes.

"Don't move," Lia whispered to Hannah. "I don't think they see us." *I hope,* she didn't bother to add. She could feel Tom's worries as vividly as her own.

Still, despite the fact that the Archons had obviously crossed her barriers, she didn't think *all* of her tricks had been cancelled. It was the way they swiveled their heads around in irritated confusion, like they were searching through a crowd. Lia believed the music and the multitude of card games playing out on the office computer were still making it look, to the otherworlders, as though they'd dropped into the middle of some weird underground rave scene. Dozens of vague identities would be wandering amongst the plants, from the Archons' perspective, appearing for a few moments and then disappearing again to be replaced by other images. Lia and Hannah would stay consistent and unchanging amidst the crowd, but there were too many fates coming and going for them to be picked out by the weird women in that manner. So they remained camouflaged. Tom, as well as Lia's own observations, confirmed it.

The two new ladydemons (the nightsky one Lia'd already pegged as Nyx and that other, the one she now guessed might be 'Lyssa,' a face and form related to Nyx that the Greeks had used to explain mental illness) both turned away and strode off toward the back of the Yard. So far the two remaining Tzitzimime had failed to join them, and Lia hoped it meant that the lady-bugs, at least, were still unable to breach her circles. She wasn't all that squeamish about bugs in general, as someone who lived in a garden, but even she had to make an exception when it came to angry specimens of unusual size.

She picked up her security branch and followed the Archons, at a cautious distance. Tom went after her, flicking his tail in agitation.

Hannah followed too, her hunched-over posture conveying a great deal of trepidation. "What are they?" she whispered when she caught up with Lia. "They're really sort of beautiful."

"Archons, I think," Lia said, looking troubled.

"Like the ant-thing?"

"More like little gods."

Hannah paused for a long moment of silent consideration. "Is it a good idea to be following them, then?" she asked, catching up with Lia for a second time. "Maybe we oughta go the other way."

"Whatever they're seeing, it's not us," Lia whispered. "Now, shhh."

The Archons paused, cocking their simplified heads in creepy synchronization. Both of them had sensed something.

Lia and Hannah crouched down behind plant cover to spy on them. Tom hunkered down too, watching the scene with his keen feline eyes.

Some yards away, a stark white skull in a worn fedora popped up from behind a broad-leafed bird of paradise bush, and *that*, at least, was obvious enough to the Archons, even amidst the flocks of normal-if-temporary individuals they thought were roaming all around them.

"*Oh*, for the love of—" Lia cursed quietly, fuming inside. It was bad enough that the otherworlders had penetrated her barriers, but this was way too much. How in the hell could that walking anatomical specimen have slipped the bonds she'd put him under?

Lia grabbed Hannah's hand when Graves broke from his cover and shot for the fence. Han, she could feel, was likewise ready to flee, in the opposite direction.

"Wait," she breathed. She wanted to see where this was going.

Graves' bones were halfway over the wall before Nyx (the black outline) grabbed his coat and Lyssa (the staticy one) seized his shinbone. They hauled him back down off the fence together and threw him to the dirt.

"So it's *him* they've been after all along?" Hannah asked quietly. "How'd he even get out of your thing?"

Lia scowled and shook her head. "I don't know," she said grimly. *But they can have him if he's gonna be that stupid.*

She felt a little ill as soon as that notion fluttered through her brain.

Dexter Graves scrambled up, but he was quickly backed against the fence by those flat woman-shapes. There was nowhere left for him to go. He held up his hands to fend them off, and he got them to pause before pouncing on him, which Lia found surprising.

"Whoa, now—" he said. "Who the hell are *you* two? *What* the hell are you two? What happened to those other ones, Hannah and Miss Lia?"

"You will call me Lady Night," the nightsky outline told him. She indicated her static-filled friend, who was standing there beside her. "This, my sister-daughter, is Lady Madness."

"Sister-daughter, huh? That must make for some weird Thanksgivings."

Those old bones sure could tap-dance for time, Lia thought, considering her options while Graves continued stalling. She was grimly satisfied to know she'd identified Lyssa correctly, even without a field guide to demons handy.

"Shut up," Lady Night said, in response to the corpse's quip. "King Caradura would hold palaver with you, Dexter Graves."

"Oh, so it's *King* Caradura now, is it?" Graves said. "That's fancy. Sounds like Hardface's head's gettin' a little too fat for his hat, you ask me."

"We will escort you to his temple now," said Lady Madness.

"And I'll escort my bony foot up your out-of-focus ass if you so much as lay a hand, sister," Graves shot back. "I am tellin' you now, *back off.*"

Lia decided what she wanted to do. Tom seconded her notion with a silent affirmation.

Quietly, she took one of her red dreamcatchers down from a nearby tree. "Hannah," she said, without ever taking her eyes off the scene that was unfolding over by the fence. "I want you to get underground. Make sure Tom is with you. Keep the hatch open and be ready for me."

"What are you gonna do?"

"What nobody else can do," Lia said. "Now hurry."

Hannah did as she was asked, padding back the way they'd come and disappearing into darkness.

Lia took up her cherry branch as well as her dreamcatcher and began to circle around, surefooted on her home turf even in the night, meaning to creep up on the Archons.

"—All right, okay, let's just talk about this now, ladies," Graves was in the middle of saying. "Emperor Hardface wants to see me, that's fine. Let's just make an appointment like professional people, and—"

Lia broke from cover and swatted Lady Madness decisively to the ground with her fat cherry branch. The dense wood cracked against the creature's featureless, scrambled-signal head with a satisfying *snap*. In the next instant Lia threw the big red dreamcatcher over Lady Night's head. She hissed "Sidestep *this*, bitch," when she did it. The ring fell as far as Nyx's star-spangled hips, erasing her from reality from the waist up.

As soon as the dream-net fell over the Archon of Darkness, night became day. Literally. Blue sky and brilliant sunlight replaced the depthless black dome overhead. Lady Madness screamed in the sudden noontime glare.

Lia, squinting in pain, grabbed Graves' emaciated hand and together they fled, racing away as fast as they could. Graves glanced over at his savior as they sprinted through the foliage and gasped: "And here I thought you didn't even like me!"

"Not sure I do," Lia replied, shielding her eyes from the blinding onslaught of off-schedule sunlight. "But I'm pretty sure I *loathe* them."

"Whatever you say, sister. I'll take it."

Nyx, somewhere behind them, must have thrown off the dreamcatcher, because night resumed in a flash. The sky and all the plant life around them turned back to black. Lyssa's repetitive banshee screaming continued on in the darkness.

Lia saw Hannah's wide eyes peering over the top of the tube as she and the bones of Dexter Graves pounded toward it, even though her night-vision was still murky after that blast of magical daylight.

"*Get down, get down!*" Lia yelled.

Hannah dropped out of sight.

Graves reached the tube and looked in over its lip. It went a long way down, and Hannah had barely reached the bottom of the ladder.

"Just jump," Lia commanded. "Go, quickly!"

She pushed him. Graves tipped into the tube at the waist, shouting. Lia grabbed his legs and dumped him the rest of the way in. He tumbled right past Hannah, headfirst, his coat flapping, missing her only by inches, and shattered against the hard concrete floor. Han and Graves both shrieked as his bones went skittering everywhere. Cat-bodied Tom had to dive under the bed to get out of the path of the bouncing skull.

Lia was swinging her legs over the lip and into the tube when Lyssa and Nyx, the lady gods, came screeching out of the trees behind her. She dropped, catching the wheel as she fell and slamming the hatch cover down after herself.

She hung there, some feet above the floor, as the Archons on the other side of the hatch jerked the wheel she was gripping back up. She screamed. The heavy hatch door lurched and clanked again, shaking Lia around like a marionette in the hands of a spastic puppeteer.

"Hannah, help," she cried. "Turn me, turn me, *turn me!*"

Hannah grabbed Lia by the hips and spun her bodily in order to turn the wheel and seal the hatch. After a few shoulder-wrenching revolutions Lia was able to throw the bolt that sealed them in, and then they were safe.

Hannah tried to catch her when she dropped and both women tumbled to the floor, hard. They stayed there for a breathless minute or two. Then Lia sat up. So did Hannah. They exchanged a look.

"I guess we can sleep down here tonight," Lia said.

Chapter Sixteen

Ingrid wasn't all that surprised when Lyssa and Nyx showed up again empty-handed. She'd been lounging languidly on a soft chaise for quite some 'time,' next to a dark teakwood throne the King had conjured for himself upon Mictlan's endless plain, and she barely acknowledged the Archons' reluctant reappearance.

Skeletal Winston quietly continued mixing martinis behind a nearby bar. Besides the bar, her sofa, and the King's fancy chair, there were no other signs of civilization anywhere beneath the slate-gray sky.

Nyx and Lyssa dropped to their knees before their King. They wore simple linen wraps, as before, and their hair hung down their backs in neat braids. They looked like more or less ordinary women over here (if strikingly lovely ones, in the classical sense). Ingrid couldn't even guess at what they must've looked like out there in the realworld, as strange and vast as they were.

"Well?" Mickey said.

Together, Nyx and Lyssa answered: "He has returned to the cold womb of the earth, Mictlantecuhtli."

Ingrid suppressed a satisfied smile.

"He's what?" Mickey said.

"Returned to the cold womb of the earth, Mictlantecuhtli." Again in unison, with submissively downcast eyes.

"I heard you the first time!" Mickey shouted.

Lyssa and Nyx wisely stayed quiet. The King jumped up, knocking over his throne, and commenced to pace. Ingrid watched him wearily.

"What are you telling me?" he demanded of his playmates. "That he dumped himself back in a hole and pulled the dirt in on top?"

Nyx and Lyssa exchanged a look and a shrug. "Yes, Mictlantecuhtli," they said together. "We no longer feel his presence."

The King righted his throne and parked his ass, pouting. He sighed. "I did not expect that," he said.

"Nor did we, Mictlantecuhtli," the Archons echoed.

"*I* might've guessed," Ingrid said. Everyone looked over at her, draped elegantly across her chaise. She shrugged. "If history's any precedent," she explained.

The illusion of a man that called itself 'Miguel Caradura' sneered. He stood again, knocking over his throne for a second time. "Go ahead and laugh, witch!" he barked down at Ingrid. "You've got plenty of time for jokes."

Ingrid swung up into a sitting position, taking a moment to arrange her skirt. "Relax a little, why don't you?" she suggested, glancing up at Mickey. "So they're smarter than you thought they'd be. I'm sure your 'companions' will find them for you soon enough."

"Yes, you should keep on hoping that," the King said.

"Oh, come *on*, Mickey!" Ingrid cried, finally raising her voice in frustration. She was more than a bit amazed that he hadn't blown this deal already by trying to get a glimpse of the witch called Lia Flores, perhaps to see if the newer model had a body he might enjoy possessing. "This has nothing to do with me anymore," Ingrid insisted. "And we had a deal."

"I am altering the terms of that deal."

Ingrid rolled her eyes. "Then I'll just pray you don't alter them further, Lord Vader," she said, trying to chide him with a joke, but Mickey turned on her with nuclear rage burning in his eyes.

"Who is this *Vader*?" he demanded. "You call me by the name of another man? Who is this person? I will eat his skin while savoring the music of his screams!"

"Mickey, my god, have a drink," Ingrid said, raising an eyebrow. "Winston?"

Winston brought over a martini on a tray. A spiral curl of citrus peel clung to the rim of the frosty glass. Mickey refused to take it. He continued to glare at Ingrid, actually expecting an answer, it seemed.

"It was a line from a movie, okay?" Ingrid told him, forcing herself not to sigh. "Remember I told you about movies? The dreams the realworlders share in common? What you said sounded like a line from one, is all." When the King didn't respond, she flashed her bright blue eyes at him and said, emphatically: *"There is no 'Vader,' Mickey."*

Mollified, King Caradura finally took Winston's proffered martini. He looked to Lyssa and Nyx, who had cringed during his outburst, but hadn't moved from where they knelt upon the ground.

"Can you find again the place where he is buried?" he said to them, after sipping his drink and nodding his approval of it to Winston. "Are you that much smarter than my idiot Tzitzimime?"

"We... we believe so, Mictlantecuhtli," the sinister sisters replied.

Mickey looked to Ingrid. "Well, *that's* something then, isn't it?" he said.

Chapter Seventeen

About a third of the impossible thing that called itself Dexter Graves sat in the middle of Bag End's cold concrete floor, intently organizing the rest of his bones. His torn trenchcoat was still in place around his ribs and shoulders. The ragged garment had held those bones together when he fell down the tube, leaving his arms attached at the torso and in proper working order. He sang softly to himself while he sorted:

"*Soooo... the knee bone's connected to the / leg bone, and the leg bone's connected to the / hip bone, and the hip bone's connected to this / other bone / but I still can't tell / what this one iiiiis...*"

Lia stepped out from behind a folding shoji screen in comfy flannel pajama pants and a faded, laundry-thinned t-shirt, and paused to watch the decayed detective for a moment. Hannah was lying on her side on Lia's bed, assembling a skeletal foot while munching cereal straight from the box. She glanced up at Lia, clearly suppressing her own laughter.

"Mr. Graves?" Lia asked politely. "Is that really helping?"

"Yeah, sure it is," Graves said. "What am I, a goddamn osteopath over here? I gotta figure this out somehow. There's about a thousand bones in the human body, y'know."

"There are two hundred and six," Lia informed him, "and not all of yours even came apart."

"Then *you* figure out where they all go, you know so goddamn much," Graves grumbled, crossing his arms in a show of weary petulance.

"All right, all right, relax already," Lia said, pulling her bobbed hair back into a blunt little ponytail that bristled like a makeup brush at the nape of her neck. "I'll help." She stepped in front of him, looking down at him squarely. "Just don't go freaking out on me again, or I'll have to put you back under glass. Understood?"

"Ha!" Graves exclaimed. "Fat chance, sister. You're not getting anywhere *near* my lighter again." He frantically pawed at the front of his coat, searching for the item in question.

Lia raised her eyebrows. She walked over to the shelf the lighter had been sitting on, underneath a waterglass, when last she'd seen it. "No? You sure about that?"

"Of course I'm sure about that," Graves shot back. "I rose from the *dead* to get that lighter. You can't seriously think I'm gonna... gonna forget... oh."

He trailed off when Lia retrieved the Zippo from the scrim of broken glass it was still lying under up on the bookshelf, then held it aloft and waggled it.

"Damn it all to hell," Graves muttered, sounding defeated.

Hannah did her best to muffle a snicker.

"Well, what do you expect?" Graves said irritably. "My brains turned to mush a long time ago."

Hannah laughed aloud at that. Graves sulked. Lia smiled and tossed him his lighter. He caught it on the fly and looked up at her, more than a bit surprised.

"You know this means I'm trusting you, Mr. Graves," Lia said. "I expect your best behavior."

Graves stared at the lighter for a long moment before he put it away inside his coat, on the lefthand side, over the place where his heart used to be. It glowed warmly through the fabric for a pulse or two before fading away, Lia noticed.

"My word is my bond, dollface," Graves swore, looking up at her earnestly. He seemed unable to keep a faint note of emotion out of his voice, and that made her smile. She knew how good it could feel to be trusted. "Dontcha ever let anybody tell ya different," the skeleton continued. "And... you *did* promise to call me Dexter, if I recall."

"All right, then, *Dexter*." Lia's smile twisted into a mischievous grin as she nodded toward the little, leftover bone in his hand that he hadn't been able to identify. "And that one's your coccyx, by the way," she said.

"My *what?*" Graves yelped.

"Your tailbone."

"Oh. Right." Graves—Dexter—examined the little calcified

nub. "Didn't think what I thought had an actual bone in it."

Hannah outright snorted with laughter at that one, and Dexter looked over at her. "Okay, *now* I'm gettin' the level of the room," he said. "I pick up on subtleties, y'know. I was a private dick before I died."

"Private *dick*?" Lia said. She hadn't heard that term before. Maybe it was from before her time, like 'groovy' or 'zounds.' It sounded nasty though, so she was intrigued. "What's that," she asked, "like a male prostitute or something?"

"A male...?" Dexter was openly astounded. "No. God, *no*. What gutter is your mind in, girly? Geez! No, a dick's a detective. A gumshoe, a seamus. You heard those vocabulary words before?"

"Sure," Lia said, grinning at his outrage. "But these days, just so you know, a dick's a penis. Unless it's a person, then it's an asshole. Just FYI."

"I got a lot to bone up on, don't I?"

"No pun intended, I'm sure," Lia said.

Mystified, Dexter looked over to Hannah for clarification. "I made a pun?"

Hannah smiled and shook her head. Lia yawned hugely.

"We borin' you over there, dollface?" Dex asked, swiveling his skull back in her direction. He seemed like he was starting to enjoy the banter.

Lia handed him a rebuilt leg and he popped it into place. The bones stayed put when they were fitted together, like they had magnets embedded in their ends, and she thought the effect was pretty nifty. "It's been a really long day for me, Dexter. That's all."

She sneezed unexpectedly.

"Plus I think I might be getting sick."

"Well, we can put out the lights and chase down some Zs, if you're feelin' the need," Dexter said, and Lia noticed his voice had become overwhelmingly protective, underneath his hardboiled drawl. Again, she felt warmly glad to have rescued him. "This's been a sorta trying sunup-to-sundown for me too, you wanna know the truth," he said.

Lia nodded. Hannah was looking at her with some concern. "Do you want a sleeping bag, Dexter?" Lia asked. "Do you get cold?"

"Y'know, I haven't really thought about it," Dex said. After a moment's consideration: "I guess I'm okay."

Lia nodded and unrolled her own bag onto the hard floor. She hadn't realized how tired she really felt until just a few minutes ago.

"Llll...isa?" Hannah said, catching herself on the verge of using Lia's true name. "Honey? Do you want to sleep in your own bed? I can—"

"Sleeping on this floor'll kill your back, Han," Lia said. "Really, I'll be all right."

Hannah nodded uncertainly. Lia wriggled into her bag, and Dexter propped himself up against the wall. Tom curled up at Lia's hip and she reached out a hand to touch his fur. Her eyes were already closing. "Can you get the light?" she said to Hannah.

"Sure."

Hannah sat up to click off the lamp, and the small bed creaked when she settled back into it.

In the ensuing silence, Lia let her eyes drift back open. Dexter Graves, lit only by the faint digital glow from her few electronic appliances, angled his skull in her direction. Something seemed almost to pass between them, some exchange or communication, although neither of them said a word.

After a moment or two Lia watched the sentient skeleton lean back and settle his misshapen old fedora down over his eyeholes to sleep.

Black Tom felt Lia's fingers twitch against his fur when she began to dream. He could've joined her, tired as he was, and he would have, had he not also been able to tell that her dreaming was of a calm and restful variety. She was all right. So, instead of drifting off after her, he stood up from his motionless catbody and shuffled his ghost over to stand in front of Dexter Graves, leaning on his insubstantial cane out of old, unbreakable habit.

In sleep, the bundle of bones wrapped in a raincoat looked about as divorced from life as a fossil should. If Tom had wandered in for the very first time he might've been tempted to believe that Graves had died trapped down here when the bomb shelter was new, and had been a decomposing part of the décor for the subsequent half-century. The clothed bones looked like nothing so much as the *Calavera* cartoons he remembered seeing in Mexican newspapers back when he'd been alive: engraved illustrations of skeletons getting drunk or riding bicycles or what have you. People still trotted out those old images of domesticated death every October, for use as Halloween decorations.

Try as he might, though, Tom couldn't sense any ill intent on *this* skeleton's behalf. Which, in truth, worried him far more than the direct menace posed by the Archons and the Tzitzimime. Dexter Graves didn't even seem to know who or what Mictlantecuhtli was, and yet Tom would've been an idiot not to assume some connection there. The mere fact of the dead man's presence meant they weren't shut of el Rey or his creatures yet, despite all of Lia's clever if desperate attempts at deflection.

He paused, listening again to his girl's (and to Hannah's) almost inaudible respiration in the darkness. Graves didn't seem to breathe, and there were no other sounds to be heard this deep underground. Tom knew they couldn't stay down here forever, though.

He was filled with a dreadful certainty that el Rey's ambitions hadn't changed at all since the night he'd broken his covenant with the King and fled from his patronage, so many years ago.

He wondered what sort of trap he'd led his girl into, and he could only hope they'd find their way out of it again.

Retrospective No.2 ~ 1910

A century ago...

Southern Pacific's Toluca Flyer pulled into the Valley Line terminus (at the busy heart of Lankershim Township, about as far to the west as one could travel by rail) right on schedule. The time was just after one o'clock in the afternoon on a temperate autumn day, late in the year 1910.

'Lankershim,' Delgado noted, with a wry arch to his brow, as the engine chugged the last few hundred yards down the gleaming tracks and into the station, finally rolling right across 'Lankershim Boulevard' itself. The broad dirt street was crowded with pedestrians, horsedrawn carts, and a surprisingly large number of those newfangled motorcars that were already becoming such a menace on the roads back east. The omnipresent name it bore was also a recent addition, both to the street itself and to the greater township at large. It had been contributed by the family of a sheep-magnate-turned-local-investor from someplace up north: one Mr. Isaac Lankershim. Obviously a humble and unassuming sort of man. Or at least that was the picture Los Angeles' native necromancer had constructed from newspaper stories during this last leg of his long peregrination across the North American continent, as he made his way back home.

Dulcé had been dead for a decade, almost to the day. Delgado had planned his return to Los Angeles to coincide with that anniversary, according to the terms of the deal he'd been forced to make in order to avenge her murder... although he didn't want to contemplate that just now. The pain of her loss had been dulled by time, but he could still feel it as keenly as a new wound whenever he made the mistake of letting memory catch up with him.

The town at the end of the tracks had still been called 'Toluca' when he departed from this same station a full ten years before. He was a native *Californio*, Tomas Delgado was, born on a nearby *rancho* in the year 1845, and he remembered back to a time when this particular place had enjoyed no proper name at all.

But then the times were changing, weren't they? Everything was changing, change was absolutely *de rigueur* these days. In the fullness of time, Delgado reflected, this little boondock situated to the north of Hollywood would probably come to be called something else again.

He eased himself down from the private car el Rey's man had chartered for him and stepped onto the wooden platform, leaning heavily on his cane.

His hip seemed to ache even when the weather was warm, these days.

At sixty-five, Tom felt far older in his bones than he did in his mind. On some days that discrepancy didn't bother him a bit, but on others, it did.

He paused on the platform while his fellow travelers milled around him, greeting families or fussing with trunks, tickets and porters, then shielded his eyes to look south.

The Santa Monica Mountains jutted up from the earth a few miles away, divided by the natural cleft once known to the old people as *Kawengna*. It was the 'Cahuenga' Pass these days, the old native name approximated by a new Spanish spelling.

Not far beyond the pass, Tom knew, was a lonely field in which stood an ancient and gnarled *encino*, or oak tree, whose limbs had always pointed up at a Hole in the Sky. A Hole where someone was currently waiting for him to climb up and crawl through, as he'd long ago promised he would... one day.

And now that day had come.

Tom sighed. He could hardly complain. He'd had a decade to roam the earth and money enough to do it in style. He'd bedded the most beautiful of women during that time; dined at the finest of tables; drunk himself stupid on the rarest liqueurs. He'd seen the cities and palaces of Europe, traveled the colorful trade routes of Egypt and India, sipped at tea or opium while conversing with silken courtesans in the lacquered pavilions of the Orient. Through the grace of his patron Mictlantecuhtli, the ancient Aztec

Rey de Los Muertos, the old sorcerer had done and seen and had just about everything he could remotely imagine doing or seeing or having, but now...

Now that he'd traveled so far to the west that he was a mere ocean away from the mysterious East again (and, more importantly, now that the bill for the whole affair was about to come due), he couldn't help but feel a touch of what the world's professional pitchmen were said to have labeled 'buyer's remorse.'

Caveat Emptor indeed, Tom thought.

Watt, the skinny Englishman whose given name was Wendell or Wilson or Webster or something like that, if Tom remembered correctly, was already waiting for him across the street. Leaning against the Japan-black fender of a brand new Model T, right out in front of the Lankershim Post Office, where they couldn't fail to miss each other.

Watt raised a hand in greeting and Tom waved back, muttering "Hijo de puta..." through a phony rictus of a smile.

He'd expected at least one night to himself. A chance to eat a last meal in a proper restaurant and sleep in a soft hotel bed. Not the King's one-man welcome wagon over there. But he knew it was in his best interests to keep a pleasant face on things.

And besides, he ought to be at least a *little* bit grateful. The Pacific Electric Railway had plans (again, according to the papers) to open a Big Red Streetcar line up from Hollywood to the recently-rechristened Lankershim sometime in the next year, but until then the only way over to the field containing the Tree That Grew Below the Hole in the Sky was via the rutted, winding dirt track that snaked through the mountain pass.

The route was known by now simply as Pass Road, though Tomas could remember a day when it had been part of *el Camino Real*, the Royal Road connecting all the Spanish Missions up and down the coast. He also knew, beyond what he could personally recall, that it'd served the old people as something that might be better described as the *Carretera del Rey*, the King's Highway (or simply the Road that Runs Past the Hole in the Sky), for some millennia before that.

Riding in Woolgar or Wilshire or Wilbur Watt's fancy new auto-mobile would certainly be easier on Tom's old bones than the joint-jarring trudge in a hired horsecart that was his only other option.

El Rey never skimped on hospitality. Not even when it overwhelmed his guests.

Wallace or Walter or Watson crouched down to crank-start the Tin Lizzie while Tom hefted his bag over his shoulder and hobbled across the street on his walking stick. He'd heard those engines had a tendency to kick back if the spark wasn't properly retarded, and he wondered if he wasn't about to witness Willie or Wally or Whatever his name was breaking a thumb.

But no, the engine sputtered safely to life, and Watt stood to shake Tom's hand. "Welcome home, Tom," the Englishman said, in his characteristically clipped and formal tones. He lowered his voice to add: "Mictlantecuhtli would see you."

Tom knew. That's why he was here.

He nodded, climbed up into the fancyass car, and held onto his hat as Winston (yes, that was it, *Winston*) Watt piloted the noisy contraption out into traffic and away down the street, frightening any number of horses.

By the time they reached the far side of the pass Tom learned to be glad that the racket kicked up by Mr. Watt's 'auto-mobile' more or less precluded casual conversation. He *also* learned, after they stopped for a gulp of water at the Eight Mile House (a small way station and hostel situated in the middle of the pass), that the infernal thing could hammer along at a pace of almost twenty-five miles per hour on a straightaway. Watt felt compelled to demonstrate that property, for some unfathomable reason, as they barreled down the southern side of the mountains.

It felt suicidally fast to Tom. He remembered the headline furor surrounding the death-by-motorcart of a man named Henry Hale Bliss way back in 1899. The accident had still been the talk of the town when he first disembarked in New York City, after leaving Los Angeles. He further remembered naively regretting that the internal combustion fad hadn't snuffed itself out before such a tragedy had to occur. Tom had been certain, back then, that the threat of violent, crushing death would finally be enough to dampen the public's rabid enthusiasm for this absurd new sport of 'motoring.'

He, apparently, could not have been more wrong about that.

Twice he and Watt met with vehicles like their own as they traversed the Carretera del Rey—noisy bouncing carriages piloted by grinning idiots swaddled in dusters and goggles, and each time such an encounter occurred one car or the other was forced to back some number of yards down the narrow dirt track until it widened out enough for someone to pull off into the weeds and let the other motorist pass by.

Tom didn't see how the Cahuenga Pass could possibly accommodate too many more of Mr. Ford's Follies. Practical considerations like geography and the availability of fuels weren't preventing people from buying the things, however.

There were exponentially more autos on the Hollywood side of the pass, Tom noted, when they rolled down out of the hills. The cars puttered and honked their way past delivery wagons and well-dressed folks perched precariously atop fat-tired bicycles. Watt drove them down Highland and past the Hollywood Hotel: a vast, white, Moorish-style monstrosity hunkered at the northwestern corner of Highland's intersection with Prospect Avenue.

All of that acreage had been devoted to beans and strawberries the last time Tom had ridden by. There were even rumors in the papers now that old Prospect Avenue itself might soon be renamed 'Hollywood Boulevard,' in honor of the ever-expanding hostelry on the corner.

The pace of development around here stunned him. There were still plenty of open fields stretching away to the horizons, but also so many large new homes and broad new streets, as well as all of the stores and schools and other businesses needed to sustain the ever-swelling numbers of brand new residents.

The thought of so many new people living so near to the Hole in the Sky left Tom feeling a little sick.

The old people—the Tongva and the Tataviam and the Chumash—had known how to respect a thing like a Hole in the Sky. Their fathers had known for countless generations, and the traditions they handed down amongst themselves had preserved the necessary balance between the elemental forces involved. Even the *rancheros* who displaced them had indulged a healthy superstition regarding old heathen magic, and they'd always shown enough good sense to leave the things they didn't need to know about alone.

These new people, though, Tom was not so sure about. They so often seemed to behave with the mindless rapacity of a swarm of locusts.

What would happen when people like that discovered a thing like the Hole in the Sky? The old deflective hexes that protected it might not be able to keep the blissfully ignorant from stumbling across the secret by accident. Only the great Tree's relative isolation and the difficulty of reaching the Hole above it had ever really prevented that.

Worse still for Tom was the thought of what might happen if the King who occupied the twin chambers beyond the SkyHole were to become infatuated with the lives these new folks were building for themselves over here, on the far side of existence.

What would become of the worlds if el Rey discovered Time, and the possibilities for growth, change, and increase that only it could offer?

Tom Delgado literally shuddered to think of it, even in the warmth of the relentless California sun.

Watt turned left at Sunset Boulevard, and when they motored through the intersection at Gower Street Tom saw it was true that the Blondeau Tavern had indeed closed down. The establishment had been doing land-office business back when Tom left town, serving Madame Blondeau's famous pigeon-&-rum omelets to oceanbound daytrippers and local farmhands, and now it was gone. Marty Labaig's older Six Mile House was still open across the street, still advertising light meals and cold drinks, although its sign now read 'Casa Cahuenga.'

Tomas nudged Watt in the ribs with his elbow to get the man's attention and then motioned for him to stop in at the old roadhouse. He didn't believe el Rey would begrudge him a quick glass of beer.

Watt cut across the street and pulled up in front of the *faux chateau*, which still had grapevines growing over its picket fence and up the sides of the house, exactly as Tom remembered. He felt relieved by the fact that something, at least, had managed to remain almost unchanged for over a decade. It was apparently quite a feat, here in the new *Ciudad de los Angeles*.

"It true they mean to shoot motion pictures over there?" Tom asked, tipping his head toward Rene Blondeau's boarded-up building across the street. "The Nestor Film Company?"

"That's what they say," Watt said, and sniffed to indicate his contempt for the very idea. "Those Selig-Polyscope people are expanding their operation up in Edendale, too. Just what this city needs: a flood of producers and writers and actors."

"Oh my," Tom said, cheered for the very first time that day by a vision of the future. He'd always enjoyed the company of actors. Well, of *actresses*, anyway. Still, the influx of theatrical types made sense. Tom knew from growing up around here that California's weather would prove much better suited to the realities of film-making (a subject that had fascinated him for some time now) than anything he'd experienced on the eastern seaboard, or out in the middle west either. He wouldn't be surprised to see the young city of Hollywood parlay the combination of Mr. Edison's remarkable new technology and its own climatic assets into recognition as one of the world's great centers of cultural dissemination, right after London and Paris and New York.

He had to guess that Mr. Watt would respond with a hollow laugh if he tried to advance this theory to him. Tom figured they'd just have to wait and see.

Then he remembered that he wouldn't be here to see how the experiment panned out. He wouldn't be here to see how *tomorrow* panned out, if things went as expected, and his momentarily-kindled spark of interest faded away.

"Well, to hell with it all anyhow," Tom said abruptly, then turned away from the movie-factory-to-be across the street and shuffled into the Six Mile House's oasis of cool continuity on his cane. "I've been sober all morning, so maybe you wanna hurry up?" he said, back over his shoulder, to a bemused Winston Watt.

Anyone watching would have assumed both Tom and Winston were well besotted by the time they wobbled out of the Six Mile House and made their way down to the grassy curb they'd parked at. Tom clambered back up into Mr. Watt's gleaming new Tin Lizzie.

He cast a surreptitious eye over at the bleary Englishman, who was pulling on his driving gloves with undue difficulty, as though he'd somehow found himself with more fingers than he remembered having.

He was too skinny to be a good drinker, as Tom had guessed would be the case. Watt seemed aware enough of his limitations; he'd turned down Tom's first offer to buy him a drink, attempting (Tom supposed) to keep things on a professional footing.

But no one who worked for el Rey de los Muertos could stay away from the sauce for long, and Watt accepted Tom's second offer. And then his third, and his fourth, and then some undetermined number beyond that. Tom did know that he was out almost five whole dollars, and he'd only bought three glasses of beer for himself. Watt had switched over from disgusting juniper-scented gin mixed with quinine water to bright green French absinthe at some point in the last two hours, and now he was crouching in the gutter to turn the Model T's handcrank.

A Prohibitionist's worst nightmare, Tom thought. *They could put this on a protest poster.*

This time the unpredictable engine did kick back, startling Watt, who leapt away from the thing with a shout, only to land on his ass in the street.

Right in front of a horsedrawn farm wagon.

The animals reared, almost upsetting the cart's inventory of vegetables and clanking milk cans. The driver cursed at Watt and called him an idiot, then pulled his team around the obstruction and continued down Gower Street. Watt responded with an obscene gesture of his own, one he directed safely at the back of the receding cart, while Tom watched the whole exchange with one eyebrow arched dispassionately.

"The roads around here are like this *constantly* these days," Watt complained. "People have no manners at all anymore. I'm afraid it's likely to get worse before it gets better, too."

Tom nodded, looking south over the fields and gardens, figuring Watt was probably right enough about that. There must have been literally a dozen houses in sight, almost all of them having cropped up like toadstools in the ten years that had passed since Tom last laid eyes upon this landscape.

Forty years before *that*, the area for miles all around the Tree Below the Hole in the Sky had still been wild. The field it stood in was a natural prairie, situated across a low shelf of foothill bedrock. Isolation had long been its best, but not its only, defense.

Back then, when Tom first came through here, he'd been on foot and in the company of his old friend Ramon San Martín. They'd been walking for some days—questing, really, one could say—eating nothing but the mix of dried cactus buttons and small brown mushrooms given to them by an old shaman in preparation for the trip. Teonanactl and Mescalito, the spirits of the plants they ate, walked with them. The spirits revealed the landscape as it was in *their* otherworldly eyes, and they guided the boys to what they sought, in their youthful foolishness: that which was rumored and whispered about by witches and sorcerers for leagues all around and had been for a thousand years or more.

The Hole in the Sky, of course. And the two rooms that lay beyond it, the King's Chambers, las Cameras del Rey. There was an antechamber, in which a man could stand and live; and then there was that inner room, the one with the blood-black altar. That was the Holy of Holies which, once penetrated, could never be returned from.

At least not without the King's permission, and even then it was only possible at a particular time of the year, the roughly forty-eight hour period acknowledged by the Catholic Church as the paired feasts of All Saints' and All Souls' days, when natural seasonal progressions brought the worlds into close alignment.

Watt the Englishman squatted again before the auto's handcrank, and this time he was able to wring the engine to life without incident.

"We all set then, Tom?" he said, swaying a bit as he got to his feet.

Tom nodded again, eyeing Watt for any signs of falsity in his behavior. He believed the man was legitimately soused, all right, but it wouldn't do to be caught out unawares. Not now. Because, at some point in the afternoon, Tom had come to a decision. Quietly, without a lot of fuss or conscious consideration, he'd realized that he had no intention of climbing up that Tree, nor of crawling through that Hole. As he sipped his few beers (using a touch of sleight-of-mind to let Watt think he was matching him more or less drink-for-drink), his true objective had finally solidified.

Now, he planned to let the King's Englishman drive him out to the field with the Tree. But then, instead of ascending, he'd find a pretense to buy some time and wait till Watt inevitably passed out from acute inebriation.

At which point Tom would tie him up, and then cut down that godforsaken oak.

That's right: he meant to chop down the Tree Below the Hole in the Sky. The ladder to the otherworld. The stairway to... well, not heaven.

He could hardly believe it himself, but when he looked into his heart, he found that it was true.

Tom looked over at Watt as the man hoisted himself up into the Model T's driver's seat. He hardly looked capable of operating the Ford's elaborate controls. Tom wanted to offer to drive, but he'd never piloted an auto-mobile before in his life, and besides, he couldn't now claim to be less intoxicated than Watt without tipping his hand, could he?

If the Englishman killed them on the road, well... then Tom figured he'd just arrive in the King's realm a little ahead of schedule.

But if they happened to survive the drive, then he might yet have his chance to turn the tables.

Part Three: All Souls' Day, Morning

Chapter Eighteen

A century later...

A tall, female figure in head-to-toe black leather stood at a scenic viewpoint off Mulholland Drive and gazed out over the San Fernando Valley as it yawned and stretched away below her in the day's clear new light. She had her helmet's mirrored visor down, obscuring her face from view. The rising sun's reflection burned across the silvered plastic in a hot white stripe.

She raised a divining rod in her right hand and flicked it with her left index finger. The rod spun wildly, like a compass needle near a magnet, round and round.

Then, with unnatural suddenness, it pulled to indicate north/northeast, and froze there.

The concealed woman nodded, zipped the rod into a breast pocket, and swung a leg over a hulking black motorcycle that was parked at the side of the road. When she kickstarted her ride and roared off a total of six big black cars trailed after her, snaking down the winding road that ran through Laurel Canyon.

Fifteen minutes later, the same woman and her six-car retinue growled to a stop for a red light at Laurel and Sherman Way, nearly halfway across the Valley's flat floor.

The foothills a few miles back had seemed a lot more affluent and pretty, in her opinion. Up here it was all blank-faced warehouses and construction-supply outlets with little knots of hopeful laborers milling around outside their parking lots. Cheery, accordion-based Mexican music blared from a nearby pickup truck that was also caught at the red.

The leatherclad, helmeted biker took her divining rod from her breast pocket and flicked it again, repeating her wayfinding operation while the six black sedans that made up her ominous entourage settled in behind her. The rod spun, then froze, pointing in a more easterly direction.

They were getting close now.

The concealed woman nodded and zipped the rod back into her pocket. She glanced over at the pickup truck that was idling next to her, raised her visor for just a flash, and the men inside the cab promptly turned their music down.

The red light changed to a green and the woman continued traveling north into the Valley, following the rod and leading her menacing procession of nondescript cars forward.

Dexter Graves popped his skull up through Bag End's already-open hatch. It was a lovely morning, bright and cool and full of birdsong. There were savory breakfast smells on the breeze.

Graves climbed up out of the tube and into the sun, glad to be, well, if not exactly *alive*, then whatever the hell this was. His bonus round. It might not've been perfect (not by a damn sight), but it sure beat the long dirtnap.

Of which he remembered surprisingly little, he found, when he stopped and gave it some thought. He had a hazy, disjointed memory of being burritoed up in a paint-spattered dropcloth then hauled out to a desert grave by Big Juan San Martín, Hardface's enforcer, whom he now regretted not shooting back when he had the chance. After that, it was like his mind had shut down in the face of unending blackness, boredom and immobility, and it hadn't stirred again until that driving compulsion to find his lighter roused him yesterday morning. Why *that* should have happened, he just couldn't say. He didn't know how these things worked. Going through them wasn't enough to make you an expert.

After a few agreeable minutes of wandering through the dew-bejeweled plant life and feeling the grasses underfoot tickle his toebones, Graves spotted Miss Hannah some way off through the greenery. She was standing in a little clearing filled with garden furniture, making bacon and eggs on a portable hotplate she'd dragged up from Lia's bunker, as well as tea with an electric kettle.

She didn't seem to see him.

Graves heard water start to run somewhere in the distance and he turned his skull in the direction of the sound, too curious about what Miss Lia might be getting up to not to check into it before he started a conversation with Hannah. She glanced up before she began setting out Lia's mismatched plates, an instant after Graves stepped behind the cover of a potted tree. Maybe she saw him, and maybe she didn't. Either way, she smiled a tiny smile and continued to busy herself with pleasant morning chores.

Deciding she hadn't seen him after all, Graves wandered off to look for Lia.

She had an old waterheater jury-rigged into the Yard's irrigation apparatus, and a soft cotton bathtowel thrown over a nearby garden bench.

She stepped, naked, into the steamy cascade of water that gushed down from a showerhead on a hose that she'd slung over a wooden arbor, one nestled amidst a bower of fragrant citrus, peach and pear trees. She knew, from Black Tom, that these tall, rooted fruit trees were all holdovers from the Valley's agricultural past.

Her private outdoor shower was Lia's very favorite amongst the many perks that came along (in her opinion) with life at Potter's Yard.

Behind her, Dexter the trenchcoat-wearing skeleton came sauntering out of the unruly foliage that proliferated back here in this far corner of the Yard. He spotted her straightaway, and she saw him duck back behind a juniper shrub, out of the corner of her eye. He peeked out from around his camouflage a couple of moments later, apparently thinking he was being subtle.

Lia smiled. *Some gumshoe,* she thought.

She was feeling a lot better this morning, after a good, recharging night's sleep. Improved enough to be feeling a touch... well, playful. Something deep in her core quivered enticingly when she imagined Dexter's eyes (or his ocular orbits, anyway) drinking in the naked sight of her.

She didn't think of herself as a necrophile. She'd never performed a peep show for a corpse before, and she'd certainly never expected to. But she was about to do it now, and she felt the strangest combination of surprise and excitement as she contemplated her own imminent behavior.

Lia washed herself, languidly, leisurely, keeping her back to Dex, whom she knew wasn't going away. She squeezed water from her hair (which looked like a spill of India ink when it was wet), and shook it out. She soaped up a second time just for show, just to let herself glisten amidst the torrent of white waterdiamonds that cascaded down all around her, basking as she did every morning in the warmth and billowing steam, fully aware that every inch of her bare, creamy skin was shining in the glory of the pure morning sun...

While one leering cadaver looked on, with his jawbone hanging open to his sternum.

Graves knew he shouldn't have been there. He knew he should've beaten a retreat already and decided, reluctantly, that he would now actually do so. Before things got weird. He turned away from the scintillating sight before him (with more than a moderate degree of personal difficulty), and ran smack into Hannah, who'd snuck up behind him with a steaming cup of tea in her hand.

Graves shouted and backpedaled, tripping over a stray flowerpot and taking a number of young Japanese maples down with him when he tumbled over backwards, landing hard enough to rattle his bones.

He lay there for a moment, in the dirt, gazing up and feeling dazed. Hannah looked down from one side of his field of vision. Lia, her black hair dripping, did the same from the other. There was nothing but blue sky behind them, piled high with bulging towers of bright white cloud.

"Tea, Dexter?" Hannah asked cheerfully. She and Lia (who'd swaddled herself in a towel) both laughed aloud.

Graves sat up. "Yeah, that's funny," he said, exaggerating his perturbation as he retrieved his hat and crammed it back onto his bony head, then got to his feet. "Real funny. What're you, the vice squad? This a sting operation? You know damn well I got no gut to dump that in," he accused, pointing imperiously at Hannah's teacup.

Lia claimed it and sipped from it herself, grinning at him over the rim. He did like being grinned at by her, he had to admit. That chopped-off haircut made her a dead ringer for pretty picture star Louise Brooks, with whom he'd been infatuated since he was about fourteen years old. All the way back in 1929.

He heard the sound of engines somewhere in the near distance, but traffic noises weren't uncommon around here, and none of them took any particular notice.

"Looks like you're feeling better this morning, anyway," Graves observed, automatically tilting a salacious socket down toward Lia's thighs, which poked out fetchingly from underneath the hem of her abbreviated towel-skirt. He hardly even realized he was doing it.

"I think I just needed to sleep," she said, stepping close and gently tipping Graves' chinbone back up so that he had to meet her eyes. "I get twitchy when I'm tired."

"Well, don't we all, sister," he said, feeling dizzily bemused and more than a little embarrassed to've been caught so nakedly eyegroping Miss Lia's gams. You'd think not actually *having* the offending orbs anymore he'd be able to keep 'em in his goddamn head, but no. Not him. No chance.

At least he couldn't blush in his current condition.

"Don't we all…" he repeated, a solid beat too late, just for the sake of having something more to say, and he was gratified when Lia nudged his femur with her terrycloth hip and smiled up at him.

Chapter Nineteen

Black Tom watched over the Yard from the peak of the office shack's corrugated roof, through his catbody's sharp green eyes. He was in the habit of giving Lia a bit of space in the mornings, so that she could bathe and see to other personal business in relative privacy.

From where Tom was crouched he could see all the way to each edge of the nursery's property, and far beyond. To the north of them, the DWP generating station's four red-&-white, candy-striped smokestacks poked up into the blue sky. Closer by, he could easily look out over the locked front gate and down into the empty street outside.

While he was lounging in the early sun and lazily watching the Yard's perimeter, a large black motorcycle piloted by a tall woman in head-to-toe black leather came rumbling down the road. She surprised Tom when she stopped her bike and let it idle right before the Yard's front gate. Half a dozen long black cars also pulled up and parked at the curbs on either side of the street.

They didn't look like landscape designers, who rarely if ever traveled by motorcade. Tom sent a note of concern out toward Lia, just one soft alarm bell. For now. He could feel his girl tiptoeing back toward her bomb shelter with her rubber shower-sandals slapping at her heels, still unclothed except for a towel she'd cinched around herself like a fuzzy white mini-dress.

The black-clad woman killed her engine and swung herself off her bike, then wandered up to the fence. Her henchmen, a full dozen of them, got out of their cars and stood around, waiting for orders.

The leatherclad Amazon took in the eyeball-covered fence, with its multiple rings of Pi digits scorch-tattooed onto the silvery wood. She raised her helmet's mirrored visor for a better look. None of the henchmen were in a position to see Lyssa's mad static revealed instead of a face, but Tom was.

Lyssa, Lady Madness, was the unknown biker. Crazy as she was, she'd somehow found her way back out here, and this time she had a different kind of reinforcement in tow: a dozen armed men with money as their motivator, in place of a handful of nightmares. Maybe things looked clearer to her by the light of day, which obviously didn't force her to retreat from reality as it did in the case of her relation Nyx, or the Tzitzimime.

Tom's psychic warning bell began to clang in earnest, in time with his catbody's skyrocketing heart rate.

He felt Lia down in her bomb shelter, throwing on clothes she'd laid out before her shower and searching under the furniture for her shoes. She was coming, but she was still far away, down below ground in the most distant corner of the eight-acre Yard. Events were apt to unfold here at the gate before she could make the scene.

Lyssa reached out and touched her gloved fingertips to the fence. "Oooooh, such an angryugly stare," she murmured, her voice gone soft with wonderment. The painted eyes didn't seem to trouble her much. "Oh, and a Pi slide; a long, long Pi slide, all the way down, down into the ground..."

Tom watched the nearest pair of henchmen exchange a clear look of no confidence.

Lyssa snapped her visor closed and turned back to them. "This is the Gravesite, yes," she said decisively, in a somewhat muffled voice. "Surround it now, you vicious boys."

For a moment, nobody moved. Then the oldest of the assembled men stepped forward. He wore a scuffed leather jacket and his face was both shaped and textured rather like a brick. He looked to be in his early fifties. "Lady, look, I know Mickey Hardface wanted you to bring us out here," he said carefully. "But ain't somebody else gonna, like, tell us what to do?" After a beat he added, hopefully: "Anybody?"

Lyssa cocked her helmeted head like she'd never seen such a thing as him before. "The Sun King reigns o'er hard, bright hours," she said, "and I walk the day by his permissive grace, but my sister-mother never can hold dominion here. Duh. But

Dexter Graves has left his grave and I can feel him there amidst the trees again. Our moment grows as ripe as the gibbous moon!"

Brickface exchanged a second look with his buddy, the one he'd shared a car with on the drive out here. It was plain enough to Tom that the faceless wackadoo's line of horseshit did not sound good to them, not good at all. It didn't sound so great to him, either.

"So... that'd be a no, then?" the pensive wiseguy pressed, still trying to get an answer on that chain of command issue.

"That'd be a find him find him find him *now*, before I bite your squishy eyes to feel them pop between my teeth," Lyssa elucidated. She then raised her voice to address the men *en masse*: "*Go and stalk your prey, my wolves!*"

The assigned-by-Hardface henchmen reluctantly did as they were told, the full dozen fanning out, while Lyssa turned back to the closed front gate and raised her leather-sheathed arms to the sky.

Mictlantecuhtli's footsoldiers moved in quick. Tom had to wonder who'd hired these men on el Rey's behalf. They seemed very well prepared for the task they'd been set to.

One of the younger men removed the lock on the front gate with boltcutters. A second kid eased the gate open. Two older guys darted through, guns drawn, and feinted to either side. The man Tom thought of as Brickface and his partner entered next, their guns also drawn, and they crouched down as they jogged for cover deeper inside the Yard.

Then Lyssa sauntered right the hell in, rendering all of that stealthy choreography pointless.

The other half of the Henchforce hurried around the outside perimeter of the fence to cover any alternate exits. Tom could feel that Lia was now above ground and coming on the run, but he dreaded the thought of her encountering any of these people.

In the moment of quiet that descended after the goon squad scrambled off to execute their orders, a half-visible thing that looked like a cross between a bulldog and a bullfrog peered around the gate, snuffling after the interlopers.

It was a Croucher, as Tom well knew. The two men assigned to guard the front entrance couldn't see it at all.

It sniffed at a new offering of fresh fruit Hannah had put out first thing that morning, considered it... then hopped after the intruders instead, snorting up their scent and baring its double rows of sharp, shark-like teeth in a hungry, anticipatory grin.

Tom watched from the office shack's roof as half a dozen more ravenous Crouchers hopped through the gate, following in the path of the first one.

Chapter Twenty

Graves relaxed while Hannah finished up her cooking. The good, homey smells of frying breakfast filled the air, making him wish bitterly that he still had the plumbing you needed to digest a strip of bacon. He was starting to wonder how long he was apt to stay like this, dead in all but the most fundamental of ways, but such thoughts were not pleasant ones and he pushed them aside in favor of more enjoyable memories of meals he'd eaten two-thirds of a century in the past.

Hannah started munching straightaway, as soon as the eggs were done. Lia's plate waited for her on the table, steaming mellowly in the mottled light that filtered down through a forest of grown trees—oaks, olives, evergreens and palms—all of which stood rooted in half-ton wooden pots. Hannah told Graves, when he asked, that they rented the exotic specimens out to film productions. There were even several stands of tall bamboo that would rustle and rattle like lonely old bones in all but the gentlest of breezes.

Graves tilted precariously back in his chair and rocked it a bit. He was savoring this quiet and companionable moment with one of his new friends when a leatherclad, helmeted woman came striding out of the foliage toward him.

He was so startled that he tumbled backwards out of his chair.

Hannah jumped up. The new woman knocked her out of the way as she made a beeline for Graves. He found his feet a second before the leather lady seized him by the throat and pinned him to a sapling tree's wooden support post.

Hannah scrambled up and ran for it, vanishing into the bush after taking one huge-eyed look back. Graves was peripherally relieved to see her escaping.

"King Caradura throws the very best parties, Dexter Graves," the disguised female said to him from behind her visor. "So what, prithee, be thy major malfunction?"

Graves deftly broke the weird woman's chokehold and headbutted the mirrored face of her helmet. The silver plastic shattered, revealing the crazy static behind it. "Awww, hell, not *you* again," he said.

"Me and all the names I call myself," Lady Madness confirmed. "Come, Sinister Dexter, the King awaits."

The being Lia had called an Archon popped her fingers into Graves' nosehole and eyesockets like his skull was nothing more than a bowling ball and then dragged him, effortlessly, even as he struggled and kicked, off toward the gate.

She waved her other hand across her visor to heal it before she pulled a tiny walkie-talkie out of her pocket. The reflective glass melted back into place, obscuring her static. "Hunt the pretty, my wolves, but don't break her," she warned her confederates via the handheld radio. "The King has all the cold girls he can eat."

"Hey, Bad Signal," Graves shouted up at her (albeit in a stifled, nasal voice). "You so much as *touch* Miss Lia and I'll cancel your broadcast for good. You hearin' me under that shell, sister?"

The woman-shaped distortion peeled a glove off her statichand and stuffed it into Graves' mouth as she dragged him along, muffling his threats. "Not anymore, Dexter Graves," she said, answering his rhetorical question.

A moment later she raked him through the parking lot gravel and threw him into the back of the nearest of her six black cars while the pair of henchmen left to guard the front gate looked on with a high degree of astonished disbelief.

A heavy steel dog screen blocked access to the vehicle's front seats and there were no door handles here in the back, as Graves discovered in fairly short order. He still had the Archon's leather glove stuffed between his teeth.

He watched her stride back into the Yard through the open front gate, past a large black cat she didn't even notice.

"Now for LisaLiaChloeMia, and anybody else she thinks she is," the unhinged otherworlder said, to nobody in particular.

Chapter Twenty-One

Hannah sprinted through the trees, racing toward Lia and the safety of Bag End with all her might. Lia was already coming on the run when she spotted her friend and angled her trajectory so their paths through the plants would intersect. She was freshly dressed in jeans that clung to her still-damp skin and her hair was barely toweled dry. Tom's frantic psychic alarms had roused her from her hobbit hole, but the images she was getting from him were jumbled and confused, with so much going on in them. The one thing she knew for certain was that she didn't have time to sort them out. Dealing with this morning's new threat, whatever it turned out to be, was going to require improvisation, since she'd had no chance at all to prepare for it.

"Han, what's happening?" she called out, through the diminishing screen of foliage that separated them. "Tom saw someth—"

A sharp, hard gunshot hammered the air, leaving Lia's ears ringing. Hannah clutched at her side and went down, driven to the ground by a bullet. She crashed out of sight into a massive billow of blue hydrangeas.

"*Hannah!*" Lia screamed, like she'd never screamed any other word in her entire life.

She brought her cherry branch up, but more gunfire tore apart a bromeliad that was hanging inches behind her head, and she shrieked as involuntary survival reflexes made her drop to the ground for cover.

She peeked up over a fern frond and saw two men coming toward her. Saw the guns they held in their hands: black and menacing things that seemed out of place here amidst the Yard's sea of living green. Faced with the weapons, the only thing Lia could do was scramble away, back into the dense camouflage provided by the enveloping plant life she knew so well.

She was shaking by the time she reached the back of the Yard, her guts knotted up with adrenaline. The men with the guns were still pursuing. She could hear them crunching and rustling through the plants somewhere behind her. Directly in front of her was a woodpile, several feet high and seven or eight feet long. A small cluster of century-old walnut and pecan trees stood off to her right. Some of them extended a branch or two out over the Yard's rear fence.

Lia looked back over her shoulder, cringing against the shots she expected to erupt at any second. Gods and demons were all a part of her program, but guns upset her badly.

For a moment, she almost didn't know what to do.

Black Tom left his catbody on the shack's roof and let his awareness bloom large, out over the Yard, then scanned the property for Lia. He still tended to think of her as his Winter Flower, the first name he'd ever known her by, especially when he was scared for her. He'd called out to her on instinct when Lyssa and her crew first pulled up, but now he regretted the impulse. Steering his girl *away* from this situation would've been the smarter thing to do.

If those men hurt his Lia, Black Tom was apt to lose his mind. At which point several distinct forms of hell were likely to break loose. Tom had never been the same man again after the last time he unleashed such a torrent of grief and rage upon others, after Dulcé died... even if the others in question *had* deserved it.

He was distracted, scattered, trying to keep track of more than a dozen people all at once, but the percussive sound of a gunshot caused him to draw all of his awareness straight down toward it.

Hannah was the one who'd been shot, he saw instantly, as he watched the man he'd labeled Brickface deftly disarm the trigger-happy fool responsible for it. Mr. Brick's technique looked like some fancy martial arts sort of thing, perhaps military training. The gunman hit the ground with a solid thud that was nowhere near satisfying enough for Tom.

"What the hell, man?" the shooter said, looking up at Brickface, who'd thrown him down and taken his weapon before he so much as knew what was happening.

"Do you know what 'alive' means, you goddamn idiot?" Brickface barked down at him. "It tends to be the exact fuckin' opposite of bein' fulla bulletholes!"

"What'd we all bring guns for, then?" the shooter asked, getting to his feet and rubbing at the back of his head.

"To point 'em," Brickface yelled. "Not to *fire* 'em! They're fuckin' motivational tools, is all."

He dropped the clip out of the grip and cleared the chamber before giving the younger man his weapon back, shaking his head as he did so. "You just better pray that Lia chick's not the one you hit," he said. "For your sake."

Tom thought he had no idea how right he was about that, as Brickface tromped off in the direction Lia had fled. His Winter Flower was all right, Tom sensed, terrified but still unharmed... which was more than he could say for poor Hannah.

She was fading. Lying in the dirt, surrounded by broken blue flowers, with both hands clamped to her injured side. Blood was soaking through her clothes. There was blood everywhere, it seemed like. Tom knew his girl would not have wanted him to leave Hannah's side, so he moved in close enough to feel her pain as well as touch her thoughts, to see if there might be anything he could do.

Hannah looked up, and Tom thought for an instant that she was somehow seeing *him*.

Then he looked back (or rather he let his disembodied self experience three hundred and sixty degrees of visual awareness. There was no need to turn around when he wasn't using physical eyes to see. Habit was always a considerable force when it came to perception, though).

Sitting behind him and looking right through him, a few feet away from Hannah, were, well, *things*. Frogdogs, was the best description Han's unstrung mind would offer. A sizable ring of them hunkered there, watching her, behaving like exemplary models of calm and patience. She had no idea what they were, or even if they were real, although Tom recognized them as the entire clan of Crouchers he and his Winter Flower had long ago petitioned to guard their front gate. The same ones that had trailed el Rey's mercenaries into the Yard a few minutes ago.

Hannah looked pale. Tom could feel that she was blacking out, possibly for good. The Crouchers all watched her in silence, with hungry expressions on their lumpy, curious faces. The man who'd shot her also stepped up to view his handywork, and Han turned her head, with an effort, to squint up at him.

The gunman couldn't see the Crouchers. Tom touched his mind and knew that it was so. All the guy saw, lying in the bushes, was a nice, mom-type lady whose clothes had gone a dark, wet red all down her left side. Tom sensed that he'd shot men before, several of them, but this, he did not feel good about.

That's much too little, much too late, cabrón, Tom thought, feeling not the slightest glimmer of pity for the gunman, even though he knew from firsthand experience what was going to happen next.

Hannah rolled her head away from her shooter in order to look back at her Crouchers, all of which squatted close to her eye level. She was seeing them, all right. They were fully visible to her. Her gunshot wound must have temporarily shocked her eyes open to the subtler aspects of being, Tom surmised. Such things were not unheard of.

He looked back down and saw that the creatures had all turned around to consider the armed intruder who'd come to stand over Hannah.

He also saw, with no surprise (before he winked away to drum up more assistance), that every last one of them was grinning.

Chapter Twenty-Two

Graves hooked his fingerbones through the unbendable metal screen that penned him into the car's back seat while the two front gate guards looked at one another uneasily, then peered back in through the car's windshield, doing precious little to conceal their stupefaction. You'd think they'd never seen a skeleton get manhandled by a crazy lady before. Their voices were faint, muffled by the heavy window glass, but Graves could hear them. He felt like a zoo animal in a goddamn cage.

"Are you seeing what I'm seeing in the back of that car?" the taller and darker-haired of the two men asked.

"I dunno. What're you seeing?" was the shorter, blond man's evasive reply.

"I don't wanna say unless you're seeing it too," the first guard said. Something darted across the parking lot behind him and he whirled around, catching the movement in the corner of his eye. "You see *that*, then?" he demanded.

"What? A cat?"

Graves, too, had seen Lia's cat, a large black tom, go bounding past the Yard's main entrance.

"No, it was a guy," the blond man said. "I saw a guy, like a little old guy! Fast like a freak, though."

Darkhair nodded and motioned that they should go and check it out. Mr. Blond eased into the Yard, clicking off his gun's safety, with his partner first covering and then following after him.

A small, bearded man in sunglasses rapped on Graves' window with the back of his hand as soon as the sentries were out of sight.

Graves, who'd been yanking on the metal dog screen, looked

over and finally thought to pull that goddamn glove out of his mouth. "Hey, pal," he shouted, raising his voice to be heard through the insulating glass. "Lemme outta here, whaddaya say? I'll owe you the moon and the goddamn stars!"

The little man, who wore a hat and carried a walking stick, opened the door and even held it for him, graciously. Graves jumped out and threw his arms around the liberating stranger, who accepted an embrace from a partially-dressed skeleton with wordless aplomb. "I love ya, man, I really do," Graves said.

Then he turned and strode into the Yard, just as the gate guards were returning to their post after a fruitless check of the parking lot's perimeter.

The dark-haired man saw him first. Wide-eyed with horror, he drew a gun with a silencer screwed onto the barrel and unloaded.

Bone chips flew from Graves' cranium and bullets cracked a few of his ribs, but he incurred no damage that would stop him. He walked right up and twisted the gun out of the shooter's grip, wrenching the man's shoulder to drive him to his knees in the same motion. Graves genuflected behind him and shoved his head back viciously, snapping the henchman's neck over his fleshless femur like a dry twig.

Done. Graves claimed the man's gun and dumped his slack body aside.

He turned on the second guy, who backed away, dropping his weapon and holding up his hands. "Hey, come on, man, we weren't gonna hurt nobody," he said. "We had orders not to—"

The silenced weapon made an anticlimactic sound—sort of a '*bzzew*'—when Graves dropped the sniveling fuck with a perfect shot through his thigh. The man groaned rather than screamed, his face turning purple as veins stood out in the sides of his neck. His eyes rolled back to the whites.

Graves walked up and loomed over the writhing mercenary, training the automatic down at him. "The minute you point guns at my friends is the minute I stop givin' a shit about your perspective," he said, although he doubted he was really being heard. "You punched your own ticket, far as I'm concerned."

The skeletal PI gritted his teeth in grim satisfaction as he drilled the blond man between the eyes with his own partner's silenced pistol. It made that distinct *bzzew*! sound again, a little bit louder this time as the baffles inside the suppressor began breaking down under the stress of so many recent firings. It was nowhere near as wrath-of-God satisfying as an *un*muffled report from a hand-cannon of this caliber might've been, but blood sprayed across the gravel just the same.

Graves spun on his calcaneus bone and headed off into the Yard, hellbent on saving Lia.

Her cat, that old tom, watched him lope away from high up in a pepper tree. Graves caught a flash of bright green eye when he strode past.

Chapter Twenty-Three

Lia, crouched behind cover, listened as the three gunmen who were chasing her crept up on the large woodpile at the very back of the Yard. She trusted that Tom was watching over Hannah for her, since she couldn't see him anywhere.

"Eddie?" one of the men said, only to be shushed by their obvious leader.

"Uh... Miss?" the one called Eddie began, raising his voice to address *her*, apparently, even though Lia knew they couldn't have seen her yet. They weren't looking in the right direction.

The guys he was with both eyeballed Eddie like he sounded asinine, and he shrugged in exasperation. He *had* sounded asinine, trying to open a dialog under these circumstances, and Lia could tell from his irritated expression that if they had a better opening line to audition, he was more than ready to hear it.

"Listen," square-faced Eddie continued, speaking up to make himself heard. "We got sent out here by a guy called Mickey Hardface. Maybe you heard that name and maybe not, I dunno, but all he wants to do is talk, okay? Now I apologize for the hostile behavior of the mental defectives I got workin' under me, and I *promise* you there is not gonna be any more gunfire. Those are Hardface's specific orders: nobody gets hurt today."

"Except *you*," Lia said, stepping out from behind the copse of trees that stood beside the men and batting the one called Eddie across the back of his head with her weighty, knot-studded, cherry branch cudgel.

He pitched forward, losing his gun along with his balance. The other two clowns both pointed their weapons and staggered back at the very same time, dancing out of each other's line of fire.

Lia stepped in to seize Eddie by the throat with both hands

before he could regain his feet. She screamed down into his face as she squeezed, with tears of near-psychotic rage streaming down her cheeks, and vines sheathed in rough gray bark twined down her arms to lend an ancient strength to their daughter's efforts.

Edwin Dane's face reddened and his eyes bulged grotesquely. Capillaries burst in the whites and bloomed there like tiny red roses. His truest name and certain of his foul memories bloomed similarly into Lia's mind.

The other two henchmen looked on in abject, uncomprehending terror as green life effloresced all around Lia Flores, sprouting and flourishing at a time-lapse pace. A camellia tree—Lia's namesake plant as well as her earliest vegetal teacher—shot up from the bare dirt behind her to a height of well over ten feet within a matter of seconds, and its flexible new limbs helped her throttle Eddie Dane until the small bones in his neck crackled and popped like twisted bubblewrap. The sound of it was audible even over the soul-deep scream that blanked out Lia's conscious mind and empowered her intentions. The earth beneath her feet shook with rage to hear its child's cry, although Lia herself barely felt it.

All she could think about was Hannah.

Shoots and tendrils grew up *through* Eddie Dane, piercing and impaling him, rooting him to the ground. His skin roughened into crusty bark, while his limbs shrank and gnarled up into brittle, leafless branches. By the time Lia ran out of breath all that was left of him was a twisted stump that looked a vague bit like a contorted, struggling man.

It was like he'd never even been.

Lia ended her scream and staggered drunkenly when she let go of the stump and stepped aside, panting for air. She fixed the other two men with her raw, red gaze.

They fled, both of them, without another moment of hesitation. One of them actually dropped his gun in his haste to get away. Lia grabbed up her cherry branch and followed after them, flashing murder from her eyes.

Tom looked down from his cat's perch in the pepper tree to see three of the men who'd gone around to guard the Yard's periphery returning to the front gate, wondering over the weird noises they heard emanating from the central depths of the property. He could tell they were feeling keyed-up after the brief jolt of an earthquake that had set off car alarms and caused a few dogs to bark, somewhere down the block.

At least they *assumed* it was an earthquake. Tom, however, figured his Winter Flower must have drawn up a walloping bolt of chthonic force and discharged it at somebody. He knew a psychic shockwave when he felt one.

As the three uncertain joes from outside the fence stood gaping over the two bullet-riddled corpses of their confederates that now lay in the parking lot, a pair of thugs Lia'd routed on her own came racing across the gravel and out the front gate in what Tom could only describe as an undignified panic. Each man hopped into a black car all by himself, and they both peeled away, in opposite directions.

Tom could not have felt any more proud of his girl.

The youngest of the three remaining gate-guards looked over at the other two. "Should we go in there?" he asked.

His nominal elders considered the question and all of its ramifications. "I think we oughta wait," one of them ventured. "Cover the exits like we were told."

"Yeah, I'm gonna wait too," the last man concurred.

Satisfied they weren't going anywhere, Tom leapt down the tree trunk in two long hops and hurried into the greenery to find his friends.

Chapter Twenty-Four

Graves came across Miss Hannah first. The lady was just then sitting up (possibly having been roused by the swift seismic kick the earth had delivered moments ago), fighting for consciousness and wincing at the obvious pain in her side that rewarded her efforts. She was banged up badly but far from finished off, he was glad to see.

Hannah looked over at a man-shaped bundle of twigs and leaves and rotted crap that was lying in the dirt beside her and she cocked her head, as if it meant something to her but she couldn't quite remember what. The pile looked like nothing so much as the husk of a mummy, desiccated beyond all recognition— although there was a gun lying next to it. And a pair of shoes at one end. Graves didn't know what in the hell that thing might've been before something sucked it dry, nor did he much care to speculate, not at the moment.

There were significant sights Hannah had yet to see.

Graves, standing a few yards away, watched as she slowly looked up further, only to find the imperious, helmeted figure of Lady Madness looming over her, with her head cocked at a curious angle.

The figure's visor exploded, showing the static behind it. Hannah flinched, and shards of tinted plastic rained down all around her.

Lady Staticface turned to see the bones of Dexter Graves pointing two silenced handguns at her, from behind. They spat quiet fire as he squeezed off every round in the magazines.

Hannah threw her hands over her head as multiple bullets perforated the Archon's black suit, traveling on an upward trajectory. Graves had been sure to shoot from the hip, to keep her safe. The spots of bright gray static that showed through Lyssa's leathers made her look like she was dressed up in costume as her absent sister-mom.

"Gin plus tonic, super plus sonic, you plus moronic, if you think that's gonna help you, Dexter Graves," she said.

Graves shrugged. "Never know until you try," he replied. Then he threw the empty guns aside and charged at her, bellowing at the top of lungs he no longer possessed.

The thing called Lady Madness hauled off and backhanded his skull right off the top of his spine, almost without effort. The skull landed in the dirt many yards away. Graves saw the rest of his frantic skeleton caroming off the trees from his new, low-angle perspective, while Miss Madness turned back to Hannah.

"LiaMiaZoeClioTia," she said. "Where is they?"

"Right behind you," answered the woman in question.

The Queen of Crazy spun around in time for Lia to ram the jagged, torn end of her cherry branch right through Lyssa's broken visor. Lia ran her backwards with it, shouting, until the leatherclad demon tripped over Graves' skull and went sprawling.

As Lia savagely ground the splintered branch into Lady Madness's open helmet, grunting with the effort of it, roots broke out through the back of the hard plastic braincase and slithered down into the earth. The demon drummed her heels and fists on the ground while the branch blossomed into a new sapling under Lia's influence, pinning her helplessly to the dirt like some monstrous approximation of a scientific specimen.

Both Graves' skull and Hannah watched this happen with quiet shock. Neither of them would ever have guessed that such a thing could occur, much less that Lia might be the one to cause it.

Her moment finally broke. Lia stumbled back from the fresh sapling and the madwoman whose head it was staked through, falling on her ass next to Graves' disconnected headbone.

She looked both stunned and depleted. Such intense acts of will took an immediate and visible toll on her.

"That thing dead enough for you yet?" Graves' skull asked. It happened to be facing the new tree, and had enjoyed an excellent view of the whole improbable event.

"You can't kill the moon," Lia said, distracted. "But that might hold it till sunset. Maybe."

She picked up his skull when she got to her feet and shoved it against Graves' ribs when the rest of him went running by. The skeleton grabbed its proffered top gratefully and crammed it back down onto its spine once again.

Lia fell to her knees beside Hannah. Her black cat came running up to them, switching its fat tail back and forth. Graves hurried over and knelt down too, quickly assessing the lady's injuries.

"Awww, hey there, that's not so bad, is it?" he said, squeezing Miss Hannah's hand. "Not deep. Just grazed your side, is all. More of a mess than anything."

"Are you sure? Dexter?" Lia sounded wobbly. He hated hearing that terrible, sick fear in her voice. "There's so much blood, I don't know what to do, oh, Hannah, I'm so *sorry*…"

"Pressure right now," Graves said, ripping the lining out of his coat. "Stop that bleeding. Here. Hold this, nice and firm." He balled up the fabric and put it into Lia's hands, then guided them to Hannah's wound and demonstrated an effective amount of force to apply.

"Yes, okay, thank you Dexter," Lia babbled, holding that wad of cloth against Hannah's hip like all the world depended on it. "Are you sure she's okay? She'll be okay? You've done this sort of thing before?"

"Back in the war, field surgeon woulda called you a sissy for wantin' a band-aid on a scratch like that," Graves said.

"Some scratch," Hannah gasped. "Feels like I've been chopped in two."

Graves looked to Lia. His manner was serious. "Maybe it's time we got the hell outta here, whaddaya think?" he whispered. "There could be a whole stack of those guys out there in the trees."

Lia thought about it, frowning. "You're right," she agreed, after exchanging a quick glance with her black cat. "But we've gotta do it carefully."

Chapter Twenty-Five

Lia's car came barreling out of the Yard's gravel parking lot, scattering the three henchmen who'd gathered at the gate after the earthquake. They must not've been watching carefully; they hadn't seen anybody get into the Mazda. They hurried to pursue it in three of the four black cars they had remaining after the high-speed defections of the terrified pair who'd resigned without notice after encountering Lia. That put the score at three dead, two fled, and three more hopelessly distracted.

A second after the cars all squealed away, Graves' stolen fancyass number blew out of the lot and skidded around the corner. It headed west, unlike the Mazda, which had gone east, toward Burbank.

The last three men covering the Yard's other possible exits ran for the front gate after seeing the shiny new BMW shoot past them, but it was moving as fast as its expensive engineering allowed, and they were already too late to keep up with it.

Lia's battered gray Mazda zoomed east on Sheldon Street, turned right onto San Fernando, and shot down toward the Burbank Airport with three V-8 predators closing in behind it.

The little car dodged around a lumbering lunch truck, pulled briefly ahead of the pursuit, and then skidded off the main drag, into an alley marked with a 'NO OUTLET' sign that was tucked in between an apartment complex and a liquor store, just past Ensign Street.

Game over, the nearest pursuer thought. That should've been it.

Which was exactly the impression Tom and Lia had planned to convey.

The nearest of the large black cars followed the Mazda right down the alley's narrow corridor. The other two stopped to block the alley's mouth. Lia's little sedan skidded all the way around at the far end of the passage and stopped there, rocking on its springs.

There was nobody in it, either behind the wheel or in the passenger seats.

Some distance back, the approaching black car also squealed to a smoking stop. Its driver frowned, realizing that the little gray car up ahead really *was* empty. His eyes weren't playing tricks.

"What the...?" he muttered, as Black Tom (who was invisible to the norms but grinning ear-to-ear nonetheless) threw Lia's car into gear and stomped the accelerator. The tires screamed against the pavement.

Hardface's man saw the empty Mazda coming at him at an already dangerous and still-increasing rate of speed. He threw his own car into reverse and mashed a blue plastic recycling bin against the side of the alley in his haste to back the fuck up.

The black car slammed ass-first into the blockade comprised of Hardface's other two vehicles, both of which failed to get out of the way in time. A second later Lia's car crashed with considerable force into the trapped sedan's front end, driving it back hard. Both cars' radiators blew simultaneous jets of steam.

The three shaken henchmen got out of their respective vehicles and peered with disbelief into the unoccupied wreck that had taken them out of commission.

This would not be easy to explain.

Black Tom lingered on for a moment, perfectly invisible, enjoying their looks of astonishment and dread before pulling his awareness back down to the Yard.

He found the only three of Hardface's henchmen remaining on-site easily enough (without bothering to reclaim the catbody he'd stowed under a bush before driving off in Lia's car). They were sidling up and trying to come to terms with the sight of Lady Lyssa, who'd somehow been spiked through her helmeted head with a living, rooted tree. Tom gave his girl high marks for style.

"Now how in the hell does *that* happen?" one of the men in the cheap suits asked rhetorically, eyeing the new sapling.

They all shouted and scattered when the presumed corpse at its base answered. "Which girl was the witchgirl was something we should've learned much sooner, is how this happens," Lyssa said. "Hello? Wolves?"

There was, by then, nobody but invisible Tom around to hear, but still she asked:

"Will one of you please find an axe?"

Chapter Twenty-Six

Graves drove his stolen car westbound down Branford, with the women socked away in its small back seat. Hannah was stretched out as much as possible, with her head resting in Lia's lap. Lia kept steady pressure on the wound that grooved Hannah's hip, exactly as Graves had demonstrated for her.

He looked again in the rearview mirror. "I don't see 'em," he reported. "I don't see anything. I think we're in the clear, ladies."

Lia nodded, squeezing Hannah's hand. Her eyes were shut painfully tight. In the mirror she looked withdrawn and lost. Graves glanced over his shoulder at her in concern.

"Say," he said, exchanging a look with Hannah, who seemed to share his worry. "Just outta curiosity, d'you know what that thing was back there? That broad with the bad reception?"

Lia had to drag herself out of her daze to think and answer. Those dark circles were starting to look tattooed under her eyes.

"That was Lyssa, I think," she said. "The Archon of Madness and Moonlight. Like a goddess, very ancient. Greek originally. Too crazy to be scared of my tricks the way the others were. Too irrational already."

"Yeah, that lunar chick was a lunatic, all right," Graves agreed lightly. "Bugs in the brainpan, you ask me. Strong, though. Geez."

He rolled his neck, cracking vertebrae all up the line. He was pleased to have drawn Lia back out of herself, even if it was only to a tiny degree. At least he knew the trauma of recent events hadn't left her unreachable.

"So," he said. "The sooner we get that wound hosed out, the less chance of infection there's gonna be. Maybe you got some kinda destination in mind, dollface?"

"Head south," Lia told him. "Over Coldwater Canyon. I know people who'll help us, up in the hills."

Graves nodded and made a left when they reached Coldwater, after another two blocks. When he looked over, the short man with the hat and the sunglasses who'd let him out of Hardface's car was sitting in his passenger seat. He grinned at Graves and doffed his hat without saying a word, like he thought he was Harpo Marx or something.

"Oh," Graves said in greeting, his capacity for surprise having been much diminished by the events of the last two days. "Hey. So you're one of Lia's sort of things too, huh? Guess I mighta known."

"Who're you talking to up there, Dexter?" Hannah asked, as he wove the fancyass car through mid-day traffic denser than any he'd ever seen. Everyone in the world had a car of their own by now, it looked like, including kids too young to enlist in the service, and all of them were on the roads all of the goddamn time.

Chapter Twenty-Seven

Ingrid watched as Winston the bony butler finished knotting Miguel Caradura's fine silk tie, then stepped back from the King. 'Caradura' turned to admire himself in a full-length mirror that appeared upon the gray plain in perfectly-timed anticipation of his desire for it.

The King had materialized another elegant, modern-day suit, Italian cut, which he now wore with his golden Aztec armbands over the sleeves and his owl-feather headdress perched upon his brow. The necklace of eyeballs was, as ever, his signature statement. If the vitreous humor that dribbled from the holes they were strung through stained his new clothes, well, then that was just as it had to be.

He turned away from the mirror. "Do you like my suit, my love?" he asked.

Ingrid looked him up and down, from where she sat reclining on her chaise. The step pyramid stood tall against the gray horizon far behind him, like a jagged Mount Fuji. "I do," she answered, truthfully enough. "You always did know how to wear your clothes, Mickey."

El Rey grinned. Ingrid figured it probably wasn't the moment to point out that his taste in accessories did detract somewhat from his outfit's overall effect.

Nyx, who was still kneeling on the bare ground, stirred and looked pained. She remained dressed in her simple linen and wore her hair in a fat, dark braid, as was her prerogative on this side of reality.

"Mic- Mictlantecuhtli?" she said.

"Yes, Nyx?"

"My sister-daughter... will not be returning, Mictlantecuhtli."

Mickey blinked calmly, several times. "And why might that be, Nyx?"

"The witchgirl grew a tree down through her head and rooted her to the earth," the anxious Archon explained. "She... she is quite uncomfortable, Mictlantecuhtli."

"I always wonder what really happened when they come out with surrealist shit like that," Ingrid said.

Mickey frowned, and Ingrid instantly regretted having spoken her mind. "Do you say their descriptions are not accurate?" the King queried. "They do not illustrate the events of the actualworld?"

"They tend to be... colorful, let's say," Ingrid said. "That's all."

"Foreigners," the King spat, sneering down at his kneebound concubine. "I wasted my efforts when I conquered your sphere, Nyx. But you were weak and it was easy, so I figured 'what the hell?'"

"I apologize, Mictlantecuhtli," Nyx said, without raising her eyes. Ingrid actually felt a little bit bad for her. "I will free my sister-daughter at dusk, if it pleases you."

"Yes, yes," Mickey said dismissively. "Now leave me. It will please me more not to look upon you for a while."

"Yes, Mictlantecuhtli," Nyx said, and vanished.

The King turned to Ingrid. "Did I use that right?" he asked. "A 'while?' The vocabulary of time remains academic for me."

"It was perfect, Mickey," Ingrid said. "Spot on."

"Like an incarnation would say it? An actualperson, not a nonbody pretending?"

"Exactly like."

"It wasn't 'colorful?'"

"Mickey..." Ingrid had to make an effort not to get frustrated with him. "It was just right. Do I have to drop to my knees in admiration before you believe me?"

She illustrated by doing so, at a distance from his pelvis that was far more suggestive than it was respectful. She looked up the silk-suited front of him, batting her lashes and making her blue eyes as large and innocent as she possibly could. "Does this make you happy?"

"Stand up, Ingrid Redstone," the King said, sounding stern and not at all amused. "Those games ended between us when you elected not to become my Queen."

"Yes, Mictlantecuhtli," Ingrid said, in perfect imitation of Nyx and Lyssa's fawning subservience.

"Stop it." Mickey shook his head, looking disgusted. "Foreign women," he mused aloud. "I should never have strayed beyond the ministrations of my Tzitzimime."

"Sure, if you like handjobs," Ingrid said, getting to her feet and brushing off her knees. "Plenty of extra limbs. I'd steer clear of those mandibles though, if I were you."

"Do not forget your place, Ingrid Redstone," the King murmured. "Do not insult my sphere or those native to it. *You* are a foreigner in this land as well."

"As if I could ever forget it," Ingrid said.

That seemed to give Mickey an idea. He paced, thinking aloud. "And yet you *are* a native of the actual," he said. "One not hampered by the necessary ignorance that blinds my living soldiers…"

"What's your point?" Ingrid asked, leading him a little, but not too much. She had to play this very carefully now. He would never send her on this errand if he had any inkling that she wanted to go.

"You could get them," the King said. "Find them, bring them. You could do this, my love."

"Do I *look* like a bounty hunter to you?" Ingrid sat back against her cushions and spread her white arms out across the back of the red velvet sofa. "Don't act desperate, Mickey. It's unattractive."

"You may command my mercenaries," he told her. "I've got all the human beings you can use."

"I don't know, though…" Ingrid said, feigning a frown and hoping she wasn't hamming it up too much. Not that a nuanced performance wouldn't be lost on Mickey Hardface anyway. "It's kind of a tall order. What can *I* do that all of your bugbabes and moonmaidens couldn't?"

"Walk the actual with some understanding of its habits and its ways, apparently," was Caradura's considered thought on the matter. "You will do this, Ingrid Redstone," he decreed. "You will do this, or you *will* become my Queen, regardless of your wishes in this matter, and we'll try this all *again!*"

Before Ingrid could respond, Mickey snapped his fingers.

She woke up on the floor outside his office within the Silent Tower. In the very place where Dexter Graves had died, in fact. Died by her hand... sort of. She *had* managed to bind a tiny spark of him to the lighter he'd dropped, the last object he'd touched, right before he passed on into darkness.

She sat up, looked around, and smoothed her hair. The hall was a lightless ruin once again, with no red carpet rolled out for her now.

"My gods, that took long enough," she muttered. She looked back at the closed door with Miguel Caradura's name stenciled on it, and allowed herself a slight, sly smile.

Ahh, Mickey, she thought to herself. *Still handsome, ruthless, and stupid. Just the way I like you.*

She got up and hurried off, down the decaying hallway, headed toward the stairs.

When Ingrid stepped out onto the street, she found thirteen new gangsters already waiting for her, with six new black cars at their disposal. These guys were younger, rougher, more tattooed and less experienced than the last bunch had been. They mostly wore hooded sweatshirts and dark jeans—a distinct step down from the ugly suits the previous, more competent-looking minions had worn.

They all fell silent upon seeing Ingrid. '*Rapt*' seemed like the appropriate word. She figured her gown was probably decades out of style (her clothes often were), but it was low-cut and form-fitting, and she didn't think the men were staring because it looked anachronistic. Her curves and her vibrant red hair never failed to make an impression.

The gang's defacto leader, a mean-looking, baldheaded bastard in sunglasses, stepped forward. "You 'Lady Redstone,' then, lady?" he asked.

"I am," Ingrid said.

"Yeah, well," the wiry man with the impenetrable black glasses continued, "I'm Xavier, okay? Miguelito Hardface says we gotta do whatever you say and guard your safety with our lives. That's the way his boy Winston said it exactly. Guard your safety with our lives, and do anything you say."

"And report to him my every move, I'm sure," Ingrid added in a pretty singsong voice, keeping it light so her words wouldn't sound like too direct a challenge.

Xavier said nothing. Ingrid nodded as if he'd answered, though.

"Very well," she said, starting down the building's front steps and heading toward the cars, parting the crowd effortlessly before her. "Allons-y, boys. Let's go."

Ingrid motioned for everyone to come along as she padded over to the back of the nearest vehicle on the balls of her still-bare feet. She hadn't thought to ask Mickey to replace her shoes, but she was still taller than most of her men, even without high heels. She opened her own door and slid into the car's back seat. Xavier closed the door for her, like a good underling should, and then went around the front to drive.

The engines started up. Ingrid's car led the pack when they pulled away from the curb, one by one, turning left onto Fountain at the end of the second block.

She thought for a while as prison-tattooed Xavier drove west toward Santa Monica, his eyes hidden behind those imposing black sunglasses. He turned right at Highland, a street name that hadn't changed in a very long time.

"Uh... Mrs. Redstone?" the unlikely chauffer said, after a few blocks worth of northbound travel, up past Labaig Avenue. "Lady? Where do you want us to, like, take you?"

Ingrid, in the back seat, continued to gaze out her window, in no apparent hurry to answer.

"We could go out to that plant place in the Valley," Xavier offered. "Where that chick's supposed to, like, work or something? Winston says he still got three guys out there, so we got a street address now, but I guess they say it don't look like nobody's comin' back there anytime soon."

"No, I don't expect they would, would they?" Ingrid said, almost to herself. "But let's head out there anyway. Maybe I can figure her out by seeing where she operates."

Xavier nodded. "Whatever you say, lady. Redstone."

Retrospective No.3 ~ 1910

A century ago…

Old Tomas Delgado nearly shit his britches when Winston Watt's motor carriage rumbled around the last ridge to the southwest of a vast stretch of grazing land that had once been a part of Rancho los Feliz and into view of the field where the Tree that Grew Below the Hole in the Sky used to be.

That's right, Tom had to tell himself: *used to be.* Past tense. Someone else had beaten him to the punch in cutting down the ancient Tree.

Somebody else had thought the unthinkable, and acted upon it. Then they'd done him one better, too. The natural prairie the live oak once dominated was now cleared and graded, and a concrete foundation had been laid down amidst a grid of newly demarcated city streets. A cage of new steel girders towered into the sky, stacked up from exactly the place where the old encino had stood for well more than a thousand years, according to the tales the old people had preserved and passed on.

"Watt, what the fuck is this?" Tom said, aghast, although it was plain enough to him what was happening. These distempered fools were putting up a goddamn *skyscraper.* Right under the Hole in the Sky, where los Muertos crossed over into the realm of Mictlan. And it already reached higher than the old Tree ever had, even in this early phase of its construction.

Anyone could find their way up there now. *Anyone.*

"Believe me, it's not my idea," Watt muttered, letting his engine stall as he coasted down to a stop in a wheelrutted lot that was stacked high with construction materials and situated across the road from the building-to-be. From the Tree-that-was, that was.

Tom could hardly believe it was gone. The landscape looked wrong without it.

He took a moment to look up at the man-made blight that had replaced the oak—that boxy metal skeleton silhouetted against a darkening sky. Watt, who was far too drunk to be in any sort of a hurry, nodded complacently over his car's steering wheel while Tom examined the newly-assembled framework that stood before them.

There were no other buildings around here like this one, not for miles. It was going to be at least ten whole stories tall, too, at a minimum. You'd have to travel as far as downtown, to Los Angeles proper, with its theater and business and manufacturing districts, to find a comparably ambitious structure. At *least* that far, if not all the way to the island of Manhattan.

It looked ridiculous, an incipient skyscraper standing alone in the middle of what was still essentially farmland.

Tom had assumed that if he cut down the Tree, it would take another thousand years for a new one to grow back in its place. The worlds would've been safe for at least that long, and his selfish, squandered life might've come to have a little meaning yet.

He could never have conceived of a project like this one, though. This incongruous erection out here on the prairie. Not in his wildest dreams or his worst nightmares. He couldn't imagine an undertaking more dangerous or more foolhardy than this, and he had to wonder just who it was that would set such a thing in motion.

"Tío Tomás!"

Tom swiveled his head toward a gang of workers who were just then coming across the road, laughing and joking with one another after a wearying day's labor. They wore coveralls and caps and carried tin lunchpails, and one of them, the foreman (a handsome young man with thick black hair and a face Tom remembered all too well from his younger days), was grinning his ass off and waving to him.

It was Oscar San Martín. Ramon's boy. He'd been a kid the last time Tom saw him. Now he was well over six feet tall and as broad as an ox through the shoulders. He looked so much like his father that it took Tom's breath away. Seeing him now was like traveling back in time.

"Bienvenidos, Tío Tomas," Ramon's boy said, as Tom made his careful way down from Winston Watt's Model T. "Welcome home."

"Oscar," Tom said, wanting to hug the kid (the 'kid' who stood more than a foot taller than him and had a rough shadow of late-day stubble growing along his jaw), but not doing it.

He and Oscar hadn't been as close as Tom might've liked after Ramon... went over.

Xochitl, Ramon's widow, hadn't really *blamed* Tom for what happened. Not exactly, and yet it had been clear enough that he was welcome to keep his distance from her boy after it was done. She hadn't wanted Oscar following in his father's (or in his pseudo-uncle's) footsteps.

Especially if those footsteps led him here, to this field. And, as much as it pained him, Tom *had* seen the wisdom in that position. It'd even been a factor in his decision to travel the world so late in life. There'd been other reasons for that too, of course, but as far as Oscar went, it'd simply been easier not to be around. Convenient.

And yet, despite the aloofness and the loneliness that resulted from it, here Oscar was. Working for el Rey. Like father, like son. The San Martín family had a legacy now.

Tom clasped the young man's large, calloused hand in both of his and held it warmly, for a long moment, looking up at him. "Gracias, mijo," Tom said. "It's good to see you again."

Oscar nodded, clearly pleased to see his father's oldest friend, yet feeling as unsure about the content of their relationship as Tom was himself.

"Oz," Tom said, as his eyes were drawn back up to the black steel bones superimposed over the purple evening sky, like some sort of artistic photographer's effect. "What is it you think you're doing out here?"

"The bidding of el Rey, Tío Tomas. What else?"

"But... this wasn't *your* idea, was it?"

"Oh, hell no," Oscar said, and laughed. He ran his hand back over his hair, a little nervously. "Don't blame me, I just work here."

"Then who?"

"La Bruja Roja," Winston Watt piped up from the Model T's front seat, jerking himself out of a drunken stupor in order to speak. He craned around to look at the other two men. "The Red Witch," he said, as if it explained something. "The Scarlet Woman."

"Who?"

"The King's new girlfriend," Oscar said quietly. Turning to Watt, he put a finger to his lips. "Shhh, now, about that."

Construction laborers were crossing the lot as they knocked off for the day, men piling onto a horsecart that would take them 'home' to a nearby migrant camp. Some got into private carriages of their own, horseless and otherwise. (Otherwise if their work happened to be of the more skilled and better paid variety, Tom supposed.)

Watt looked the dispersing workers over and nodded sagely to Oscar, preserving the secret they both were in on. *Very craftily, too,* Tom thought, raising an eyebrow.

"Have you two been drinking?" Oscar asked quietly.

"Watt insisted we stop," Tom said, under his breath. "El hombre es un borracho, you know."

Oscar nodded, watching as Watt observed the last of his crew departing for the day. The final few stragglers were heading home on foot. Within minutes, Tomas, Oscar, and Watt—the preservers of the mysteries of Mictlantecuhtli—were all alone in the gloaming.

"A witch?" Tom said, turning to Oscar for clarification as soon as the last of the workers were out of earshot. "Like a person, a woman?"

Oscar nodded.

"Not a nymph or a succubus or some damn thing like that from over on el Rey's side of the sky?"

"An actual person," Oscar said. "Alive. Flesh and bone. And she comes and goes as she pleases, if you can believe that."

"What, between the rooms?" Tom asked, his tone filled with disbelief. His old friend, Oscar's father Ramon, had showed them both what was likely to happen when a human being stepped through the door between the worlds and into the King's sacrificial chamber.

It was supposed to be a one-way trip.

And yet Oscar nodded, verifying that he had indeed observed this thing they'd all long assumed to be impossible. A living, human woman who could cross at will.

"I can't believe it myself," Oscar said. "But I've seen it happen, once or twice. She walks across like it's the door between the kitchen and the dining room, and nothing more."

"She visits so bloody often she needs a mechanical lift," Watt said contemptuously, reeling a bit when he stepped down from his car's running board. "She's hardly the sort to keep climbing up and down a tree."

"What's her name?" Tom asked.

Oscar and Watt exchanged a look, and then a shrug. Neither of them wanted to admit to having that piece of information, although Tom suspected Winston Watt might've known more than he was owning up to. Oscar might as well, for that matter.

"She doesn't bother conversing with the help," Oz said. "Keeps her own counsel."

"Mictlantecuhtli says she's to be his Queen," Watt informed them. "We're to call her '*La Reina de los Muertos*,' once she's crossed over for good."

This was sounding worse and worse by the minute to old Tom Delgado. He couldn't help but feel a stab of jealousy when he contemplated this unnamed woman. Not only did the stranger share in his hard-won secrets, she'd also been allowed, somehow, to experience the otherworld without forfeiting her life and her freedom.

It didn't seem fair. Not when Tom had sold his very soul for a journey far less exotic, for initiations far less significant and experiences that hadn't done a fraction as much to satisfy his lifelong curiosity about the nature of the worlds as one single day spent freely exploring the possibilities of Mictlan would have.

Tom had to wonder what this new witch offered, that she enjoyed such favor with the King. It occurred to him that the ambitious crazywoman would soon be *his* mistress, too (and not in the way he liked to have a mistress), according to the letter of Mictlantecuhtli's contract.

Well, he wasn't having that. And that's all there was to it.

"We can go right up to the top if you're ready, Tom," Watt said. "There's a temporary elevator set up."

Wonderful, Tom thought. They'd thought of everything. While none of the half-baked plans *he'd* been incubating had ever anticipated a scenario like this one. Tom was at a loss. What sort of excuse could he plausibly make?

It was Oscar who saved him, or at least bought him some time. Thank the Powers That Be for Oscar.

"Maybe you could hold your horses for just a minute there, Mr. Watt," the young man said. "Mr. Delgado and I have a lot of catching up to do."

"You can still talk to him once he's gone over, and the King wants him as soon as possible."

"Well, it'll be possible in a few damn minutes, okay?"

Tom was getting the impression that Oscar cared as little for the King's Englishman as he did himself.

"It's not the same once people go over," the young builder said. "Besides which, you might've taken a pass on those last few glasses of gin I can smell on your breath if punctuality was your big concern."

Watt frowned and shot Tom an irritated look, but he was chastened enough not to argue or make accusations. "Fine," he said. "I think I'll go up to the Hole and wait for you there."

"You do that," Oscar said, looking at Watt in a way that was quietly confident yet not quite combative. "Tio Tomas and I will be up directly."

The Englishman didn't know what to do, other than slink away. Tom and Oscar watched him cross the absurdly wide street (you could walk three dozen sheep abreast down a trail like that one, and no other sort of traffic was likely to use it), and a few moments later they heard the gasoline motor that powered the rickety-looking supply elevator cough to life. As the lift platform ascended, up the girders that framed the structure's southwestern corner, they saw Watt's skinny silhouette looking back down toward them.

"How are you really, Oz?" Tom asked.

"Married, for one thing," Oscar said, holding up his left hand so that Tom could see the gold band around his ring finger. "Last spring. Almost an architect too, one more semester till I have my degree, and I just found out I'm gonna be a father."

"Congratulations," Tom said, feeling his heart sink as he

wondered whether a third generation of San Martíns would now be pledged to the service of the King. Architecture also surprised him as a career choice. Tom didn't recall him ever expressing an interest in any such thing, but then he supposed a lot really could change in the course of ten years. "Got names picked out?" he asked.

"Not yet." Oscar grinned. "Maybe Juan, after Connie's father, if it's a boy. I think she'd like that."

Tom nodded. "He'll be a big one, if he takes after you. Hope your missus knows what she's getting herself into."

Oscar laughed and nodded, then turned quiet. "I know you're shocked by all of this, Tio Tomas," he said, nodding over at the partially-erected skyscraper. "But I don't think it's the first time there's been a building here."

"What are you talking about?"

"When we cleared the site," Oscar said, "there were bits and chunks of old broken mud bricks, all over the place. For miles around, too. Like maybe something was built here a long time ago and then got torn down again, and the bricks got scattered everywhere. And then the old Tree grew up in its place."

"Like somebody planted it to mark the spot," Tom mused.

Oscar shrugged. "Maybe," he said. "They smashed up what they built, but somebody didn't want to forget what's, you know... up there. That's what it made me think of, anyway, finding all those little pieces of brick. Farmers around here tell me they've been plowin'em out of their fields since the beginning, just thinking they're dirt clods that have edges and corners for some reason. They either crush 'em up or throw 'em away."

"Huh," Tom grunted, thinking of the tales los Muertos sometimes told about the Great Step Pyramid that stood on the other side, beyond and beneath the King's unbreachable chamber. On this side, a Hole in the Sky, stationed a hundred feet above the earth. On that side, a monumental Pyramid with stairs down each of its four faces and doors that opened onto other worlds. Old Ramon's bones had spoken of it to Tom more than once, while standing at the door between the Chambers. The conversation of the dead tended to be disjointed and rambling, however, and many of the things Ramon said after his death had made little sense to Tom.

Ramon had died crazy, guilty to the point of madness over some cataclysm he believed he'd set in motion. Over some secret he said he'd given away. That betrayal had been enough to send him over the threshold between the rooms, and Tom had never even figured out what it was he thought he'd done.

Tom now wondered if people older than the old people had long ago erected a real-world counterpart to the Temple of Mictlantecuhtli right here in this field. Perhaps the ancient forbearers of the Aztecs themselves had done it, before moving south from their mythic homeland of Aztlán. Maybe their temple had even been the original, and the one lingering on in the otherworld was a copy. Who but el Rey could know?

Tom also wondered who'd torn the structure down again, feeling a certain kinship with those wise folks, whoever they may have been.

"Makes me think of what the dead say, about what's outside the second room," Oscar said, echoing Tom's thoughts uncannily. Of course the younger man would've heard the same stories. Even from some of the same ghosts. "You know, about the pyramid el Rey's supposed to have over there, in the land of Mictlan."

"Me too," Tom murmured. "So what's the plan here, anyway? How're you supposed to keep all those men from finding out about the Hole?" He waved an indicative hand in the direction most of the departing workforce had taken.

"Well, I'm to finish off the top floor myself, for one thing. At least the rooms right around the Hole, me and maybe a few handpicked guys."

"And you think you can expect them to keep the secret?"

Oscar shrugged. "Not really. I've been thinking it might go better if I give the work to some of the men I hate, like the ones who get drunk and punch their wives for fun on a Friday night, and then when they're done just, you know... push 'em through."

"That's coldblooded, mijo," Tom said. It was also smart, he reflected, and safer than letting rumors of the Hole spread amongst these new people. Still, he couldn't quite bring himself to encourage it out loud.

"I know it, Tio," Oscar said, lowering his voice. "But the King's reach into this world is getting long enough already, I think."

Tom looked up at him. "What do you mean?"

"He has money of his own now," Oscar said. "Investments, bank accounts. He owns land. He's got people on a payroll who think he's completely human, just a weird recluse. Watt handles it all for him, for now, but he's gonna snap under the pressure soon. He's wound too tight for it."

"Is it that bad already?"

"Things are moving fast, Tio. The King's even picked himself out a name to use in the realworld: 'Miguel Caradura.'"

"'Michael Hardface?'" Tom said. "I guess that fits."

"I think it was the witch's idea of something clever," Oscar said. "He's working on a face and a body to go along with it. He stands there in the second room wearing a suit to practice looking like a real person. I think he means to hold business meetings and crap like that when the building's done. He's already had me drag office things up there so he can start learning to handle them."

"Oscar," Tom said, looking up at the younger man. "Do I have to tell you how bad an idea all this is?"

"Not really, Tio," Ramon's boy said, and Tom felt both relieved and proud of him upon hearing it.

The curtain came down on his moment of hope when Oscar took a small gun from inside his overalls and pointed it, reluctantly, right at him.

"But I still have to take you up to the Hole, and watch you go into the second room," Oz said.

Tom looked at the gun. "You gonna shoot me? What would be the point of that?"

Oscar also looked down at the sorry little pistol in his hand, acknowledging the absurdity of it. He put it away, tucking it in at the small of his back. "Not much, I guess," he said. "You need to give up your flesh of your own free will if you're to be useful to the King. It's the deal you made with him. I just need to make sure you honor it."

"How come, mijo?" Tom said softly. "What arrangement has he made with you?"

Oscar's face creased with shame and sadness. "My son," he whispered. "The child Connie's carrying right now, Tio. The King says he won't call for him when he's older, if you make good on your promise."

Oh. Tom might've known. He nodded.

"Let's go, then, if we're going," he said, and Oscar looked down at his boots, unable to meet Tom's eyes.

Part Four: All Souls' Day, Afternoon

Chapter Twenty-Eight

A century later…

Graves thought his stolen fancyass car looked made for the driveway Lia instructed him to pull it into. An automatic gate closed behind them as they glided up towards a sprawling, Spanish-style mansion perched on a rocky outcrop high above the city, way up in the exclusive Hollywood Hills. Graves didn't know what sort of architectural magic kept it up there. Every house they'd passed on the drive up winding, twisting Coldwater Canyon looked like it could've gone sliding down the side of its mountain at any second.

Lia was out of the car almost before it stopped at the top of the circular drive, leaving the passenger door hanging open and dashing up the walkway at a full run. She pounded, urgently rather than politely, on the big house's carved mahogany front door.

A smartly-dressed and somewhat nerdish young hipster opened it right away. Lia threw herself into his arms with obvious gratitude. "Riley!" she cried.

He squeezed her briefly and then appraised her at arm's length. "Lia," he said. "You look like hell. Seriously. Your friend's in the car?"

Lia nodded and he was on his way down to the drive, without another word. Black Tom, the voiceless little man with the cane and sunglasses, got out of the car on the passenger side, and Graves realized that this Riley person didn't—and perhaps *couldn't*—see him. The same way Miss Hannah couldn't. That privilege seemed to be reserved for Lia, and now for him as well.

"What happened, anyway?" Riley was asking of Lia, over his shoulder, as she trotted back down to the car at his heels. "Who'd shoot at you? You're not in some sort of—whoa."

Graves stepped out of the car on the driver's side, and *him*, Riley saw.

Lia's friend stopped, stunned, and then broke into a grin, his face glowing with genuine wonderment and geekish delight. "Oh, Lia…" he breathed, unconsciously raising a hand to his mouth. His eyes even glistened a little. "Oh. You are… an *artist*, girl. That is just incredible." He turned to her. "I could go straight for you if I had to," he said. "I'm serious. Maybe no oral stuff, y'know, but I can get it up for anyone who can do *this*."

Graves could only stare at him, at a rare loss for words.

"Riley, my friend is bleeding," Lia reminded.

Riley tore his attention away from the skeletal spectacle of Dexter Graves, arisen from the thing that shared his name. "Right!" he said, snapping out of his rapture. "Right, although I don't really see what you need me for when you can raise the dead…"

He leaned into the car. Graves looked at Lia across the top of it.

"Hey, Ms. Potter, I'm Riley, remember? It's been a while," Riley said, from inside the cockpit, craning over the passenger seat to greet his patient. "Why don't you show me where it hurts?"

"This guy's a doctor, is he?" Graves muttered.

"Well, he has a medical degree," Lia hedged, "but not a license to practice. It's a long story."

"That's reassuring," Graves said. "Beats the local veterinarian, I guess." Then he saw how weary and worried Lia really looked, and felt abashed. "I'm sorry," he said. "She *is* gonna be fine, you know."

Riley helped a wincing Hannah out of the car. Graves stooped down beside her so she could throw her arm across his shoulderblades and let him bear her weight.

"He's right, you guys were lucky," Riley said. "I'll irrigate this and dress it, and I think I've got some antibiotic samples kickin' around, so she's gonna be okay."

Lia nodded, looking like she could've cried from relief. Graves helped Riley help Hannah up toward the house, carefully, taking it slow so as not to pull at Hannah's wound.

Lia followed them. After a moment she asked, "Riley… is Steb around?"

"What's a steb?" Graves said.

Riley nodded uneasily. "Upstairs, yeah," he said in response to Lia. "He oughta be awake soon. He's been working a weeklong operation, and you know how he gets."

"So it's a bad time to be here, then," Lia said.

"Well… there does tend to be that, you know, spillover, when he's practicing."

"No, really, what's a steb?" Graves asked again. "Is it a guy?"

"Esteban de Rojo," Lia said. "Steb."

"Her ex," Riley and Hannah both told him, in unintentional unison.

"*No*," Lia said. *Quick to protest*, Graves noted. "No. Not my ex. We had an *affair*, not a relationship. A fling."

"Her flingerer, then," Riley said. "Whatever that means. I don't know what sort of sick shit you people get up to. I really don't like to think about it."

Graves tried, unsuccessfully, to conceal his jealousy. He knew Hannah felt his spine tightening up. "Well, hey," he said, way too jovially. "Let's shake that deadbeat outta bed, is what *I* say. I'm damn curious to meet the man who can tame our Lia."

"Can you guys just stop it?" Lia said. "Please?"

They all looked at her. Her eyes were bloodshot and more than exhausted. Graves thought she looked absolutely spent.

"Lia…" Riley said, his brow creasing with concern. "Are you really okay?"

"I'm fine," Lia said, rubbing at her forehead. "But maybe I could lay down… somewhere… for just a little… little bit…"

Her knees buckled and she collapsed to the driveway pavement. Graves could see she was unconscious before she hit the ground.

Riley and the short phantom with the cane were at her side in less than an instant. Graves lurched back over with Miss Hannah draped across his shoulder so that they might help her, too.

Chapter Twenty-Nine

Graves brushed an unconscious Lia's hair back from her forehead, taking care not to scratch her with his bony fingertips.

That Riley character and his people had laid her out on a big, comfortable bed in a palatial guest room. It had rough plaster walls with dark wood trim, in the old Mission style, and there was a lush Persian carpet spread out on the red tile floor underfoot. The rug felt soft and rich against Graves' exposed metatarsals.

There were also a number of framed movie posters decorating the walls. One eye-catcher advertised a flick called *Pulp Fiction* and featured the image of a dangerously beautiful woman with Lia-style black hair. Another bore the title *Scarface*, which Graves figured might refer to Al Capone, ol' Public Enemy No.1 (although the film's skinny star, some mug named Pacino, bore no resemblance whatsoever to the pudgy criminal visage he'd seen staring back at him a hundred times from the front pages of newspapers).

The poster right over Lia's bed, however, was related to a picture Graves had actually seen before, all the way back in '46. *The Big Sleep*, starring Bogart and Bacall. He'd even read the novel it was based on, and it'd given him an idea for something he might do with himself after the war. The paper the poster was printed on had turned brittle and yellowed with age, but the artwork was still vibrant, and long-faced Bogie still looked cool in his floor-length trench and canted hat.

Graves adjusted the lapels of his own copycat coat, feeling a touch self-conscious about it. He pulled a light blanket up to Lia's chin and straightened up to go out into the hallway.

The ghost Lia had said was called Black Tom (after Graves

confessed to seeing him on the drive up here) remained at her bedside, sparing the departing skeleton only a momentary glance and a brief nod before he went out the door. Graves felt good about that. He trusted that Lia's tightlipped and selectively visible pal would come to fetch him at the literal instant anything about her condition changed.

There were two guards stationed out in the hall, both of them wearing black suits with skinny black ties and holding automatic weapons the like of which Graves had never seen before. One man stood to either side of the bedroom's arched doorway.

Graves ignored them, and they returned the favor. His footbones clicked against the corridor's terracotta tiles.

He went out into a living room crowded with party people. It had yet another cadre of those blacksuited guards stationed around the doors. The wood-beam ceiling above was vaulted; the room flooded with natural light from high windows. There were big canvases covered in splotches of paint that didn't look like anything hanging in frames up on the walls. Like someone was excessively proud of their toddler. Music poured from unseen speakers and frenetic images of a longhaired, half naked guitarist flashed too fast to follow across a cinema-sized screen that was set above a fireplace you could've barbecued an ox in. Riley's guests held colorful drinks in their manicured hands while they socialized, many of them showing each other pictures and video clips on tiny personal viewers that somehow doubled as telephones even though they were thinner than a pack of cards. People either wore a lot of black or else wore very little at all. The crowd that had gathered for whatever the hell this was—some sort of a cocktail soiree held in the middle of a weekday afternoon—felt moneyed yet bohemian to Graves, with his plainly outdated point of view…

But they still weren't jaded enough not to fall silent when a skeleton in a trenchcoat made an entrance, as he was quietly pleased to notice.

He felt like a movie star in this room.

Graves turned to a nearby hipster in a crisp new fedora. He plucked the guy's hat right off his head and replaced it with the chintzy replica he'd been making do with since his spontaneous exhumation yesterday morning. The kid's only response was a single gulp, as audible as a sound effect in the hushed, cavernous space.

"Thanks, pal," Graves said, adjusting the brim of his newly-acquired skullcozy. "I owe ya one."

Graves nodded to Riley on his way across the subdued room. Riley nodded back, and everybody in the joint gaped at him, impressed by his connections.

Graves went out a sliding glass back door that rumbled on a metal track, shaking his head. "You'd think they never seen a fella that looks good in a hat before," he muttered to himself, emerging onto a back deck that boasted a predictably spectacular view of the descending foothills. The vast LA basin stretched away beyond that, the city awash in autumn sun.

Hannah was sitting at a small café table at the far end of the deck, taking in the scenery with an unlit cigarette waiting in her hand. Somebody'd dug up a pair of bluejeans and a clean white t-shirt for her to wear, both garments free of bloodstains and bulletholes.

Graves stepped up beside her and clicked his old Zippo alight. "You gonna fire that thing up or what, sister?"

Hannah looked up at him, then down at her cigarette. "Oh... no," she said, after a moment's consideration. "I suppose not. Lia made me quit. A long time ago, actually. She hates these things. Says they dishonor the relationship the old people had with an important plant."

Graves shut his lighter and pocketed it. He sat down in the chair opposite Hannah's. "I guess she'd be the one to know about that," he said.

Hannah nodded and shrugged, still contemplating the efficient nicotine delivery device trapped between her first two fingers. "She says the same about teabags, though. And it can still calm me down to hold one of these things, sometimes."

"Sure it can," Graves said. "Gives those nervous hands something to do. I getcha. I sorta think that's the whole reason I ever took it up in the first place. My hands were nervous a lot, back in the war."

Hannah nodded. They looked at the view together. The sun was warm, the breeze cool. Tall clouds marched across a crisp blue sky, casting large pools of shadow onto the landscape below. The tower-clusters of Century City and downtown jutted up in the southeastern distance like strange crystal formations. They both could smell the ocean on the winds that gusted in from the west. It would rain in the next few days. Graves could feel that in his bones—not that he could expect to feel it anyplace else.

"Doctor Ironic says it looks like she's just exhausted, by the by," Graves said, feeling no need to state that he was talking about Lia. She was right up at the forefront of both their minds. "Needs some rest. Guess it's no big wonder why."

"That's his full name?" Hannah said. "Riley Ironic?"

"What he's got that pack of sycophants in there callin' him, anyway. Don't know who he thinks he's fooling, myself." Graves huffed in frustration, and Hannah glanced across the table at him. "Miss Hannah, who the hell *are* these nutcakes?" he asked, searching her face for answers. "This place is just plain *weird.*"

"I've heard Lia call them 'operators,' I think," Hannah told him. "Operators for hire. Steb, I know, does his thing for gangsters and smugglers and such, for a lot of money. As you can see. Riley said he likes to have people around to help him celebrate when he finishes a job. So they're sort of like Lia, I guess... to varying degrees."

"Riiight," Graves said. "Widely varying, I'd say. If a dozen of those clowns in there are worth one Lia, I'll eat my fine new hat."

Hannah nodded her agreement and looked back out at the becalmed view. "Still, it's good of them to help us out."

"That it is, sister, that it is," Graves agreed. "So. What kinda history's she got with this 'Stub' creature, anyhow?"

"It's Steb, Dexter, and *she* dumped *him*, if that's what you're wondering. Three years back."

"Won't say it hadn't crossed my mind," Graves confessed. He supposed he was doing a piss-poor job of concealing his envy. "You've known her for quite a little while there yourself, haven't you?" he asked.

"Since she was about sixteen or so, yeah. Going on... god, almost ten years now, I guess."

"Wow," Graves said, genuinely impressed. "Don't think I ever knew anybody for a full ten years, 'cept for some of the guys I was in the service with. How'd you two, y'know, link up?"

"That's a story too," Hannah said.

"I'm all, well, not ears," Graves said, touching the side of his skull. "Sound holes, maybe. Words still go in there, though."

Hannah smiled. "Actually, Lia was already living there when I bought the Yard," she said. "It'd been empty for a long while before I took it over. Many years. Lia'd gotten into that old bomb shelter all by herself, somehow, and the place was so overgrown that I didn't even know it was there. She was growing vegetables for food and marijuana for pocket money. She wasn't ambitious about it, she was just… there. Doing her thing in that little back corner. She actually hid from me for almost a year while I was getting the place ready to open, thinking I'd throw her out if I knew."

"Reasonable worry," Graves said. "Guess I didn't realize that place was yours."

"Oh yes, all mine," Hannah said, turning wistful. "I- I had a husband once, Dexter," she explained. "His name was Warren, and he was good to me. He had insurance. A lot of it. After he was, you know, gone, I wanted to do something different. Warren was a software developer, and I'd been a project manager at the company he founded right from the very beginning. It was our life together, and after twenty years I needed something that was just *opposite*, I guess. Something that would be healing and soothing, so the Yard's what I bought with all that money. Plants, life, earthiness, you know? Roots."

Graves nodded. He didn't know what 'soft wear' was (like maybe they'd had a lingerie business was the way he interpreted it, that they'd been involved in the garment trade in some fashion), but he didn't want to interrupt her to clarify.

"Anyway," Hannah continued, "going into my first full winter there, Lia got very sick. I found her one morning passed out near the spigot behind the office. That old shack off the parking lot, you know? Laying there curled up on the bags of potting soil. I guess at some other point in my life I would've called whoever it is you're supposed to call when you find unconscious teenage squatters on your property, but I didn't. For whatever reason, I just didn't. I think maybe I needed to take care as much as Lia needed to receive it. Does that make any sense?"

"Sure it does."

Hannah nodded. "I'm pretty sure it was just a bad flu, for all that," she said. "But the fever gave her nightmares and awful hallucinations, and I know she thought she was dying. I fed her soup and kept her warm, nothing much more than that, and when she was better she said her name was Camellia Flores, but I know it's one she chose. Flores was the name of a foster family she liked when she was younger, before someone had medical complications and she ran away rather than go back into the system. She told me that story once and I could never get her to talk about it again, like it's gotten hard for her to recall. I don't know if she even remembers *who* she was, originally."

"I grew up kinda the same way," Graves said quietly, thinking back on it for the first time in a long time. "Joined the Navy soon as they'd let me, just to get the hell outta there."

Hannah tipped her head, empathizing. "Looking back," she said, "I think maybe that time was when Lia started to be, well, what she is now. A witch, I guess. An 'operator.' And I also think that maybe, for some reason, maybe just because I was there, that I'm a part of that for her. That I mean something to her, beyond being the lady she works for."

"I know you do," Graves said. "She'd knock the sun out of the sky rather than see you hurt."

"She already did nail down the moon." Hannah's eyes crinkled with pride and pleasure as she smiled about it.

Graves laughed softly and nodded. He took out his lighter and played with it idly, clicking open the lid and closing it again, as was his habit.

"I guess that's got to have a story behind it too, doesn't it?" Hannah asked, tipping her chin at the Zippo. "You came back from the grave to get it, after all."

Graves considered the old lighter. It glinted, caught there in the frail net of bones that was all that remained of his right hand. "Well, yeah," he said, "I suppose it does at that. I'm not in the habit of boring nice ladies with old war stories, though."

"I'd like to hear it," Hannah said. "I'd like to know."

Graves looked her in the eye. He hesitated. He'd never told this story to anyone before, nice lady or otherwise, and when he started to speak he found he had to look down at the lighter, instead of at Hannah herself.

"Well…" he began. "A kid named Dave Normoyle tracked me down and gave it to me after the war. Davey. Guess I pulled him outta the water on Easter Morning of 1945, during the battle of Okinawa. That's what he told me later on, anyway. I wouldn't have remembered the date, myself."

He paused, gathering his memories before going on.

"I can't even describe to you what those days were like, Miss Hannah. The Japanese were using a tactic they called the 'wind of the spirits,' the *kami-kaze…* "

"Their airplanes," Hannah said softly.

"Yeah, exactly right, their airplanes, crashin'em into the ships, plane after plane after plane. I still say they must've gone through thousands, even though I know that sounds like I gotta be exaggerating. Still, though, it's what I remember. One of 'em hit a deck I was standin' on, not fifteen feet behind me. Piece of its engine caught me in the ribs and knocked me into the drink before I knew what was going on."

He looked away toward downtown, feeling troubled by the recollections.

"I remember that, and I remember the dawn," he said in a voice pitched barely above a whisper. Hannah leaned in close to hear him. "That sunrise, well, it was about as gorgeous as any sunrise I've ever seen. Which I guess was sorta the worst part of that morning, in a way."

He glanced up.

"You see," he continued, averting his eyesockets before Hannah could ask him for clarification. "It, well… it hurt me, frankly, to think about how things like the dawn go on being beautiful for reasons all their own, even when you're right in the middle of learning firsthand the ugly truth about how easily people can, you know… get themselves broken."

Hannah nodded, thinking back to a thunderstorm she'd once watched from a hospital room window, now more than a dozen years in her past—a fact she could scarcely believe. Lightning bolts had forked and clashed all night long. She'd had little to do but watch them sear the sky while she sat there helplessly, feigning calm and waiting hour by hour as a cancer crushed the final drops of life from the wasted remnant of her husband, her Warren, whom she'd married in the spring of 1980 and had truly loved every day thereafter with every last ounce of her soul.

The memory of that spectacular storm hurt worse than the bandaged bulletgroove in her side. She thought she understood what Dex was saying.

"Things like the dawn don't care how messy and painful and scary it gets when people break," he said, directing his words toward his lighter. "I remember thinking, while I was floatin' in the blue, half-drowned and losing blood and dumb-lucky to've grabbed hold of a liferaft myself, that that old sun comin' up on the far horizon there wouldn't mind if I bucked convention and did something a little bit different that morning, like saving one little life. Hell, why not, I figured. As if it could matter anyway, one life, when so many others were comin' to bad ends all around me, but Davey Normoyle was the closest body still twitching in the water, so he got hauled aboard. And then I don't remember so much after that, for a time."

When Graves chanced a look up at Hannah she was rapt, her eyes full of gentle sympathy. Almost more than he could bear. He turned away again, looking out over the view, although he barely registered it by now. The eye of memory was doing all his seeing for him.

"Wasn't till a few years after that he finally tracked me down," Graves said. "I didn't really know the kid. I was in the intelligence service, moving all around the Pacific theater during the war, so he wasn't on my ship or anything like that. But I guess I must've told him my name at some point, 'cause he found me later on through a buddy of mine. Charlie Lurp, up here in Los Angeles. Just a couple of months before I, y'know, died. Davey by then had a missus and a baby girl and a life he was glad to be living, which I guess he thought he owed to me instead of to a shellshocked whim that happened to hit me one weird morning. But he was serious about it. Said an angel or some such shit came in a dream and told him that really, he'd been slated to buy it in the surf that day, and his life had been returned to him for the sole purpose of giving this particular lighter to *me*, Dex Graves."

Graves shrugged, examining the thing. It looked old, but otherwise unremarkable.

"He came up from San Diego to do it, even. Begged me to take the damn thing. Said the angel told him that if I didn't then he *would* have died that day. That he would've gone under before I ever found him and his happy life would be erased, nothing more than a dream before drowning. Crazy, sure, but hey, war is. Guess I don't mind telling you I wasn't always the world's cheeriest fella after I came back myself. So of course I took it. I was glad for the gift. I let it remind me that something I did one time, whatever my reasons, made a difference for somebody. And I needed that." He fixed Hannah with his empty sockets. "Like you needed to help out Miss Lia, I suspect."

"Yeah," Hannah said. "Just like, I'd think."

She took and squeezed Graves' bony hand. He squeezed back, kind of hard, but she held on.

She felt sure that she could trust this man (or whatever he was), this Dexter Graves, to watch out for her Lia, come what may.

He knew the true value of things.

"So, there's the tale, anyhow," Graves said, feeling a little awkward by the time he was ready to let Miss Hannah take her hand back. "What it means to me. Wouldn't have guessed it'd be enough to drag a dead man outta the dirt, but hey, like the poet once said: I guess there's more between heaven'n earth."

"Hey, uh… guys?" Riley said from behind them.

They both looked over, their moment gone. Graves put the lighter away.

"Not to interrupt the sharing, which I think is really sweet, but—"

Graves stood up. "Is she awake?"

"No, not yet," Riley said. "But her cellphone keeps ringing."

Chapter Thirty

Lia had a sense of something happening nearby, something her friends were concerned with, something that probably could've used her attention, but the pull of deep sleep was too strong for her to keep an eye on it properly. She drifted off instead, despite her efforts, sinking away from conscious awareness and down into the deep psychic blackness where the eternal currents churn. There could be other things besides herself moving through this sort of darkness. Shapes ancient and vast, leviathans of the imaginal sea that might, for an instant that would seem to contain the entirety of time within it, turn their alien-yet-familiar brand of awareness toward *her*.

Lia never liked it when that happened. It inspired as much dread as it did awe. At least she knew the things she needed to say to keep herself safe out here. She pitied the poor bastards who found themselves lost in these nether spaces due to madness, coma, or sheer unpreparedness for the experience before they intentionally set out to visit—all conditions that left them with little hope of escape or reprieve. One of those shapes that was too large to really comprehend would gobble up such cases sooner or later, but Lia had no way of knowing whether or not that ended their torment.

Danger, however, was not the only thing to be found down here. This ocean-between-minds was the font of individual consciousness, a primal headwater, older by far than human form itself. The currents here ran pure and strong and could be aligned with in the name of healing and growth, or to aid in the acquisition of knowledge. This was Lia's own territory, in a way. Black Tom had long ago taught her to use these confusing, often disturbing, yet meaning-saturated dreams as an opportunity to better understand herself, if and when she found herself having them.

They were important. They always meant something.

Lia quit resisting, letting the unconscious show her what it would, and almost that quick the featureless blackness around her transformed into rain-whipped foliage that shivered and danced in a cold, gusting wind.

There was nothing Lia loved better than a rainy night, but the pajamas she found herself wearing—her standard t-shirt and soft, loose pants—were insufficient against the weather, which felt as real as anything. Her bare arms pebbled up with gooseflesh as she hugged herself against the cold and hurried for shelter. She was also wearing a pair of her favorite dainty, soft-soled Chinese slippers, but she ran on the balls of her feet anyway, in a vain attempt to keep her cuffs up out of the mud and damp.

There were prefab gazebos and patio tents on display on the west side of Potter's Yard, and Lia found herself in the shelter of her favorite example, a large pavilion with mosquito-net sides that could be zipped closed, without really having run the full distance. She was just sort of there, more or less as soon as she decided where she wanted to be.

Her sleeping bag was waiting for her, already unfurled across the old futon she kept for nights like this, when the turbulent weather most made her feel like sleeping outdoors, where she could feel close to its wild energy.

Lia was shivering badly, her shoulders quaking, the point between her shoulderblades that always got sore after too much heavy lifting tightening up into a painful knot. She kicked off her sodden slippers and shimmied out of the pants that had gotten pretty well soaked despite her efforts to keep them dry. Clad in just the t-shirt and her underwear, Lia dove into the sleeping bag and huddled up with her head inside it, waiting until enough warm breath and body heat had accumulated to make her comfortable. Then she poked her head back out, so that she might listen to the rain drumming on the tent's canvas roof.

It woke something in her, the rain did. It always had. She found it soothing and nourishing and deeply sensual, and she imagined that the plants around her responded to it in just the same way. She could feel their delight and sense of release, and she longed to experience more of the latter for herself.

Lia rolled over, thinking that one of Riley's backrubs would've felt like heaven just then, and even as she recalled it his touch became real, palpable, and deeply appreciated. He knew how to work out that recurring knot in her back in a way that felt so good it made her want to go crosseyed.

She'd spent more time than she liked to admit pining after Riley. Her signature haircut, that sleek little bob, had been his suggestion, and the elegant style continued to make her feel coolly alluring, even to this day.

They'd met at Valley College, where Lia had taken a few random courses in literature, philosophy, history and other things that interested her, at Hannah's urging. Riley had been a brainy and fun new influence at that time, into things like books and bands and cool movies, always full of ideas for things to do and places to go all around the city. People liked Riley. He could talk to anyone and make them laugh, and Lia admired that. They'd been more or less inseparable, for a time.

He'd always been affectionate with her, Riley had, willing to give massages like this one or simply hold her while they talked, and he'd certainly never made her feel threatened by intrusive or demanding sexuality. Not even a little bit.

Not even when she wouldn't so much have minded.

It wasn't because he didn't care, or didn't find her pretty. He was gay and that was all. He tried to make it work for a little while only because he *did* love her, as dearly as she loved him, and knowing that let Lia feel better, a little less rejected... if still unfulfilled.

If Riley had been all air—intellect and humor—then his best friend Esteban was all fire.

He and Lia had sparked off each other from the moment Riley introduced them. As she thought about Steb, her sweet sense-memory simulacrum of Riley changed, and she felt herself rolled over onto her back. She felt Steb's hard, wiry body on top of her own as he kissed her hungrily, like he meant to consume her.

A lack of passion had never been part of their problem.

No, their problem had been the sheer force of Steb's personality, and the way it made Lia feel overwhelmed and embattled, like she was in danger of losing herself. Which wouldn't do, as she *liked* herself, and enjoyed her quiet little life. She cherished the time she spent learning from the plants and from Tom, as well as the regular *al fresco* breakfasts she shared with Hannah and the occasional DVD nights spent down at Han's cozy house in Studio City. Lia imagined her own personality as made up of equal parts earth and water (with a touch of air and just the right amount of fire mixed in), representing inclinations toward patience and understanding, manifestation and gradual growth. She was a meditative, reflective sort, while Esteban could barely sit still.

It wasn't that he couldn't be tender. He could be, as well as incredibly observant and thoughtful. He also had money, which she'd judged to be a good thing at the time. He'd kept up a steady stream of gifts and bombarded her constantly with invitations to travel or dine at fancy restaurants. It made her uncomfortable to turn him down, but she liked to stay close to the Yard, and she preferred to eat at familiar, comfortable places, if not cook for herself with the herbs, spices, and vegetables she grew. Besides, accepting those lavish offers always left her feeling awkwardly obligated. The financial disparity between them ultimately proved to be a source of friction, but it was just one amongst many by then. She'd never been able to properly relax in Steb's company, for any number of reasons.

She pushed him away, and he dissolved back into dreamstuff without a qualm.

She was alone with the rain.

It saddened her to think that she'd never yet gotten a chance to make love under this tent, on a blustering night like this one. The timing had never worked out. She'd never shared her futon-and-sleeping bag arrangement with another, except in her dreams. It would still have to wait, for a different lover and a different night.

She found her mind wandering in the direction of Dexter Graves. Not the talking skeleton she knew, so much, but rather the ghostly image she'd conjured the day before, when she bound him and de-animated his bones.

It had been a brief encounter, but she'd gotten an idea of what his smile had been like in life (mischievous and quick to appear), as well as how good he'd looked in that old-fashioned hat. He had the height and the width at the shoulders to carry off those long coats he liked, too. She'd felt compelled to flirt with that ghost almost as soon as it appeared, she remembered, and her knees had felt a little weak when she climbed back up the tube. Dex had apparently been a sailor in life, before becoming a detective, and those occupations suggested to Lia that he had strong affinities with air and water—qualities that had tempered his fiery and earthy aspects into something like steel.

Lia sat up, asking the rainy night to go away, and it was as compliant with her wishes as Esteban's image had been a moment before. These dreams weren't always like that. Sometimes she had very little say in what happened in them, even as regarded her own actions.

But this time the lively, rainy darkness disappeared, and a cool, bright morning dawned in its place.

Lia found herself standing amidst the Yard's old camellia trees, her favorites amongst all the plants, wearing nothing but a robe delicately stitched together from their fresh, translucent leaves. She looked down at it, marveling at the intricacy of its construction. The leaves were small, paper-thin and plastic-shiny—springtime foliage, vivid green and bursting with new life. When Lia moved she did so carefully, taking pains not to tear the fragile, living garment.

Thock!

Lia turned at the unexpected noise. She knew the sound of wood being chopped, the thud of the axe head when it bit into the grain followed by the quick clatter of two half-logs tumbling to the ground. The familiar sound reached her again:

Thock!

Lia headed toward the woodpile at the back of the Yard. She came out of the trees in time to see Dexter—a living, vital Dexter—bringing down his axe to bifurcate another length of wood.

Thock!

He was shirtless and sweating a bit from exertion. Lia liked watching the way the muscles worked in his back and arms when he swung the axe. He was built like a long, inverted triangle: broad at the shoulders, tapering down to small hips.

Thock! Another log cracked and split. Dexter bent to pick up the halves and set them aside, and that's when he noticed Lia.

He straightened up, not saying a word, giving her that knowing look and that lopsided grin. He was quite a bit taller than she was, big and solid through the chest, with a flat, firm stomach. Lia didn't quite realize she was biting her bottom lip while she eyed the point where his flesh disappeared behind the crisp front of his well-fitted work pants, just below his navel. He had an appealing air of genial masculine beastliness about him. A certain quiet confidence and maturity that Lia found lacking in so many of the other men she knew or regularly saw, when she compared them.

Dexter set the axe aside as Lia padded over the soft earth to stand before him, opening her weightless leaf-robe and letting it fall back from her shoulders. Dexter stepped closer, put an arm around her, and drew her to him, chest to chest. She was sure he must've felt the thudding rhythm of her heart both under her left breast and right through the planes of her back.

At that moment a jolt of alarm straightened Lia's spine. Dexter let her go and stumbled back—almost recoiling, you could say.

Lia looked down and was horrified to see her own hands stripped bare of flesh, the bones bleached to a chalky white. The leaves that made up her robe were all brown and dead and curling.

She willed the images and sensations away, but that driving urgency only intensified. There was something happening back in the waking world that needed attending to. She could feel her friends' distress over it quite keenly now, and she began the long upward struggle back toward them and toward consciousness, leaving her strange, intimate moment with an impression of Dexter Graves unconsidered. She didn't understand what the vision meant, but didn't feel like she could spare the time to wonder about it, either.

Chapter Thirty-One

Graves stepped in close to Hannah when she checked the front display on Lia's wireless telephone. Riley and Black Tom also crowded in and craned their necks to look over her shoulders. Lia was still sleeping soundly on that massive four-poster bed, behind them.

"Someone you know?" Graves asked, pitching his voice low so as to not disturb Lia's rest. "Those tiny phones are goddamn amazing, by the way, that they tell you who it is that's calling..."

"No," Hannah said, frowning over the caller ID. "It says Ingrid Redstone. Not a name I've heard before."

"Ingrid Redstone?" Graves repeated. He didn't think he could've heard her right.

"It's *been* ringing," Riley said. "This must be at least the third re-dial."

"Should I answer it?" Hannah asked.

"Yeah, do it," Graves said. "But keep it vague. Wish there was an extension I could listen in on."

"I can put it on speaker," Hannah offered.

Graves nodded his approval, quietly impressed.

Hannah unfolded the phone. "Hello?"

The caller hesitated for a long while. Then, "...Lia?"

"Ah, no," Hannah said. "No, Lia's not, ahh, Lia can't come to the phone right now, but I'll be happy to give her a message, if you like."

"Who's this?" the caller asked sweetly. Her name was Ingrid Redstone, if the 'caller ID' was to be believed, and Graves had to admit that the honeyed voice did sound the way he remembered.

"I'm, uh... Lia's boss," Hannah said. Graves guessed she was being mindful of Lia's wariness regarding names, which he figured was probably smart. She was improvising, although she was neither a performer nor a deceiver by nature.

"Lia's boss at Potter's Yard?" the woman calling herself Ingrid asked.

"Umm, yeah," Hannah said, after a longish beat. "Yeah, that's me, all right."

She was at a loss for more to say. Graves folded his arms, frowning and thinking.

"Well," Ingrid continued, "my name is Ingrid, Ingrid Redstone, and I was really hoping I might speak with Lia. Do you know when she'll be available?"

"Well, she, she's a little busy right now," Hannah said. She was floundering, not quite sure what was required of her, or even what was going on. Graves had a notion rattling around in his head, but he wasn't ready to let the rest of them in on it yet.

"She's organizing a lot of new stock, you know, waaay out back," Hannah continued. "She forgot her phone up here in the office."

"Oh, did she?"

"Yeah, yeah, she did," Hannah lied. "And it's a pretty big place, so I'm not exactly sure where she is right now, but I'll sure tell her you called, miss, ah, Redstone, was it?"

"That's right, Ingrid Redstone. Lia's been working on a... a project for me, and it's really quite important that I speak with her as soon as possible."

Graves could stand the charade no longer. "Yeah, I just *bet* it is, Ing," he snarled down at the little phone Hannah was holding up. "Tell me—this *'project'* of yours gonna end with Lia's gray matter spattered all over Hardface's door, or was that just how things shook out with me?"

"Dexter," Ingrid said, after a moment. "That's you, isn't it?"

"In the... well, hell, I was gonna say 'in the flesh,'" Graves said, aware of the inadequacy of the expression. "But yeah, it's me. How've ya been, dollface? Hope the years've been kinder to you, 'cause they've sure taken a toll on me."

"Welcome back," Ingrid said, and Riley and Hannah exchanged a glance. "Dex," Ingrid hesitated on the other end of the wireless phone line. "I- I want you to know that what happened, back in 1950? That was... well, it was a complicated situation. What I did to you, I didn't do lightly."

"Glad to know you didn't blow my brains out on a goddamn whim, Ingrid."

"Dexter, I had no other *choice*," Ingrid exploded, suddenly emotional. "You have no *idea* what would've happened if you'd gone through that door!"

"I sure didn't then," Graves said. "My horizons have broadened since."

"You may think they have," Ingrid shot back, "but you still don't know what's really at stake." When she spoke again she pitched her voice very low. "Dex, this isn't the very best time for me to talk about all this. But there are things you need to know. You and Lia both. And you need to know them before dark."

"Yeah, regarding Lia," Graves said. "You come anywhere *near* her, and my head won't be the only one with a hole in it. You get me?"

"Nyx will be coming at sunset," Ingrid warned. "And Lyssa, and the Tzitzimime, too. None of them are finished with you, and they're not the last Caradura has to send. Meet me before the sun goes down—"

"Nuts to that, sister!" Graves said. "Our social life ended when you pulled that trigger."

"How's Lia feeling, Dexter, why don't you tell me that?" Ingrid challenged, trying a different tack. "Still on her feet?"

Everyone in the guest room looked over at unconscious Lia, and then back to Graves.

"And what would you know about that?" he said darkly. "*What did you do to her?*"

Hannah jumped when he shouted.

"Oh, it's not me doing it, Dex," Ingrid said. "It's *you*."

Graves hesitated. Hannah, Riley, and Black Tom all stared at him. "What the hell are you yappin' about, Ingrid?" he said. "I'm not doing a damn thing to Lia. I wouldn't ever."

"Haven't you stopped to wonder how it is you're up and walking around?" Ingrid asked. "What do you think is powering that? Chthonic potential is what. Earth energy. The sort of force that needs a channel."

"Then you tell me how to change that channel."

"When we meet," Ingrid said. "Before sunset."

Dexter shouted down the line at her: "You must already have a hole through your goddamn head if you think I'm gonna meet you anywhere outside of *hell*, sister! Now you tell me how to fix this, you tell me *right now*, before I—"

"What? Come after me?" Ingrid said, cutting him off. "Oh, no! Whatever will I do? I'll just have to cower here at Potter's Yard until you track me down, Sherlock. Just be sure you do it before dark. Seriously."

Ingrid broke the connection, and Lia's phone burbled a dropped call tone.

Nobody knew what to say. Hannah, Riley, and Black Tom looked up at Graves, but all he could do was shrug, helplessly.

Chapter Thirty-Two

Ingrid closed her phone and wandered away from the Lyssa tree—a source of amazement for her henchmen that in Ingrid's opinion almost amounted to an art installation. She was trying to avoid the avid attention of that creepy Xavier, whom she knew had been eavesdropping during her call. The other men hadn't wanted to hang around the leather-suited Archon with the sapling tree growing up through her head after she tried to talk to them, but Xavier hadn't been deterred. He hadn't let Ingrid out of earshot since arriving at the nursery.

Her bare foot encountered something soft and yielding on the ground. Something lying concealed under the cover of a low shrub.

Looking down through the foliage she parted, Ingrid found a black cat. It hadn't moved, despite being accidentally kicked. It was alive, no doubt about that, yet unresponsive to stimuli. Ingrid made a gesture to knot the oddity up in a precautionary binding hex, one she could shore up later if she saw a need. Then she put away her phone and picked up the limp animal, frowning.

This meant something. She was sure of it.

She was looking critically at the inert black cat when Xavier crept up behind her. "So," he said out of nowhere. "You think they gonna come, or what?"

Ingrid turned, startled, but kept it cool. She betrayed nothing. She fixed Mickey's footsoldier with a contemptuous gaze of a sort that usually made men feel self-conscious, to say the least. Xavier had sidled up a lot closer than she might've expected. She looked him up and down dismissively, then looked at the cat again, and grinned. "You know, I have a feeling they will," she said.

Ingrid tucked the animal under her arm and strutted off,

through a thicket of potted palms, pointedly ignoring Xavier as he watched her walk away.

He lingered, waiting to make sure Ingrid was really gone. After the Red Witch wandered out of earshot, he fell to his knees and ripped his own face off, gasping. 'Xavier' was nothing more than a disguise. While he caught his breath, Winston, the King's skeletal servant, looked disdainfully down at the floppy face in his hand.

"Bloody hell, I forgot how *hot* these things can be," he muttered, his voice and manner changed completely from those of his crudely-drawn character. As if servitude weren't enough, the final indignity was that he was now being forced to *act*, like some vagabond gypsy player prancing for coins on a rickety stage.

He looked again at his false face, which was stubble-scalped and marked with a teardrop tattoo at the corner of the left eye. It'd been flayed off a recent arrival in Mictlan mere hours ago. It felt moist, and smelled meaty.

"How *do* the living tolerate it?" Winston wondered aloud.

He heard a rustling in the oleander behind him and threw his face back on. It shrink-wrapped down onto the bones of his skull. He still had no eyes (the ones that came with a fresh face were impractical, as they tended to deflate or turn cloudy so quickly; and besides, the King prized them as jewelry), but he covered up that fact with his sunglasses and got to his feet before two of the gunmen he'd enlisted 'rolled up on him,' to employ the vernacular of the day. He recognized them as Top Shelf (aka Reggie White) and his shadow Andrej Mirovic (known amongst his confederates as the Silent Soviet, due to his lack of English). Winston had hand-picked each member of this crew himself.

"Dude, what you doin' back up in here, anyways?" Top Shelf said. "Takin' a leak?"

"Yeah, why," Winston shot back, dropping into character as Xavier once again. "You wanna watch?"

Top Shelf snorted in contempt and wandered off in the direction Ingrid had gone, with quiet Mirovic trailing along behind him. Winston stared after them through Xavier's dark lenses.

"Wankers," he muttered.

Chapter Thirty-Three

Lia got out of bed. Nobody saw her. Nobody was looking in her direction. She was still fully dressed, except for her shoes. She suspected her hair was mussed and she smoothed it self-consciously, probably not doing it any good.

"Dexter?" Hannah said, breaking the silence that filled the guest room at Casa de Rojo. She still hadn't folded up Lia's phone, although its screen had gone black. "What are you gonna do?"

"You're gonna tell me how you can possibly know Ingrid Redstone, for starters," Lia said, from behind them.

There was a mass turn. Hannah, Dexter, Riley and Black Tom all wheeled around. Hannah ran over and hugged her, hard. "Lia, honey!" she exclaimed. "How are you? You fainted dead away, we were so scared—"

"I did not faint, don't you say that," Lia admonished her. Hannah let her go and she slipped back into her shoes. "I never faint. I don't want to be a girl who faints." She turned to Graves. "Dexter?"

"What, how did I know Ingrid?" he said. "I met her back in the '40s, before I... well, you know. She was a singer in a bar I spent kind of a lot of time in back then. She's gotta be into her nineties by now."

"If she is, she's got a great plastic surgeon," Lia said. "I saw her yesterday morning, and there's no way she's more than thirty years old."

Dexter looked confused. "But that's not possible," he said.

"Says the Crypt Keeper," Riley piped up.

Dex glared at him like he meant to rejoin with something snotty, but then relented. "Yeah, good point," he admitted. Then:

"Lia, she said there's things we need to know. She said I'm here, somehow, because of *you*."

"Not to the best of my knowledge," Lia said. "And I do think I'd notice. What am I, reanimating in my sleep?" She frowned. "But I guess I *did* find your lighter in a place she sent me to…"

"Can you undo it?" Dexter asked. "Whatever it is she did to me that's hurting you?"

Lia shrugged. "I don't even know what it is. This's beyond me."

"That Ingrid woman didn't seem to think so," Hannah said.

"No," Lia agreed reluctantly. "No, I guess she didn't." She looked up at Dexter. "So, Dex. We gonna go talk to her, or what?"

"Hell no, we're not gonna go talk to her!" Dexter said. "You know how to spell 'trap,' sister? That'd be I-N-G, uh," —he thought about it— "R-I-D."

"But what about all those 'things we need to know?'" Lia asked.

"That's a bluff," Dex said. "She's bluffing. It's bullshit."

"What if it's not, Dexter?" Hannah asked quietly.

Hannah and Dexter exchanged a private glance, and Lia knew they were both thinking of her. She must still have looked pretty worn out. She hadn't really expected that three hours of sleep would erase those dark, haunted circles from underneath her eyes.

"If that's the case," Dexter reassured Hannah, "then we'll find out what she knows some other way. But playing by Ingrid's rules is not gonna be the smart move, here, I'm tellin' you. I'm getting a notion she's a better tactician than I ever knew."

"You guys are welcome here for as long as you need," Riley said. "We're defended. Let 'em come."

"Thank you, Riley," Lia said, touching his arm affectionately. "But I don't think that's really gonna work."

"Why not?" Dexter and Hannah said together.

"It's nice here," Dex elaborated. "Swanky."

"And safe," Hannah supplied.

"You'll see, if we hang around long enough," Lia told them. "Riley, can I have a drink of water? Maybe a sandwich or something, before Steb wakes up? I don't know if I can handle him today."

"Of course you can," Riley said. "You can have roast duck and chilled caviar, if you like."

"PB&J'll be fine."

Hannah meekly raised her hand. "I might try the duck and caviar."

"Come on," Riley said. "We just restocked the kitchen."

They all filed out into the hall, except for Black Tom. Lia noticed, but she figured he'd be along directly. He wasn't her shadow, after all.

Chapter Thirty-Four

Graves realized that Casa de Rojo's party people had come to terms with his *memento mori* presence much more readily than most crowds would have. The decayed Dick Tracy, Riley, and Hannah hung out amongst them in the main hall and talked amidst their chatter while Lia finished off her snack: two sandwiches, a banana, and a glass of sweet iced tea.

Hannah nibbled at a leg of crispy duck and sipped from a glass of champagne.

Truth be told, Graves was almost as startled and captivated by Riley's guests as they were by him, now that he had a chance to look them over. He'd gotten used to the idea that Hannah and Miss Lia wore dungarees all the time, and he figured it had to do with their soil-centric line of work out at Potter's Yard. (Although Lia's pants didn't quite fit, like she'd bought them in the wrong size. They showed off her belly button and a good two inches of skin below that. Not that Graves meant to complain about it, mind you). But the women in this room, as well as some of the men, all wore jeans that barely covered their pubic bones, if not 'skirts' that seemed to be little more than narrow bands of fabric stretched taut around slender hips. Shapely legs and plumped-up breasts bulged everywhere he looked, like a part of the décor, and these kids were about as tattooed as a tribe of South Seas savages. Graves had known career Navy men who didn't sport as much ink as any random twenty-year-old girl at this party, which had apparently been going on for some number of days already.

O brave new world, thought Dexter Graves. These young people had grown up with choices and freedoms arrayed before them that nobody born in his era would've been able to imagine.

Graves believed in freedom, as an ideal. He'd fought for it in the big WW, and he was more gratified than he would've guessed to see this future generation using it as they were, to strike out into the unknown countries within and between themselves. What sort of new continents might explorers like these discover, given time? Graves may have been overwhelmed and intimidated by their liberally-displayed beauty, but he wished them all the best just the same.

While he was idly musing about days and wonders yet to come, a double-door at the top of the stairs banged open and a wild-eyed figure who could only be freelance shaman Esteban de Rojo (known in some circles as Steb) burst back into the everyday world after an unbroken week of isolation.

All conversation ceased; all heads swiveled up toward him. Graves, Lia, Hannah and Riley all stood up.

Steb zeroed in immediately on Lia.

"*Brujachica!*" he screamed.

The new lunatic with the flair for entrances leaped down the stairs in three large bounds to seize Lia's hand. He had a shock of black hair, small glittering eyes, a sharp wedge of a chin, and the letters of some arcane alphabet tattooed down his forearms. "You have returned to me, as I always knew one day you would," he said.

Graves didn't know what to think.

"Hi, Steb," Lia said. "I haven't returned, I'm just stopping by."

"Ahhhhh, you say that now but wait," Esteban chided. "You've yet to see the newest wonders we've evoked. There is no place else you will care to be once you've seen the works that we're performing here."

Finally he noticed Graves and was visibly taken aback.

"Whoa," he said, looking to Lia. "You've been scaling new heights too, haven't you, brujachica?"

"Steb," she said, "this is Dexter Graves. Dex: Esteban de Rojo."

Turning to Graves, Steb said, "Charmed, I am certain."

"Not so much for me," Graves replied.

"Lia, la brujachica," Esteban said again, delighted nearly to the point of rapture by the mere fact of her presence. "How can you stay away, mi corazon? What hospitality can I offer you?"

"Riley just made me a sandwich."

"A *sandwich*? A fucking *sandwich*?" Steb turned on Riley. "Why would you make her a sandwich when anything the world can offer is hers for the asking?" he demanded. "What is the matter with you?"

"It's what I asked for, Steb," Lia said. "It's what I wanted."

"But—"

"You know I hate being told what I'm supposed to like."

"You always did, didn't you, brujachica?" Steb smiled. "Hannah Potter," he said, taking note of the lady for the first time. "I remember you." He grabbed Hannah up in a bearhug and whirled her around. Riley'd scrounged enough Vicodin for her that it didn't appear to trouble the slice on her hip at all.

"Hi, Esteban," she said. "It's good to see you again."

"And you as well, Doña Hannah."

"What've you been working on, Steb?" Lia asked. "You seem a little... wired."

"Yeah, man," Riley said. "Even for you."

Steb set a slightly dizzy Hannah down, and Graves steadied her.

"Scrying the aethers, mi brujachica," Steb told Lia. "I've been scrying the aethers and such wonders I've seen! You must join me. Really, you're my only peer."

"What is he, hopped up on bennies?" Graves whispered. "Benzedrine?"

"He's been in a deeply altered state all week," Riley said. "He's supposed to ground himself better before he comes out of seclusion, though."

"*Brujachica*!" Steb jumped up onto a coffee table to grandly assume the center of the room. The crowd of hipsters and hexy girls parted around him, except for four female stereo bearers who raised four identical boomboxes (in what Lia and Riley thought of as a Lloyd Dobbler style) and started them all playing the same song.

Steb's dark eyes blazed with excitement. "I want you to see what I have brought back from the edge of the 30th sphere," he cried, when he had Lia's full attention.

Esteban began to dance to the dark, manic beat that poured from the sexy caryatids' upraised radios. Slowly at first, then faster as the tempo increased. All of his attention was focused on Lia, who wasn't intimidated one bit.

Hannah had to smile, Graves noticed.

"Steb, what are you doing?" Lia asked.

"Just watch, brujachica," he said. "Unless you are moved to join me."

Esteban raised a hand and the half-dozen party people nearest to him simultaneously joined in his choreography. Their moves looked expertly coordinated.

"Theatrical bunch, ain't they?" Graves muttered to Hannah.

Lia twitched her hips as Steb danced at her, not joining him, exactly, but matching his steps a bit. It was a weird tango she wasn't quite participating in, although she didn't shy away from it, either.

"You like my dance, brujachica?"

"If it's leading where I think it is, I might not," Lia warned over the music.

The song's intensity redoubled at the chorus and Steb threw his head back in a scream that had the effect of drawing all of his blacksuited bodyguards into the number with impeccable timing. They doffed imaginary hats and spun their big guns like canes. It was both absurd and scary. People instinctively scrambled away from the whirling weapons. Graves and Hannah were stunned, as were the guards themselves, judging by the looks on their faces.

This wasn't choreography at all. It was mind control.

"All right, Steb, I'm impressed," Lia said. "*Really* impressed. But I'd like you to stop now."

"Ohhh, why don't you just *loosen up*?" Steb shouted. He raised his arms above his head and the remainder of the room (including Graves, Hannah, and Riley) were all compelled to join the dance.

Only Lia, the demure axis of all that energy, remained immune. She smiled at Steb's antics, and Graves thought he sensed in her some desire to take part in the madman's reel. She clearly knew the steps. She could probably have shown this 'Steb' a move or two. Together they'd be plain dangerous.

For the first time, Graves thought he understood Lia's full potential for terrible and terrifying beauty, like that of a firestorm or a raging angel. She and Esteban could have danced across realities together and molded the worlds anew, into whatever strange and striking forms they might've fancied, with no regard for any rules of gods or men.

If she'd wanted to, that was. Graves was glad she didn't.

Lia edged away toward the door, drawing the whirling crowd along after her.

"Dance with me," Steb dared, screaming it over the music.

"You mean you're not gonna force me to?" Lia shouted back.

"Ha!" Esteban laughed. "Never you, brujachica. As if I could."

"Yeaaah, anyway," Lia said, "I think it's time my friends and I were going, now." She slipped out the front door, pulling Hannah and Graves along with her. Control of their limbs came back to them when she took their hands.

Steb and all of his guests and guards spilled right out the front door after them. A team of gardeners attending to the grounds joined in the crisply-executed dance routine, spinning rakes and smashing garbage can lids together to amplify the beat. Involuntary partiers gyrated on the lawn, more than a few of them still clutching the remainders of spilled drinks in their hands.

"But my operation has just ended, and my party has just begun," Steb said, pursuing Lia as she backed away down the steps. "We are as one mind with many bodies. Imagine the possibilities!"

"That's not my kind of party, Steb," Lia said sadly. "It's too much. These people aren't toys. This kind of thing is the reason we can't be together, and you know it."

"You limit yourself. Why, brujachica? Why will you not think of what we, together, could be? What more must I do to prove my passion?"

"Nothing!" Lia pleaded. "Please, gods, nothing more. You take risks that scare me, Steb. You sell your skills in ways I can't abide. I don't want to change you, or stifle you, or tell you who to be... but I also can't stand by. And we've been over this before."

At the apex of the song, Steb let the number stop.

The music died away and the dancers quit. Some fell to their knees in fear and relief, while others turned around and went back into the house, in search of fresh drinks.

Steb turned sad and earnest. "But I love you, brujachica," he said. "I always will."

Graves looked on, with his ulnae and radii folded across his ribs. Hannah pulled him toward the car. They both got in, Graves in the back, Hannah in the driver's seat, as Lia kissed Steb's cheek.

"Take care of yourself, Esteban," she said. "Don't let yourself do things you'll regret. People's choices have to be their own."

She pulled away from him, pained by the disappointment evident in his eyes. She turned and took Riley's hands. "Thank you, Riley, for patching up my Hannah," she said. "Oh, and that Pi trick you taught me worked *really* well! I'll have to tell you about it sometime."

Riley nodded and Lia hopped into the passenger seat of Graves' stolen fancyass car. She waved out the window when they pulled away, angling down the long, curving drive.

Esteban watched them go from where he stood on the front steps, looking quietly brokenhearted.

"**All** right," Graves said from the back seat of the car as they wound their way down the hill. "Can I just ask, what the *hell* was that?"

"That was Steb," Hannah said, without looking back from the driver's seat.

Lia said nothing at all. She stared out her window at expensive houses and sun-mottled vegetation as they rolled silently past.

Then, out of nowhere she shouted: "Wait a minute, where's Tom?" She looked around, with panic written across her face. "Hannah, *stop the car!*"

Hannah did so, wide-eyed, skidding to a stop in the middle of the road. Thankfully there was no one behind them. Lia was openly panicked, trying to look in every direction at once, it seemed like.

"I can't find Black Tom!" she shrieked.

Chapter Thirty-Five

Tomas Delgado—Black Tom, as Lia called him, and others had called him before her—stood alone in the middle of Casa de Rojo's guest bedroom, testing an invisible boundary like a mime without an audience. He hadn't been able to move or project himself at all for some minutes now.

At his feet, three lines of fire spontaneously ignited and grew together to form a triangle around him. Tom watched this occurrence curiously until he realized that the well-appointed guest room outside the firelines was fading away and changing, becoming the familiar, engulfing greenery of Potter's Yard.

The stunning redhead who'd introduced herself to Lia as Ingrid Redstone (first by e-mail and then in person at Paty's coffee shop not two weeks before), looked on as she forced him into visibility within a space she'd defined by drawing lines in the dirt between three lit candles encased in tall glass jars. Black Tom looked down and saw his catself lying at his ghostfeet. He couldn't send himself out any further from the cat, nor could he fully re-enter and wake it up. His captor had set her candles around an inverted fishtank, under which she'd trapped his catbody, intuiting that the stuporous animal had to be more than it seemed. She'd been right enough about that, and he'd been too distracted with concern over Lia to feel her sneaking up on it.

He looked up and considered Ingrid.

He may not have known how this was happening, but he thought he finally knew who this was, at least: the King's Girlfriend. The Red Witch, or la Bruja Roja, as an acquaintance of his had once called her, long, long ago. The mystery woman whose name old Tomas Delgado had never learned, back at the start of the twentieth century.

How the hell could he have known she'd still be alive? How the hell *could* she still be alive, alive and unchanged, untouched by age? He'd long ago deduced Mictlan to be a realm devoid of time, because he and other clever necromancers had discovered they were able to communicate with the *future* dead, with the possible ghosts of generations-yet-to-be as well as with their ancestors, at the pleasure of el Rey. It was where the mantic or prognostic part of the art came into play, really. Could the time-free property he'd observed possibly allow a witch equipped to cross from one world to the next also to hop around the ages with no regard for linear chronology at all?

Time-travel went well beyond any grace of Mictlantecuhtli's Tom had ever experienced, or heard tell of either. This woman was obviously no ordinary initiate, however.

He'd been taken in utterly by the lies she'd told to Lia. He'd wanted to help her, even more than Lia had. He'd also wanted to keep her safe from the influence of the King, as soon as he realized exactly where it was she thought her 'brother' had gone.

Well, he always had been an idiot for a pretty face. This was one of the few times he'd ever regretted it. He acknowledged that Lia's instincts on this had been better than his own, right from the start.

"Here, kitty kitty," Ingrid cooed. When Tom was visible enough to recognize, she said: "Ohh, I remember *you*, you're the one who thought I didn't see you at the restaurant yesterday. Or the other time, either."

Black Tom folded his arms.

Ingrid's cellphone rang almost as soon as he'd materialized all the way, into full visibility, despite his continued efforts to send out or otherwise break free of her reinforced trap. Smiling, she answered the call.

"What did you do with him?" Lia shouted down the line. The volume on the little device was turned up high enough for Tom to hear, though Lia's side of the conversation sounded tinny and distant.

"Lia," Ingrid said brightly. "So nice to hear from you again."

"Who are you, anyway?" Lia demanded. "*What* are you, Ingrid?"

"Why Lia, I would have thought you'd have that figured out by now. I'm just like you."

"That whole sob story you told me about the missing brother with the occulty friends was bullshit too, wasn't it?"

"Well, yes, I suppose it was," Ingrid said. "But that doesn't matter now."

"It matters to me!" Lia yelled, loud enough to make the phone's speaker crackle and Ingrid wince. "I don't like being played with, and I don't like being lied to. And if you've hurt Black Tom I'll, I'll—"

"Lia, you don't understand. I can help you, but you have to trust me. If you'll just for gods' sake come back out here with Dexter, then we can—"

Tom saw Ingrid spot a liberally-tattooed henchman in sunglasses watching her from a distance that probably left him within earshot. She abruptly changed her tone.

"—we can, ah, talk over all the things that Mr. Caradura wants me to, you know, tell you. It's important. Trust me, and I won't have to do what I don't want to do. To your, you know, your cat."

Ingrid turned away from the inked-up creep, grimacing. She looked to Tom like she knew this conversation was going poorly, but she couldn't say more with that baldheaded lurker so plainly listening in. Tom guessed that all of this would get back to el Rey, then. Everything the man heard. So Ingrid had to choose her words with care, and hope they'd play the way she needed them to, for both of the audiences who'd receive them.

Tom could tell when somebody was working both sides of an angle. He didn't yet know *why* she was doing it, however. Couldn't fathom it. Nor could he reach out to communicate with her from inside her hex. Not without the benefit of a voice he could raise.

"Trust doesn't apply when you take away somebody's options," Lia said darkly, from the speaker on Ingrid's little phone. "But you win, Ingrid. I'm coming. I can't do anything else."

"Just do it soon," Ingrid said. "Please." She dropped her voice to a whisper. "It's already late, and there won't be a damn thing we can do after dark."

Black Tom looked on calmly as Ingrid broke the connection, appearing frustrated and pensive. She turned on the henchman with the dark glasses, away from Tom, and snapped: "It's hard to work with a fucking audience, you know."

The tattooed man said nothing, but he stepped creepily back into the foliage and out of sight.

Ingrid looked back to Black Tom, who raised an eyebrow at her.

Chapter Thirty-Six

Lia folded up her phone, scowling and thinking. "She's an operator," she said, meaning Ingrid. She, Hannah and Dexter were standing on the shoulder of Mulholland Drive, where Lia had paced back and forth during the call. "She's like me. I guess maybe *better* than me. I think I'm still aging at a normal rate." She looked to Dex. "She's bound my Tom the way I did you, yesterday, Dexter."

"How do you know?" Hannah asked, having never seen Black Tom out of his catbody before. She'd parked their car at a scenic overlook, though none of them had eyes for the view. "How *did* you know?"

"Normally I see him, or at least I feel him," Lia said. "He's always with me, in one way or another. And now he's not."

"Always?" Hannah said, thinking about it. "*Always* always? Does he look like a cat?"

"No, he mostly looks like a man," Lia said. "Like he looked when he was alive. He was an operator too, years and years ago. His patron was Mictlantecuhtli. That's how I know about the Tzitzimime and all that stuff, from him. But he skipped out on the deal they made when he died and escaped into another body. A cat's body. My cat's like his tenth or twelfth ride. So if Ingrid's aligned with Mictlantecuhtli, and it's pretty clear by now she is, then Tom's in real danger."

"What's a Mictlantecuhtli?" Dex asked. "Like an imported beer or something?"

"He's the Aztec personification of Death, Dexter," Lia said shortly. "The King of the Realm of the Dead. You've heard him called Miguel Caradura or Mickey Hardface, I guess."

"Hey," Hannah said, as a weird thought occurred to her.

"Does that mean the Aztecs had the right religion, then? Lia?"

"It means everything that can be dreamed or imagined lives a life in the otherworld," Lia said.

Dexter looked thoughtful. "Ingrid told *me* Hardface was just a mobster," he recalled. "Or at least implied it. She was pretty vague, but I chalked that up to her being scared for her life. She said she got mixed up with Caradura, said he was crazy and threatenin' to kidnap her off to Mexico or someplace and force her to marry him, if she wouldn't tell him where to find a baby of his she'd given up to get adopted." He paused, touching the ragged exit hole above his eye socket. "Then she went and shot me through the head when I was trying to rescue her from that."

"Hannah, give me the keys," Lia said.

Hannah did so without hesitation. Lia went to the car that was parked some yards behind them. Dexter followed after her.

"Lia, we are *not* goin' out there. Not without a plan," he said.

Lia opened the driver's side door, but stopped and stared at him over the top of the stolen BMW before she got in. A soft tone chimed to remind her the door was ajar. She looked to Hannah, too, who was visibly frightened.

"You're right," Lia said, coming to a decision, although it still fell pretty far short of anything that might be called a plan. She'd hoped to have more time up at Esteban's extravagant estate to formulate one, but it hadn't been in the cards, and all she could do now was trust in her instincts. "It *is* too dangerous for us all to go out there. That's why I'm going, and you're staying here."

"Lia, *no!*" Dex shouted.

She ducked into the car, shut her door, and hit the locks. Dexter saw the plastic nub drop down into the passenger-side doorframe, but he scrabbled at the handle anyway, scratching up the paint with his calcified fingertips.

Lia downed the electric window just enough to be heard when she spoke. "I *have* to go, Dexter," she explained. "I owe it to Black Tom. You guys walk down to the park on Coldwater and wait for me there, or call a cab and go to Hannah's house. I'll find you when this is finished."

"Dammit, Lia, don't be stupid," Dexter snarled, pounding on the tinted window like he meant to smash it in. He might even manage it, with a few more blows. "Take me with you, at least!

I'm not breakable like you are."

"I don't know what you are, or *why* you are, but Ingrid does," Lia said, leaning across the passenger seat to look up into Dexter's empty sockets, which were like a pair of shadowed caves underneath the brim of his fedora. "None of us are safe if she gets anywhere near you, is what I think."

"Lia, I swear to whoever you want, you can trust me," Dexter said, abandoning his assault on the window glass. She didn't doubt that he meant it. His voice was so earnest it practically broke her heart. But it didn't change the facts.

"I'm trusting you to take care of Hannah, Dexter. Please do that for me."

Dex nodded helplessly, agreeing that he would of course do that in any case, while still trying to organize an argument. Hannah crowded in beside him, stooping to peer through the chipped passenger window. "Lia, don't do this," she said. "Don't go back there alone."

"Hannah, she has my *Tom*."

"Then let us at least come with you," Han pleaded, echoing Dexter. "Maybe we can help."

Lia shook her head, eyeing a fresh red spot of blood on the side of Hannah's borrowed white t-shirt, which had seeped through the bandage beneath. "I can't have you hurt on my account. Not any more than you already have been. I *can't*, Hannah. Please try to understand that I have to do this, and I can only do it alone."

She stomped the accelerator before either of them could wedge another word in. She knew she wouldn't have withstood another round of protestations. Her wheels spun on the loose dirt of the shoulder before catching pavement. Dexter took one last parting shot at the passenger window with his bony fist, and this time he managed to crack it down the middle, but he was too late.

Hannah yelled and ran after the sportscar as it shot down the snaking length of blacktop that led back down to the Valley, still begging her not to leave them at the very top of her lungs.

Lia glanced back in the rearview mirror in time to see Dexter catch her friend when she stumbled and almost fell into the shallow depression at the side of the road, clutching once again at the bleeding wound in her side.

Retrospective No.4 ~ 1910

A century ago...

Oscar closed the metal gate across the front of the platform and advised Tom to hold on before he started the construction elevator's noisy gasoline engine. The lift rattled and clattered as it carried them up toward the Hole in the Sky. The Hole that would be enclosed by an office at the top of a thirteen-story building within a matter of months. Maybe before the year 1910 had run itself out.

Old Tom Delgado looked north, toward the surprising number of lights (warm tongues of kerosene flame as well as steadier electric glows) that were then coming on in the windows of the distant houses of Hollywood. It looked like a handful of flickering stars had been strewn across the black foothills.

This world was already changing faster than he could follow, and it was about to change so much more.

Now that he'd seen the architectural evidence of el Rey's ambitions, Tom thought he finally understood how his patron intended to use him. As a placeholder. A bookmark. As something to wedge into the imaginal space Mictlantecuhtli was meant to occupy while 'Miguel Caradura' projected himself out into the living world as he desired, in subversion of the ancient laws that bound him.

King Death himself could never travel beyond the Hole in the Sky. He came right back when he tried, like a dead man arriving. Tom had witnessed it before. Los Muertos, the ordinary denizens of Mictlan, lacked even the ability to step into the first chamber (*or the second one, from their point of view*, Tom supposed), except on the two nights that followed Halloween, when the worlds experienced a flash of precise synchronization that made such crossings possible. They could exit only then, should their King elect to grant his subjects permission to walk the earth. Which he rarely did, as there was nothing in it for him, generally speaking.

But Tom's demise would be unique. Mictlantecuhtli meant to flay him bare with his obsidian blade at the door between the worlds instead of on the second room's altar stone (as he did with all of the regular dead). In this special case he'd leave Tom's freely-offered pelt out in the first of his Chambers and wear it into the realworld, rather than feed it to his creatures. Tom himself would become almost the opposite of the King's emancipated mistress, in effect—a ghost that could never leave the Chambers at all. He'd be deprived of his body but not freed from its obligations, trapped forever in the two-room airlock between life and death that the twin Chambers comprised.

While the King would walk free, slipping into the space left empty by Tom's unfinished death.

El Rey had bought a body from his minion rather than a soul. He'd purchased a niche in the realworld with a tawdry currency of toys, travel, and sex—the pursuits Tom had chosen to drown his pain in after his love had been taken away. (And even *that* loss had most likely occurred through the machinations of his King, he realized, much too late).

He was about to pay dearly for those indulgences now. As was everybody else. King Death had been privy to every trick discovered and every truth divined by a thousand generations of sorcerers, and Tom couldn't imagine a greater threat to the worlds than an unbounded, incarnate Mictlantecuhtli. Restraint had never been a part of his patron's nature.

Tom figured the plan also included using the rest of him, the disembodied remainder, to conduct el Rey's brave new endeavors in this unsuspecting world on a full-time basis. The King needed an administrator more capable and effective than old Winston Watt, whose brain was burnt already after a mere two decades of service. Tom's ghost, on the other hand, would be hanging around the office for the rest of forever, fully able to manage Miguel Caradura's affairs with his living employees from there, so his afterlife wasn't even going to be his own. There'd be no post-mortem reunion with Dulcé, or with Ramon, or with anyone else he missed. The physical pain of being torn between life and death might well be with him for an eternity, too, since the King sure as hell wasn't going to bear it.

Tom could still run (like he'd meant to after cutting down the Tree, a plan that now seemed to have been formulated at some irrelevant point in distant antiquity), but if he did so his old friend Ramon's boy Oscar and his yet-to-be-born grandson Juan would be the first to pay the price.

Poor Oscar had yet to look up from his shoes. Tom didn't blame him for the 'betrayal,' such as it was. Their King had been playing a very long game, and they'd all been his unwitting pawns.

When the lift reached the top of the incomplete structure's bare steel skeleton, Tom noticed a small, gray, feral cat that had climbed all the way up here to soak in the view, his lofty ambitions almost a feline equivalent to the King's. Seeing him there gave Tom an idea.

Years ago, when he and Ramon had first come to this place, each of the boys had met his *nagual*, his spirit-animal, so to speak. That particular creature with which he had a special affinity and which might, if asked, guide him across the dreamscapes revealed by vegetal friends like Teonanactl and Mescalito.

Ramon's nagual had been the lizard—cool, thoughtful, and prone to disappearing in a flash.

Tom's had been the mountain lion. The prince of cats who stalked these hills and canyons. He silently asked the brave little birdstalker who was flashing his eyes from the far end of a girder for a very great favor, and received the animal's consent.

Tom sent out his mind and switched places with the cat. He wasn't sure it would work with such a small specimen, one that resembled a lion about as much as a chihuahua did a wolf, but work it did. After a sickening instant of vertigo those reflective green eyes were his, and he was looking back up at his own human body as the catspirit he'd swapped with steered it down the foot-wide girder and toward the Hole in the Sky, holding onto a rope the work crews had strung between the steel supports for balance.

Oscar, following behind it, seemed none the wiser.

Winston Watt was waiting for him, standing inside the first of the two rooms beyond the Hole. The chamber's rough, torchlit adobe walls remained as Tom remembered them from the old days, although brand new carpeting had been laid down over the floor's ancient flagstones. Watt cocked his head at an odd angle and examined with a critical eye the awkward, shuffling progress that Tom's cat-piloted body was making in his direction, but he said nothing about it.

So far so good, Tom thought. This little catbody's vision was so much brighter and sharper than what he was accustomed to that the rising moon seemed to cast almost as much light as a midday sun.

He acknowledged that he'd sold his flesh and bones, and was obligated to send his mortal form through the door between worlds of his own free will. It'd never been stated, however, that he had to be the one driving it at the time. The King was bound by his own rules once he established them, and loopholes in his contracts could be slipped through, if you could find them. Tom had even seen it happen, once or twice before.

As his aged body stepped through the Hole in the Sky for the very last time and stood before the door to the second room, the altar room, where the King waited to receive all souls, he hoped he was about to see it happen again. Through a cat's eyes and from a safe distance, this time around. The familiar skeletal image of Mictlantecuhtli hadn't appeared at the door yet, but Tom trusted that he would, blade in hand, and probably at the very last moment. His patron did have a flair for the dramatic, after all.

His body only needed to take a few more steps.

"Tio Tom!"

*God*dammit, Tom thought. *Feel guilty tomorrow, why don't you?*

"Tio, I'm *sorry*," Oscar wailed. His guilt and anguish were real, and so overwhelming that his voice broke, making him sound for a moment like the boy Tom remembered. "Please forgive me, I didn't have any choice!"

The catspirit walking Tom's body to the door stopped and turned back, unsure.

Just go, Tom thought at it, and thankfully the catspirit did. Without a word to Oscar, as it had no capacity for verbal language.

"Tio, *say* something, at least," Oscar cried, when Tom's body headed straight for the inner sanctum. "Please, don't go through there yet. Please, *wait!*"

The young man lunged after what he thought was still his

father's old friend, trying to catch him by the back of his shirt before he went through Mictlan's one-way door.

Winston Watt, who'd been silent all this time, now charged after Oscar, flailing his arms and screeching madly. Both Oz and the catspirit inside Tom's body whirled around, startled by his manic display.

Tom himself, the part that counted, was in the process of jumping from the borrowed cat and back into his rightful head when a large black mockingbird landed on his furry shoulders. It stabbed painfully at the catbody's neck with its beak, and Tom experienced a sensation that felt like something vital tearing loose from his throat.

Then he was back in his own body, looking out through his own human eyes, but totally unable to speak. He found he had no voice with which to explain himself to Oscar. No words at all to warn off the younger man.

Watt shoved him aside and he staggered back, tumbling through the doorway between the rooms before he could catch himself against the stone jamb. He abandoned his skin with an instant to spare before his now-empty human form fell across the barrier, turning skeletal before it hit the floor. The special flesh Mictlantecuhtli had bargained for was gone. Wasted, just like that.

Amorphous, disembodied Tom rejoined the cat's body even as the vicious mockingbird clawed at its back and sides.

The bird threw its head back and shook it, swallowing, choking down Tom's voice once and for all. A tiny, purplish-white wheel of energy the bird had ripped out of Tom's neck disappeared down its feathered gullet. "What's the matter, Tom?" it squawked, in a grating, inhuman, yet conscious and comprehending voice of its own. "Cat's got no tongue?"

Tom realized it was Watt, Winston Watt, in a nagual form of his own—that of an irritating, sarcastic bird.

Fitting, he thought, before he reared back with a hiss and clawed one of the bird's beady eyes right out of its head.

It shrieked hideously and beat at him with its wings while Oscar, back inside the first room beyond the Hole in the Sky, punched Watt's birdridden body in the face for having pushed what he thought was Tom and not an empty husk into the second chamber. The bird inside Watt's skin screeched and clawed and thrashed at Oscar with unwieldy human arms, and Oscar leaned in to pummel its torso with both fists.

Tom's cat raced down the cold steel girder on nimble paws, bleeding from a dozen punctures and lacerations but still sporting the proper number of eyeballs—which was more than he could say for Winston Watt's animal form. The half-blind bird swooped down after him, keeping its head cocked to one side so that it could see. He sank his claws into Tom's back and plucked him off the beam, letting him loose into empty space.

He fell, thrashing and twisting, with an extended, echoing yowl.

Watt reassumed his human body in time to experience Oscar San Martín kneeing it in the crotch. He slumped, groaning, and crumpled to his knees, clutching at the front of San Martín's stained coverall.

The builder gripped his throat with both strong hands and throttled him, slamming his head back against the brick wall in a steady, bonecracking rhythm.

Tom abandoned his borrowed catform in freefall and caught hold of a mountain lion that was hunting a quarter of a mile away, which was as far as he could reach in the split-second available. He ejected the lion's indigenous tenant from its seat of consciousness an instant before the honored stray's small body smashed against the future building's hard concrete foundation.

The gray cat was dead in a flash.

Tom hoped he'd felt no pain.

Watt, his ears ringing like tuning forks while large black roses bloomed across his field of vision, caught hold of something solidly metallic that was tucked into the back of San Martín's coveralls, at random, as he flailed for his life.

He got his finger into a ring on one side of the metal object and squeezed.

Tom's new wildcat heard the small-caliber shot clearly, even at a distance. He raised its head from the still-twitching fawn it had brought down right before his unscheduled arrival in its brainspace and listened for a second shot, but there was nothing more to hear. Nothing but crickets and the suddenly enticing rustlings of small rodents in the brush. Even more vivid than those were the rich smells of blood and life all around him, which hit these new predator's senses of his like a symphony.

Tom sent himself out again, without letting go of the big cat entirely. He figured he was going to need a safe place to store his soul for a while.

Up in the first room beyond the Hole in the Sky, Winston Watt's vision swam back into focus. The piercing note howling in his ears died away, like someone had turned down the volume on a particularly pointless and obnoxious phonograph recording.

Oscar San Martín lay beside him, gasping like a landed trout as his life's red blood pulsed out from the gash a bullet had torn through the small of his back. There was blood all over the new carpet.

Winston had never even gotten the handgun out from under the man's coverall, but that hadn't stopped it from doing its deadly work, had it? Bang, right through something vital. Oscar was bleeding out fast.

Watt felt a little sick. It could've been due to concussion, he thought. (It never occurred to him that Tom might be lingering nearby, projected out from his new lion, and that he might be catching a ghost of a ghost's reaction.)

The King's Englishman pushed himself into a sitting position, then got to his feet, bracing himself against the wall for balance. He waited for his head to clear, then turned around to face the door that opened onto the next room. The one with the bloodcaked stone altar at its center.

"Mictlantecuhtli?" Watt called into the empty, echoing chamber. "Hello?"

On the floor behind him, Oscar San Martín breathed his last. His chest rattled when his lungs settled and then failed to reinflate.

In the next instant his coverall-clad bones materialized from a wisp of smoke right before Winston's eyes, on the other side of the doorway, while his inert flesh lay cooling in the outer office.

"The King's not in right now," San Martín's skeleton informed

Watt, reaching out and slipping a bony hand around the back of his neck to yank him face-first through the doorway. "Why don't you come inside and wait?"

Winston shouted and staggered forward, pulled off balance by a man he'd just killed, then toppled gracelessly into the realm of Mictlan. His living flesh sloughed away from his bones like so much fine, dry dust when he pitched across the threshold.

He'd never walk the realworld again, he knew, save possibly for one weird weekend each year, and only then with the express permission of his King... except that boon was almost never granted, was it?

Winston pounded the stone floor with his unfleshed fist. He wanted to cry, but there wasn't enough moisture left in his bones to form tears. Tom Delgado's abandoned, unmanned skeleton lay motionless on the floor beside him. It was nothing but a worthless relic now, already disarticulating, softening and collapsing in on itself. Soon it would break down completely, with nothing inside to maintain its integrity.

When Winston looked up Mictlantecuhtli was there, standing beside San Martín's skeleton at the altar and staring down in disappointment from out of the shadows that pooled under his heavy gray cowl.

T om left them as soon as he felt the presence of the King, drawing his thoughts back into his new feline head. He'd come close enough to the Hole in the Sky to see for himself what had taken place, even though he had too clear an idea already. Winston Watt was dead, as he'd hoped would be the case after hearing the gunshot, but then so was Oscar. His boy Juan would have to grow up without a father, now. There was little enough that Tom could do about it, though. Not with his body ruined and his delicate arrangement with the King in disarray. Death had been denied, and that meant it was no longer safe for Tom to hang around this place. Mictlantecuhtli would know he'd tried to cheat, to breach their contract, and that meant he had no patron anymore.

He'd been lucky to catch the mountain lion that was currently the only thing anchoring him to the living world. Having a form to cling to meant that Death wouldn't be able to claim his ghost, despite owning his bones. He wouldn't be able to stay in a cat forever, obviously, but at least he'd bought himself a little time to try and think of another option. He was sure he'd have an idea before too many hours or days had passed.

The former necromancer turned and ran up into the hills with his commandeered catamount, into the wild and away from the comforts of civilization, putting as much physical distance between himself and the King's Chambers as he possibly could.

Part Five: El Dia de los Muertos
(The Day of the Dead)

Chapter Thirty-Seven

A century later...

Black Tom, still trapped out amidst the hibiscus blooms where Ingrid had evoked and bound him earlier in the afternoon, watched as the tattooed man who'd been spying on her padded silently out of the greenery.

He circled around Tom's invisible enclosure, looking him over slowly and thoroughly. Tom did likewise. His examiner's hair was shaved down to a shadow, and his dark jeans and sweatshirt were each voluminous enough to conceal multiple weapons. He had a greenish-black teardrop inked under the outside corner of his left eye. His sunglasses' thick frames didn't quite cover it up.

"You Tomas Delgado, ain't you?" the gangbanger said. "I get it—del Gato. That's cute, esé. That's real clever."

He got close and looked Tom in the eyes. Through his shades, of course. They were each wearing their own set of impenetrably dark lenses.

"You recognize me, then, esé?" the gangster asked. "You remember me, Tommy del Gato, mister black magic man? Huh? Do you?"

Black Tom shook his head.

Winston pulled off his disguise. His fleshmask, 'Xavier's' secondhand face. "Perhaps this helps to refresh your memory, Tom?" the skeleton underneath asked in his familiar, dry British accent.

Tom felt his eyes go wide behind his glasses. He beat and scrabbled at the walls of his invisible cell in a way that made

Winston's uncovered skull seem to grin. He knew by now that he couldn't get out, but he was unable to keep from trying again anyway. Like a wild animal caught in a trap.

"Ahh, yes, there we are," the skeleton on a two-day furlough said. "I didn't think you'd forget me so soon. You must have known that *someone* would have to fill the position you were groomed for when you opted to breach Mictlantecuhtli's contract." He leaned in and said, ominously: "Do you know how *long* time feels in Mictlan, Tom? How many millennia of servitude I've already endured? Because *you* opted to ditch *your* freely assumed obligations?"

Winston stepped back and slipped his face on. He covered his empty sockets with his shades and grinned Xavier's vicious grin at Black Tom.

"Hardface be comin,' esé," Winston said, dropping back into his character's voice. "An' he is gonna mess you *up*. If not him, then me. Count on it."

Chapter Thirty-Eight

Lia blasted back toward North Hollywood in Dexter's sleek BMW at wildly excessive speeds, cutting in and out of traffic as she shot up Laurel Canyon Boulevard and accelerating through yellow lights at Ventura, at Moorpark, and then again at Riverside in the last nanoseconds before they changed over to red, eliciting honks and shouted curses from the disgruntled left-turners she darted past.

She'd never driven so fast in her life.

Eventually, perhaps inevitably, Lia blew past a motorcycle cop's speedtrap while rocketing east on Sherman Way. Blue and red lights burst like a fireworks display in her rearview mirror and a siren chirped, making her jump in her seat and yelp in startled response. She pulled over into a Home Depot parking lot, feeling sick.

The officer who'd snagged her removed his helmet and left it on the seat of his hulking motorbike before hitching up his gun belt and approaching. He didn't bother to take off his silver, aviator-style shades.

"License and registration please, ma'am," the cop said, when Lia rolled down her window to speak with him.

"I... I don't have them with me," she said, only then realizing that she really didn't. Her purse was down in her hobbit hole. She could see her own dismay reflected twice in the officer's shiny lenses.

"I'm gonna ask you to step out of the vehicle then, ma'am, and turn around and put your hands on the side of it."

Lia had little choice but to comply. The motorcycle cop (who was tall and young and under better circumstances might've been somewhat attractive) frisked her efficiently.

"I just forgot my purse this morning, officer, is all, I really don't think—"

"Ma'am, this vehicle was reported stolen yesterday afternoon, so unless you can produce some ID and a good explanation, I'm gonna have to ask you to put your hands behind your back."

Lia did as she was told, and the cuffs closed around her wrists with two decisive clicks. A few do-it-yourself shoppers watched the sorry drama from beside their parked SUVs, but all of the day laborers gathered around the hardware store had scattered when *la policia* arrived.

Shitballs, Lia thought.

She was fucked and she knew it.

The tall cop guided her to a seat on a concrete block at the front of a parking spot. She was cuffed tight. Black Tom could've let her loose in an eyeblink, but he wasn't available right now.

The officer paused to jot down some notes. Lia noticed a small black tattoo in the shape of a dog on the back of his left hand when he flipped open his notebook.

She felt a small kindling of hope.

"Hey. Blackdog," she said.

The cop slowly turned his head. "What did you say?"

"Your tattoo," Lia said. "You're a Blackdog."

"And what would you know about that?"

"Before you call this in or whatever," Lia begged, "will you do me one favor? Will you call Frank Chudabala for me? Captain Chudabala? Please?"

"And what would you want me to tell him?" the cop asked.

"Tell him Lia la brujachica needs the Blackdogs," she said. "Tell him I've fallen down a well."

The young patrolman didn't stop frowning, but he did pull a personal cellphone out of his pocket and dialed it, never once taking his mirror-covered eyes off of Lia.

Chapter Thirty-Nine

Ingrid Redstone stood in the door of the Yard's ancient office shack, leafing through a dog-eared paperback copy of *The Portable Dorothy Parker* she always carried in her purse and waiting as the day grew long. Her gangsters hung around their cars out in the gravel parking lot, most of them smoking nasty, chemical-scented, factory-rolled cigarettes. A bit of a surprise, that was, really. At least to Ingrid. It'd seemed to her that people didn't do that so much anymore, in this baffling new madhouse of an era.

The twenty-first century had been on for over a decade already, if you could believe it. The fateful events of 1950 seemed like they'd happened a few short months ago (which, for Ingrid, they sort of had).

The important thing was that Dexter was really back, in this time and place, after sixty years in the dirt.

Ingrid was quietly awed by the idea. He wouldn't be quite *alive* again, yet, but he was above ground at least. Walking the earth. Hearing his voice over the wireless telephone had finally made it real for her.

She'd been sure (well, pretty sure) that he wouldn't die all the way when she shot him in the head so far back along this new timeline. Dexter was different, due in part to the feelings she had for him and the protective net of hexwork she'd once wrapped him up in, quite without his knowledge. He was special. She'd gambled that Mictlan would have no authority to draw him in if and when he 'died' in the realworld. She'd bet that he, his soul or whatever, would stay with his bones for as long as they lasted. The only way Dexter Graves would ever cross the threshold between the rooms was by agreement, as an act of his own free will.

It was good to see her theory finally borne out. The stakes on that wager had been so very high, and they remained so now, really. Her whole plan could still go wrong in any number of ways.

Ingrid had many regrets when it came to Dexter, not the least of which was that she'd never been able to tell him the truth about herself. She'd never gotten to know him as well as she might've liked. It had simply been too dangerous. She hadn't dared to let him meet the King—not when he might've taken Mickey up on the offer she knew he intended to make. Dexter had still been raw from the experience of war as of the winter's day in 1950 on which he'd expired. Physically healed from his wounds, yes, but still ungrounded, adrift and in need of an emotional reconstruction he had no idea how to perform. The escape from remorse the King would've promised might have sounded all too enticing to a man in that precarious frame of mind. A man with little to nothing anchoring him to the ongoing life of his world.

Shooting him had been easier than facing the consequences, ultimately.

But Mickey found out about him anyway, of course. Mickey's influence in this world was limited, to say the least, but even so, he had his spies everywhere.

If she'd just run away when she first realized that the cons outweighed the pros when it came to being Mickey's Queen, if she'd just left the city and put as much distance between herself and the building Mickey'd erected for her as she possibly could... then none of this would've happened.

But she'd exited the otherworld into 1950 instead, and that hadn't been enough distance in either time or space. Mickey's Tzitzimime tracked her easily across the years and he sent a new man (a big fellow called Juan, the son of architect Oscar San Martín in fact) to fetch her back to him. She might've done better if she'd just stayed when she was and put more miles between them, like maybe the span of a continent or an ocean.

Now Dexter was yet another pawn in her long chess game with Death.

That Mickey'd been willing to make a deal at all, that he'd given her this chance to find an understudy for her role in this production, was an indication of how desperately he coveted what Dexter and Lia, together, might be able to do for him.

Her King was only diplomatic when he absolutely had to be.

Still, Ingrid's upper hand could only be played for so much advantage here. Turning up another operator like herself—an initiate of the eternal cycles of generation and decay, one thoroughly schooled in the mysteries of the tripartite plane of being—had proved difficult enough that Mickey'd missed out on the entire twentieth century while Ingrid searched, and questioned people, and tracked down leads across any number of decades. All he had were the tales and memories that trickled into Mictlan along with the dead, and he was *pissed* about what he heard. He mourned Studio 54, and bemoaned his missed opportunity to attend a thing called 'Woodstock.' Burning Man was still on his agenda, even though he'd heard by 'now' that it was becoming too commercial.

Commitment to a timeline was a new and frustrating experience for the King.

Witches of Ingrid's caliber were rare and independent creatures, though, clever and wary of those who sought them out. Not easy to track down, and less so to set up. Ingrid had taken a good long while to find Mickey his girl. She'd been sure to. She bought time by obfuscating the issue and doing what she could to cover her tracks, but her King's patience was far from endless. She'd finally had to deliver her discovery, Lia Flores, little Camellia Flower herself, here in the second decade of the mindbendingly distant twenty-first century.

That Dexter Graves was up and ambulatory was proof that the first phase of her operation had succeeded. Lia *had* picked up that lighter, the link to Dexter, despite her protestations to the contrary. Her touch had sparked Ingrid's long-dormant hex to life, and Dexter's bones along with it. Lia's abilities must have been the full equivalent of Ingrid's own, or else the enchanted symbol would not have awakened for her. Had Ingrid ever returned for the lighter herself during the intervening sixty years, she would've been right back on Mickey's hook.

She sighed, thinking about it.

She couldn't help but identify with Lia, this young operator she'd uncovered, and she didn't want to see her hurt, above all things. Lia's basic affinities seemed to be vegetal rather than mineral, like Ingrid's own, but they still had an amazing amount in common.

That knowledge made her wistful. Equals in her field had, in Ingrid's experience, been few and far between. It took a fortitude few possessed to live full-time in the actual, when the real was the only world most people would let themselves believe in. The otherworld could be scary, since it was but partially mapped and minimally understood. Daunting as it was, though, most folks at least acknowledged its existence as a metaphor or a frivolous fantasyscape, if nothing more.

The actual, though... hidden in that subtle distinction was the witches' world, the liminal tract of headspace wherein events deemed impossible or untenable by the standards of the realworld might nonetheless occasionally occur, to be remembered, contemplated, and learned from, by those who dared.

Ingrid had good reason to believe Lia knew that territory as well as she did. She'd sensed it from the moment they first corresponded, through the mediation of an entity called Craig who kept lists of the messages posted to the incredible public internetwork. Ingrid imagined he needed a staff of thousands. The planet's new invisible information-sharing web seemed to her like nothing less than a man-made astral plane, one summoned up with secret words and viewed through flat black scrying-screens, very much in the classical tradition. The greatest of medieval sorcerers would've killed to possess even the cheapest example of the computation machines that made it all possible, and today they were used by everyone, including children.

Ingrid shook her head. So much had changed, and yet a lot remained the same.

Her old familiar loneliness felt like an ache in her chest today. She longed to be able to talk with Lia about any of these things. Ingrid's modern-day counterpart was sure to be versed in concepts and cosmologies similar to the ones she employed.

What a relationship they could've—and *should've*—had.

She truly did hate manipulating the girl, but it had to be done, for now, in the name of manipulating Mickey.

If only she'd never found her way out to that goddamned Tree...

But no, Ingrid thought, she didn't really feel that way, not even now. She didn't regret her long-ago choice of the left-hand path. Only one particular betrayal by Mickey had ever brought her close to sentiments like that.

She couldn't imagine renouncing the wonders she'd seen as a result of that choice, including this, the incredible opening of a brand new era, a full hundred years beyond her time. Ingrid was a true innovator in her ancient art, the first human being ever to time-hop like the imaginals did, and that privilege was a direct result of her relationship with Mictlantecuhtli.

Ingrid fingered the large garnet she wore on a silver chain around her neck. A dark red stone on a thin tether of shiny white moon-metal. It was the only thing that let her find her way back to herself from the unfamiliar ages she visited. Timehopping required that she use her true name, all the time, even in her own head and when it was inconvenient, or else risk losing her identity through the subtle split that existed between the other and the actual worlds. You had to know exactly who you were if you wanted to step across a seam like that. The gem that symbolized her to herself was *it*self an imaginal artifact, a thing from the otherworld, a gift from the figment of myth that now called itself Miguel Caradura, after her own suggestion.

His patronage had been her ticket to the initiatory level beyond the poetry and semiotic mindgames of the Hermetic Order of the Golden Dawn, where Ingrid began her occult career. In London, this had been, around the turn of the previous century. Though she'd been born in San Francisco she'd spent her early twenties trying to make a name on the West End stage... or so she'd told herself, even at the time. What she'd really done was earn her keep as a box jumper, a stage magician's lovely assistant (easy work for one sexy enough to get it), and then spent the bulk of her time attending the parties and pub-crawls of the theatrical set. That had led her to the alluring, exotic and slightly dangerous Golden Dawn (where she befriended a young painter from Jamaica named Pixie Smith, whose Tarot deck was still in print and popular today, and enjoyed several secret assignations with the poet William Butler Yeats, initiates of the mystic Order both).

It was through such acquaintances that she first heard the tales of a Hole in the Sky situated above a tree that grew back home, in distant California. She'd crossed an ocean to hear a local legend, ironically.

She followed one of the very earliest film production companies back to Los Angeles in 1908, blazing a trail that uncounted numbers of the world's pretty people had apparently followed after her. A dear old friend from the Alcazar Theater Company in San Francisco (of which both her parents had been a part), directed the first movie ever to be filmed entirely in Los Angeles. He'd shot it in the drying yard of a downtown Chinese laundry, and in it Ingrid played an heiress who marries a gambler who does a good deed. She'd found similar trophy-women reiterated in the films of every decade since, and she had to smile every time she saw the well-earned love of a special girl held up as a symbol of healing and redemption. Even though the motif had been a staple of vaudeville too and probably went back to the goddamn Greeks, she still felt like she'd started something.

It amused her to recall how intimidated she'd been by the bulky, hand-cranked wooden camera with its single unblinking glass eye, so different from today's 'digital' devices, which fit into the palm of a hand and yet shot both in color and with sound. The newfangled apparatus of 1908 had struck her as menacing and judgmental, whereas a live audience, at least during a good performance, always felt receptive and warm. People's applause was like an embrace. The camera, however, claimed far more than an audience did, and it gave next to nothing back to the performer. Ingrid had known enough by then about the nature of images and signifiers that she hadn't dared to let the contraption possess her true name, fearing the obsessive pull the thing exerted. Instead, she substituted the slightly awkward pseudonym 'Silent Tower.'

The stage name was an in-joke between herself and the film's director, Francis Boggs, who'd also been her first and only vocal coach a dozen years before. Ingrid had stood 5'10 by the time she was twelve years old, and was painfully, awkwardly shy—until she learned to sing on stage. The Silent Tower had been Uncle Frank's nickname for her, an affectionate nudge to coax her out of her shell, and Ingrid knew he'd been touched when she chose to immortalize it in the credits of his movie.

Well, semi-immortalize, anyway, as only a handful of her

friend's two hundred or so single-reelers seemed to have survived the century, despite his pioneering efforts in the world of filmmaking (as Mictlantecuhtli had once warned her would be the case). To the best of Ingrid's knowledge her piece, entitled *The Heart of a Race Tout,* was not among the survivals. Her source on that, however, was again the modern-day 'internets,' and it had to be said that the information they turned up often seemed somewhat fragmentary and vague. 'Googling' herself had proved neither as pleasurable nor as revelatory as she might've expected.

Appearing in that one early flicker show was the only acting she ever got to do in Los Angeles, but that didn't matter to her, much. It was fun, but it wasn't what she'd really come for. There was magic in the movies, certainly, but by then she'd needed more stimulation than shadow, light, and make-believe were able to provide.

Instead of pursuing theatrical ambitions, she talked her way into the Golden Dawn's sister organization here in Los Angeles: the Ordo Aurea Catena, or the Order of the Golden Chain. Their attitude had proved rapacious, however, their rituals staid and uncreative. Ingrid stayed with them only until she managed to goad one of their initiates into showing her a map drawn and sold to the association years before by a penniless independent named Ramon San Martín, a jealously-guarded map that showed the infamous SkyHole's secret location…

Her education had mostly been her own affair, after that.

Hers, and Mickey's.

The King was an experience like no other at first. His attention was exhilarating, his company exciting, the physical presence he put on for her erotic and enticing, modeled as it was after her own personal aesthetic ideals.

It was the subtle changes wrought in her by the practice of her art, she believed (the alignment with the earth's secret graces that such work engenders, especially in a woman who starts young) that imbued her with the rare ability to cross back and forth between the King's Chambers, and that made her tantalizing to Mickey, captivating and bewitching, at least as much as he was to her.

She was a unique creature according to him, a nonpareil, completely free to walk the worlds, and she'd fast become the favorite amongst his handful of human servants. Really she'd been more like a protégé. Together they'd made of her an unassailable independent operator in an age when magical practice was dominated by rigid and phallocentric orders with classical pretensions. It was a rather unusual accomplishment. Ingrid felt daring and dangerous simply for knowing King Death, while his lusts for her, his fascination with her living flesh, had known no satiety.

She might've guessed at the ways in which their relationship would get out of hand, but at the time she'd been too willing a beneficiary of the King's largess to bother with things like worrying about the future or planning ahead. Her magical ambitions had grown to quite an unsupportable size by then. She'd actually imagined she could rewrite the ancient inequities of the realworld from the absurd office building she talked Mickey into erecting around the Hole in the Sky, almost by accident.

That place was her own Silent Tower, a crazy brick-and-mortar monument to her dreams. The King had altered the pasts of certain of his human servants in order to produce a man capable of putting up the structure and then charged him with the task, merely as a demonstration of his transworld influence and generative prowess. The Tree was gone and the building was up, almost before she challenged Mictlantecuhtli to prove himself. Workmen arrived on-site at the literal instant in which Ingrid joked that a smart new skyscraper might be better suited to the sensibilities of her twentieth-century world than was some root-rotted old mistletoe factory.

It was how she first learned about Mictlan's special relationship with human time. The King might almost as easily have remodeled a much larger chunk of architectural and social history in order to make the building appear in a complete, fully-realized form as soon as she imagined it, but thankfully, he hadn't yet learned to think that big.

Not then, anyway.

Mickey, who aped every trait of hers that fascinated him, especially her passions for creation, novelty, and change, soon enough seized upon the example of her aspirations to begin laying schemes of his own, on his side of the barrier. He conquered and claimed foreign mythological ground in the name of his kingdom, taking over moribund animist pantheons by the score and rearranging a large swath of the otherworld according to his own lights in the process. You couldn't put an idea in his head that he wouldn't extrapolate to the furthest degree. Before long, he even had designs on those unwieldy monotheisms that still dominate so much of humanity's imaginal space.

Otherworld victories weren't what he really coveted anymore, of course, but for quite a while Ingrid's native reality remained, for the King, just tantalizingly out of reach. The barrier between worlds held firm, even as she foolishly plotted to help the relentless monarchetype transcend his limitations, in the belief that her own power could only increase with his.

That it'd all seemed romantic and magical rather than mad at the time was all she could say about it now.

Then Mickey went and surprised her in a way that changed the terms of their relationship forever.

Ingrid sighed again, reflecting on the unprecedented turns her life had taken.

She'd tried her best to right her King's wrongs, and she was trying still. If Dex and his dirtgirl would now get their asses back *out here*, before night fell, then maybe the three of them together would still have a chance to turn this thing around, before it ended badly for everyone but Mickey.

Chapter Forty

A hoodie-shrouded homeless man pushed a woman wearing a fedora down a Studio City side street in a rattling, clanking shopping cart. Other pedestrians ignored them with a zeal that rendered them effectively invisible. Lia herself might not have recognized them as Hannah Potter and Dexter Graves.

"I seem to recall Miss Lia sayin' something about us takin' a cab...?" Graves said ruefully. He was in the process of discovering that his reanimated bones could still ache like a bastard when he'd been on his feet for a while. It was going to be a long walk back to North Hollywood.

"Yeah, well, I didn't bring my purse, or my phone, or anything," Hannah said. "I didn't expect to be leaving the way we did."

"And I didn't guess we'd get dumped off at the top of Mulholland Drive."

They rumbled past a pair of very old men playing chess out in front of a rundown nursing home, a few blocks north of Ventura. One of the players was very big, as well as very old. Large enough that sheer size must have been his defining feature for his entire life.

Graves stopped the cart and came back after a moment, to have another look at the big fella, but Big Fella wouldn't look up from the chessboard.

"Hey," Graves said, after a moment of silence. "Your name's Juan, ain't it? Juan San Martín?"

Big Juan kept his eyes on the chessgame. "Not if you're a cop or a process server, it ain't."

"Nah, nothin' like that," Graves said. "This is strictly

personal."

Big Juan looked up, and Graves pushed back his filthy hood, revealing the bullet-cratered bone beneath. "If I recall," he said, "you were the only schmuck that showed up at my funeral."

Big Juan leapt to his feet, upsetting the chessboard, and booked it (as fast as a fat nonagenarian dragging an oxygen tank could, anyway), shuffling off down a nearby alley.

Hannah hopped out of the shopping cart and was after him in a wincing, relative flash, limping along in deference to her bullet-grooved side, but Graves and the second old guy who'd been playing chess had seen one another by then, and for them, time had all but stopped.

The antique looked up like he was seeing a ghost. He wore a stiff Navy baseball cap with the insignia of the *USS Jubal A. Early* embroidered across the crown.

"Dex?" he said, squinting like he expected his vision to resolve into something he could process. "Dexter Graves? Can that really be you?"

"Holy shit," Graves said. "It's Charlie Lurp! Brother, you got *ancient.*"

"Dex, am I dyin'?" Charlie looked like he really needed to know. "Is this what happens? Old friends come back to meetcha?"

"I don't think so, Charlie old pal. At least not today," Graves said. "I got special dispensation, is all."

"Last time we talked was when I helped my buddy Dave track you down," Charlie said. "You disappeared right after that."

"Yeah, well, I woulda phoned… but you know how it is." Graves tapped his exit wound and Charlie nodded as if he did indeed know how it was to be shot in the brainpan and buried for sixty years.

Graves threw off the hooded sweatshirt he'd scrounged from the same roadside gutter in which they found the shopping cart he'd been pushing Hannah along in since her feet had started to blister during their downhill trek. He shrugged back into his long coat and headed down the alley, feeling little need to hurry after Hannah's low-speed pursuit of Big Juan. Graves kept pace with Charlie, who followed with the aid of a walker, bumping along step by step. The thing had slit-open tennis balls crammed onto its feet, for some reason.

"Big Juannie wasn't the one that done that to you, was he, Dex?" Charlie asked, pointing up at the exit hole in Graves' forehead. "Wouldn't put it past him—the asshole cheats at chess. Poker too."

"Nah," Graves said. "But he used to work for the guy that had it done. And he *did* dump me in a hole, way out in the desert."

"That dirty son of a bitch," Charlie said.

They came upon Hannah, who was crouched over the prone and wheezing form of Big Juan, way down at the litter-strewn end of the alley. So that was that. Chase over. It hadn't been much of a horserace.

Hannah looked over her shoulder as first Graves and then Charlie stepped up behind her. Graves took his hat off her head and settled it back onto his own. Then he leaned over Big Juan, getting right down into the old henchman's face.

"I need some intel before you shuffle off there, big fella," he said. "You worked for Hardface once. You know his ways. Spill what you know about his fetish for earthy girls, and maybe I won't come after you on the other side."

Chapter Forty-One

Lia's handcuffs came off less than fifteen minutes later, and the young officer's attitude had changed markedly by the time they did.

"Guess the Captain thinks pretty highly of you, Miss Brujachica," he said, using the Spanish description like a surname. "Says you've consulted on SWAT operations before?"

"Remote viewing, yeah," Lia said. "Looking into places people needed to go. I've also helped on a forensic case or two."

"Well," the young cop said, "the Cap pulled me and three other units off our assignments and says we're to help you. Blackdog guys all. So it looks like you're getting a police escort. I'm Ben, by the way, Ben Leonard."

"Lia Flores." She shook his proffered hand and considered him, feeling curious. "So, Ben Leonard, were you really there?" she asked. "The Night of the Blackdogs? I've heard the stories for years."

Ben Leonard nodded. "A thousand black ghost dogs," he said, "all barking in unison, all at once, witnessed by dozens of cops from a dozen divisions, warning us off from a building that collapsed not three hours after. It was like nothing I ever knew could be. Changed me, frankly. Changed every guy who saw it. Showed us all a wider world."

"Sure you didn't eat some funny mushrooms earlier that evening?" Lia kidded.

"*No*, I didn't," Ben said, "and why does everyone I ever tell ask me that? No, I was sober and lucid and in my right mind. We all were." He looked Lia over in his turn, as curious about her as she was about him. "So," he said. "You're, like, an 'independent operator'?"

Lia nodded.

"More of you on the street than there used to be," Ben said thoughtfully, re-appraising her. "Guess I never met an actual witch before, though. A real one who can do things, I mean. Most of the ones I've run across were sort of pretending."

"No warts, no broom, no pointy hat," Lia said. "Hope I don't disappoint."

Ben smiled. "I wouldn't say that, exactly."

Three LAPD cruisers pulled around the corner and into the Home Depot parking lot, and Ben raised a hand to their drivers in greeting. Then he turned back to Lia.

"Your motorcade awaits," he said. "Let's leave that stolen thing for somebody else to deal with. You can ride in one of the cruisers... or I guess you can ride with me. If you like. I don't think the Captain expects normal regulations to apply."

Lia thought about it, then broke into a grin.

She was still grinning some minutes later, gleefully, under a helmet and perched on the back of Ben's motorcycle while it and the three cruisers flew up Vineland at an insane rate of speed, flashing lights, blaring sirens, and parting traffic like a blade.

Chapter Forty-Two

Graves got Big Juan sitting up and propped him against a discarded, cushionless sofa some slob had dumped in the alley. Within minutes, the fat man was breathing better.

Graves paced while he interrogated, his bony feet crunching over dead leaves and bits of broken glass. Hannah and Charlie Lurp looked on.

"This world is what he wants," Big Juan said, in answer to the walking skeleton's most fundamental question. "Mictlantecuhtli. He's obsessed with it. They all are, over there. In love with the flesh. You said 'fetish' an' you were sorta kidding, but that's really what it's like. They envy every moment of our stupid little lives."

"Daylight's burnin'," Graves said. "Cut to the part about the girls."

"You mean Ingrid, don't you? Ingrid Redstone, that singer shot you in the back of the head?"

"You're a quick study, you are."

"Way it got explained to me, she was gonna be Mictlantecuhtli's Queen," Big Juan said. "It was a deal they made: she was gonna give up her life so he could have one. Mictlantecuhtli needed someone with her kinda skills an' her connection to the earth to break all the way through the wall between worlds an' take over an incarnation. Guess that'd be where *you* come in."

"Why me?" Graves asked.

Big Juan shrugged. "I dunno. Why not, I guess? But that Ingrid, she got cold feet. She couldn't do it to you, even though it woulda ended with her becoming Queen of all Mictlan. She stopped you goin' in to talk to Hardface the only way she thought she could."

Graves was troubled by this interpretation. "What'd Hardface have to say about it?" he asked.

"I dunno about that either, man," Big Juan said. "That was it for me, I planted you for Caradura an' I was out. Stopped operating altogether. El Rey shut his place down afterwards, after you died, so I got a real job an' had a different life. Learned to bake, opened a shop, sold cakes and donuts for near forty years."

"Never even occurred to me you might still be alive," Graves said.

"Well, me neither, tell you the truth, but I'm scheduled to hit the century mark next summer," Juan said, nodding. "Willard Scott's supposed to say happy birthday on the TV, an' all that shit."

"Runnin' across you here was pure dumb luck," Graves said, speaking less to Big Juan than chasing down his own train of thought. He looked to Hannah, and then to Charlie. "What're the odds of something like this happening, d'you think? All of us being here at the right time and place?"

"I think it's what Lia means when she talks about 'synchronicity,'" Hannah said quietly. "The past and the present harmonizing. Maybe the future, too."

"Yeah, that's how these things like to work," Big Juan confirmed. "Like maybe it couldnta happened any other way. You get used to it after you been operating for a while."

Graves and Hannah and Charlie Lurp all looked back down at him.

"I do know one more thing," Juan wheezed. "El Rey didn't kill that Ingrid to bind her in Mictlan. He wanted that project to work, an' I guess he still needed a witch."

Hannah looked to Graves. "Like Lia," she murmured.

"Must not've panned out for 'em, though," Big Juan said.

"Why do you say?" Graves asked.

"Because the world's still the world, amigo," Big Juan replied. "I can't imagine it would be if Mictlantecuhtli had got out into it."

Graves nodded and extended a hand. He, Hannah and Charlie pitched in to haul Big Juan to his feet, Iwo Jima style. "All right," Graves said, once the giant was upright again. "I'm calling us square. Go on livin' out the rest of your different life, Big Juan."

"Thank you," he said. "Gracias. I was sorry about what

happened to you, man. You coulda killed me that day, but you didn't. I remember that. And I know you were only there to save that lady. I wouldnta chose to see it work out like it did."

"Guess I appreciate that, for what it's worth." Graves nodded and looked to Charlie. "Charlie, you wouldn't happen to have a car, wouldja?"

"Not no more, but I know where there's one you can use."

"Dexter?" Hannah said. "What are you gonna do?"

It seemed like it was becoming a standard refrain.

"I'm thinkin' it's time I paid this Hardface a visit," Graves growled. "Look him square in the sockets and see what sort of personification he is."

Graves and Hannah waited in the small staff parking lot behind the nursing home while Charlie Lurp and Big Juan San Martín shuffled around to the front of it. Juan needed to refresh his tiny oxygen tank. Charlie returned alone after less than ten minutes, slipping surreptitiously out a back door that banged shut anyhow when he turned to rest his weight on his walker. Graves and Hannah hurried over. Charlie thumped the hood of another fancy modern car (a Jaguar, this time) that was parked in a spot with a sign reading 'RESERVED FOR DR. WALSH.'

"Doc locks hisself up in his office to look at that internet porn and sample the pharmaceuticals on most afternoons, but he leaves his keys in his jacket on the coat rack," Charlie said, holding up a jingling ring on a leather tab embossed with the Jaguar logo. "So this ain't gonna be missed for at least a couple of hours."

"Ahh, thank you there, Charlie old pal," Graves said, accepting the stolen keys from the wobbly old man. Back in the war, Charlie'd had a knack for acquiring whatever a guy might happen to need, from a bottle of whisky or an extra carton of cigarettes on up to a jeep or a box of grenades. Graves was glad to know he was still getting up to his old tricks. "If I get through this I'm comin' back here," he promised. "We'll play a game of chess ourselves."

"Just like that weird old movie," Charlie grinned. "I'd like that, Dex, I really would."

They shook hands, holding them clasped together for a long and meaningful moment. Charlie's frail bones were almost as prominent as Graves' own. Then they broke contact, and the skeleton got into the new car with Hannah.

Graves saluted his old (now elderly) friend and Hannah waved as he backed them out of Dr. Walsh's parking spot and pulled onto the street, heading east down Ventura, in the direction of the Cahuenga Pass. Charlie Lurp shambled out to the sidewalk and watched them go, with his withered chest puffed up and pride shining in his eyes. Graves glanced up to see him receding in the rearview mirror.

It didn't take them long to get over the hill and down into the streets of Hollywood, now that they had wheels. Even after sixty years Graves was able to find the old Silent Tower, the Office of the King, without too much circling around. Today it looked derelict: besmirched by graffiti, with many of its windows broken out and covered over with plywood. It had been in good repair and apparently a part of the regular world, the last time he saw it.

Now it looked like the world had passed it by.

Graves still didn't know why Ingrid had chosen to involve him in any of this (him of all people, involved so deep that he'd crawled back out of his grave to play his part), but he figured he'd come to the one place in all the worlds where he might be able to pose that question and actually demand an answer.

He and Hannah got out of their stolen Jaguar. Graves held out the keys. "Here, take the unauthorized requisition back to where we got it before old Charlie gets in trouble, willya?"

"Forget it, Dexter," Hannah said flatly.

"Miss Lia'll kill me if I let anything happen to you," Graves said, laying it out there with no further pretense.

"That Ingrid person apparently beat her to it, so what are you afraid of?"

Graves looked up at the old, ill-maintained building. "Last time I walked in there, I didn't walk back out," he said. "I'm not ready to see that happen to you."

"Then we'll make sure it doesn't," Hannah said. "But you can't ask me to stand by when Lia's in trouble and there might be something I can do. Isn't that why we came here? To see if we can help without getting close to Ingrid? If you're going in there, Dexter, then I am too."

Her mind was made up and she would not be dissuaded. That much was abundantly clear.

Graves loved her for it.

"Mrs. Potter, for a lady, you've sure got some balls," he said. "Brass ones, if that ain't too crude."

"Mr. Graves, it's the sweetest of compliments, coming from you."

Graves nodded and kicked the building's front door open almost casually, the same as last time. Then he and Hannah strode on in together.

As they entered the broken-down lobby, through those old double-doors that still hung askew after Graves' long-ago fight with Big Juan, the lights came on and the foyer restored itself to greet them.

Hannah seemed quietly awed by the special effects. Graves refused to be impressed.

A pristine elevator car descended into the gaping shaft and the bell dinged. They got in when the doors opened.

"This floor: notions, housewares, and self-repairing lightbulbs," Graves said in a mocking, nasal voice. The elevator doors slid closed and the car started to rise. "Next floor," he continued, "Aztec hell. And we're up, up and away…"

Chapter Forty-Three

Ingrid came to attention at the sound of an engine just outside the fence, and she set aside the book she hadn't really been reading.

Some distance away, Mickey's man 'Xavier' readied himself as well. She saw him from the corner of her eye.

A small, metal cylinder came sailing over the fence to land in the middle of the parking lot. All of the gangsters looked at it quizzically. Only Ingrid caught on in time to turn away and cover her ears before the police flash-bang grenade went off as advertised. (She didn't know what in hell the device *was*, not by any contemporary name, although the intention behind it seemed plain enough.)

Stunned gangsters fumbled with guns and scrambled for cover while a coordinated team of six LAPD officers poured into the lot, wearing riot helmets with protective visors and carrying clear plastic shields. They took out three of Hardface's hired men straightaway with handheld devices that delivered an electrical jolt, and then cuffed them.

The unit's apparent leader downed that idiot 'Top Shelf' with a nonchalant punch to the face as he and Lia strode into the Yard, right behind the initial wave of cops.

Xavier ran for it, Ingrid saw, vanishing into the thick cover provided by the Yard's vegetation, as did the dozen or so other gangbangers still at large.

The cops gave chase.

"That one, Ben," Lia said, spotting Ingrid and pointing her out from across the parking lot. "Over there."

Oh, for fuck's sake! Ingrid thought. She spat and made a hex sign in the air before turning to flee, wondering how in the *hell* Lia had managed this.

Lia looked on as Ben Leonard drew his weapon, trained it on Ingrid Redstone's leg—and then realized that the .9mm in his hand had somehow turned into nothing more than a red plastic water pistol. A toy. No cop was armed with anything else, to their very great dismay. Lia saw it as clearly as they did. The guns might still have worked if they'd tried them (Ingrid's trick must've been perceptual, Lia figured, hypnotic, something easier to accomplish than an act of physical transmogrification), but none of the Blackdogs questioned the evidence of their senses enough to make the experiment. They were disarmed, for all intents and purposes.

Gunfire nonetheless broke out deeper in the Yard. Ben threw his shiny toy pistol aside and powered after Ingrid, vanishing into the greenery.

Lia followed after him.

Chapter Forty-Four

When the bell above the sliding door rang, Graves and Hannah stepped out of the elevator. The Silent Tower's top floor hallway was pristine and ready for them. To Graves, it seemed not to have changed one iota since the last day of his natural life, all the way back in 1950.

They walked up to the office door. The coat of Graves' blood that obscured Miguel Caradura's name looked as red and fresh as if it had just been sprayed there in the wake of a high-velocity projectile. Graves paused to contemplate it.

"Here's as far as I got on my last visit," he said. "Never did make it through that door."

"Are you ready, Dexter?" Hannah asked, looking over at him.

"As I'll ever be, I guess."

Together, Graves and Hannah pushed open the office door, which had once been a mere Hole in the Sky, although neither of them knew it.

The King's office was immaculate, elegant, and timelessly appointed. There were traces of Art Deco in the space's design, as well as evidence of the post-war trends toward bolder colors and straighter lines that had been starting to assert themselves when Graves died. There was a lot of polished wood, not to mention a few very modern touches, such as a flat-screened television setup mounted on the wall like a framed painting. Graves got a sense that this room was supposed to feel like it could've been anywhen in the twentieth century, stylistically speaking.

In the suite's second chamber, the freshly-flayed figure of Mictlantecuhtli sat behind his desk, in his robes, watching another, smaller flatscreen while snacking on human hearts. A pile of them glistened on a silver tray beside him. He washed them down with what smelled like blood (hot blood, from a steaming skullmug), like it was morning coffee.

He rose and turned to greet his guests when they stepped into the first room.

Graves moved forward to meet him at the threshold. Except for their different costumes (Graves' coat and fedora versus Mictlantecuhtli's reaper robes), the two skeletons might've been mirror images facing each other through the doorless doorway between the chambers.

"Dexter Graves," Mictlantecuhtli said. His voice was deep and sonorous. "Our moment arrives."

"Yep," Graves confirmed. "Greetings and salutations."

"Come," Mictlantecuhtli said, "and walk beside me as my guest, and see what I have summoned you to offer. Bring your soul, but leave your body at the door. I shall then have no power to prevent your resuming it as you desire, upon my unbreakable word."

Mictlantecuhtli made a gesture, and Graves stepped forward. His bones and clothes fell into a heap at the threshold when his ghost stepped through the doorway, which neatly separated it from his mortal remains. Lia'd done the same thing to him yesterday afternoon, so the sensation was not unfamiliar. This time his unrestricted spirit was free to move around, and he had to admit he preferred it that way.

Having crossed into the inner sanctum, Graves' unencumbered ghost-form raised its eyebrows at the instantaneous changes he noticed all around him. It was like a painted veil had been yanked away. The modern-day office trappings he'd seen through the door had all disappeared. In their place were dim torchlight that flickered off of mud-brick walls, and a bloodcaked stone altar where the desk had previously been.

Mictlantecuhtli had also changed, into what Graves guessed was supposed to be 'Miguel Caradura,' also known as Mickey Hardface. The tall skeleton in a cowl had become a living man, a muscular and dark-complected one, with black hair and small, knowing eyes. After that, the anthropomorphic illusion fell apart a little bit. The Aztec King's attire consisted of a modern-day suit that might've looked pretty sharp if he hadn't gone and further adorned it with a headdress made from a skull and a fan of long feathers, hammered golden cuffs that he wore over his coat sleeves, and a necklace of what appeared to be semi-fresh human eyeballs looped twice across his broad, pin-striped chest.

Graves looked back at Hannah, who was still standing behind him in the outer office, which hadn't changed at all, it seemed.

"Your guest may wait," Caradura said. "I have provided magazines."

"That sit all right with you, Miss Hannah?" Graves wondered if the inner sanctum was still an inner office from Hannah's point of view, and if Caradura still looked like fleshless Mictlantecuhtli. He guessed that *he'd* still be the same gray ghost of himself, in either case. His bones, coat and hat were out there on the carpeted floor, but he felt like he'd be able to get back into them when he wanted to. Felt it instinctually, and he'd learned long ago to trust his gut.

"Oh, I'll be all right," Hannah said, in answer to his question. "Besides, I have a weird sense I wouldn't be able to walk through that doorway and survive. Feels like looking over the edge of a tall building."

"You are likely correct, Lady," Mictlantecuhtli told her. "Only an initiated practitioner of ancient earth magicks could hope to cross that threshold and retain her living flesh."

"So there, you see?" Hannah said. "Thanks for the warning. I'll just park it here and catch up on which celebrities are screwing."

"Very good, Lady," Mictlantecuhtli said, but he was Caradura again when he turned around to address Graves' ghost.

"Come," he said, in his grandly booming voice. "Let us walk, and talk, and hold palaver, Dexter Graves."

Miguel Caradura guided the ghost past the altar and toward the rough door in the second chamber's far wall, the one that opened onto the undiscovered realm beyond the rooms. Graves glanced back one last time to see Hannah finding a seat, then making a sour face when she picked up one of those magazines Caradura had mentioned. It, like all of the others fanned out on the low table in front of her, was brittle and faded, dating from the 1940s.

Graves turned away from Hannah to follow the King and found

himself stepping outside onto the top of an enormous Aztec pyramid, one every inch as tall as the skyscraper that stood in its place on the other side of reality. He paused to admire the view.

There was a leaden sky above, and an endless chaparral plain below. The landscape was dotted with twisted, leafless, and black-trunked oaks. Slow mists rolled between the trees, billowing in ways that suggested the shapes of people or buildings or vehicles for an instant or two, before the breeze pulled them apart again.

"So this is Hell," Graves declared thoughtfully. He'd seen some things in his day, but this took the goddamn cake. "I was told I should expect something warmer."

"It need not be hell," Caradura said, sounding almost defensive about it. "It is Mictlan—a paradise for some and a torment for others, and even these fates are their own creations, deriving from their feelings about the lives they chose to lead."

"All of the dead come through here?"

"Yes."

"Regardless of whatever they believed?"

"Yes, Dexter Graves. Death wears many faces. My cult of worshippers persists in this City of Angels, however. It was *their* actions, not mine, that first opened the Hole in the Sky, more than a millennia before your birth. Their attentions have helped me to retain this form over generations, while others less remembered by the living world have faded to obscurity, if not oblivion. Mictlan is as vast as memory, and all of this, my kingdom, can be yours... if you desire it."

Graves' ghost chuckled at the assertion. "You don't say," he said. "For how many easy payments?"

Chapter Forty-Five

Ingrid slid on her bare knees into her makeshift Tomcat trap, scraping herself badly as she knocked over the still-lit candles and threw aside the fishtank to grab up the cat before one of her own men could accidentally shoot her.

If she died now, or if the sun went down on them, then all was truly lost.

Lia's aged spirit familiar disappeared from sight at the instant she had hold of his living anchor. She forced the old sorcerer's ghost down into the cat and fixed it there with a fierce effort of will. She could hardly afford to let the crafty spirit roam free. She'd need a bargaining chip just to buy a chance to explain herself now, and there was so little time left in which to pull off this operation.

All around the Yard, well-armed gangsters pinned the cops down, firing at them with foliage-rending automatic weapons when they tried to move from cover. The henchmen laughed and cackled, feeling triumphant and having a perverse sort of fun, at least for the moment.

Lia and the cop she'd called Ben came upon Ingrid as she was getting to her feet, with blood streaming from both knees and a black cat cradled in her arms. She slid a knife from a secret sheath on her thigh and angled its point toward the animal's neck, for emphasis.

Lia grabbed Ben's arm.

"Now you stop right there, Lia," Ingrid said, panting for breath. "This has gotten out of hand. Where's Dexter, is he with you?"

"I came alone," Lia said.

Ingrid's face fell. She could actually feel herself wilting. "Oh,

Lia, no," she whispered. "Please say you didn't."

When Lia said nothing Ingrid shook her head.

"Then it's already too late." Her last hopes vanished, extinguished like a match pinched between two fingers. She felt almost sick with despair. "The sun's about to go down."

"Too late for what, Ingrid?"

"For us to finish resurrecting Dexter," Ingrid said, like it should have been obvious. "It would kill either one of us alone, but *both* of us, working together, we could survive. We could *have* survived, that is, and hidden him from Mickey. Mictlantecuhtli. But if Dexter can't be here within a few minutes, there isn't anything more we can do. You'll be dead before dawn, Lia, and I'm sure I'll be right there with you."

She looked down at the cat in her arms, and sighed. "No point in keeping the pawns once the game is lost," she muttered, mostly to herself.

As soon as Ingrid dropped the cat, Xavier, her driver, of all fucking people, swooped right out of the glowing sunlit bushes and snatched it up at a run. Ingrid yelped involuntarily. So did Lia's cop, Ben. Lia shot right after the fleeing gangster with no hesitation, showing them the soles of her shoes.

Ben tackled Ingrid from the side before she recovered from her very genuine surprise, driving her to the dirt with all of his considerable, athletic weight. Her bone-handled knife went flying. Ben cuffed her before she could move her hands enough to do anything useful with them, and then jumped up to follow after Lia.

Tom hissed and flailed when Winston Watt—whose false face was beginning to peel around the edges as it dried out—held him up in one hand. Watt also had a fully automatic gun of some kind clutched in his other bony claw, and he fired chattering bursts of lead into the air as he ran. Tom's sensitive feline ears rang from the staccato gunshots. It felt like having his head clapped between a pair of frying pans a dozen times per second. Ingrid's rough hexes still had him tied inextricably to his cat, so escape by sending out into another animal wasn't going to be an option.

"*Lissen up, esés,*" Winston yelled, still posing as Xavier, the gang's appointed leader. The non-Spanish speakers amongst them must have wondered why he'd address them like they were book reports. "*Is time for plan B,*" the disguised manservant shouted. "*Shoot the pigs and catch the women. I'm givin' the orders now!*"

Winston skidded to a stop and held the cat up at eye level, looking it in the eyes through his shades.

"But first," he said, "we deal with—"

A frightful screech and a blur of flailing paws interrupted him when Tom brought his untrimmed and razor-sharp claws slashing down around the henchman's undefended head.

"*No!*" Winston screamed, trying to shield himself with his forearms as Tom raked the sunglasses right off his fake face. The eyeless skeleton beneath the skin shrieked, feeling with both hands that his borrowed forehead and cheeks were shredded into bloodless ribbons. He dropped to his knees and scrabbled around for his lost sunglasses, and Tom seized his moment to run for it.

Lia and her new friend Officer Ben came upon the scene, but gunfire from another of el Rey's henchmen sent them diving off in opposite directions, into the vegetation. They called out to one another and Tom knew that neither of them had been hit, without breaking his fastest four-legged stride.

Winston jumped up. He crammed his sunglasses back onto his torn face. "Get the cat and the witch," he shouted in a rage, and Tom could hear him crashing and crunching through the plants behind him. "Consiga el gato y a la bruja," he bellowed. "*Get the cat and the goddamned witch!*"

The chase was on.

Two bulky gangsters who looked like they'd probably been playing high school football not too many years before came at Tom from either side and he darted away at the instant they both dove for him. The men collided face-first, with a solid, meaty *smack*. They fell away to either side, knocked unconscious, upsetting two stepped racks of culinary herbs that rained down around them in a noisy avalanche of tiny plastic pots.

Tom's mischievous old heart surged with wild joy as he fled.

Then one of the older guys almost had him—got a grip around his middle, even, for about half an instant—before tripping over his own feet and somersaulting into a steel-wire shelving unit that housed terracotta pottery. Hundreds of pounds of it. The rack itself was eight feet high, and its entire payload of fired clay came crashing down onto the man's head and shoulders before he had a chance to exclaim. It sounded to Tom like God's own busboy had dropped a bin full of plates somewhere behind him.

If ten large men chasing one puff-tailed tomcat wasn't a recipe for physical comedy, then he didn't know what was. Tom would've been having a blast, frankly, if he hadn't been so afraid of somebody shooting his Lia. His Winter Flower. There were far too many guns around his girl just now, and that really would not do.

Blackdog cops obligingly tackled, disarmed and cuffed another pair of men when Tom lured them through a cluster of potted fan palms, right past the officers he sensed were concealed there, waiting to pounce when they saw a chance.

That left eight of Mictlantecuhtli's men in black still standing, by Tom's hasty count. 'Xavier,' known to him a century ago as Winston Fucking Watt, was one of the few still on the loose.

Chapter Forty-Six

The King snapped his fingers and they were down upon the plain, under the sunless silver sky. The pyramid they'd been at the top of a moment before now stood tall on the dark horizon behind them.

It was a pretty nifty trick, Graves thought, in spite of himself.

Miguel Caradura turned to the soul at his side. "You should know, Dexter Graves, that I am a powerful king," he said. "My reign extends even beyond the boundaries of my native Mictlan. The territories of my weaker brethren have also become my own as their rulers have lost coherence and their worshippers have died out."

Hardface sounded exactly like a salesman, in Graves' opinion. Not one he'd buy a bridge from, either.

Mickey Caradura raised his arms, and rank after rank of his conscripted troops appeared from out of the smoke when he spoke of them. They stood at attention, silent and still, awaiting their orders. They were creatures out of myths and dreams, a few of which Graves recognized from stories (such as dragons, centaurs, and what he thought might've been a gryphon), although there were many more he could not identify. So many that it boggled his mind to look at them. They became little more than a mass of vaporous, insubstantial sketches as their ranks faded back into the gray distance.

"The domains of Olympus and Luxor have long been under my control," said the King. "As have the spheres of the Kami, the Fair Folk, and the Shemhamephorash. All of those our brothers whose ties to the realworld have slipped away are now my conquered minions to command. My Army of Imaginals. I am Mictlantecuhtli, King of the Forgotten, Lord of the Shades,

Emperor of the Archaic and the Arcane—and you can be too, Dexter Graves."

"Hey, that all sounds swell, it really does," Graves said, cocking a ghostly hat back on his transparent head. "But I just know there's gotta be a catch."

He was getting bored with the hard sell already.

Caradura lowered his arms and let his armies fade until he and his guest were all alone again upon a rolling, empty plain that never seemed to end. "But a small one, Dexter Graves, so hear me out," the King said. "I, you see, am possessed of ambitions beyond the ordinary dreams of my kind. I would have what no nonbody is ever given to have. Sensation. Experience. The World. *Your* world. I will walk it, I will conquer it, and it will be *mine*, the crowning glory of my vast empire!"

Caradura shouted this mission statement up into the gray sky.

"But to achieve this," he said, turning back to Graves, "I will need a body. I need *your* body, Dexter Graves. I therefore propose that we effect a trade. I will walk the actual in your flesh and with your bones, while you remain here and reign in my stead as Lord of all Mictlan."

The King raised his hand and a dozen podiums emblazoned with treble clefs sprang up from the soil like a row of improbable crops. Tuxedoed skeletons coalesced out of the mists to stand behind them, and musical instruments appeared in their hands.

"Everything that memory contains is available to enjoy," Caradura assured Graves, raising his voice over the big bony band when they launched into a lively swing number. More skeletons appeared around them, dancers hopping eagerly to the beat. Flesh and clothing swirled together to cover their bones by the time the band had played three or four bars, and then the gray plain looked like one of the USO shows Graves remembered from the war. Sailors in their whites spun and shimmied with pinup girls who might've stepped right down from the nosecones of airplanes and into three glorious dimensions. Their lips were as red as exotic fruits and their legs went on for miles.

"You will want for nothing in this place," Caradura promised. "The totality of experience will be yours to recreate."

"You really tellin' me you'd trade in all this fine and shiny kingliness for the chance to catch a cold or stub your toe or get shot to death for no good reason in some idiotic war?"

"I would, Dexter Graves, I would," Caradura said. He made a slashing gesture across his throat and the band went silent on the very next note. The dancers stopped and turned to look at them from where they stood, waiting in expectant silence. "All such experiences would shine as jewels in the dark depths of my long memory."

Graves laughed at that, one terse bark that had no trace of humor in it. "Spoken like a man who's never had much shrapnel impacted between his ribs," he said.

Caradura frowned, and the party he'd conjured to tempt his guest with dispersed back into smoke. Only the distant pyramid remained. It seemed to be the one landmark that never changed within this realm that could become a copy of any time or any place, according to its ruler's will.

Graves paused, soaking in the immense, empty landscape before him as he considered the King's words, and considered them carefully.

"So," he said, grabbing the conversational reins when he sensed that Hardface was about to launch back into his sales rap. "Say I actually bit on this line of shit. How would we arrange the trade?"

"Therein, Dexter Graves, lies your 'catch.'"

"It's Lia, right?" Graves asked, although he didn't really need a confirmation by now. "Ingrid wanted outta your deal, so you made her scare up Miss Lia as a replacement."

"Their homegrown brand of witchwork is rather rare, Dexter Graves," Caradura said. "Such women are as strange flowers grown up in the cracks between worlds."

"But helpin' us to swap would grind her into mulch, wouldn't it? That's why Ingrid wouldn't do it, in the end."

"You are correct, Dexter Graves. Acting as our bridge will cost the witch her life. At which point she will become your servant here in the kingdom of Mictlan, and subject to your every whim. Think about it. I believe this is what you incarnations call a 'win-win situation,' is it not?"

Caradura's grin as he delivered this last line was as wide and bright as any politician's.

Chapter Forty-Seven

A bullet whizzed past Lia's head like an angry, supersonic bee when she snatched up her tomcat at a lucky moment and ran for it, ducking under branches and distancing herself from the gunmen behind her. She was far more agile around here in the gathering gloom than they could ever hope to be. She knew this ground better than anyone ever had.

The sun's upper arc had sunk dangerously close to the western horizon. The vegetation around her blazed with the last of the afternoon's smoldering light as she tore across the property, sprinting as hard as she ever had. It was the hour of day Lia normally loved best, although she had no time for smelling roses now.

Her heart was thundering by the time she reached the back of the Yard. Her teeth tasted like copper and she had a deep, lancing stitch in her side, one that threatened to seize into a cramp when she pulled up short and paused in front of the eight-foot-long pile of cordwood that was stacked almost as high as the rear fence.

As vast as it was, the nursery couldn't go on forever.

The odd, misshapen stump that had been a man earlier that morning was rooted deeply into the earth before the woodpile, like it had been there for a century. Lia let Tom out of her trembling arms and he leapt down onto it with easy, feline grace.

Her first instinct was to run for Bag End, which lay off to her left, but Tom gave her to know that men were coming from that direction, and less than a second later she heard their swift if clumsy approach with her own two ears. So that wasn't going to work. There'd be no hiding underground.

The thing with a false hood of skin hanging askew over its ivory-yellow facial bones was much nearer, practically in sight of her already and closing fast, by the sound. It would seem to be another reanimated skeleton like Dexter, which both awed and bewildered Lia. There were old trees to her right, the same trees she'd hidden in before (as well as one new, magically-sprouted camellia), but she only had a moment left in which to bolt for cover and the woodpile was closer by.

She snatched up Tom and ducked behind it right before the corpse with the secondhand face burst from the potted treeline at her back. He had at least half a dozen of Mictlantecuhtli's remaining henchmen at his heels.

Lia felt sure they'd seen her. They must have. She couldn't have been fast enough. As a hiding place, the woodpile was shot. It was good for nothing but cover now.

Still, she cowered there, trying to breathe quietly while her lungs burned and her blood thundered in her ears, just in case she was wrong and they hadn't spotted her after all. She clutched her bristle-tailed Tom against her breastbone, wishing as hard as she could that her pursuers would move on.

"All right, now, brujagirl," the dead henchman in charge said, dashing any hope of a reprieve. "We're done with this, so come on outta there. You ain't gonna be happy about it if I have to send my people in."

With a glance, Tom let Lia know that this was likely true. He'd known this man before, in another era, and was willing to vouch for him as a serious threat. She therefore set her cat down and complied with the skeleton's order, holding up her hands and stepping out from behind her small mountain of split-and-stacked firewood.

She broke a small branch off from the new camellia shrub as she did so. Almost a twig, really. And yet it was still a wand—a symbolic channel for her will.

She glanced west at the moment the sun finally disappeared from the horizon, leaving the sky above a cloudless cerulean blue that would bleed away to starry blackness within minutes.

It was officially night, and all the worlds' nocturnals were free to roam.

"Where, pray tell, is the bloody cat?" the dead man with the torn face asked, switching from a Spanish to a British accent for no reason Lia could begin to fathom.

She looked right at him, into the lenses of the cracked sunglasses he hadn't yet removed, in spite of the gathering darkness. They were the only thing holding his face in position. Lia was no longer afraid, even though she could see teeth through the bloodless rents in his stubbly cheek. A strange calm descended over her, and a subtle breeze she couldn't feel against her skin nonetheless stirred the leaves of the nearest rooted plants. The trees around her hissed as if in quiet anger, and the living men glanced around themselves nervously, even though they all were armed and Lia plainly was not.

Except for the crooked little stick she raised and pointed in their direction.

She gasped in a breath and straightened her spine when a semi-perceptible shock rolled up her legs from deep within the earth, igniting each of the seven chakra points that ran up the median line of her body as it traveled all the way to the crown of her head. Rising ethereal energies rippled across her skin, trailing fever-waves of gooseflesh after them. Her intentions could now be grounded into manifestation, and she reached out with her mind to share the current, brushing the last of Ingrid's binding hexes away from Black Tom.

"Boys," Lia said, smiling wickedly and training her makeshift wand on the gunmen, each in turn, stopping on their leader. "There's something the old people used to say that I believe applies to this situation." She let her conscious mind unfurl down the wand's shaft, pushing at the men's perceptions with the full force of her will as she quoted a Zuni proverb she'd once read:

"'After dark, *all* cats are leopards.'"

Before any of the men could ask Lia what in the name of hell she was talking about, a sleek, black mountain lion stepped out from behind the woodpile and nuzzled its head against her hip, purring like it had an eight-cylinder engine buried within its massive chest.

The observing gangsters were staggered. Lia saw their eyes go wide, and the color drained from their faces. Late-to-the-show cops looked merely confused as they emerged from the trees.

The enormous black cat, easily the size of a full-grown tiger, roared and pounced on the dead leader with the torn face without further ado. The costumed skeleton went down screaming. The wildcat planted two fist-sized paws on its chest and clamped its leathery skull between his jaws, then shook it with all the force those powerful predator's shoulders could muster.

"*Get him, Tom,*" Lia shrieked, her voice gone high and wild as she cackled with crazy glee. "*Chew his goddamn face off!*"

Incredulous, Ben Leonard stepped up beside her, taking in the surreal scene. Lia barely noticed him, or any of the other officers, either, as she was so busy cheering. Her champion had long ago been christened in honor of his maternal grandfather, a man named Tomas de Leon, Tom the Lion, and Lia knew that one's true name was always the key to one's true nature. She knew it because he'd taught her everything he could, and never asked for anything in return.

The six or seven henchmen looked on in horror; the cops in weird wonderment. Nobody could quite countenance what they were seeing, although all of them believed in it. In her fever pitch of excitement Lia was catching impressions from their minds without even trying to. She was sending and receiving all at once, exquisitely aware of every emotion within the vicinity.

Ben Leonard looked down to see Tom the plain old housecat clawing at a screaming, flailing perpetrator—one that happened to be a long-dead skeleton dressed in black jeans and a hooded sweatshirt. (The sort of shit that would never wind up in any report, he thought).

Hardface's henchmen, however, saw a man-sized, melanistic wildcat, as Lia intended them to. (The police officers hadn't been within her spell's sphere of influence when she cast it, and so remained untouched by its effects.) The monstrous cat stopped shaking the gang's freakish leader by the head and looked up, flashing green eyes at the final lingering knot of the King's hired men. The mountain lion lowered its head and lunged at them, almost playfully, although it was more than enough to send them screaming away through the darkened trees.

The puzzled Blackdogs saw only a small, ordinary tomcat hissing and puffing its tail after the half-dozen sizable gunmen it'd somehow routed, all by itself. They exchanged confounded looks before they remembered their jobs and went chasing after the escaping suspects.

Ben Leonard walked over and cuffed Mictlantecuhtli's

partially-disguised manservant, tightening the bracelets all the way down to the very last notch to enclose his bony wrists. Lia smiled, watching her new friend restrain the rogue cadaver like a pro.

They could play Ingrid's brand of mindgames too, she thought, as she picked up and hugged her Tom.

Chapter Forty-Eight

Nyx descended unseen into a quiet pocket of Potter's Yard, in the form of a matte-black sphere that barely stood out at all against the night's clear and moonless sky. She touched down without a sound and assumed her best humanoid shape: that of a flat female outline aswirl with distant galaxies.

She looked critically at the cherry sapling Lia had generated from a broken branch earlier that morning, then seized it by the trunk and hauled it back up out of the earth, lifting her trapped sister-daughter by the head along with it.

She set Lyssa on her feet, broke off the top of the green young tree, then spun Lady Madness around. Nyx grabbed hold of the tree's roots and kicked her insane relation off the far end of the splintered trunk with a foot planted in the small of her back. Lyssa staggered forward and fell flat on her face. Her motorcycle helmet's open visor bit into the earth like a shovel blade. Nyx threw the sapling's rootball aside.

Star-like points of light that would soon become Wasp and Mantis descended and began drawing local insects together while Lyssa got up, tossed her broken helmet away, and began peeling the black leather clothing from her jittering staticbody.

Lia and Ben hauled Ingrid to her feet and marched her out toward the parking lot together. The towering redhead's feet were bare and quite dirty, Lia noticed. She would've stood as tall as Ben if she'd been wearing heels. Her satin gown was torn and stained with blood from her scraped knees. She looked around everywhere as they went, wide-eyed and frightened, although it could easily have been an act. Ingrid was an excellent liar. Black

Tom's image sauntered along in Lia's peripheral vision, leaning on his cane. (He'd socked his catbody away deep underneath the office shack, where it wouldn't be disturbed again until he came back to it.)

"Lia, please," Ingrid pleaded, cringing back from a frond of dark foliage that brushed her shoulder. "You can't leave me handcuffed. Nyx is here already, she has to be. Lyssa won't be far behind, or the Tzitzimime either. Maybe we can fight them if you'll let me use my hands."

"I'd rather let a pyromaniac smoke in a fireworks factory," Lia said, prompting a laugh from Ben.

They emerged from the dark trees and into the parking lot, with Ben leading Ingrid by the arm and the rest of the Blackdogs following behind them.

Lyssa and Nyx were waiting there, blocking the front gate, their paired outlines filled with static and stars, respectively. Everyone stopped where they were and gaped.

"See, I told you, didn't I *tell* you?" Ingrid screeched.

Lia *had* anticipated that Nyx would uproot the tree she'd pinned Lyssa down with as soon as the sun could set. Ingrid didn't need to warn her about that. She'd just hoped they might find a few more minutes in which to make a getaway, or devise some new defense.

But no.

Insects boiled up out of the gravel and clumped together into tall, churning, half-human suggestions of a Wasp and a Mantis. The buzzing clusters solidified fast, becoming angular mutations that could've sprung forth from Pablo Picasso's worst cubist nightmares. Stark white light from a nearby streetlamp shone on their armored thoraxes, and their large, faceted eyes glittered like alien gems.

The quartet of feminoid imaginals had indeed been expecting them.

Ben stepped forward to confront the creatures, despite Lia's grab at his arm. "All right, ladies," he said in his most authoritative tone. "I don't know who you are or what you are, but *we* are here as representatives of the laws of men, and we are prepared to tolerate *no form* of aggression—"

Which was all well and good, until Mantis leaned in and

scissored his head right off his shoulders with one single clash of her wicked green mandibles.

It happened almost too fast to process. Black blood fountained up from the sliced-off stump of Ben's neck. Mantis knocked his spurting body aside and the severed head landed in the gravel at her feet half a second later. The Blackdogs could only stand frozen and stare at the six-foot insect with their colleague's blood on its jaws, aghast and unable to absorb this sudden reordering of their command structure.

Wasp opened her translucent wings, rose up into the air, and buzzed toward them, angling her jagged stinger forward.

"*Move!*" Lia screamed, snapping everyone out of their shock. Horrified cops scattered for cover back inside the Yard, seeking shelter anywhere they could find it. Lia grabbed Ingrid's still-cuffed arm when she stumbled and dragged her along, chasing after the Blackdogs while two furious Archons and a pair of hissing Tzitzimime pursued them all.

Tom spun around and hurled his cane like a javelin, skewering Wasp through the thorax with it as she dove down through the trees, aiming for Lia. Wasp detonated into a swirling maelstrom of individual hornets and yellowjackets, which made the situation exponentially worse. Mantis joined her sister in bursting apart only to funnel her hopping insects in around Lia and Ingrid, encircling them and backing them against a clump of magnolia saplings.

Separating them from the remaining cops.

Lia tore down a new branch and swung it, swiping it uselessly through amorphous clouds of bugs and brandishing it when the contrasting shapes of Lyssa and Nyx slunk closer, hemming them in. Mantis and Wasp melted back together out of the loose, whirling swarm in order to flank them. Black Tom had no defense against the Archons whatsoever, but he caused Ingrid's handcuffs to fall away when Lia silently asked that he remove them. Ingrid rubbed at her chafed and reddened wrists, surprised but free now to defend herself, if she could. It only seemed right to Lia.

Then they heard the thudding bass pulse of a car-mounted subwoofer booming toward them through the empty streets outside the Yard. This wasn't an uncommon noise out here in the

Valley by any means, but the snarling roars of several large, overtaxed engines made even the ladydemons turn toward the fence an instant before a black Cadillac SUV came slamming through it about a dozen yards down from them, scattering planks and kicking up dust into its own dazzling headlight beams.

Esteban leapt out on the driver's side and Riley did the same on the other, before the big vehicle had entirely come to a stop, while it was still rocking on its springs. Their amped-up dance music was louder and clearer now, with both doors hanging open, and the beat seemed to cancel out all other sound.

Three more SUVs skidded up outside the ruined fence and disgorged a team of Steb's personal security guards in their interchangeable black suits (the guys Lia thought of as his Reservoir Dogs). Each man was armed with a large aluminum light housing and carried a batterypack slung on a strap over his shoulder.

Steb, ever the showman as well as the shaman, leapt forward and raised his arms when his musical selection reached a dramatic crescendo.

Except for Lia and Ingrid, every human being present— Esteban's mercenaries and Blackdog officers alike—all turned toward the demons and stomped the earth, simultaneously assuming an identical, cross-armed fighting stance. Every other conscious person for five miles in every direction probably did the very same thing, by the feel of it, each of them wired into sequence by the force of Esteban's projected will. Lia sensed that force radiating off him in rhythmic waves and she recognized what was happening, although this display was so much grander in scope than the tiny demonstration her former lover had arranged for her earlier in the day that it was scarcely the same experience at all. The scale of his intention here was overwhelming, like watching a tsunami rush toward you. Lia had no doubt at all that he'd be able to make half the population of the San Fernando Valley dance the Spanish Panic against their will, if that was what he meant to do.

Making them fight to the death on her behalf wouldn't be any more of a trick.

"Esteban, don't you *dare*," she shouted at him, raising her voice over the music as a pregnant pause in the song came to an end and its tooth-loosening beat began pounding once again. "These people aren't yours to use!"

Steb looked disappointed, but he lowered his arms and released the cops, the guards, Riley, and everyone else in the surrounding neighborhoods from his thrall. He killed the power to his car stereo with a chirp from a tiny handheld remote, and evening quiet rushed back in like displaced water.

"As you wish, brujachica," he said. "We will do this the hard way."

He bowed to Lia from the waist, then turned to face Wasp and Mantis.

"*Bugbitches!*" he challenged, at the top of his voice. "I am Esteban de Rojo." He drew a razorsharp machete from a sheath on either hip. "And I have come to *dance!*"

They flew right into it. Wasp slashed at him with her broken stinger, Mantis snapped her mandibles, and Steb sliced, bobbed, and wove in an explosive outburst of acrobatic martial art. *Capoiera*, Lia thought the style was called. From Brazil, where Steb had spent a portion of his youth. She'd seen him practice its backflips and windmill kicks before, but had never seen any of the techniques actually put to use. Machete blades struck sparks off the bugs' barbed carapaces when the witchman and the dreamdemons hacked at one another.

Lia and Ingrid were both taken aback by the sudden ferocity of the fight, as were Lyssa and Nyx. Ingrid half-consciously touched a hand to her breastbone while she tracked Esteban's wild moves with her eyes, and Lia thought she looked thoroughly impressed. At another time and place it might've made her jealous.

Somewhere behind them Riley shouted: "*Spartans, ho!*"

The guards all raised their light housings like shields and turned the power on. Their lamps produced an instant, retina-searing glare, one that turned the world into a washed-out photograph. Lia covered her eyes and Ingrid turned away, but Nyx reacted to it like she was on fire, shrieking and flailing and racing off blindly into the Yard's sheltering darkness.

The men with the lamps chased after her.

"Hey, Lia!" Riley chirped, pausing to chat while his troops pursued the inky Archon. "Check it out. Hydroponic grow lights.

Full spectrum UV, pure artificial sun.   Pretty freakin' nifty, dontcha think?"

"Riley, I can't believe you guys came," Lia said.   She'd explained their situation to him earlier, in some detail (even claiming credit for last night's burst of magical daylight, which the news had tried to write off as some sort of atmospheric anomaly), but she'd never asked for nor expected anyone to come riding to her aid.

"You don't really think I could've talked *him* out of *this*, do you?" Riley asked, nodding toward Steb and his ongoing three-way fight with the Brobdingnagian bugs before hurrying off after his men.   Ingrid went after them too, and Lia didn't know how concerned about that she needed to be.   She realized with a twinge of panic that she couldn't account for staticy Lyssa's whereabouts anymore, either.

Lia dropped to her knees and closed her eyes, sending out effortlessly.   Black Tom joined her.

She first perceived Lyssa, Lady Madness, cowering in a far corner underneath a large-leafed palm, feeling overwhelmed by all the shouting and unexpected intrusions.   Lia sensed the psychotic Archon was terrified by the clarity of thought and ingenuity behind the tiny captive suns the new arrivals had brought to prod Nyx with, and she didn't care to see what they might have in store for her.

Deciding to cut her losses, Lyssa simply disappeared, and Lia couldn't tell where in the worlds she might have gone.

Next she spotted that second animated skeleton, the one who still had shriveling skeins of borrowed flesh plastered over his facial bones.   *Winston*, she learned, catching his name from his thoughts and feeling Tom confirm it.   Winston could hear Esteban's commotion from afar, from the distant quarter of the Yard where poor Ben had cuffed him and left him less than twenty minutes ago.   Unaware that both Lia and Black Tom were watching with their minds' eyes, he laid his head down onto the dirt and decayed.   His bones crumbled to a soft, powdery dust that the earth absorbed.   His clothing, his sunglasses, and even his shoes went with him.

He, like Lyssa, was gone in a wink, leaving nothing but his handcuffs behind.

Earth was Lia's element, however, and in this case she could follow him down into its fecund blackness. She listened hard for his fading thoughts, holding on to her last impression of his mind, even though it was difficult to do. She'd never sent herself out this far before. She felt Winston reconstitute his bones from the soil of the empty lot across the street from Caradura's office building, and caught an image of the place through his eyes. He rose up from the dirt, shook it off his shoulders in a dusty cloud, and then went sprinting for the Tower's front door, darting around the back end of a new Jaguar that was parked out in front of it.

Lia lost her sense of him when he went inside. The place was warded up pretty good. She could've sawed her way through the old hexes with a bit of effort, but there was so much still happening back at the Yard. She could hear the extravagant noise of Esteban's clash with the Tzitzimime through her physical ears, although it sounded much more distant from her than it actually was.

Tom's spirit shot right after Winston, faster than a thought, bashing through the wards before Lia could so much as ask him what they ought to do next. He was diffuse and invisible, so he couldn't nod his customary acknowledgement, but Lia felt him vanish when he ducked inside the building.

Chapter Forty-Nine

Lia pulled her thoughts back into her head as soon as Tom was gone. The clanging of cold steel against rigid exoskeletons grew in volume and she opened her eyes in time to see Steb nailing Mantis to a sturdy pear tree. Right through the middle section of her segmented body, with one of his machetes. The damaged Tzitzimitl's chitinous armor bubbled, rippled, and almost broke apart into a cataract of bugs, but resourceful Esteban looped a beaded bracelet over the serrated equivalent of her wrist and then looped it again around his own.

"Oh, no," he admonished, shaking a finger in her triangular and out-of-focus face. "That would be the coward's way out!"

Mantis re-solidified against her will, her disintegration canceled.

Esteban next swept Wasp to the ground when she snuck up behind him and pinned her face-down in the dirt with his second machete. He bound her with a bracelet as well, preventing her from coming apart with the same hex he'd used on Mantis, although he was now effectively tied between the two of them. Wasp's twitching wings crackled and snapped like crumpled cellophane when she tried to rise and fly away.

Lia could also hear Riley and his people in the distance, shouting to each other while they chased Nyx around the Yard. The sky above flashed blue every time they startled the frantic Archon with their lights. The ultraviolet bulbs inside them burned with the intensity of tiny suns and cast weird, dancing shadows all down the long rows of leafy trees.

Dawn broke with full and instantaneous force and held onto the sky for almost half a minute when a number of the black-clad security specialists managed to surround Nyx, hemming her in from all sides with phony daylight until she arced out over the top of their circle and raced off into the darkness that resumed as soon as she could turn her featureless face away from their lamps.

Closer by, Esteban's two pinned specimens writhed and screamed in the stuttering flashes of inappropriate daytime, but they couldn't escape him, not even under conditions that normally would've cancelled out their existence.

He turned to face Lia as night spread out above and held its place. She assumed the Archon of Darkness must've pulled ahead of her pursuers. Nyx wasn't easy to see in the shadows, but she'd need a minute to gather herself before she could vanish the way her missing sister-daughter had, and Lia didn't think Riley's people were going to give it to her. The thrashing bugwomen relaxed a little in the restored gloom, but Steb was still physically tied to them. He'd achieved a stalemate here, at best.

"These things never die, brujachica," he said to Lia. "Now they know you, they will never leave you be."

"I have been worried about that," Lia confessed.

"Yes," Steb said, confirming that she *should* be worried. "But I do have one idea."

He bit at the empty air, catching something in his teeth. It was nothing more or less than reality itself, Lia knew: the actual fabric of being. It wrinkled where his incisors sank in. He pulled at it, tore at it, worried it open like a dog ripping into an unsecured sack of kibble. There was weird light beyond the flap he tore out of existence.

"I've held a ticket to oblivion for a long time now," Steb said to her, when he'd gotten the hole well started and widened to about half the size of his head. "What better occasion to make the trip? I'll even have traveling companions this way. Incredible dancers!"

"Steb, what are you talking about?"

"The spaces between the worlds, mi brujachica," Esteban explained. "Limbo. Oblivion. Nowheresville. Nobody comes back from there."

"Don't be crazy," Lia said. "Those bonds you made won't be enough to pull them in with you. You'd be killed and it wouldn't even help."

"No, you're right," Steb said, and yanked both his machetes loose from their moorings, unpinning the bugwomen. They both instantly impaled him, Wasp with her broken-off stinger and

Mantis with one slim, barbed, raptorial forearm. He looked to Lia and gasped, "…but *these* links, I think, should do."

"Steb, *no!*" Lia howled, shocked to her core by the sight of him run all the way through in two different places. There was surprisingly little blood. "No, you can't do this, *please don't do this!*"

But Steb only smiled. He *could* do this. He was perhaps the only human being alive capable of doing this, and she could tell that he meant to see it done. For her sake.

"Te amo, brujachica," he told her. "Remember me."

"Oh, Esteban…" Lia said, brushing his cheek with her fingertips before stepping back from him, out of harm's way. "You know I always will."

Esteban de Rojo grinned and then, with a shout, the freelance witchman swung his twin machetes around in a wide X. They caught in the gap he'd torn from reality and sliced it open further, just long enough for the resulting rift to suck him and his dance partners into the white nowhere zone beyond the worlds, before it sealed itself back up.

And then they were gone, all three of them.

Lia dropped to her knees, unable to breathe. This was too much to cope with. It was too real. Too irrevocable. Esteban was worse than dead, he was *gone*. Extinguished. She recalled, randomly, how he'd always brought her cut flowers when they'd been together, even though she lived in a world of flowers, because he somehow knew that contemplating their fleeting beauty as they faded moved her in an odd and personal way. He'd viewed her through a lens no one else ever had, understood feelings she'd never even tried to articulate, and now she'd never see him again. Not in this life or the next one, either. The weight of the sacrifice he'd made on her behalf was devastating.

Lia felt sick and desolated, too gutted even to cry.

Chapter Fifty

Black Tom condensed himself down into the first chamber at the top of the Silent Tower. Winston Watt may have channeled himself across miles through the medium of earth, but he still had to climb a dozen flights of stairs before he'd reach the King's Chambers, so non-corporeal Tom beat him to the top by a handy margin. He couldn't tell where the Archon Lyssa had gotten to, either, even though he'd sensed this place as a destination in her mind as well, right before she winked out of existence.

What really surprised him was finding *Hannah* up here, well ahead of anybody else. She was standing at the door between the rooms and staring through. Lia hadn't sent her; Tom was certain he would've picked up on such a memory had it existed anywhere inside either of their heads. The only sign of Dexter Graves in evidence was a deflated mound of clothing and bones that lay on the floor at the lady's feet.

Did that mean Graves had gone over already? Made a deal with el Rey? Not yet, Tom thought, although Hannah seemed to believe they might be negotiating when he touched her mind.

She wasn't focused on Graves at the moment, however. She was instead remembering the Crouchers Lia had taught her how to feed. Recalling the shock of wonder that accompanied the experience.

Tom could guess at what she was about to do next and he dreaded seeing the results, although he also knew that Hannah couldn't really help herself. He understood the fascination she felt as she stood there at the boundary between the worlds. His Lia had always been possessed of that same sort of curious nature.

Hannah put her hand through the doorway to the inner office.

The air seemed to ripple around it, as if she'd touched a plane of glassy-still, vertically-suspended water. But her hand went through, and on the other side it looked to be just fine. The flesh stayed on her fingers. It was hard to say that anything unusual had happened at all.

She put her face through next. Panic spiked Tom in the chest and he leapt toward her instinctually, even though he knew he'd have no chance of pulling her back if going over was her intention. He was no more substantial than a breeze.

Hannah wasn't yet that bold, however. She stayed right there on the threshold but opened her eyes, like a child dunking her head to look around underwater. She gasped in surprise at what she saw.

Tom touched her thoughts and shared the vision with her. The second chamber was not an office anymore but rather the old inner sanctum of the Temple of Mictlantecuhtli, as Tom had known it back in its Hole in the Sky days. The carved altar stone crouched where the desk had been, and a rough doorway in the wall beyond it had replaced the illusion of panoramic windows. The impression of modernity the King liked to affect was gone: a projection visible from the first room only.

Hannah pulled her head back across the threshold. She looked all right, as far as Tom could see. He could further tell, from both her expression and her thoughts, that the fancy, well-lit office with the desk was once again what she saw on the doorway's far side. One image replaced the other as soon as her eyes crossed the dividing line. It was like seeing two television channels switched back and forth.

"Huh," she said.

Then she bent over and retrieved Graves' lighter from his bone pile, digging it out from the inner pocket of his ratty, crumpled raincoat. She clutched it to her heart as she straightened up and faced the doorway. She took a single deliberate step inside, setting one foot onto the inner chamber's stone floor and then planting the second right down beside it. Tom cringed, expecting to see her flesh slide away from her bones like so much loose sand, the way his friend Ramon's had done so many years ago.

Hannah's skin didn't do that, though, and after a few seconds she opened her eyes again. She seemed unchanged, to both her own and to Tom's very great relief.

Behind her, back in the realworld, shred-faced Winston Watt burst into the outer office, banging the bloodstained door off the wall. His black sweatshirt and jeans looked beige with embedded dirt.

Hannah whirled around at the percussive sound of his entrance.

Watt saw Graves' cigarette lighter in her hand. He pulled a gun from inside his soil-caked sweatshirt and marched right into Mictlan without undergoing any more metamorphosis when he stepped through the portal than Hannah had a moment before. Tom was indistinct enough to go undetected by both of them.

Hannah put her hands up, clutching the lighter in the left one, when the desiccated gunman shoved his weapon into her face.

"I thought only a bonafide dirtwitch or whatever he called it is supposed to be able to walk through that door," she said to him, shying back as far as she could without letting her ass come into contact with the grisly altar.

Winston ripped off the remainder of his Xavier mask, sunglasses and all, revealing the bare and eyeless skull beneath it. "Here's *my* dirty little secret," he said over Hannah's involuntary shriek. "Now what, pray tell, is *yours?*"

Chapter Fifty-One

Daylight flashed again in the sky above Potter's Yard, as bright and sudden as thunderless lightning. It disappeared as quick, leaving Ingrid's night vision obscured by brilliant, overlapping afterimages. She'd gone with Lia's friend, the one called Riley, to see if there was any help she might offer, or anything else she might be able to do. There wasn't, really, but she was too fascinated by Riley's technological solution to the Archon problem not to see how his approach panned out.

She saw Nyx duck into an outlying shed and slam the door, pursued by a team of those identically-dressed guardsmen. It seemed that Mickey wasn't the only individual in town who maintained a small army of mercenaries, and these people behaved like they'd even been trained, in sharp contrast to the motley assortment of lowlifes her King had sent her out here with. Ingrid knelt down some yards back from Riley's men and closed her eyes, latching onto the perceptions of the ancient entity inside the shack. She caught an impression of the guards' lights illuminating the windows before Nyx dropped down to the floor.

Outside, Ingrid opened her physical eyes to watch the guards ring the shed, three men to a side as well as one at every corner. The combined glare of their electric sun-lights made the boxy little structure at the center of their circle stand out with hallucinatory clarity. She could feel Nyx cowering under a table, in there.

Riley stepped up next to Ingrid and put his hands on his hips, assessing the situation.

Inside the room, on the floor by her head, Nyx noticed a strip of electrical power outlets, as well as something attached to it. Ingrid felt the attentional snag, closed her lids, and turned her mind's eye toward the object of the Archon's focus. It turned out to be a complex, boxy device plugged into the power strip, one that Ingrid guessed to be a timer of some sort, based mostly on the fact that it had a numbered dial on its face. Nyx, she sensed, had no idea what the mechanism was called, although she understood that it was counting down, and that something would happen when it finished.

The timer clicked over to the next hour, and more dazzling sun lamps came on above to nurture a prolific crop of fat, red tomatoes.

Nyx yowled in the lamps' glare like a boiled cat and Ingrid pulled away from her, back into her own headspace.

Opening her eyes, she found that it was now daytime outside the shed. It just *was*, despite being nearly eight o'clock in the evening, according to reason. A beautiful mid-morning blue hung over all of Los Angeles (and maybe over all of everywhere, as far as Ingrid knew, since Lady Night was currently unable to fulfill any of her duties).

She got up from her knees and brushed them off. She didn't want to think about how ragged she must've looked in the harsh light of day. Riley nodded, appearing rather pleased with himself when he grinned at her. "I think that'll do," he said.

Ingrid had to shade her eyes to look at him. She was apt to freckle now, because of his tricks, and yet she couldn't help but smile back.

The men in the black suits began propping their burning lights up around the shed, and she and Riley started back toward the last place they'd seen Lia. Nyx went on wailing, unharmed but unhappy about being trapped in the light of an artificial day.

When they came out of the trees, Lia was kneeling in the dirt where the young man called Esteban had been fighting with Mickey's Tzitzimime. Weird tracks proliferated, scattered across the dirt in no discernible pattern. Ingrid didn't see any other trace of the bugwomen, but then there was no sign of Lia's friend, either, and her heart sank. She didn't know the particulars, but she got a sense of what must've happened, all the same. She hoped it hadn't been terrible for Lia to watch, but she could tell just by looking that the hope was in vain.

"Lia…" she said, very softly, coming up behind the smaller woman and hesitating for a moment before placing a hand on her shoulder. "We're both alive. They can't have switched yet. There's still time. Maybe we can close that door to Mictlan, if we hurry."

Lia looked up. Her eyes were black and cold.

"All right," she said. "Let's go do that."

A column of three police cars blasted down Lankershim Boulevard, their lights flashing and their sirens wailing. Lia sat in the front passenger seat of the lead car. Riley and Ingrid were in the back. Lia was all too aware that theirs were not the only flashing emergency lights out here on the roads. Accidents, awe, and the evidence of panic were everywhere to be seen, right outside her window. Madness and wonder wandered freely through the streets while people stared up into a blue mid-day sky that should've been as black as midnight, according to their watches or the clocks on their cellphones.

"They must all think it's Jesus coming home to roost or Superman turning the planet backwards or, well, shit, I don't know *what* they must think," Riley said, staring out through his own window as they turned onto Ventura from Lankershim, heading into the Cahuenga Pass. It was a rare thing to see either his vocabulary or his imagination desert him, Lia knew.

Panicked crowds were pouring down the hill from Universal Studios, making the intersection all but impassable. Their police car eased past a mad-eyed, bearded man wearing a sandwichboard too-tightly packed with apocalyptic text for any of it to be legible. He harangued anyone whose eye he could catch about the pressing need to repent, and Lia looked away from him. They'd driven past a surprising number of individuals who seemed to share his attitude already. Lia wondered when they'd had the time to hand-print all those 'The End Is Nigh' signs. She hated to think that people had them pre-made and socked away in garage rafters or under their beds, in case an unscheduled end of the world should ever catch them unawares.

Lia ignored the hysteria as best she could. She figured people's existing beliefs would help them reassemble their conceptions of reality later on—assuming that things eventually did return to normal. There were no guarantees on that score, she reminded herself. This was unprecedented territory.

Their cruiser sped up again once they entered the Cahuenga Pass itself. From here they'd reach their destination within minutes, and Lia already knew she meant to send the police escort away as soon as they arrived—using Esteban's brand of influential tricks, if necessary. The Blackdogs were needed out on these streets more than anybody, and, after what had happened to Ben Leonard, Lia didn't want any more of their blood on her hands.

Chapter Fifty-Two

Black Tom stood by in the waiting room, helplessly watching Winston Watt's old bones threaten Hannah inside the second of the King's Chambers. Tom knew he couldn't cross the barrier the way they both had and retain his will, as he was technically dead already and therefore a subject of el Rey's (even if he'd been absent without leave for the last hundred years). He'd be rendered helpless by Mictlantecuhtli's influence as soon as he stepped across the threshold, and he'd be no good to anybody, then.

"But I hardly know anything about these things!" Hannah protested, staring down the barrel of Winston's gun. Tom had no idea what would happen to her if she got shot while standing in the realm of the dead. "I didn't even know things like you could *be*, outside of movies," she insisted.

"The dead like me can walk the earth this time of year, with permission from our King," Winston informed her. "But a living thing like you has no business being here. You couldn't be, unless you know *some*thing more than you're letting on, my dear."

"I really swear I don't," Hannah said.

"It doesn't matter to me," Winston replied. "All I want is for Black Tom Delgado to take over my position in Mictlan. Do you think your Lia will trade *him* for *you*?"

"I... I have no idea," Hannah said. Tom didn't either. He was glad that Winston couldn't see him.

"I think you'd better hope so," Watt said. "Now, summon Dexter Graves. He will bring Mictlantecuhtli, and Mictlantecuhtli must approve the terms."

"I don't know how to summon," Hannah said. "I missed that class."

"I am getting a *bit* tired of this obtuse routine, lady."

Hannah sighed. "Okay, I can try," she said. "But I wouldn't expect much." She put the lighter to her forehead and closed her eyes. "Hannah to Dexter," she said in a dopey nasal voice. "Hannah to Dexter, come in Dexter…"

Winston looked like he was about to say something pissy in response when Graves' ghost appeared beside the altar stone.

"Wow," Hannah said, looking as startled as anyone. "Good reception. There must be a hellphone tower near here."

King Caradura appeared a moment later, looking none too pleased. "What is the meaning of this?" he demanded of Hannah. "Why have you summoned Dexter Graves from our palaver?"

Black Tom faded further back, making himself as hard to perceive as possible. Only distraction was keeping el Rey from spotting him out here. He thanked whatever other gods might be that Mictlantecuhtli wasn't *quite* omniscient.

Hannah cocked her thumb at Winston. "He placed the call," she said. "I'm just the operator."

"Winston?" 'Miguel Caradura' said, raising his dark eyebrows. El Rey was fully dressed as a living human being for this performance, a form in which Tom had rarely seen him. He was even wearing a modern-day suit, one with big shoulders and pinstripes.

"Tomas Delgado is with them, Mictlantecuhtli," the bony majordomo said. "The witch Lia will trade him for this one. I humbly ask that you force him to assume the mantle I have carried in his place. I'm tired. I just want to sleep. Please, Mictlantecuhtli."

"I have a better idea," Hannah said. When she had the King's full attention, she continued. "Look, in case you haven't noticed: I'm in here. I walked in and I didn't melt. Guess that must mean I'm a witch, huh?"

"It… would seem so, Lady," the King said. "Yes."

"I've helped Lia with her work," Hannah said. "I've fed the doorway demons, and I think I've seen them too. I make my living helping things grow out of the earth, and I just now summoned up a ghost. I guess that's enough to qualify me as a witch or an operator or whatever it is they're called, technically speaking. And I hear you need one, Mister, um… Death. Sir, I mean."

"You hear true. What then do you propose, witch?"

"Leave Lia out of this. Do what you've gotta do with me."

"That's a really bad idea there, Miss Hannah," Graves' ghost said.

"Very good." Caradura agreed with a nod, ignoring Graves utterly. "I accept your terms. Let us, as they say, 'do this thing.'"

Hannah nodded too, and they shook on it, her slender hand disappearing into el Rey's powerful mitt. Winston looked on, completely flummoxed.

"Hannah *no*," Graves protested. "You can't just—"

"Hannah!"

Everyone within the second chamber whirled around when Lia, Ingrid and Riley burst into the office. Winston Watt raised his gun and fired. Whether he did it reflexively or on purpose was more than Tom could say. The shot resounded in the tiny, crowded chamber, making every living ear ring.

The bullet caught Ingrid square in the chest, slamming her back against the door and exploding the garnet pendant she wore on a silver chain. Tiny shards of the stone rained across the floor like drops of crystallized blood. Everyone shied back against the walls of their respective chamber, except for Winston and el Rey. Ingrid sank to the first room's carpet amidst a stunned silence, leaving a dark red smear down the door behind her. It matched the evidence of Graves' long-ago death that still decorated the other side of the deeply-varnished wood.

Graves' ghost dove back into his bones and they flew across the barrier at Winston, decking and disarming the dirt-encrusted skeleton in one decisive move. The action left him inside the second chamber, though, and Black Tom didn't know if Graves would be able to exit back out into the realworld again, now that his physical remains had entered Mictlan.

Hannah stepped aside to let Graves' skeleton bum-rush the trigger-happy manservant out into the first chamber, where Riley caught him, slapped binding bracelets on him, and dumped him to the floor.

Lia, still in the first room, was staring down at Ingrid. She and Tom hadn't had time to acknowledge one another yet. She knew he was with her, though, and he could feel the dizziness the sight of Ingrid's scarlet blood caused her. It looked garishly bright against the redhead's pale skin.

"Thank you, Lady," Caradura said to Hannah, startling her by snatching Graves' lighter right out of her hand. "But your services will no longer be required. My first choice just became available."

Caradura crossed into the outer office, through the barrier, becoming skeletal Mictlantecuhtli in the blink of an eye. Tom knew from experience that el Rey could go no further than this first room, nor could he assume a false form out here, this close to the realworld. No more than his Tzitzimime or his conquered Archons could.

"You stay away from her!" Lia snapped, interposing herself between Mictlantecuhtli and a gasping, trembling Ingrid. "You stay where you are," Tom's girl yelled at el Rey, although she might as well have yelled at the ocean for all the good it would do. Mictlantecuhtli was no more reasonable than the waves or the tides or the axial tilt of the earth.

Riley wisely grabbed Lia and yanked her aside. The cowled, emaciated figure of Death strode past them without so much as a glance and bent over dying Ingrid. He took her hand and pressed Graves' old cigarette lighter into it, then made a gesture like a benediction over it, severing one attachment in favor of another. The Zippo's metal case sizzled against the redhead's palm, and Tom thought he saw a wisp of either smoke or steam rise from it. Ingrid looked up at her King, and her blue eyes were wide with terror.

"At last, my love, you'll be my Queen," Mictlantecuhtli said, and even as she was on the verge of death, with her life's blood burbling out through a hole that didn't belong in her chest, Ingrid's expression crumbled. Her eyes turned glassy as they filled up with tears of despair.

With her dying breath, Black Tom heard her whisper: "…no…"

As soon as Mictlantecuhtli put the lighter into Ingrid's hand, Lia felt the connection diverting her life force away to animate Dexter click off as neatly as if someone had thrown a switch. Strength she'd barely realized she was lacking returned to her limbs like a flood of adrenaline. The drain had been subtle and slow enough that she'd chalked its effects up to a lack of sleep, or possibly an oncoming cold.

She understood that Ingrid and her King had been setting her up since the moment Ingrid first contacted her, baiting her good nature with a story that would tempt her up here, to these Chambers, and right into their trap. Dexter's Zippo lighter had always been the link, and she'd been entangled with him from the moment she picked it up.

But then it seemed like Ingrid hadn't been able to go through with the plan, or maybe she'd meant to double-cross Death all along.

Either way, she was paying the highest possible price for her schemes now.

Lia looked to Dexter, through the doorway between the King's Chambers. The membrane between the worlds shimmered between them, a barrier so subtle it hardly seemed to be there at all.

"She said restoring you would kill either one of us, but together we could both survive," she told the skeleton in the hat. She glanced back at Ingrid, lying on the floor behind her and losing her struggle to breathe through a newly-perforated sternum. "That's what she wanted to do before dark, back out at the Yard."

It might be too late for them to share the entire burden now, but Lia thought there was still a little something she might be able to do, for someone who'd at least *tried* to be of help.

The lighter was right there, and Mictlantecuhtli's shrouded back was to her. He only had eyes for Ingrid, at the moment.

"Lia, you don't have to," Dex warned, guessing at her intentions by tracking the movements of her eyes.

"I know," Lia said, then scooped the lighter out of Ingrid's hand and threw herself over the barrier between worlds. Mictlantecuhtli shouted in surprise and made a grab for her back, at the very instant in which Ingrid expired.

The witches Dexter Graves was bound to—one by fate and the other by design, one still alive and the other freshly dead—entered Mictlan together, and Graves' flesh grew back in a flash when they did. Nerves and veins and musculature, organs and skin and hair, all of them knitted together faster than he could put on a shirt.

Then his clothing went and regenerated, too. Gum-soled shoes, a good-looking suit, and his favorite floor-length trenchcoat all appeared around him, all as good as new. The pristine fedora he'd taken from one of Riley's party guests was the only item of clothing he wore that magic didn't bother to replace.

His connections to life and the world had been re-forged. Graves was alive again.

Alive *and* in Mictlan, he couldn't help but notice, even as Lia shouldered past him like he was still a ghost, invisible.

Dex spun around in her wake and saw what she saw: a red-haired skeleton draped in Ingrid's ragged gown standing right behind him, next to the inner chamber's round limestone altar. Hannah also noticed her there and gasped in surprise. Ingrid now uncannily resembled a Catrina, Lia thought—an elegant 'Lady Death' figure of the sort she associated with traditional Dia de Los Muertos decorations.

Lia seized the new skeleton's cold, bony hand and shoved the still-warm lighter into it. Most of Ingrid's vital force had siphoned off into Dexter's restoration, although the link between them, Dexter's Zippo, continued to smolder with the last of her transferred energy. Lia hoped that giving the tiny spark back to her would let Ingrid keep her voice and her own free will, at least for as long as she held onto the talisman.

Mictlantecuhtli would want to divert that final glimmer of her life to serve his own purposes, however, and that didn't leave them with a lot of options. He'd need to do his thing fast, before either the lighter or Ingrid's realworld corpse turned cold. Further complicating matters was the fact that Lord Death was currently standing out there in the twenty-first century waiting room, also known as the first of his chambers. His shrouded back was turned to Riley, Black Tom, and the only exit, barring the rest of them from escaping out into the land of the living (where all of them but Ingrid still technically belonged).

"I'm standing over here," Dex noted aloud, prodding the torchlit chamber's adobe wall with his regenerated fingertips. "Thought I couldn't do that, in a body."

"There seem to be a lot of loopholes," Hannah observed.

Mictlantecuhtli displayed no intention of crossing the barrier after Lia. He stopped short in the doorway instead, leaving Ingrid's slackening body to cool on the First Chamber's floor behind him. He held a black obsidian blade in his hand, the one he used to cleave souls from their attachments to the living world. Riley and Black Tom both scooted around the perimeter of the room, staying well out of Death's way.

"Now we cross into one another, Dexter Graves," the skeletal King said. "I assume your form on this side, you my attributes on that. Quickly, before the Red Witch's heat can dissipate. Our link must not grow cold."

"There's one thing I still don't get, though," Dexter said, completely ignoring Mictlantecuhtli's declaration of urgency. "Why me? And how am I standin' over here, all in one piece? I thought you needed special clearance for that."

Skeletal Ingrid Catrina and fleshless Mictlantecuhtli exchanged a loaded glance, through the doorway that separated them. Dexter stood back next to Lia, folded his arms, and waited to hear what they were both plainly reluctant to tell him.

"Dexter... you have it," Ingrid Catrina said carefully. "Special clearance, I mean. You've always had it. Don't you know who you are? Haven't you put it together yet?"

"You, Dexter Graves, are my son," Mictlantecuhtli said. "Rightful prince of all Mictlan."

Ingrid touched his living arm with her now-ossified hand. "And I am—or, well, I *was*—your mother," she told him.

Dexter stood there for a moment, stock-still and unable to process the news. Nobody else was doing much better. Lia, Riley and Hannah all gaped at one another in open astonishment.

Then Dexter cried, "Oh, my *God*," and continued on bellowing like a crazy person, clutching at his head. "Awwwwww, for cryin' out loud," he yelled at Ingrid's bones. "Come on, say it ain't so! Do you know the *torch* I carried for you, lady? *Do* you? Awww, hell, this makes me wanna tear my new eyeballs outta my goddamn head!"

Nobody noticed when Lyssa re-appeared behind Lia during the commotion of Dexter's outburst. Not even Tom. Hannah and Riley were trying too hard not to laugh over the content of Dex's reproaches. The Archon looked like a normal enough, dark-haired woman clad in a simple linen dress here on this, the otherworld side of the barrier, inside the second of the King's Chambers.

She darted forward and seized Lia in a chokehold.

Chapter Fifty-Three

Hannah shouted and it was the last thing Lia heard before the Archon put a hand over her face and sent her quietly, catatonically mad in less than a second, by pointing out in a deft succession of mental images the contradictions and rationalizations Lia needed to remain personally unconscious of in order to function. The memories and knowledge she could not abide. The truth of her past, her childhood, the years before Black Tom, before foster care even, came bubbling up: a swamp of guilt, grief and confusion as noxious and suffocating as the black goo that bubbled out of the earth itself down at the La Brea tar pits.

The girl whose name had not then been Lia came awake rolling in darkness, bouncing down a hillside, torn at by thorns and branches before coming to a quick, jolting stop with her left arm angled under her body in such a way that it snapped audibly, as neatly as a twig. The wave of pain that surged out from the breakpoint made her lightheaded. She thought she might throw up, or pass out.

She did neither. The screams brought her back around. She raised her head and saw the undercarriage of a minivan angled up at her from where the vehicle lay, some yards further down the embankment, lodged in a copse of thin trees. Its headlight beams lanced through the branches and dissipated into the empty blackness beyond. The girl who was not then Lia remembered they'd been driving home through Topanga Canyon after a weekend at the beach up in Ventura County. She'd been asleep in the rear compartment, behind the big car's last bench seat, which her mother thought was unsafe but which seemed ironically to have resulted in her being thrown clear when their van went over the side of the road.

Her mother and father and younger brother were still inside it, screaming for help.

Screaming for *her* help, she thought, as she sat up and hugged a broken arm to her skinny chest. It was a climb down to where they were, and she didn't know if she could make it. She couldn't even gauge the drop beyond. It was too dark for that. The scraggly saplings the minivan was lodged against made for a precarious brace. The car looked like it might fall at any minute, and the girl was terrified of falling with it. She didn't know what to do. She had no experience with emergencies.

Lyssa made Lia watch herself sit there and consider her options. Made her aware of just how *long* she'd mulled them over while her family screamed in pain and terror, instead of scrambling down the embankment as fast as she could to help them, to save them, to do something other than *sit* there like a terrified rabbit...

And then the trees gave way. The car plummeted into blackness, crunching several times as it tumbled out of sight, down the side of the canyon.

For a moment there was only silence. Then came a vast airy *whooooooshh* and a fireball rolled up toward the star-filled sky, painting the night in garish shades of orange and gold.

She hadn't saved them. She hadn't even tried, not in time, and it made no difference to her own heart that she'd only been ten years old. Only a child, and in shock. But Lyssa wouldn't let her forget what she'd failed to do, and Lia's shrieking psyche responded in the only way it could: by shutting down.

Lyssa flashed a smile and eyes of static up at a startled Graves when he spun around. She looked human in every other way.

"Oh, I am just *sick* of you," Graves yelled. "Let her go!"

"After you've kept your promise to Mictlantecuhtli," Lyssa said, "I'll think it over."

"No dice, sister."

Mictlantecuhtli could contain his frustration no longer. He crossed back into his altar chamber, where all of his power was at his command. His cowl lost its integrity and loosened into a caul of smoke, then concretized down around his bones to make a convincing illusion of muscular, tattooed flesh. The King eschewed his double-breasted suit for this iteration, costuming himself instead as a bare-chested Aztec lord from centuries past, with reed sandals on his feet, a loincloth tied at his waist, and an elaborately-woven cape drawn around his shoulders. His skull headdress and eyeball necklace, the indelible symbols of his office, were the only things that stayed the same.

"Don't make me throw you through that goddamn door, my son," he said to Graves.

"Like to seeya try, pops."

Enraged, the King shouted and ran at him. Graves sidestepped and shoved him into the bloodcaked altar, which stood only a little higher than his knees. The King pitched across the round slab gracelessly, face first, and caught himself with both hands before his jaw collided with the flagstone floor. His ceremonial headdress flew off and went skittering right past Lyssa and Lia (who didn't so much as turn her head to acknowledge it).

It looked to Graves like she'd checked out completely.

Pre-Columbian Caradura was up in half a second and Graves darted in to deliver a fast combination, opening with a jab at his face to get the King's hands up. He followed that with a hard shot to his liver, then finished off with a devastating left hook that connected so hard with the side of Caradura's head that it ruptured the cartilage in his ear.

Graves had been in bar fights on three continents, and if there was one thing he knew how to do, it was throw a goddamn *punch*.

He socked Caradura in the gut while the King was recovering his balance, driving him to his knees, and Caradura seized the opportunity to bite deeply into Graves' calf. Graves bellowed and kneed Caradura in the face, knocking him aside and sending several teeth flying. Caradura shook his head, spraying strings of blood and spittle, and Graves tackled him with his full weight, sumo-style, before he could get to his feet again.

They rolled across the earthen floor, grappling and tearing at each other's hair. Before Graves quite knew what was happening they'd wrestled each other out the far door, and then they were spilling over the edge of the giant pyramid's steep stone steps, with Mictlan's gray sky spinning wildly above them.

He caught a last glimpse of Hannah, framed up there in the rough doorway, watching them tumble away.

"Oh, God, that can't be good," Han said, stepping out into the grayish, sourceless daylight and peering over the stairway's edge to watch the pugilists roll and bounce as they receded down the Aztec temple's stepped side. The artificial mountain was taller than seemed credible to her, like a structure in a dream.

Ingrid's skeleton hurried past her, after the combatants. She held up the hem of her skirt to keep from tripping over it as she dashed down the steps, and the bare bones of her feet rattled against them with a sound like dice being shaken in a cup.

Hannah glanced back over her shoulder to see Riley standing on his tiptoes and craning his neck, trying to watch the action through the far doorway, from the safety of the outer office. He seemed to know instinctually that stepping through the portal was not a thing the living were meant to do. Hannah remembered feeling the same sort of existential dread when she first stepped up to the doorway, and she hoped that Riley wouldn't try his luck against it in the same way she had.

King Caradura and Dexter Graves hit ground level and continued to bash the crap out of each other down on the plain. Neither of them was doing any real damage here on this side of the barrier. Their injuries righted themselves almost as fast as they could be inflicted. Both combatants were too much a part of the realm of the dead to be significantly hurt within it, even by each other.

"You wasted a witch, making me come back over here," Caradura barked, snapping his head back to fore after taking a solid right across the jaw. "We'll have to burn another one to effect the trade now."

"Gee, ain't it a sin to be wasteful?" Graves mocked, ducking a punch that whistled over his head before throwing one of his own right back. "Maybe we'll have to skip the whole damn thing."

"*That*, Dexter Graves, is *not* an option," the King roared, lowering his head to charge like an angry bull. His solid battering ram of a cranium hammered into Graves' midsection, expelling the air from his lungs as Lord Death seized him around the ribs and drove him backwards, tackling him to the dirt.

Black Tom clung to the jamb opposite from Riley, watching as Hannah turned away from the pyramid's magisterial view of Mictlan's gray plain to come back inside the altar room.

Her eyes went straight to Lyssa, Lady Madness, and her hostage, both of whom were still crouched in a corner of the sacrificial chamber. Lyssa had her pale arm wrapped around Lia's throat. Lia's eyes were empty and staring, while Lyssa's crackled with silver static.

Hannah approached the grinning Archon cautiously, speaking softly and making no sudden moves.

"Lia said your name was Lyssa, I think," Hannah said, keeping her voice gentle and pitched to soothe. It was, in fact, the very tone she'd needed to use with skittish young Lia years ago, when they'd first met. Tom remembered it well. He also remembered the gratitude he'd felt for this kind woman who'd come to love his girl as much as he did, back when she first appeared in their lives.

"The Goddess of Madness, right?" Hannah prodded, easing nearer to the Archon and crouching down before her. "I think we've looked into each other's eyes before."

Winston Fucking Watt wormed his way out of his bead-bracelet bonds before Tom knew what was happening and then the sweatshirt-clad skeleton was up and on his feet fast, rushing at Riley's back. Tom condensed into visibility as fast as he could, hoping to warn Lia's oblivious friend, but he was much too late. Watt's filthy bones collided with the thin young man in the narrow-cut suit, propelling him forward through the doorway even as he turned his head in surprise at Tom's unheralded appearance.

Riley's flesh vanished when he fell across the threshold, in the manner Tom had come to expect. He shouted when he hit the second chamber's cold floor on bony hands and knees. He jumped back up and tried to cross back over... but no. It was too late. Riley was a part of Mictlan already, just like that, and the empty doorway might as well have been a solid wall, as far as he was concerned.

Women seemed to have much better luck when it came to that sort of thing, Tom couldn't help but notice. He wondered sickly if his long lost Dulcé might not've fared as well as Ingrid, Lia, and even Hannah, if his own stern warnings (based on the experience of watching Ramon go over) hadn't kept her from ever trying.

Watt dashed away, out of the King's office and back into the world, and Tom almost chased after him, but he didn't really know what to do about him.

And besides, he wasn't yet prepared to leave his Lia.

He turned back to face the inner sanctum, where Hannah had never quit trying to communicate with Lyssa, Lady Madness. Tom realized that Han was so intent on the Archon and her captive that she hadn't even noticed poor Riley's unceremonious demise.

Tom's instinct was to rush across the barrier and wrestle Lia out of the Archon's grip, but he knew he wouldn't be able to do it. He'd be subject to el Rey's will as soon as he crossed, and unable to intercede. Lacking words, he wouldn't even be able to negotiate.

Hannah at least could do that.

"You're mad," he heard her say, addressing the insane otherworlder face-to-face, crouching to look into her static-filled approximation of eyes. "You're angry. But it's because you're broken, and in pain. I know that. I know *you*. There was a time when I might've lost myself in you. You almost walked the world with me."

She seemed to have Lyssa's full attention. Tom thought maybe the Archon's grip on Lia's throat had even loosened, a tiny little bit.

"But then I helped to heal this girl," Hannah continued, reaching out to touch Lia's cheek with such tenderness that Tom could hardly bear to watch them. "And that wound up healing me."

She looked up, into the ancient entity's silver eyes.

"You can let her go, now, Lyssa," Hannah whispered. "You can come to me. I have room enough inside to hold you now. Come, and let me show you peace."

Lyssa let go of Lia, allowing her slack body to slump against the wall, and tentatively stood to accept the embrace that Hannah offered. Tom wilted with relief to see his girl released, even if she remained as limp as a ragdoll.

Hannah enfolded Lyssa and they merged together. Then Lyssa

vanished, absorbed.

Black Tom looked away, preferring not to witness what happened next to Hannah Potter.

Instead he watched Lia's blank expression clear. She blinked, coming back to herself by slow degrees. She sat up from where she'd been lying crumpled in the corner, but then she remembered where she was, as well as what was happening, and she looked around for her friends in sudden alarm.

Her eyes grew wide and welled with tears at what she saw.

"Oh, Hannah, *no*," she whispered, and Tom forced himself to look up again, too.

Hannah now looked as skeletal and Catrina-esque as Ingrid, her human life having been used up in accepting Lyssa's office. Her flesh had already dusted away. She looked down at her rescued friend, her daughter in every way that counted, and was obviously relieved to see her restored, although she also seemed anguished by Lia's evident pain.

When Riley's bones stepped up next to Hannah, Lia broke down completely. The young skeleton squatted and drew her into his skinny arms.

While Lia wept, grieving for her lost friends and family (even though they were, in some sense, still right there in front of her), Hannah looked over and spotted Black Tom standing alone in the outer office, wringing his insubstantial hands.

She came over to the doorway and tested the invisible barrier with her bony palm, just to confirm that she really could go no further.

"You're Black Tom?" she asked straightaway. "Lia's Tom?"

He nodded. Hannah's empty sockets now saw everything her living eyes never had—including him.

"Nice to meet you," she said. "You heard of a retired operator called Big Juan?"

Hannah Catrina was obviously grasping at straws, but it seemed she couldn't let herself stand by without doing *something*. Not when people who didn't need to be were dead. Tom liked that about her.

"Juan San Martín?" she continued. "He knows an old friend of Dexter's, Charlie someone or other, in Sherman Oaks? You think you could find him?"

Black Tom nodded again. Yes to both. Oscar's boy Juan, Ramon's grandson, was the one she meant. Tom would always be able to find *him*, if he tried.

"Then I need you to deliver a message for me," Hannah said. "The thing that killed Riley and Ingrid is loose in the world. It's dangerous. You have to tell Mr. San Martín to, oh, I don't know… to *warn* somebody, at least! He used to know about these things, maybe he knows people who can help."

Black Tom nodded a third time, agreeing that Juan San Martín might indeed still have connections. Winston Watt had also killed Juan's father, Oscar, more than a century before, and Tom would be able to communicate his memory of that event directly, mind to mind. He imagined Juan was going to be quite interested in finding the King's rogue manservant, even after all these years.

Hannah Catrina returned his nod before turning away from the door between worlds. She went over to join Riley's remains in trying to soothe an inconsolable Lia, leaving Tom to vanish in pursuit of his final errand.

Chapter Fifty-Four

Ingrid reached the bottom of the pyramid's staircase at long last. She knew how she must've looked by now, stripped bare of her flesh but still draped in her long satin gown: like a redheaded version of *La Calavera Catrina*, a famous old piece of Mexican folk art.

The King and his heir were exchanging futile blows down near the structure's base, neither of them doing or incurring any damage that didn't right itself within seconds.

"Dexter! Mickey!" Ingrid's breathless skeleton scolded. "This is pointless, you can't hurt each other over here, so *stop it*."

"Sorry, mom," Dexter said, infuriatingly. "But you don't get to show up at this late date and start bossin' me around."

"You have to push him out that door between the rooms at the top of the pyramid without you," Ingrid told him, her ribs heaving for air even though she had no lungs to fill anymore. "You can't beat him over here."

Mickey snarled at her, but he couldn't silence her. Her voice was still her own, thanks to Lia. She would hold on to that much of her life's free will until the lighter in her hand grew as cold as the corpse she'd left behind, back out in the realworld. Her King wouldn't control her fully until then.

"I will throw *you* through that door and burn away the life of your pet witch, Dexter Graves," Mickey spat. "Why do you fight this? She will still be yours, yours in every way!"

"Yeah, to dress up and pose and play with, like a frilly, pretty doll," Graves sneered. "Right. Gifts like that don't count unless they're freely given. Like I once heard a wise woman say: people's choices gotta be their own!"

Dexter punctuated his declaration by throwing his father-figment over one extended leg and slamming him to the ground. "Thanks for the heads up, Ing," he said, and then looked back down at Mickey, who was laid out flat on his back, dazed and staring up at them. "C'mon, dad," Dex teased, planting his hands on his knees and leaning over to look down into Mickey's face. "Let's play *catch*."

He turned on his heel and raced back up the side of the pyramid, taking the narrow steps three at a time. Mickey leapt to his feet and powered right up after him. Neither of them experienced any physical limitation over here in Mictlan. They could behave like cartoon characters for an eternity if they felt like it, bashing away at each other relentlessly, without suffering any lasting consequence.

Ingrid Catrina sighed and began dragging her own weary bones (which were subject to a very different set of rules) back up the endless steps after them.

Graves led King Caradura in a chase back up to the top of the pyramid, running effortlessly, magically, as though they were in a dream. It was fun, if anything, but Graves was already coming to see that no escalation in the level of violence was ever going to put him on top of this situation. He and Hardface were too evenly matched for that. Ingrid hadn't been lying. Not on that score, anyway.

A re-awakened Lia and two new skeletons he was pained to recognize as Miss Hannah and that Riley guy all stood aside when he blew past them upon reaching the summit, ducking under the temple door's low stone lintel and darting back into the King's inner sanctum. He didn't know how Lia's friends had come to lose their skins, but this hardly seemed like the time to ask.

Caradura burst into the dim, torchlit chamber after him. Graves positioned himself in front of the doorway on the far side of the altar stone, the one that led out into the empty antechamber and then the realworld after that, taunting the King.

"C'mon, pops, gimme a push," he teased.

Caradura jumped up onto the altar and leapt at him from it, his small eyes glittering with rage. Graves dodged aside at the last second. Caradura nearly tumbled through the doorway barrier, but caught himself against the jambs before he fell. Graves tried to push him out of the chamber and across the dividing line before he could scramble back from the threshold, but the King grabbed hold of his arm and swung him hard against the mud brick wall. The impact was concussive enough to break Graves' nose. It sent one of the torches that had flickered for ages tumbling from its sconce, and Graves' injury evaporated before it went out in a burst of orange sparks against the cold flagstone floor.

Ingrid's elegant skeleton led Lia and the remains of Hannah and Riley back inside the temple, away from the Mictlan-side door. Lia was the only one of the bunch who still looked alive. There was no sign anywhere of the Archon who'd taken her captive. Graves assumed the creature had been dealt with—at the cost of Riley and Hannah's lives.

"Dexter," Ingrid said, raising her voice to be heard over the ruckus he and the King were making. "If you go through that doorway first, what he is goes with you and it'll take over your body. You'll be him, not you. You've got to throw *him* through on his own, into the realworld, and someone on this side has to willingly assume his office, so he can't come back."

"Who's that gonna be?" Graves gasped, craning his head to see her as he struggled with Caradura at the doorway.

"Me!" Ingrid's skeleton said. "I'll do it. I'm ready. And I bore his son, so I have a right to succeed him."

"Your tortures for this treason will never end, Ingrid Redstone," Caradura bellowed, while Graves tore at his hair. "You've *refused* to be my Queen before!"

"Oh, I'll be Queen, Mickey," Ingrid said. "I just won't be *yours.*"

Enraged, Caradura seized Graves by the shoulders and launched him bodily at the doorway to the living world. Graves caught either side of it and felt himself stretched across the opening like a trampoline skin when Caradura slammed into his back with all his weight, fighting to ram him through. He peripherally saw the skeletons that had so recently been Hannah and Riley freeze into place before they could join the fray (according to their King's will, he supposed), but Ingrid and Lia ran over to beat on Caradura's back with their fists, trying to help.

Caradura turned away from Graves for an instant, knocking

them both aside almost without effort.

Knocking Lia to the floor.

Graves saw her fall and his vision went red.

King Caradura hesitated just long enough to make sure his merchandise wasn't damaged. Lia was the last living witch to've touched the lighter, so it was *her* life that would be forfeit if they made their trade now.

Graves knew it too, and he seized the momentary distraction to come around punching.

He caught Caradura straight across the jaw, first with his right fist, then with his left. He bashed Hardface across the room and out the far door, driving him back with blow after crunching blow to his face.

Nobody hurt his Lia, Dexter Graves thought grimly. *Nobody.* Not even the big bad king of the goddamn dead. Not without answering to *him*.

The King missed tripping over his own altar again by bare inches before he staggered out the far door, fighting to keep his balance under the onslaught. Graves discontinued his rain of knuckles when Hardface pinwheeled backwards on the very edge of the pyramid's steps… then blew on him, sending him tumbling all the way down to the distant chaparral plain below.

He turned to catch Lia up in an embrace when she ran to him, out the door and into his arms. It was the first time she'd gotten a good look at Mictlan proper, and she couldn't help but exclaim over the breathtaking view from the top of the pyramid. The land of the dead seemed to go on forever, its low hills stretching off toward every horizon.

Caradura was on his way back up to the top again literally as soon as he landed, his bare feet beating a fast tattoo on the rough stone steps. It wouldn't take him long to regain the pyramid's summit.

Ingrid's bones turned to Graves. "Dexter," she said, looking as though she'd had a sudden flash of inspiration. "It's still November second out in the world. The dead can walk today if they have permission from the King. Maybe permission from the Prince will do. Call for help to drag him over the barrier!"

It sounded like a decent plan.

Graves looked out across Mictlan. He could see smokestreets

and nebulous cities and possibly millions of tiny costumed skeletons in the far distance, if he tried. There were sure to be a lot of disgruntled dead out there. Plenty of possible allies.

King Caradura was about a third of the way back up the stairs.

"I think I can go you one better," Graves said, looking away from Ingrid Catrina to wide-eyed Lia while he imagined them all, the forlorn dead of every era.

He knew in a flash what he wanted to do.

Graves leapt up, found a handhold between two mud bricks, and hauled himself onto the sanctum's flat, square roof, onto the absolute top of Mictlantecuhtli's pyramid. He bent down to help Lia up, too.

He didn't have to wrack his brain to know how she'd choose to handle this situation.

So he put two fingers in his mouth and whistled. The shrill shriek cut across the plain like a sharp sonic knife. Skeletons going about their business on the vague smokestreets down below all turned toward the distant pyramid. Even King Caradura paused in his climb. He was more than halfway up the staircase.

"*Listen up*," Graves called, projecting his voice easily, as though it were somehow amplified. "Son of Hardface says it's play day on the earth plane, so all of you—*get those bony asses on the streets!*"

His penultimate order rolled across the realm of the dead like a peal of thunder, and the Prince's directive was heard by one and all.

The entire skeletal population of Mictlan, down on the ground and numbering so many billions strong, all paused and looked to one another. They were uncertain for an instant, but not one of them needed to be asked twice. The dead dropped whatever they were doing and stampeded across the plain, converging on their King's pyramid from every side.

All of them. Every one, without exception. After a moment an ocean of bones spilled over the hazy mountains that ringed the far horizon and flooded down their foothills—a multitude of tiny skeletons coming on the run, in numbers too great to comprehend.

No similar offer of freedom had ever been extended before, not to everybody all at once, not even in the dustiest and most disused corners of any of their memories, and it woke a hunger in the dead for the pleasures of the living world that the realm of Mictlan could no longer contain.

King Caradura, still stranded partway up his own pyramid, saw everyone who ever died pouring toward him across the vast, barren landscape at an unbelievable rate of speed, raising great billowing clouds of grayish dust that hung in the air behind them. The rumble of so many fleshless feet pounding the earth rose to a sustained roar.

The King screamed and sprinted upward as the first wave of skeletons swarmed the pyramid's base and stairs. He made it back to the summit within a matter of seconds, but while el Rey may have been supernaturally fast, he was nowhere near fast enough to outpace the motivated mass of his subjects. The wave of eager dead caught him and bore him up the last few steps, through the exterior door, and back into his own temple.

Graves and Lia watched all of this in delighted astonishment, from the safety of the pyramid's small, squared-off rooftop, both of them leaning over its edge to look down between their feet.

Inside the sacrificial chamber, the flood of jubilant skeletons herded their King across his own inner sanctum. He clung to the altar by his fingernails until they yanked him from it, muscling him toward the far door in spite of his violent, clawing struggles and the snarled invectives he hurled at them.

Ingrid Catrina watched it all as it happened, from a safe corner of the room.

King Caradura turned into fleshless Mictlantecuhtli when the dead shoved him across the barrier and out into the first chamber, ahead of them. He had no chance to slow down before the crush of animated bones pushed him through the modern office suite's main door—the one marked with the name of his favorite avatar and the blood of his human family.

Then he was out in the corridor. Out in the realworld, beyond the Hole in the Sky, where he'd never been before.

Which could only mean that Dexter's extravagant, extemporaneous experiment had miraculously paid off.

Ingrid Catrina stepped forward to help her fellow skeletons uproot Mictlantecuhtli's round limestone altar and rumble it out the office door after him, like a massive grinding wheel. She stepped back and stood her ground on the spot where the altar had always been, in the center of the sacred chamber, at the very seat of Mictlan's authority. The tidal flood of fleeing dead parted easily around her.

"Goodbye, Mickey," she murmured, and could hardly hear herself over the roar of celebratory noise. "We loved each other as best we could."

She watched the dead slam their King's shrouded, skeletal form against the corridor's far wall, then mash him there with his own rolling altar stone. He couldn't come back to his realm while Ingrid was standing where the symbol of his purpose belonged. White plaster dust puffed out around his robed bones. Skeletons fought to roll the stone back as more and more of the unbreakable dead jostled out into the hall behind him, crowding the narrow space past its reasonable capacity within a matter of seconds. They hefted the altar up off the floor and used it like a battering ram, grinding Mictlantecuhtli deep into the drywall before the century-old masonry behind it simply shattered from the force and burst open in a shower of brick and plaster.

Ingrid Catrina shaded her bare eyesockets against a wash of brilliant, realworld daylight as the dead leapt through the breach after their former ruler, pouring out of what the old people had always known as the Hole in the Sky.

Mictlantecuhtli's robe fluttered and snapped as he fell, screaming, and crunched against the cracked blacktop, thirteen stories below. His ancient altar landed on top of him and broke apart into several large pieces.

Skeletons in clothing from every era rained down upon Mictlantecuhtli's remains, smashing them first to gravel against the pavement, then to powder, and then finally to the dust to which all things are said to return. The durable skeletons themselves landed unharmed and pranced away, out into the streets, elated over the prospect of being free.

Up on the roof of the Temple of Mictlantecuhtli, Graves and Lia continued staring down at the mass exodus taking place not three feet beneath the soles of their shoes.

Fresh droves of skeletons kept coming, pounding up the pyramid's steps and even climbing its stacked sides, pouring in from every corner of Mictlan's plain like a blanketing swarm of locusts.

There seemed to be no end to them, from one horizon to the next.

Dexter Graves and Lia Flores looked up and grinned at each other like a pair of delighted children.

The dead partied outside the Silent Tower and all over the rest of the city, badly disrupting the 'real' world of natural laws and social habits. They burrowed out of the ground and broke out of crypts, so hungry for the life they'd been denied that they were unable to wait in an orderly line at the door between worlds any longer.

In cemeteries across town, bones boiled out of manicured plots. Mausoleum slots blew open and whirlwinds of ash danced around the memory gardens with unrestrained glee. So many of the dead sought to act on the permission they'd been granted that the inviolable veil between life and death might as well have come unraveled. Los Angeles was the event's epicenter, but its results were going global, spreading more swiftly than the planet could turn.

Los Muertos went nuts as soon as they were loose, too overwhelmed and overjoyed not to celebrate their liberation. The blue sky above was a miracle to them—even if the bright sun, which was currently facing a different hemisphere, was nowhere to be seen within it. They hardly noticed such a trifling detail as that after having endured the tedium of Mictlan's never-ending gray for so long. Their raucous behavior freaked out the living (who were having a hard enough time dealing with the improbable daylight as it was). It looked as though a sepulchral spring break had been declared on the streets of LA. The dead were on holiday, and they meant to make the most of every second they had.

On paved avenues that had once been dirt roads, *ranchero* skeletons riding pale horses fired their guns into a blameless blue sky. Tribal bones wearing tall fans of feathers performed wildly whirling ghost dances in intersections they remembered only as crossroads, while dead musicians carrying instruments of every stripe gathered together to make as much lively noise as they possibly could. Skeletons in the costumes they remembered best from life danced and twirled and laughed and sang, all of them intoxicated by their unexpected taste of vitality.

Many of the living (who were still horribly confused, but starting to get over that first, debilitating shock that always accompanies an experience of the impossible) began recognizing ancestors. Joyous reunions broke out everywhere, in yards and in stores and on streetcorners, as the liberated dead sought out children, grandchildren, or descendents too far down the timeline for anyone to reckon. Even expired pets, cats and dogs by the skeletal score, hurried home to check up on the friends they'd loved so well in life but had to leave behind.

For one moment, unique in all of time (like every other moment, of course), the living and the dead celebrated together, and all of them believed wholeheartedly, if only for a little while, in the glorious future of their kind.

Chapter Fifty-Five

After what felt like well more than an hour Lia and Dexter hopped down from the roof of Mictlantecuhtli's temple and crowd-surfed back into the world. Lia had to coach Dex on how to do it, as he'd missed out on the era in which the practice was born by a number of decades.

Celebrating skeletons obligingly bore them across the two rooms of the office suite, then on down the stairs and out through the lobby's double doors, finally depositing them right on the cadaver-crowded street in front of the Silent Tower.

Hannah Catrina and Riley's well-dressed bones were dancing a sprightly jitterbug together, and they both waved a cheerful hello.

"You like what I did here, dollface?" Dexter asked, grinning his biggest lopsided grin when he turned to face Lia. "It's the Day of the Dead. I uncorked the otherworld for you!"

"I love it, Dexter, I really do," Lia said, and cast her wondering eyes around at the cheekbone-to-jowl crowds packed into the narrow street before them. When she looked up at Dexter again, his silly smile only widened. "I think it's the most wonderful thing I've ever seen!"

She touched his thoughts and was humbled to know that Dex had pulled this incredible trick because he believed *she* would've done the exact same thing, had the power been hers to use.

His eyes told her the same, and his lips confirmed it when he seized her and dipped her in a deep, triumphant kiss.

Skeletons all around whooped and applauded, whistled and cheered, many of them reminded powerfully of a famous old photograph of a sailor kissing a nurse that had once, for so many, symbolically sealed the end of their world's great war.

Dexter straightened up and set Lia back on her feet, ending

their breathless moment. The crowds all around fell silent, and they both looked up to see Ingrid Catrina, the new Queen of Mictlan, smiling down upon them.

Ingrid's bleached skeleton wore a regal costume now: a long-skirted suit and a broad-brimmed hat pinned over her lustrous, dark red hair. To Lia she seemed to embody everything that was dignified, elegant, timeless and wise, like the Elizabeth of the Otherworld. The dusts of this world swirled about her before settling down onto her bones in a flawless facsimile of flesh. After a few moments her face looked as smooth and radiant as it had in life, and her occluded eyes cleared to a blue as bright as sapphires. She was one of los Muertos now, as well as their Queen, and on their day she could walk the worlds beside them, on her own recognizance. Unlike her imaginal predecessor, this was a Death who had *lived*.

"Ingrid," Dexter said, taking off his hat in the presence of royalty. "Or should I say your majesty?"

"Ingrid's fine," the new Queen offered. "Or mom. If you like. Not ma, though, please. That's a sound a sheep would make."

"But…" Dexter started, then hesitated. Lia looked up and saw that his eyes were full of need and a brand of pain she understood all too well, being an orphan herself. She also knew that the world's mythologies were rife with tales of semi-divine parentage, and of progeny hidden away by human mothers until such children could come of age to claim their birthrights from otherworldly fathers. The pattern was a classic one, reiterated time and time again.

"Is it really true, what you told me about being my… you know, my mother?" he whispered. "How *can* it be? I mean, look at us. I'm *older* than you are."

"Dexter…" Ingrid explained gently. "I had you in 1915, back when I'm originally from. I left you in the realworld to keep you safe from Mickey, but then I jumped to 1950 to meet you. To see what sort of a man you'd become. I jumped to now to find Lia after Mickey tracked me down again and wouldn't let me go till I promised I'd deliver you. I've taken trips all over time. Any point in human memory is accessible from Mictlan."

She brushed his face with fingertips of dust-sheathed bone.

"I'm sorry I was never a parent to you," she said. "I had no idea how to be. I was never very good at normal life. Maybe now... I can be of a different sort of use."

"Yeah, you'll make that otherworld a better place, I just know you will," Dexter said. His voice went hoarse with emotion when Lia unobtrusively took and squeezed his hand. He held on gratefully. "Get out there and liberate those mythologies," he suggested.

"That already has been done," pronounced the Queen. Her gaze was growing distant, her focus already turning inward, toward the otherworld's eternal mysteries.

"Well all right," Dex said, beaming. He pushed his hat back on his head and looked around, at the dead who still crowded the streets, milling about and chatting. "What about the rest of the mess I made?"

Queen Ingrid shrugged. "The dead will return when their day is done," she said. "And the living will recall this only as a dream. The realworld defends its boundaries too well to let this be remembered. Nyx, I believe, remains your prisoner?"

"Back at the Yard, yeah," Lia said.

"Free her as it pleases you," the Queen instructed. "Until then... let the dead enjoy their day."

Queen Ingrid Catrina, the new Reina de los Muertos, bowed to her son and to Lia before she turned back to her building, the Silent Tower, the thin façade worn by her ancient temple in that patch of the actual currently known as Hollywood. The torrent of still-exiting skeletons parted before their new sovereign to let her enter the building, all of them kneeling and bowing their heads when she passed. No longer out of fear, as would've been the case with the previous monarch, but rather as an expression of adoration, admiration, and genuine gratitude.

"I'll be seeing you," Ingrid told her son, waggling fingers over her shoulder without turning back. The dust-flesh fell away from her bones as she did so.

"In all the old familiar places," Dexter replied, in a murmur only Lia was close enough to hear.

Together they turned away as the Queen returned to her realm and its faraway concerns, only to be confronted by Mictlantecuhtli's dead manservant Winston, who stuck his rusty gun into Lia's face. She cringed back against Dexter, who moved to shield her with his body.

"Black Tom Delgado," skeletal Winston rasped. "It's not *fair* that he should get away with what he did to me. The degradations I've endured. The *centuries* of humiliation. If all I can do to hurt him is kill what he loves, then that's what I'll bloody well do!"

Lia and Dex both flinched when the small gun burst apart, taking most of Winston's mummified hand along with it. His finger bones went careening off in every direction. One stray knuckle bounced harmlessly off Dexter's chest. They heard the shot whole seconds later, and were slow to realize that it hadn't come from Winston's gun.

Neither of them was hit.

Lia looked up to see a distant sniper atop a tall neighboring building taking aim in their direction through a riflescope. She shouted and jumped when a team of six black-clad Navy SEALs burst from concealment behind parked cars and tackled Winston the would-be assassin to the blacktop, before she or Dexter had any idea what was happening.

Dex drew Lia close while one masked and helmeted member of the SEAL team trussed Winston up with plastic zip-strip restraints and the other five covered him with drawn sidearms. She couldn't have been more astounded when a gray Seahawk helicopter diced the air above, rising from a helipad atop the sniper's building and whirring to a three-wheeled landing in the empty lot across the street from the King's tower. (Make that the *Queen's* tower, she corrected herself.) Skeletons ducked and parted to make room for the incoming aircraft. The gunship had a United States Navy insignia on its side, barely visible through the haze of brown dust its rotors kicked up.

It was the same symbol that graced the front of Dexter's lighter.

Two very old men (one dressed in a heavily decorated Naval uniform) and a skeletal version of Tomas Delgado stepped out of the flying eggbeater, ducking under its roaring blades.

"Black Tom!" Lia cried, feeling limp with relief upon seeing him again, when she hadn't been at all sure she would.

"Hey, that looks to be my old pal Charlie Lurp with 'em," Dexter said. "And... holy hell, I think that's—can that really be Davey Normoyle? *Admiral* Davey? Still in the Navy!" Dex crowed, sounding more than amazed. He and Lia ran up to meet the new arrivals. Dexter embraced the shriveled Admiral and pumped old Charlie's gnarled hand. Lia hugged Black Tom's bones.

"I called in the cavalry for ya, Dex," Charlie bubbled, plainly enjoying himself more than he had in years. "Your friend Tom there came and Big Juannie knew it meant you was in trouble, but *I* knew the Admiral here would wanna help you out."

"Davey, I can't believe you did this," Dexter said. "After all these years!"

"Years I only had because of you, Dex," the wizened old sailor said.

"Well, all *right*," Dexter repeated, and Lia thought he couldn't have wiped that smile off his face for all the tea in Tokyo. "But isn't hijacking a helicopter to chase down a ghost story gonna do some violence to your storied career, there, Admiral?"

"Ahhh, hell, they'll just retire me quiet and chalk it up to Oldtimer's Disease," Davey said, waving an arthritic and liver-spotted hand dismissively in the Seahawk's direction. "That's if anybody even knows the whirlybird is gone. I got a feeling a lot of things might escape notice to... day? Night? Which is it right now, anyway?"

Dexter saw his point. Lia did too. The bright blue, sunless sky made them feel as though they were somehow paused at the climax of an inverted eclipse, in defiance of all known natural laws. Shadows didn't know which way to fall.

"Yeah, I guess you might fly under the radar at that," Dex said. He pointed to Winston's twist-tied remains, which were lying face-down on the pavement beneath a number of black combat boots and the full weight of the men attached to them. "What about him, then?"

"Hold onto him till dark," Lia advised. "And keep him off the dirt. He'll be the Queen's problem after that."

"I think my boys can execute that order," Admiral Normoyle said. He grinned at his old friend Dexter Graves when Dex slipped his arm around his best girl. Lia laid her head against his chest.

"Say, do you two need a ride or anything?" the elderly admiral asked.

Chapter Fifty-Six

The Navy helicopter's pilot found room to set down in a wide intersection a block away from Potter's Yard. Lia, Dexter, and Black Tom's reconstituted skeleton all hopped out and waved when it took off again, rising up into the blue sky on the swirling winds its rotors generated. Davey Normoyle and Charlie Lurp waved back, leaning out the open door in the Seahawk's side and grinning like a couple of foolish kids.

Skeletons and live folks were still partying and chatting and hanging around the neighborhood, every neighborhood, all over the city and by now the world, everyone glad to be at least sort of alive and enjoying their day in the sun.

Dexter slid his arm around Lia's waist as they walked into the Yard through the open front gate. They fell into step together easily.

Tom's catbody was curled up and sleeping on the steps of the office shack when Dex, Lia and the mortal remains of its longtime psychic jockey came crunching across the gravel lot. Black Tom Delgado's bones, which he could once again call his own, stooped to scratch the animal behind the ear.

Tom felt the old King's death when it occurred, as had other earthbound ghosts all around the planet. He'd explained it to his Winter Flower on their brief flight home, as best he could, in that wordless way they had. Now that he no longer had to hide from el Rey he was free to show up in whatever form he wished, be it phantasmal or physical. With *his* skills he could have put his human face back on, if he'd wanted to, the way the Queen had, but for the time being he was happy enough just to wear the visage that all of us share in common, underneath our skins.

He parted from Lia and Dexter at the edge of the parking lot, letting them wander off into the emerald trees together. They needed their space, and besides, there was a party going on out in the world that he did not intend to miss. More than a party, really—the occasion being celebrated out there in the streets was nothing less than the coronation of a new Queen of the Dead. Such an event was likely to be anticipated by the past as well as remembered in the future, Tom guessed. The memory of Mictlan deferred to neither clock nor calendar, and all of los Muertos would recall this day, regardless of when they died. The realworld's annual Day of the Dead celebrations would therefore always be—and would also always *have been*—observed in honor of the ascension of la Bella Muerta, the Beautiful Death, whose realm could now be a place of reunion and rest rather than one of torment and loss. The transfer of power involved in the Red Witch's ouster of Mictlantecuhtli was the singular event that had drawn the worlds close enough together for the dead to cross between them, and a sympathetic echo of that happening would forever be reiterated once each year, just after Halloween. Was, had been, and would always be, both backwards and forwards in time, like ripples in the ocean of history.

Tom found the notion delightful.

He turned around, listening to the sounds of music and laughter that floated to him from the neighborhoods nearest the Yard. Everyone who ever died was out there, somewhere, looking for their loved ones.

Tom took a small skull molded from bright white sugar crystals out of his pocket and paused to examine it, striking what must have looked like an alas-poor-Yorick pose, with the little calavera resting on his palm and peering back up at him.

The name written across its forehead was *Dulcé*.

Black Tom set off to find her amongst all of the liberated dead, grinning his amiable grin as he followed the sound of their distant, happy voices and swinging the walking stick he had no real need to lean on anymore, but still enjoyed carrying.

Neither the bodies of the dead nor the handcuffed hoodlums were anywhere to be seen inside the Yard, Lia noted, experiencing twin pangs of relief and remorse when she made the observation. They'd been swept under the rug already, through the auspices of the LA Blackdogs.

Blackdog operations were always kept secret, whatever occurred, so Lia knew there would be no inquiries or repercussions over the death of Ben Leonard... beyond those her own guilt might devise.

Hannah's hydroponics shed was still ringed with dimming grow lights when Lia and Dexter walked up to it. Nyx still whimpered pitiably within.

Lia stepped into the ring of high-intensity lamps and went around to the back of the little outbuilding, to find its circuit breaker. Dex followed.

"Are you ready, Dexter?" she asked.

"Ready for night to fall on the day of the dead? Yeah, brujachica. I suppose I am."

Lia killed the power to the shed.

There was a moment of silence... and then a column of starry darkness blew off the hydro shack's roof as it shot for the sky. It dripped liquid night down the sides of the atmosphere's vast blue dome, all the way to the horizons.

The bright, distant sounds of laughter and music faded away to be replaced by the peaceful and soothing noises of evening at Potter's Yard, of crickets and sprinklers and leaves whispering their secrets to the wind.

They were some of Lia's favorite sounds in all the worlds.

"Y'know, I spent a little time on a farm as a kid," Dex said softly, in deference to the stillness that now enveloped them. "Soybeans and corn, mainly, out near Riverside. That wasn't the worst of times for me. Not the worst at all."

"Then I hope you'll stay here, Dexter," Lia said, squeezing his hand and looking up at him with those large, dark eyes that he adored. "Stay for as long as the times are good."

Dex smiled. "May they never be any other way, little witch," he said, and Lia knew that he meant it all the way down to the bone. "May they never be any other way."

They embraced in the darkness and the quiet, tenderly.

After a time, the witchgirl took the former dead man's hand and led him away, through the shadows and the trees, to her little home sunk deep beneath the nourishing earth.

Epilogue

San Diego, California. All Souls' Day, 1949.

Young Captain Normoyle woke with a start in his bed, just before dawn. Annie, his pretty wife, slumbered on beside him, beneath crisp white sheets.

At the foot of the bed stood Ingrid, in her most regal robes; and Hannah, looking smart in a tailored suit. They each glowed with their own inner light, while Ingrid's wrap and fox-colored hair billowed in a wind that wasn't otherwise there.

"Hear me, Davey Normoyle," she said, raising a pale hand as she pronounced: "I am Mictlancihuatl, Queen of the Shades, once called Ingrid, now called Doña Catrina, la Dama Muerte, the Lady Death. This, my Prime Minister, is Hannah Potter. And we—"

Hannah handed Ingrid a Zippo lighter. The Queen held it up. The gold United States Navy insignia on its silver case was clearly visible, even in the bedroom's nighttime gloom.

"We have a task for *you*."

The End

—for my wife, and for the flower girls

ACKNOWLEDGEMENTS

There are a number of people I'd like to thank for their help with this project. First off, my parents, who've supported my ambition to write ever since I first learned how to read. Alan Brennert's generous advice on the craft and business of writing novels has been truly invaluable to me. Ric Feliz and my sister Cara were the first to read the manuscript, while Will Perlis and Grant Mahnken offered sharp editorial insights. Vinnie Torres and Otto Kitsinger helped me carve out my own little corner of the internet. Jamie Neese provided me with awesome cover art (illustrated by Eric Clark), as well as incalculable amounts of inspiration and enthusiasm over the years.

And of course Tam, my lamb, who's been with me every step of the way.

ABOUT THE AUTHOR

Sean Patrick Traver is the author of what you just read. Unless you're looking at the last page first, in which case you should go back to the beginning, and we'll talk later.

www.SeanPatrickTraver.com